BUILDING

EMPIRES

SHERRYL D. HANCOCK

Published by Vulpine Press in the United Kingdom in 2017

ISBN 978-1-83919-245-6

Cover by Claire Wood

www.vulpine-press.com

To my mom, Pat B., she always got to read everything I wrote first and she's always loved everything I wrote. Thank you, Mom, for always being my biggest fan!

To Jill (Kila) Krueger. This started with our habit of avoiding home/class work in high school ... and look at it now!

Last but by no means least, thank you to all law enforcement personnel, the blue line between us and the bad guys. Thank you for all that you do for all of us!

CHAPTER 1

San Diego, California, 1980

"We're gonna take 'em," Thomas Chevalier bragged to his girlfriend Sandy. "No one fucks with Midnight and walks away clean," he went on, nodding at his sister who stood a few feet away.

As if sensing he was talking about her, Midnight walked over to where her brother stood.

"The Piranhas are gonna be hurtin' tonight, huh, Mid?" Thomas asked, grinning down at his sister.

Midnight nodded, her look steely. "They'll pay for messing with me and mine, yeah."

"See," Thomas told Sandy cockily as he reached into his pocket and pulled out the butterfly knife he'd been practicing with all week.

With a flourish and a flick of his wrist, he whipped the blade into place. Midnight watched the action with a sense of dread. Every day Thomas was becoming more the gang member and less the younger brother he was to her. It scared her.

"Look," Midnight said, looking up at him, "I want you to be careful tonight. And don't give me that look, Thomas. I know you think you're getting real good with that blade, but this gang ain't playing around, okay?"

She could see she wasn't getting through to him. He nodded and looked over her head down the street. Midnight grabbed him by the front of his jacket and shook him.

"Thomas! Are you listening to me?" she snapped impatiently.

She hated that his hormones had kicked in. At sixteen, he was becoming someone she didn't know anymore. He was becoming a man. If they'd had a father that was worth anything, he could have sat Thomas down and told him the facts of life, about sex and all that. There was no way Midnight could do it; hell, she was still a virgin herself. She never let anyone get close to her; she always wanted to be able to see their hands, literally and figuratively. Sure there were health classes in school, but they didn't tell kids the real down and dirty stuff that teenage boys should know about. Again, she cursed her parents for all their shortcomings.

"Yeah, Mid, I'm listening," Thomas said, smiling down at her.

Midnight smiled in return, she couldn't resist his smile. He looked like a little boy when he smiled. The thought stabbed at her again. She knew that he shouldn't be in the gang, but what else could she do? Give up and turn him over to Social Services? No way, not while she was there to take care of him.

Midnight had just graduated from high school the day before, not that anyone had cared. She hadn't even gone to the graduation ceremony. She told her parents that she'd graduated with a 4.0 grade point average, but they just nodded and stared at her blankly. It was as if they were strangers that lived in the house with her and her brother, they were not interested in anything their children did. She hated herself for bothering to tell them, and felt irritated that she had tried for their approval at all.

As Midnight looked up at her brother, she realized that she was tired of having to worry all the time, and wondered what she would do with her life. She'd been accepted to a local college, but how could she go? There was no money, and who would take care of Thomas when she was gone? Still, she didn't regret all she was going to give up for him. He was her brother and she loved him more than anything. He was the only person she trusted. Though, that didn't always make it easier to sleep at night.

"I love you, creep," she told him, uncharacteristically impulsive for a moment, "and don't call me Mid, I hate that!" She scowled and shoved him away from her.

"Hey!" he exclaimed, laughing as he stumbled backward.

"Cool it," she muttered to Thomas as she saw that the Piranhas were coming down the street, "and get back behind me. I don't want you on the frontline tonight."

"But Midnight," he began to protest.

"Tom!" she whispered harshly. "Just do what I tell ya."

Talma Hooks, the leader of the Piranhas walked up and stood toe-to-toe with Midnight. The rival leader was almost a full foot taller, and outweighed Midnight by at least thirty pounds. The Piranhas' leader thought that gave her the edge, but that was how Midnight won every time. Midnight's motto was, "Never underestimate your opponent, it'll get you killed."

"Ready for me to put you down, little Midnight?" Talma asked arrogantly.

Midnight gazed back at Talma, her look supremely confident. Her eyes flicked past the bigger woman to the gang spread out behind her.

3

"That your whole crew?" Midnight mocked. "You shoulda brought your mama too."

"Even my mama could cap your ass, bitch!"

Midnight grinned, enjoying that she'd gotten to the bigger woman. "Better run home and get her then," Midnight said as her grin faded and her eyes narrowed, "'cause you'll need 'er."

"Bitch!" Talma screamed as she threw a punch at Midnight.

She missed, because Midnight had jumped out of the way. 'Damn the bitch is fast!' Talma thought. Just then Midnight's fist connected with her jaw. The fight was on then; the two gangs started throwing punches.

Midnight fought fiercely, it was her way of life, what she had to do to protect her and Thomas. Somehow, in the midst of all the yelling and movement, Midnight heard Thomas cry out. Her head snapped around as she tried to locate him in the crowd. Talma landed a hard right cross to Midnight's face, stunning her momentarily. Midnight shook it off, twisted around, and kicked the other woman in the stomach. Then she ran toward Thomas. He was lying on the ground, while people still fought around him.

"No!" Midnight screamed when she saw him. She dropped to her knees next to him and frantically located the wound. His stomach was bleeding badly; there was already a scarlet pool of blood soaking the concrete beneath him.

"Oh God, no! Thomas, *no!*" she cried out.

She pulled him up and cradled his upper body against hers. Tears streamed down her cheeks as she begged him to be okay.

But, he was already dead. Her only reason for living gone, just like that.

She sat there, holding his body against hers, and rocked back and forth. That's how Tom Ryan found her.

Ryan, a cop with the local police department, was on duty that night. He'd run into Midnight and Thomas often on his patrol, and had frequently attempted to get them both to quit the gang life. When he heard the radio call about a gang fight, he knew it was on Midnight's territory. Then he'd heard the call for an ambulance and that there'd been a stabbing.

When he arrived, he noticed a few hangers-on standing off to one side, members of the Vettes, Midnight's gang. They were watching their leader fall apart.

Ryan heard the ambulance coming and he moved to Midnight's side. Her shirt had a large bloody stain on it and her jeans were covered with Thomas's blood. She didn't notice Tom Ryan come up beside her; she was completely focused on Thomas.

Ryan had time to check for a pulse before the ambulance arrived. He didn't feel one.

Midnight cried out when the paramedics took Thomas's body out of her arms, but Ryan was there and he took her in his arms and rocked her as she cried.

"I killed him," she whispered, totally devastated, "it's my fault."

****

It had been three months since Thomas had been killed. In that time, Midnight had come to look on Tom Ryan as the father figure that she had never had. He took care of her, when no one else cared and she would be eternally grateful to him for that. Now they were headed down the freeway toward the University of California, at San Diego.

She was starting her first day at UCSD. With Tom's help, she had gotten a grant and he had helped her register for classes. After much thought and many late night discussions with Tom, she had decided that she wanted to study law. She also planned to apply for the San Diego Police Department when she was twenty and a half. Tom had been surprised by the second half of her plan when she'd told him a little while ago.

"Why do you want to become a cop?" he had asked, puzzled.

"What d'ya mean, why?" she had said, looking at him as if he was crazy. "I want to bust punks like Talma." Then she had looked thoughtful. "Maybe someday I can work on a way to get rid of all the gangs." Tom hadn't replied, he had just looked at her, unsure of what to say. She had been looking out his kitchen window with sad eyes, her mind far away. He knew she had been thinking of Thomas.

Now she was on her way to the college, starting a new life. She was going to be staying on campus and no one would know she had been a gang member, although she had taken her Vettes jacket at the last minute. "Security blanket," she had explained to Tom unnecessarily. To the people at the University of California, San Diego, she would be just another beautiful new freshman. Tom was hoping that she would find herself some normal friends and be able to lead some semblance of a normal life. At that point he was just happy that she was going forward in her life to a new level; for now that was enough.

He looked over at her, struck again by how beautiful she was. He knew she was going to be the heartbreak of the whole campus. Strangely, he felt very proud of her, she wasn't afraid of this new phase in her life, even if it was something totally foreign to her. She was taking it head on, like everything else. *UCSD had better watch out,* Tom Ryan thought as he pulled into the parking lot.

San Diego, California, 1983

The sun was shining brightly on the graduates. Midnight sat with the rest of her class as the graduation ceremony progressed. She reflected on how far she had come. She'd received her bachelor's degree in psychology a full year early and received the distinction of being awarded Summa Cum Laude with a 4.0 GPA. She had also already started applying for law schools. Now, here, she was graduating top of her class, with honors in hand-to-hand combat and use of baton, from the San Diego Police Academy. She was happy, for the most part, but part of her still burned with the need to avenge her brother's death somehow. Although it was now a positive vengeance she sought.

Tom Ryan sat proudly in the audience watching Midnight. Over the last three years, she had become the daughter he had never had. She had sought his advice and counsel constantly while in the academy. Now she was number one in her class, which even in these modern times was still a major accomplishment for a woman. Ryan had helped Midnight financially as much as he could the first year, although in the end she had more than qualified for financial aid. She had received numerous grants from the police department and other law enforcement agencies. She had even received a grant from the California Peace Officers Association after Ryan had written them a letter telling them of her past and her future plans. The association had responded almost immediately, asking for Midnight and Ryan to attend their annual conference in Sacramento, where they presented Midnight with a large grant check and a certificate of recognition for her perseverance in the face of overwhelming odds.

Midnight Chevalier had become a regular celebrity in the law enforcement community, with her past plight and current accomplishments. Having already taken and passed the LSAT test for law school with an astounding score of 175 out of a possible 180, it was no wonder that her application for the San Diego Police Department was given the seal of approval almost immediately. And now here she was graduating. Midnight was sworn in on stage with all her classmates, and as she repeated the Oath of Allegiance tears came to her eyes. She knew she was moving toward what she wanted and it made her sad and happy all at the same time. The allegiance over, and the swearing in complete, all the new officers threw their hats up into the air and hugged each other. Midnight walked off the stage and went to find Tom Ryan. When she found him, he grabbed her up in a bear hug, kissing her cheek.

"You looked great up there, Midnight," he said, his voice proud.

"Thanks," she said, smiling up at him. But a shadow of sadness crossed her face.

"Hey," Ryan said, touching her under the chin, "don't be sad …" he said, seeing the look on her face. "Thomas would have been proud of you today." Her eyes filled with tears at the mention of her brother's name.

"I just wish …" she said, shaking her head, then burying it against Tom's shoulder.

"I know," he said and hugged her to him. The chief of police came up to them, and Ryan stepped back from Midnight, although his hand remained on her waist.

"Well, young lady," the chief said, looking down at Midnight, "you certainly made your mark here." He extended his hand to her and she took it. As they shook hands, he watched her intently; she was such a beautiful girl with such an intense look about her. The chief had the feeling he'd be hearing from this one again and again.

"Congratulations," he told her, squeezing her hand. Then he moved on to congratulate other graduates and meet their families, but his eyes kept straying back to where Midnight Chevalier and Tom Ryan stood talking. Yes, he was sure he'd be hearing from her in the future.

San Diego, California, 1986

Three years after becoming a police officer, Midnight received her law degree. It had been a grueling three years. She'd gone to school all day, starting at eight in the morning until one in the afternoon. After school she would go home and study for three hours and then sleep for five. She'd get up and go to work, starting at ten p.m. as a patrol officer, and she'd be on until six in the morning. Then she'd study until she had to be at school again. On her days off from school and work, which fortunately coincided, she would sleep for half a day and study for the other half. She continued this schedule for the full three years that she was in law school. When she graduated from law school, Tom Ryan was again there for her.

She took the sergeant's exam that same year, and two weeks later, she was called into the chief's office. The chief of police himself informed her that she was being promoted to the rank of sergeant. He also informed her that since she had placed first on the test that she could have her choice of assignments. Tom Ryan was there too; he had been invited to witness the announcement, considering that he was basically the motivation for her achievements.

Midnight gave the chief a measured look, wondering if she should bring up the idea she'd been mulling over in her head for a couple of years.

"So, what unit would you like to work for Ms. Chevalier?" the chief asked, pronouncing her last name wrong as usual, but of course she ignored that.

"Well, sir …" she said, looking at him, still debating with herself.

"Go on, Midnight," Ryan said, knowing what she'd been think-ing, since she'd discussed the idea with him endlessly.

"Well, I did have this idea … it's for helping with the gang prob-lem …" She looked at the chief to see if he was even receptive to the idea; he seemed to be so she continued. "Well the way I see it, gang members respond best to someone they relate to … and well who better than an ex-gang leader." She gestured to herself. "Anyway, I had the idea that if I could get together a group of ex-gang members, and ex-leaders, we could get into the gang from the inside and basically break them up from the inside."

The chief was listening looking very interested. "And what would this entail for the department?"

"Well, all we'd need is some office space and some staff …"

"And how would we deal with ex-gang members?"

"What do you mean?" Midnight asked sharply, thinking that he was saying that ex-gang members were uncontrollable.

"In terms of status, pay, and all that," the chief said gently, knowing what she had been thinking.

"Oh," Midnight replied, looking chagrined, "well I was thinking that I could start them out as informants for me, we could pay them by the case, like we do our regular informants. Then from there, if they proved reliable, after a background check and, lacking a serious criminal background, we could put some of them through the level one reserve academy, and make them non-designated level ones. That way they'd only have peace officer powers on the job. Maybe eventually we could put the level ones through the full academy, if they made the cut."

"Have you got anything written up on your idea?" the chief asked, looking impressed. She'd obviously thought this out thoroughly.

"As a matter of fact …" Midnight said as she pulled a document from the leather-bound folder she had on her lap. She had hoped to have an opportunity to talk to him about it. She hadn't realized she was getting a promotion and her choice of assignments.

The chief laughed. "Always prepared aren't you?" he said to her, while grinning at Tom Ryan.

"Well, you never know," Midnight said, handing him the document.

The chief stood, taking the report and shook her hand. "I will read this with interest *Sergeant* Chevalier, and I'll let you know."

Midnight and Ryan left. Once outside of the building, Midnight and Tom laughed and hugged. "Well little girl," Tom said. "You're certainly on your way now."

"Sergeant," Midnight said, trying out the title. "Holy shit!"

Later that week Midnight received word that her plan for her Former Organized Riot Seekers, FORS, was a go. She was ecstatic.

San Diego, California, 1987

Joe Sinclair lay sleeping on his stomach when the sound of someone pounding on his front door woke him. He turned over with a groan and glanced at the clock on his nightstand.

"One o'clock in the fucking morning?" he muttered to himself in his thick English accent. "Someone better be dying," he growled as he hauled himself out of bed.

Reaching up to rub sleep out of his light blue eyes, he walked through the house turning on lights as he went. When he reached the front door, he ran a hand through his long dirty-blond hair. He was ready to take the head off of whoever stood there.

At the front door, he paused. "Who is it?"

He heard a woman's voice say, "It's me."

He was fairly sure it was Midnight, his partner of just under a year, but her voice sounded strange. He opened the door and saw her leaning against one of the pillars on his front porch. At five foot five tall, she was a tiny little thing, compared to his six foot two height. She was wearing her standard uniform of jeans, a cotton button up shirt, boots, and her leather FORS jacket. Joe always thought of her as his little powerhouse of a partner. She was small in stature, but dangerous as hell in a fight. He was frequently thankful that they were on the same side.

Joe noted that her face was devoid of all makeup, which in and of itself wasn't surprising as Midnight didn't use a lot of makeup. What was a surprise was that she looked like she'd been crying. Crying was not something Midnight Chevalier did. She tended to hold her emotions inside and take them out at the firing range, or, more often, on the gas pedal of her classic Corvette.

"Midnight …" Joe began, not sure what was going on and, therefore not sure what to say, but she cut him off with an angry look.

"What the fuck were you thinking?" she asked, her gold-green eyes flashing in the dim light of the porch. "Where was your head?"

Her voice had a slightly hysterical ring to it, but he wasn't sure how to answer her question. He'd been involved in a shooting that day, but he knew it had been a good shoot. The kid had pointed a MAC 10 at him, with his finger on the trigger and had said, "Move and you're dead, cop!" Joe had dropped to one knee, drawn his weapon, and fired before the kid could even blink. The department had already given him a preliminary clearance on it, so why was she freaking out?

"Night," Joe said, his voice calm and low, "why don't you come inside?"

She hesitated for a moment, obviously debating his offer, which was strange for her. In the year that they had worked together, Midnight and Joe had gotten very close. They had spent many nights working until dawn, doing their best to make Midnight's brainchild, the gang task force, "FORS," work.

"Come on, Night," Joe prompted gently.

Finally, she walked inside, her eyes flicking up at him as she walked past. He closed the front door and turned to her. In the light of the entryway, Joe could see that her eyes had a glassy look to them. She had obviously been drinking. She was definitely not leaving in her own car tonight. Joe made a mental note to get her keys when he could.

She stared at him with an angry look on her face. Joe was used to seeing that look turned on other members of FORS, but she had never turned it on him. He decided he'd better be really careful, she was in a real knot over something and he didn't want to make things worse.

"So what's going on?" he asked, trying to sound casual as he walked back toward his bedroom to put on a shirt.

Midnight followed him, silent for the moment. Joe wasn't sure if she was trying to rein in her emotions or if she was gearing up to tell him something she didn't think he'd want to hear. He went over to his bed and picked up the shirt he'd discarded earlier. Sitting down on his bed, he pulled it on without bothering to button it.

He sat with one foot up on the side rail of the bed and one arm resting on his knee as he watched Midnight pace. She walked back and forth in front of him for a long time, without saying anything, without looking at him.

"Midnight!" Joe yelled finally, losing his patience. "What the fuck is going on?"

She stopped pacing at the sound of his voice and focused on him. "I just want you to tell me," she began, her voice steely, "where your head was. What were you thinking, Joe? You blew away a kid!" On the last word her voice rose hysterically, and a chill ran through Joe's body at the sound of it.

"What do you mean, what was I thinking?" he asked hesitantly, trying to test out her state of mind. What was she trying to get at? He knew that kid would have blown him away without a second thought. What did Midnight think he could have done differently?

"You know what I mean, Joe!" she exclaimed, shaking her head as if she couldn't believe that he could be so dense. "Why did you have to shoot that kid?"

Now Joe was getting mad, was she crazy or what? He didn't know what was going on, but he definitely didn't like the direction this conversation was taking. She strode over to him, stood directly in front of him, and stared at him accusingly.

"Midnight," Joe began. He was angry now, but he spoke slowly and deliberately, like he was speaking to a child. "You know bloody well why I had to shoot that kid. It was him or me!"

"Bullshit, Joe! You didn't have to kill him!" Her voice was ragged. She shook her head, as if she didn't understand what he was saying. "He was just a kid, he was only sixteen! Just a kid …" Her voice trailed off as she walked over to his bedroom window and stared out into the night.

Joe stood and walked over to her. He put his hands on her shoulders and turned her around. She looked up at him and he could tell she was still mad, he just didn't know why.

"What is going on with you, Midnight? You know that I did what any other well-trained cop would have done. What even you would have done in my shoes."

"Like hell I would have!" she yelled. Stepping back to get away from him, she found herself against the window.

15

Joe moved a step closer to her, determined to get to the heart of the matter.

"What's really going on, huh?" he asked, his voice gentle, but she wasn't taken in.

He was surprised when she slapped him. His left cheek stung. He was so shocked for a minute that he didn't hear what she was saying.

"And how dare you say I could kill a kid." She was crying now. "You cold bastard! That kid was the same age as my brother when—" She drew a jagged breath.

"Whoa!" he said as he stepped back from her. "That's what this is all about?"

Midnight wiped her hand across her eyes, brushing away her tears, and shook her head vehemently. He could see that she was trying desperately to hold onto her anger, and she was doing a damned good job.

"You don't know what the fuck you're talking about Sinclair," she said, but her voice wavered, and Joe moved in for the kill.

"You're thinking of your brother. That kid wasn't like Thomas, Midnight. That kid was a killer, a born killer," he said, trying to get through to her. "This isn't about me, is it?"

She went quiet and almost retracted into herself. He could see she wasn't going to let him talk her out of this. When she looked at him, he could see that fire blazed in her eyes, she was not about to calm down that easy.

"No," she said, her voice angry and sarcastic, "it is about you!" She shoved him away from her.

He was surprised by her strength, as many had been before him; he actually stumbled back from the force she'd used. When he saw her hand come up to slap him again, he grabbed her wrist.

"Oh no, not again!" he said to her, his voice gravelly with anger.

Seeing her attack thwarted, Midnight balled up her other hand in a fist. When she brought it up to strike him, he grabbed that wrist as well. She struggled with him furiously, trying to wrench free of his grasp, but he was too strong.

"Let go of me!" she roared.

Both of her hands were balled into fists now and Joe knew if he let her go, she'd probably do some real damage. He decided that getting the crap beaten out of him would not be productive at this time.

"Midnight! Stop it! Calm the hell down!" he yelled, but her struggles only increased at the anger in his voice.

In a last ditch effort he turned to lay her on the bed and moved to straddle her. He put just enough weight on her to keep her from kicking him, and increased the pressure on her wrists until she cried out. She calmed down then; she knew she couldn't win this one. He outweighed her by about seventy-five pounds of extra muscle.

"Now are you going to relax?" he asked, calmer now, and he smiled down at her. "Or do I have to slap you?" There was humor in his voice, but he was serious.

"Joe," she said her voice still harsh, but less hysterical, "get the fuck off me!"

She stared up at him, she seemed calmer, but Joe knew better than to trust her, and he didn't, not one bit.

"Like hell I will," he said to her. "Now," he began, his voice soft and encouraging, "talk to me, Night, tell me what's going on with you." Her eyes welled up with fresh tears. "God, don't do that, Midnight. Just talk to me, babe," he said, hating the look in her eyes.

Joe hadn't realized until this moment how much she had come to mean to him over the past year. She'd always been the fiery sergeant that had hired him to be her second in command. The one that had told him straight out the first time they'd met that she didn't go for any of that "chasing around the desk crap." Midnight was the head-strong, hard-as-nails woman who, in seven short years, had gone from being a gang member to being a sergeant with San Diego Police Department with a bachelor's degree in psychology and a law degree. She took no crap from the members of her task force, hardened ex-gang members and leaders of some of the fiercest gangs in the country. She was a woman who could throw down with the most dangerous gang leaders and come out on top every time.

Suddenly, Joe was seeing her vulnerable side. He'd never seen her with her guard down before. Her attitude was that men would trample her heart while they were making their way to her bed. Now she was hurting, and he knew that he cared about her a great deal, more than he'd thought possible. She was his friend, his confidant and his partner. It made him all the more determined to help her through whatever was hurting her. Still, she said nothing; she just stared up at him. At least the look she was giving him wasn't accusing anymore.

"Night, come on, talk to me," he pleaded with her again.

She shook her head and closed her eyes, like she was trying to block out his words.

"Night!" he yelled then, his voice cutting through her reserves.

Joe was frustrated, he knew that she needed to talk through this, but if he couldn't get her to calm down long enough to do that, they weren't going to get anywhere. He knew that whatever was bothering her would be left to fester inside her. He didn't want that, he knew what that could do to a person.

Without stopping to think about the consequences, Joe moved his lips to hers and kissed her softly. Shocked at himself, he pulled back, his face still only inches from hers, as his eyes stared into hers. He hadn't really intended to kiss her and he began to wonder what she would do. The look in her eyes wasn't angry, but surprised. He stared at her, searching her eyes for some reassurance. They had never crossed this line before, and the idea of doing so scared him.

They were inexplicably drawn together, and Joe leaned down again to kiss her, and felt her respond to his kiss. After a few minutes he let go of her wrists and she immediately put one hand at the base of his neck, while the other grabbed a handful of his long hair. He gently cradled her face in his hands. Their passion increased and he pulled away again to look down at her.

"Night," he said breathlessly but with concerned eyes, "is this okay? Are you okay?" His voice conveyed his confusion at their new intimacy. Their friendship meant everything to him; he didn't want to lose it just for the sake of sex. If she had any doubt, he was willing to stop this now.

In response to his question she tightened her hold on his hair and pulled his head back down to hers.

When their lips met again, Joe knew there would be no more questions, no more talking, just what had been inevitable for them from the beginning.

His hands slid over her clothes, outlining the body that many men dreamed about. Her hands tightened in his hair, as she pressed closer to him. Encouraged, Joe tugged the tails of her shirt out of her jeans and reached down to unbutton it. She pulled his shirt off his broad shoulders, and grasped at them.

Midnight was petite, but with just the right amount of curves to make her exceedingly attractive. With her beautiful face, that never required a lot of makeup and her long copper-blond hair, Midnight could bring just about any man to his knees with a look. Midnight was the kind of woman that had a natural, sexy beauty; it lay in her fire, in her passion for what she did.

When their clothes lay in a pile on the floor next to his bed, Joe's hands slid over her skin, skimming her breasts, and Midnight gasped against his neck. In response, she kissed his neck, making him groan. There had always been fire between them, usually restricted to witty banter and passionate arguments about work. Now the fire that burned between them was a different one, and they took everything it had to offer.

By the time his body finally slid inside hers, Midnight was clinging to him in desire. Joe knew it had everything to do with the sexual tension that had been building between them since they'd met.

Afterwards, they lay together panting and attempted to catch their breath. Midnight nuzzled his neck, feeling both drained and exhilarated. She smiled in the semi-darkness of his room, thinking that this had indeed been worth waiting for. She thanked God that Joe had turned out to be not only a great lover, but also smart enough not to make some stupid comment when they were finished making love. Well, at least he hadn't yet, she corrected herself.

Midnight had thought Joe was drop-dead handsome from the first time he'd walked into her office. Of course, she'd never really let on that she thought that, God knew men didn't need their egos fed any more than necessary. He had long, dirty-blond hair that fell two inches past his shoulders, a strong, chiseled jaw, and a handsome face. On top of that he had light blue eyes that practically glowed against his tanned skin. He was tall, with broad shoulders, a tapered waist and long legs. There wasn't a damned thing wrong with the man; he was gorgeous. Women in the department thought he was a God.

Joe lifted his head and looked down at her, his light blue eyes searching her face.

"So what really happened to your brother?" he asked gently.

Midnight looked back at him for a moment, and then settled herself more comfortably in his arms. Her finger traced the muscle that stood out on his upper arm that he had wrapped around her waist. His other arm was under her neck, and he reached around to hold her shoulder, his thumb stroking her skin as he waited for an answer.

"He was stabbed in a gang fight," she told him, looking innocuous.

"He was in your gang?"

Midnight nodded, averting her eyes.

"And you feel guilty about it," he surmised.

She looked at him, her eyes reflecting surprise at his statement. Finally, she nodded.

"I let him in my gang," she said, shrugging. "He should have been a football star, or some glee club member or something. Anything but a gang member, Joe, he was only sixteen."

"And how old were you?" Joe asked.

"Old enough to know better," she replied.

"What? Maybe seventeen, eighteen?"

"Eighteen."

"Not exactly worldly wise, love," he told her, his finger touching her lips.

"I'd been in the gang since I was fourteen," she said, shaking her head. "I knew what it was about. In my neighborhood you were either in a gang or had your ass kicked by one."

"And that's why he joined your gang too," Joe replied.

Midnight pressed her lips together, unwilling to be excused for her actions. "I could have kept him out," she said stubbornly.

Joe shook his head. "Nothing would have kept him out."

Midnight knew he was right. Thomas had even threatened to join someone else's gang if she wouldn't let him join The Vettes. She'd figured he'd be safer where she could look out for him. She'd been wrong, and she had no intention of forgiving herself for that.

"So where did you learn to fight the way you do?" Joe asked, having been curious about her abilities ever since he'd met her.

Midnight laughed softly. "Well, now that's a little bit of a story …"

San Diego, California, 1974

"Move it you stupid puta!" the short stocky Mexican girl with braids snapped.

Midnight glanced over her shoulder, shocked at the girl's tone. "I can't move any faster, there's a line," she said, gesturing to the other kids standing in the lunch line.

"You can get the fuck outta my way," the girl said, brandishing a meaty fist at Midnight.

"Dream on …" Midnight muttered, half expecting the other girl to start a fight, feeling that chill of fear run through her. The people at this school were a lot more adversarial than they had been at her last school. She guessed that was the difference between Chula Vista and San Ysidro. It was a poorer neighborhood, so there were tougher kids fighting for their share.

"You're new here, huh?" asked another Mexican girl who stood at Midnight's side suddenly. This girl was taller than Midnight by a good six inches and she had a tougher look to her.

"Yeah we just moved here," Midnight said, already hating this new school.

The taller Mexican girl nodded, looking considering, and then her eyes flicked to the girl behind Midnight. Glancing back, Midnight noticed the smaller Mexican girl shrink back a bit.

"Como te llamas hermanita?" The taller girl was asking Midnight what her name was

"Midnight, yours?"

The girl smiled widely. "You understand Spanish?" she asked, sounding surprised. "My name's Blanca, and you and me, we're gonna be friends."

"We are? Why?" Midnight asked in spite of herself.

Blanca's dark eyes sparkled with humor. "'Cause you're cute, and I think you're gonna need a friend here."

Midnight was shocked, and wondered if the girl was just putting her on. But true to her word, Blanca became her best friend for the next two years of school. She soon found out that Blanca was the toughest chick at school, and she knew how to fight, having learned from her five brothers. She taught Midnight everything she knew. She also introduced Midnight to the gang life. She was the first friend Midnight ever lost to gang violence, but definitely not the last.

****

Midnight told him the whole story, and had Joe shaking his head in commiseration with her.

"That sucks," Joe said simply.

Midnight shrugged. "Hey, what she taught me has kept me alive."

"True."

"So what about you?" she asked Joe. "What's your story?"

Midnight had heard the rumors about Joe, that he was actually independently wealthy, worth several million dollars. The house they were in was in the richest part of San Diego, a beach community called La Jolla. The house itself had to be worth millions. Why was he a cop? He'd told her that he had as good a reason to be in FORS as anyone did, so what was it?

It was Joe's turn to hesitate.

"My father owned a publishing company in England, a very successful publishing company. Our family name was on the best society rolls in England," he said, not sounding too impressed. "I was an only child, so my father expected me to take over the business when he retired. I had no interest in that. I also had no interest in the bloody debutantes or the high society parties or anything else to do with his money. I wanted to make them happy, but I couldn't do that. I knew I'd fail at being a publishing magnate; it wasn't what I wanted. So I hid."

"In a gang," Midnight said, knowing it was true.

Joe's fighting ability, and his knowledge of gangs was innate. He had told Midnight he'd been with the Sheriff's Department's gang task force before he'd come to work for San Diego PD. He'd said that she'd had the right idea about how to stop the gangs in San Diego, using ex-gang members against current gang members. Gang members could walk the walk, and talk the talk, better than any cop.

Joe nodded, confirming her statement about him being in a gang.

"It was me and my best friend Rick, he was from a good family too, so I guess we were hiding out together," he said with a bemused grin.

"What happened?"

"I never took the gang too seriously," Joe said, his eyes taking on a faraway look, "but apparently other people did. There was a gang leader, a crazy Irish guy. He wanted to make a big man out of himself, so he challenged me to a fight."

"And you kicked his ass, didn't you?" Midnight replied, knowing how good of a fighter Joe was, having seen it firsthand a number of times.

"Yeah," Joe said, sounding annoyed by the memory, "and embarrassed the shit out of him in front of his gang. Didn't think anything of it, but this guy was determined to win no matter what. I didn't realize how determined."

"What did he do?" Midnight asked warily.

Joe's smile was wintery and far from humored. His eyes misted with tears as he said, "He cut the brake lines in every car in my parents' garage, including my Porsche."

Midnight nodded, watching him closely.

"My parents were headed down to London that evening for a party. I offered to drive them since my father had forgotten about it and had given their driver the night off."

Midnight closed her eyes, nodding slowly.

Joe shrugged. "There was a cliff and there were no brakes," he said, his voice trailing off for a moment. "My parents were killed almost instantly and I spent six months in the hospital."

"Jesus, Joe," Midnight breathed, realizing now why he was so dedicated to eradicating gangs too. "Did they catch the bastard?"

Joe nodded. "He bragged about doing it. His girlfriend told Scotland Yard. Lucky for me," he said, his lips curling in disgust.

"What do you mean?" Midnight asked, her brows furrowing.

"Scotland Yard was convinced I'd killed my parents to keep my inheritance."

"What?" Midnight exclaimed, affronted for him.

"Nice, huh?"

"Assholes," she said, disgusted.

Joe smiled. It felt good to have someone totally on his side.

They lay together for a long time, each lost in their own thoughts. Midnight rolled onto her stomach and propped herself up on her elbows to peer down at him. Joe's eyes met hers and he smiled almost sadly.

"We're both basket cases," he told her.

"No," Midnight said, shaking her head. "We're both kicking ass and taking names to get back some of our own."

Joe considered that thought, then nodded slowly. He looked directly into her eyes. "This is going to get complicated, isn't it?"

Law enforcement was dangerous enough, but they worked with and against gang members so the stakes were much higher for them.

She closed her eyes and nodded.

"Well," he said, expelling his breath. "I guess we'll just take it as it comes then." He reached up to touch her cheek.

"Yeah," she said.

She leaned down to kiss him on the lips, but even as she did, she knew they were in for some rough times. Her only hope was that their friendship was strong enough to weather it. At that moment, though, being with him was what she needed. She needed his strength and his warmth, as he needed hers. They were two people adrift in a big ocean and they were clinging together for as long as possible before the world crashed in and pulled them apart.

CHAPTER 2

Four hundred miles away in San Francisco, Daniel Robbins was getting his release papers from San Quentin. He'd just done a nickel, five years in jail, for aggravated assault. Not that it was all he'd done. The plea bargain and snitching on an asshole that would have ratted him out had taken care of the armed robbery and assault charges.

Robbins grinned at the cop that handed him his property back. *Fuck you piece of shit pig,* he thought.

"Robbins!" a tall black man outside the gates called, waving him over to the car.

"Who're you?" Daniel asked, looking suspicious.

"Rivera sent me," the man said, "the names Baker." Robbins nodded and looked over the car.

"I need a beer and a broad," Daniel said.

Baker shook his head. "Rivera wants to meet with you first."

Daniel bit back the reply that came to mind. The Riveras were the money.

"Let's go then," Daniel said, then walked around to the passenger side of the car and got in.

Ten minutes later, he was sitting in front of Carlos Rivera.

"Is everything in place?" Carlos asked, picking at his nails with a switchblade.

"Yeah," Daniel said, "just gotta get my ass to San Diego and start up shop."

Carlos nodded. "And you're sure you have our transportation problem handled?"

"It's handled," Daniel said.

"And you trust the people working with you?"

"They're fuckin' gang members, how trustworthy could they be?" Daniel said, impatient with being questioned.

"Then how do you know my product will be safe?" Carlos asked.

"Because I'll kill anyone that crosses me," Daniel said simply.

Carlos Rivera nodded again, pleased with his answer. Robbins was a mean bastard; he'd already heard that. The man in jail who had attempted to kill Robbins had found himself gutted with a fork. Robbins had managed to take his revenge quietly, so much so that the guards never figured out who killed the guy.

Carlos was very pleased with this arrangement; he only hoped it would go as smoothly as Robbins claimed. If it didn't, it would be Robbins that ended up dead.

****

Spider, as he was known in the unit, noticed something different about Joe and Midnight right away. There was a new closeness to their relationship that hadn't been there before. As an original member of FORS, Spider felt he had the right to ask. So he did the very next time Joe and he were on a case together.

"You and Midnight," Spider began, his grin saying what he didn't.

"Me and Midnight, what?" Joe asked, looking up at the younger Laotian man.

"You two, uh, you know?" Spider vacillated.

Usually a man with Spider's background, the ex-leader of a deadly Asian gang in Los Angeles, wouldn't hesitate to use the words to describe an intimate relationship. The difference in this case was that Spider respected Midnight, and in turn Joe, more than any other people he'd ever met.

Joe grinned at the other man, inclining his head in answer to the unasked question.

"About fucking time," Spider muttered with a grin.

Joe shook his head, only rolling his eyes in response. As the heads of the unit, Midnight and Joe were basically the leaders of the FORS gang. It was natural for the members to want them together.

Spider and Joe stood in a run-down building in one of the worst neighborhoods in San Diego. Joe leaned casually against one wall, while Spider was keeping watch out of a second-story window.

"So, what do you think Joe?" Spider asked after a few long minutes. "You think they'll show?"

Spider trusted Joe's instincts; he hadn't been wrong yet and they had been on a number of assignments together.

Joe looked at his watch again, then back at Spider and nodded slowly. "They'll show." He watched as Spider paced back and forth. "Spider," he said, "relax."

"Yeah, man, I know," Spider said, moving back to the window.

He stood there for a few minutes, looking out. Joe could see from the faraway look on the younger man's face that he was thinking about another time and place.

Pushing off of the wall, Joe walked over to where Spider stood. Putting his hand on Spider's shoulder he asked, "You okay?"

Spider glanced at him, as if just coming back to the present. "Yeah," he said, but his voice cracked.

Joe's hand tightened on the younger man's shoulder. Spider nodded, acknowledging the show of empathy. Two years before, Spider's entire gang had been wiped out by the Bloods in Los Angeles. Spider had been the only one to survive the ambush. He'd barely survived. It had been his desire to avenge the other members' deaths that had driven Spider to join FORS. It was what drove most of them.

Joe's eyes shifted to the window then and he saw some guys from the gang they were waiting for coming down the street.

"Come on," he said authoritatively. He couldn't have Spider lose it now. "Let's do this."

Together they turned and walked out of the room and down the stairs to the first floor of the abandoned building.

The Apostles were looking for their leader, Dave Dibbins, nicknamed "Dibbs" for reasons other than just his last name. Someone had tipped them off that Dibbins was cutting himself a bigger piece of the pie that was their drug trade. A stranger had wandered into their favorite pool hall one day and had placed that bug in the ear of one of the members. This stranger had just happened to resemble Joseph Michael Sinclair. By the time Dibbins had showed up at the pool hall, his own gang had been ready to kill him. Joe had hoped that the problem with that gang would end there, but Dibbins had gotten away, barely, and had gone into hiding.

Joe and Spider knew where Dave Dibbins was. He was sitting in a musty room in the abandoned building, handcuffed to the floor radiator. Once again, someone had tipped the Apostles off as to the location of their dethroned leader. Spider had planted that bug.

Dibbins was sitting on the floor, his eyes glassy. He looked and acted like he was stoned out of his mind, he was also feeling very sure of himself. He figured Joe and Spider were there to protect him.

He was only half-right.

As they listened, they could hear the Apostles coming up to the building shattering glass and shouting angrily. Dibbins's eyes, bleary as they were, reflected fear now.

"What the …" he said his voice trailing off as he saw Joe smile evilly.

Joe walked over to him, reached down, and unlocked the handcuff that held Dibbins to the radiator. Pulling Dibbins to a standing position by a handful of his shirt, Joe unlocked the other cuff and pocketed them.

"What the fuck, man!" Dibbins exclaimed, surprised at being free, but suddenly afraid they were just going to hand him over to the Apostles.

"Shut up!" Joe roared.

"They're almost here," Spider said as he looked out the window.

"Let's go," Joe said, shoving Dibbins ahead of him.

Joe had been listening for the approaching footsteps and trying to gauge how close they were. He could hear them flaying chains in the air, breaking glass, and laughing. Dibbins could hear them too and he tried to backpedal to get out of sight, but he ran up against the six foot two blond-haired Englishman, who promptly reached out and shoved him forward. Dibbins stumbled, then with surprising agility turned to face Joe.

"What the fuck's goin' on, man! You're the fuckin' cops, you can't let them kill me! I got rights!" he yelled, his voice and body shaking violently.

Joe snatched Dibbins up by the front of his shirt, dragging him off his feet. Turning, he slammed him against the nearest wall and brought his face inches from Dibbins's. When he spoke, his voice was pure ice.

"I know you're stupid so I'm going to say this slowly, but I'm only going to say it once. You got no rights. You got that? You don't have any 'cause you're a low life piece of shit that preys on little kids and old ladies to get your kicks. I don' have to do nothing for you, so don't piss me off!"

Dibbins cringed at Joe's words, now he was really scared. He had figured that knowing they were cops was his ace in the hole, but it hadn't quite worked out that way.

Spider put a cautious hand on Joe's arm. "Let's let his friends take care of him, huh?" Joe pinned Dave Dibbins with a deadly look, as if trying to get a final point across, then he released him. Dibbins leaned against the wall, taking quick gasping breaths. For an instant, he had been afraid Joe would kill him.

"Come on," Joe said, turning Dibbins to face the doorway, then he shoved him through it. "Your friends are here, why don't you go on out and play." His voice dripped with sarcasm.

Dibbins stood motionless for a few seconds and listened as his former followers grew ever closer. Then, in desperation, he turned to the two members of FORS.

"Look," he said, "please, you gotta help me. I don't wanna go out there, they'll kill me! Can't we make a deal?"

"You're days of dealing are over," Spider said, his voice cold and hard.

"Come on, man," Dibbins said, the desperation in his voice raising to the point of being hysterical. "I have information you could use, ya know, about the local dealers and shit." He looked from Spider to Joe. "Please man!" He almost screamed when Joe looked uninterested in what he was saying.

Joe and Spider exchanged looks and shrugged. This is what they had been after all along. It was a chance to make some good busts and put some key players away for a while.

"Well what do you think, Joe?" Spider asked, his eyes sparkling with suppressed anticipation.

"I don't know, Spider. Should we trust him?" He gestured to Dibbins, clearly mocking him. "He's a gang member, you know."

"Aw, come on man!" Dibbins whined, as he watched their conversation. The Apostles were only one room away now. "Gimme a chance!"

Joe shrugged and Spider stifled a laugh when the Apostles entered the room.

"There he is!" one of the members of exclaimed.

The group surged forward toward their former leader. Joe acted quickly: He grabbed Dibbins and shoved him back behind him and

Spider. He produced a nickel plated .45 caliber Smith and Wesson from his shoulder holster. He glanced at Spider who now held a weapon of his own.

At seeing their enemy and the two men standing in front of him with guns, the Apostles hesitated.

"Who the hell are you?" asked a short-haired, lanky looking man in the front of the crowd. Joe looked him up and down and decided he'd been on one too many crystal jags.

"We're people you don't want to fuck with," Joe said, his voice commanding. "So just turn yourselves around and get out of here."

Joe eyed the crowd, weighing the odds. They didn't seem to have guns, only knives and chains. *They probably couldn't afford guns,* Joe reflected, after their leader pilfered all of their drug funds.

"Yeah?" someone yelled from the back. "And who don't we want to fuck with?"

"FORS," Spider interjected, his tone one of an informative businessman, "maybe you've heard of us?"

Spider was standing legs apart, gun in hand, but it was down at his side. Joe stood in much the same manner, his arms were crossed and his gun rested in the crook of one arm.

"Yeah, so?" the man in front said, glancing behind himself meaningfully. "There are twenty of us and only two of you."

"Well, I'll tell you what," Joe said, fingering the trigger of his gun and looking at it thoughtfully. "This here is a forty-five caliber with eight rounds in the clip and one in the pipe, and oh yeah, if you get hit with a forty-five, you don't get up. And Spider what do you have there?" He looked over at his backup. Spider held the gun up obligingly. "Ah yes, that's forty-five caliber Glock, if I'm not mistaken." Spider nodded in acknowledgment. "Twelve rounds in the clip and one in the pipe. So that makes twenty-two rounds. Oh, and it's actually only eighteen of you, perhaps you should spend more time in school." Joe paused, smirking at the young man in front again. "So that makes four extra rounds for us, and since Spider here and I are expert marksmen I'd say the odds of you getting us before we get you are slim to none."

As he wound up his assessment, Joe reached over and pulled the slide back on his gun. Spider did the same.

"First two are ready, who wants to die first?" Joe asked. His voice was the only sound in the room.

Dibbins had been surprisingly silent through the whole thing, but now he stepped forward, past Joe. He held a broken bottle in his hand, and eyed his former allies meaningfully.

"And anyone they don't shoot, I'll take out myself," Dibbins said, his voice dangerously low and strangely devoid of the stoned slur it had previously held.

There was a lot of shuffling of feet at what had been said. Joe looked over to Spider, catching the Laotian man's eye he nodded almost imperceptibly.

"So what do you say man?" Joe asked, looking at the young man up front. "Call it a draw?"

There was silence. The young man who had taken over leadership of the Apostles, eyed Joe and Spider and then his eyes came to rest on Dibbins.

"Let's just forget it, Jess," someone said from the crowd.

"Yeah, he ain't worth dyin' for," someone else seconded.

Jess was apparently considering his options. He put a nervous hand through his hair. Joe pinned him with a look.

"Yeah, Jess," he said, "why don't you wise up, so you can grow up."

More silence ensued.

"Come on Jess," someone said.

Joe could see that the crowd was already thinning out. *Good* he thought to himself.

He didn't like the idea of having to use a gun on kids. He knew if it was him or them he would, but he didn't like it.

Finally, only Jess remained. He stood eyeing Dave Dibbins.

"What's it gonna be?" Dibbins said, watching Jess closely. "You gonna try me?"

Suddenly, Dibbins didn't act like the stoned loser that Joe and Spider had seen. He stood taller, with more authority in his voice. Joe and Spider exchanged surprised looks, but they stayed out of it.

Jess's hand tightened on the length of chain he held as he eyed the three of them. Finally, he let out his pent up breath in a rush.

"Forget it," he said, dropping the chain. He turned and left.

To Joe and Spider's surprise Dave Dibbins turned to them, his eyes a lot less glassy than before. He was very aware of his surroundings now.

"Okay, so," Dave said, tossing the broken bottle aside. "Now what? Do I join FORS, or do you kill me now?"

Joe and Spider broke into laughter. Obviously, they had a new teammate.

****

Joe and Midnight's relationship proved to be a benefit for each of them. Although they cared very much for one another, they both knew that they were not "in love" and for that reason those all-important three little words were never spoken. It was something they didn't discuss, they just knew. It was a kind of a healing stage for them both.

For Joe it was a way to cure the loneliness he had felt since his parents' death, and since leaving England. For Midnight, it was learning to trust a man for the first time and to realize that she could rely on him.

The relationship was, however, very intense. The highs were very high, and the lows fiery. It was the simple fact that they needed to be close to each other in every way at that point in their lives, and being so close made for strong emotions and strong fears.

A couple of months into the relationship, however, Midnight started to feel increasingly stifled; Joe had become overly protective of her. Without meaning to, Joe had unconsciously put all of his dormant fears of losing someone he cared for onto Midnight. He was constantly after her to be more careful, to take more backup. They fought about the issue regularly, usually after she'd been hurt working a case and he'd overreacted to her injury.

One of those fights occurred when Midnight was hurt while he was out of town for three days. He had traveled up to Sacramento, in Midnight's stead, to represent FORS at a conference sponsored by the State of California, Bureau of Investigation on Organized Crime and Criminal Identification. Midnight had been too busy with a case and had asked him to attend in her place. The day he was to return,

Midnight went on a raid with three other members of FORS and a San Diego Police Department entry team. Her backup, a huge Samoan man nicknamed Tiny, had fallen behind her going up the five flights of stairs in the apartment building they were hitting. So she had been alone when she had entered the apartment door they had just forced open.

The officers searching the apartment didn't know the suspect had been hiding in a hall closet. He was on his way out of that closet when Midnight started to open the door. The man was heavy set and easily three times Midnight's weight. He threw the door open, pushing Midnight into the wall behind her. She cried out as her head hit the wall, and that alerted the officers that were farther into the apartment. They came on the run but it was Tiny, who had finally made it up the stairs, who rushed the suspect who was headed out the front door at a full run.

By the time the officers had secured the suspect, and someone thought to check on Midnight, she was sitting on the floor, knees up, arms folded, with one hand holding the back of her head. There was blood seeping between her fingers. Tiny picked her up in his arms and carried her downstairs, Midnight all the while telling him she was fine.

The big Samoan stood by impatiently as the paramedics checked her out and stopped the bleeding. It was that same big man who almost passed out from relief when they told him she would be just fine. She had a nasty cut on her head, and they said she'd have a headache for a few days. Tiny thanked the paramedics profusely. He looked at Midnight apologetically as she got up from the curb. Tiny rushed to help her. With exaggerated care, he walked her over to her car, asking her over and over if she needed a ride home.

Midnight only shook her head. "I'm okay, Tiny, but I'm taking the rest of the day off."

"You sure you don't want a ride home?" he asked, his big brown eyes looking worriedly at her.

"Yes I'm sure!" she said laughing. "But I will let you write the report on this one, okay?"

He looked down at his shoes then, still feeling very bad about the whole thing. He nodded solemnly. "I really am sorry, boss."

"Hey, you got him didn't you?" She smiled at him, stooping down just slightly to get under his eyes, which were still focusing on the ground. It always surprised her that someone like Tiny, who had been a hardcore gang member until about a year before, could turn into such a good ally. Disillusionment in the gangs tended to send its neglected or abused members in the exact opposite direction, and that's what FORS was all about.

"Go on, Tiny, get out of here before I change my mind and run you over." She laughed and saw a slow smile starting on his face.

She got into her Corvette and left the scene. Her head did hurt a great deal. She was glad that Joe had taken his car to the airport so she didn't have to pick him up that night when he came in.

Midnight went straight home, which was currently Joe's house. She had left her house in the capable hands of the now retired Tom Ryan. He kept an eye on it and occasionally she would let members of FORS stay there when they were in between places.

Tom Ryan, the man Midnight credited with her survival after her brother's death, had opened a restaurant/bar called The Pit. It was a block from the police department so a lot of cops frequented the place. Midnight and FORS had a permanently reserved table and Midnight's unit gave Tom a lot of business. She figured it was the least she could do for him, since he had helped her so much throughout the years. He'd become the father she'd never had.

At Joe's she took a double dose of aspirin and closed all the blinds in the bedroom, but left the windows open so she could hear the ocean. She kicked off her boots, stripped off her jeans, and discarded the white cotton shirt that now had her blood on it. She pulled one of Joe's shirts out of the closet, put it on, and lay down.

She tossed and turned for a while, unable to find a comfortable place on the pillow, where it didn't bump the cut on the back of her head. Finally, she settled on her side and listened to the sounds of the ocean, loving the smell of the salt air and the coolness of the breeze coming through the windows. She was asleep ten minutes later.

She awoke with the sensation that someone was in the room. Opening her eyes, she saw Joe's silhouette by the closet where he was hanging up his jacket. By the light of the hallway she could see that he was wearing jeans and a sweater, with his shoulder holster over it. She watched with an appreciative eye as he moved quietly about the room, pulling off his holster and hanging it on a nearby chair. She liked to watch him move; he was fluid, like a big cat. She realized she had missed him a great deal over the last three days.

He turned then and, walked toward her. As he neared the bed, he could see that she was awake watching him, and he smiled down at her. He sat down on the bed and touched her cheek. Leaning down, he kissed her lips, and the kiss quickly turned to passion. When he reached his hand up to touch her hair, she stiffened. He had touched the cut.

He pulled back immediately, surprised and instantly worried. "What?" he asked, his eyes searched her face.

"Oh," she said casually, "I just got a little banged up today, that's all."

She reached up to pull him back down to her again, but she could see from the look on his face that he wasn't going to accept her vague answer.

Oh boy Midnight thought, *here we go again*! She kicked herself for flinching the way she had, but she knew she wouldn't have been able to hide her injury from him for long. He'd see the accident report, if nothing else.

"What the hell happened?" his asked, his voice strident.

Midnight shrugged trying to keep the whole discussion light. "No big deal, I just banged my head today on a raid. Now tell me about the conference, was it as good as we've been hearing?" She was trying to distract him, but she could see that wasn't going to work.

"To hell with the conference, Midnight!" he said, exasperated. "Who the fuck was your backup?"

Sighing, Midnight sat up. "Tiny, but there were about five flights of stairs and you know how big Tiny is, it wasn't his fault, I—"

"What the hell do you mean, not his fault? Like hell it wasn't!" He cut her off. "Can't he do his job now? If his size is becoming a problem, then he'll have—"

Now it was her turn to cut him off. "Joe! It's still my unit and if I say that it wasn't Tiny's fault, then it wasn't. You got that?" She was as angry as he was. She was tired and all of this was making her head hurt again.

"Yeah," he said, his voice quieter now, but his eyes burned with anger.

Joe stood up and looked down at her. If he'd been paying attention he would have seen how beautiful she looked at that moment. With her hair hanging loose and wild around her face, wearing his shirt, her tanned legs tucked up under her, eyes a fiery green. But, he was pissed and he didn't notice. He was too busy thinking if he had been with her she wouldn't have gotten hurt. His frustration from knowing he couldn't be there all the time had been building for some time. Now it spilled out in anger at her for pulling rank on him in a personal situation, which it really wasn't, but in his anger he saw it that way.

"Yeah," he repeated, his voice harsh and angry, "I got that. And I guess I'm some dumb fuck who just walked in off the streets that don't know jack about anything? Yeah, well fuck you Midnight!" He turned and left the room, slamming the door on his way out.

Midnight was out of the bed like a shot and followed him down the hall. She didn't catch up to him until he was outside and almost to his car. She was worried, because she knew how mad he was and how dangerous it would be for him to be driving. She also knew he had taken off his shoulder holster and so didn't have his gun with him. In the type of business they were in, someone was always gunning for them so going anywhere without a gun was a bad idea.

"Joe!" she yelled at him, determined to stop him.

He turned and saw her standing on the front steps, in nothing but his shirt. The wind was blowing and he could see her shiver. But she wasn't paying attention to the cold; she was watching him. He strode back over to her, his anger lengthening his already long strides. He was face to face with her within seconds. They stood eye to eye staring at each other angrily. Joe broke the stare first; he looked away and over her shoulder.

"Get back in the house before you freeze to death," he said, but even his concern for her health came out harsh and angry.

"Fuck you!" she snapped at him, her eyes blazing. "What part of this don't you understand, Sinclair? That I'm a cop or that I won't stop being one because you and I are together? I'm not going to stop going on raids and taking cases because you might worry. If you're worried about me that's your fucking problem and you better get over it fast!"

Stepping down two of the stairs, she reached out and snatched his keys out of his hand then stormed back up to the front door. She turned again to face him. He was staring at her dumbfounded by her outburst.

"And you aren't driving in the state you're in right now. As your supervisor it is my job to look out for the well-being of my subordinates!"

She stepped back inside the doorway and slammed the front door.

She stood inside, taking deep breaths and shivering. She hated it when they fought. She was always worried that this time one of them would go too far, say the wrong thing and their friendship, which was the most important thing in the world to her, would be irreparably damaged.

Midnight leaned against the entryway table, closed her eyes, and tried to calm down. Her head was pounding wildly now from the yelling she had done. She didn't hear the front door open, and suddenly Joe was there, pulling her into his arms, murmuring apologies in her ear.

"I'm sorry, babe," he whispered.

He lifted her face to look up at him, and he could see that she was in pain. His eyes reflected his chagrin at having inadvertently caused her more pain by trying to protect her. Joe lifted her up in his arms and carried her back into the bedroom. He laid her on the bed carefully and went to get her some aspirin. After she had taken them, he lay down next to her and pulled her gently into his arms.

Midnight put her head on his shoulder and threw a leg over his. He held her and soothingly stroked her hair. After a while she looked up at him. He was staring off into space, but at her movement he looked down at her with solemn eyes. She reached up and touched his lips with her fingertips as if trying to hush his self-effacing thoughts.

"I'm sorry, too," she said quietly. "I'll be more careful."

He smiled at her then as if she had missed the whole point of the argument, but that he loved her anyway. They said nothing else about the incident. He continued to worry about her, but he tried to be less vocal about it.

****

A month later, the culmination of all of his fears came to bear. While on an undercover case, Midnight was stabbed by the gang leader she was working against. Like a dog that smells fear, the girl had sensed Midnight's caution. She decided Midnight was a cop and knifed her in

45

the back. Though she had tried for Midnight's heart, she hit her lung instead.

Joe was listening in on the tap when it happened. He threw down the headphones he was wearing and leapt out of the surveillance van, not caring if he blew their cover. He went through the door to the house with his weapon drawn. He intended to get to Midnight even if he had to blow away everyone in his path. The door to the room was open when he got there. He saw the gang leader stood with her back to him. She was standing over Midnight's motionless form. Midnight's blood pooling around her. Without stopping, he moved toward the woman standing over his partner. He placed his foot square in the small of her back and shoved her as hard as he could, sending her flying into the wall. She sunk to the floor unconscious. He holstered his weapon and dropped to Midnight's side.

"Midnight!" he said, touching her face. "Come on, babe, give me a sign." He felt for a pulse, and was relieved to find one, but it was weak. He knew he had to hurry.

Pulling out his radio he yelled, "Eleven ninety-nine! Officer needs help! Officer down!"

He called out their location and heard an instant response on the radio. He knew he had to get Midnight out of that house. There were other gang members in the house who would gladly kill them both, given the chance. Joe lifted her up and ran through the house. As he broke out into the afternoon sun, he saw four police cars screech to a halt. He could hear the ambulances coming too. They sped around the corner as he watched.

Joe was afraid to lay her down. He was afraid if he didn't have contact with her she would slip away from him. Other officers ran up to assist him, but he shook his head.

He looked back at the house. "Get the bitch that did this. She's in that back room." His voice was deadly calm, although his pulse was racing.

The paramedics were there and they took Midnight's still unconscious body from his arms. He stayed right next to where they were working the whole time, watching them intently as if he could keep them from losing her that way.

"We've got a pulse," the paramedic said, "but it's thready. She's losing a lot of blood. We better get her in now!"

Joe rode in the ambulance with her, holding her hand the whole time. She stirred and groaned, and he squeezed her hand encouragingly. She opened her eyes and looked straight at him, but he could see she was in a great deal of pain. The paramedics had an oxygen mask over her face, and it was obvious by the way she clawed it she wanted it off.

"Leave it on, Midnight," Joe said, keeping his voice calm for her. "You're going to be okay. Just lie there and let them take care of you."

She shook her head and there were tears in her eyes. She said something, but he couldn't understand her because of the mask.

"What is it, Night?" he asked, looking up at the paramedic for permission to remove the mask for a moment. The paramedic nodded.

Joe pulled it down, his eyes watching hers. "What is it?"

She swallowed and looked up at him. "I was being careful," she said, almost as if she was apologizing to him. Her voice was so quiet he had to bend down to hear her.

She closed her eyes again and her breathing was labored. Joe put the mask back on over her mouth. Her eyes opened again and she waited for him to reply.

"I know you were, babe. Just rest right now."

He knew she'd been too careful, that's what had tipped the gang leader off, and it was his fault. Midnight had closed her eyes again. As the ambulance sped to the hospital Joe prayed that he'd get a chance to tell her how sorry he was and how much he cared about her.

The next four hours were a nightmare. Many of the FORS team joined Joe in the waiting room as they waited for news of their leader. Joe sat in a corner staring at the floor, his thumb rubbing absently at the palm of his other hand. No one approached him. They knew the private hell that he was going through; they, too, were dealing with their own fears.

Midnight had recruited each and every one of them. She had at one time or another helped them with encouragement or a sympathetic ear. She'd earned the respect of every member of the unit, and as diversified as the members of FORS were, that respect was a hard-won prize. Joe was well respected by the team as well, but the brunt of the awe and loyalty fell on the small shoulders of the woman who had single-handedly begun the unit they all belonged to and for whom they would each give their own lives.

Midnight had made them respectable. She'd made them into people that commanded respect rather than fear. Midnight had made them human beings again, instead of the animals that they had become in the gang; killing machines with no thought or emotion. They were people again because of Midnight Chevalier and for no other reason. So they all waited for word of her condition with their hearts in their throats.

When the doctor came out, she was assailed with questions from all directions. She was trying to answer everybody at once, not having much success, when Joe, who stood a head taller than most of the crowd, pushed his way through.

"Hold it!" he commanded.

Everyone fell silent.

He looked down at the doctor. "How is she?"

"Ms. Chevalier is in critical condition at this time," the doctor said, trying to keep her officious tone, but having difficulty with so many rough looking people eyeing her. "The knife punctured her left lung, and she lost a great deal of blood." She paused, giving them a moment to process everything. "We'll know more in the next twenty-four hours."

"Can I see her?" Joe asked, his light blue eyes begging the doctor.

"She's in the recovery room. It's not normal procedure ..." she began to say, but hesitated, seeing the devastated look in the Englishman's eyes.

The doctor had heard about her patient and how she had been injured. She'd also heard about what Midnight Chevalier did for a living, and that this man was her partner. The doctor considered their mission a very noble one and because of that felt a special desire to reassure them, even if she didn't know the eventual outcome of the small blond woman in the recovery room. She rubbed her eyes wearily and looked up at Joe again. "You can come, the rest of you will have to stay out here." Joe nodded and looked over at Spider and Tiny who were flanking him.

"Keep it together guys, I'll come back and report," he said. Then he followed the doctor to the recovery room.

Midnight looked very pale lying in the bed. She had two different IVs in her hand, and various other monitoring devices.

"She's been sedated for now," the doctor explained, "because the damage to her lungs will make it difficult to breathe. She will need to stay calm to heal properly and the best way to do that is to keep her sedated."

The doctor was glad she had allowed Joe in the recovery room, even if she was going to catch hell for doing it. She watched as he stared down at his partner with such unabashed distress. She found herself having to look away before she could get emotional too. "You can sit here with her for a while. I'll get you a pass, so that you can go and tell your friends how she's doing, and come back."

Joe gave her a weak smile, barely pulling his gaze away from Midnight. "Thanks."

It was a week before Midnight even stirred, and even then she didn't wake up. She was being kept thoroughly sedated. The following night she stirred and then slowly opened her eyes. Joe didn't move; he was afraid he was seeing things or dreaming. She looked at him for a moment and then smiled. It was a small, weak smile, but to Joe it was fantastic.

"Hey!" he said, overjoyed at seeing her awake.

"Hey," she responded weakly. She moved as if to try to sit up, but Joe put his hand on her shoulder.

"Don't try to move around yet, Night. You need to rest."

Midnight nodded slowly, out of breath from just attempting to move. She moved her fingers and Joe took her hand in his. She settled back and closed her eyes.

Three days passed before Midnight could move around and actually hold a conversation without gasping for breath all the time. By this time, the doctors had upgraded her to stable with a good prognosis, but they were still watching for signs of infection. She had been moved to a private room and the hospital was allowing short visits from the members of FORS, since she didn't have any immediate family that would come to see her.

Tom Ryan stopped by and he looked her over worriedly. "Damn kid," he muttered good-naturedly, "always trying to give an old man a heart attack!"

Midnight laughed at that, clasping his hand tightly. "That's what you always say," she told him.

San Diego, California, 1980

After Thomas's funeral, Midnight stayed at Tom Ryan's house. He took her there after Thomas's death, knowing that she wouldn't get the support or the sympathy from her parents that she needed. At Thomas's funeral, Jack and Carrie stared at her as if she were the murderer of their son. Suddenly he was their son. He had meant nothing to them

51

alive, but suddenly in death he was their baby. Every member of the Vettes was in attendance, but Midnight stayed with Tom. Suddenly her gang was the root of her anguish, and she couldn't stand with them on that day. She leaned heavily on Tom Ryan, her eyes covered by sunglasses. She was trying desperately to keep from throwing herself on the coffin, wanting to be dead too. She wanted to stop the hurt that was eating her alive. She felt like the whole world had turned upside down, and Tom Ryan was the only person that cared.

For the most part it was true; Tom Ryan was the only person that cared if Midnight Chevalier lived or died. Her parents certainly didn't. As Midnight laid the long-stemmed red rose on her brother's coffin, she swore to herself that she would get revenge for his death. Grief, anger, and hate coated her like armor and she became obsessed with the idea of killing the leader of the Piranhas.

When Midnight voiced her intention to Tom Ryan the next day, he shook his head. "Do you think that killing Talma Hooks is going to bring Thomas back?"

Midnight stared at him in disbelief, he wasn't going to turn on her too? "I think it will make me feel better …" she said, standing to leave.

Ryan reached out and pulled her back, pushing her into a chair at his kitchen table. Ryan's house was small, and cluttered. His wife of ten years had left him a couple of years before, and he wasn't much for cleaning up, except for the necessities. So the place got messy. One of the few rooms in the house that was fairly neat was the kitchen.

He looked at Midnight, concern and anger evident on his face. "Midnight, the only thing that will accomplish is to put you in jail, and I think you could do a lot more than that with your life."

"Yeah?" said, not believing him for a second. "Like what?"

"Like college, like a career, something," Ryan answered.

Midnight laughed hollowly, wondering how much Ryan knew. "Oh yeah, right."

"Yeah, right," Ryan persisted. "For all the trouble you were in, you still got pretty good grades in school. I know, I checked." He gave her a direct look. "And yes I know you were accepted to UCSD."

Midnight eyed him suspiciously. "What made you want to check up on me?"

"Because," Ryan said, touching her hand, which she promptly pulled away, "I think you have a lot more potential than being top gang leader of the heap."

She eyed him warily, what was he trying to pull? "The Vettes are all I have left."

"Oh Christ I hope not," Ryan said wryly. Midnight just stared at him, narrowing her eyes. "I'm sorry," he said looking serious again, "but that gang is not gonna do anything for you, except land you in jail someday. Or maybe you'll just follow Thomas ..." To his surprise her eyes dropped from his when he said the last. "That's what you're hoping, isn't it?" he asked, reading her face so easily. "You want to die now too. Am I right?"

Midnight moved to stand again. He grabbed her arm and, even though she struggled, she couldn't pull away. She turned to look at him and to her astonishment, she saw tears in his eyes. He couldn't actually care if she wanted to die. Managing to pull away from him, Midnight stood up shrugging into her Vettes jacket.

"I have to go," she said, her eyes averted from Ryan's. She didn't want to see his sympathy. She knew what she had to do.

"Where are you going?" Ryan asked.

She cracked a wintery smile. "Date with death, maybe," she said and walked out of the house. Once outside, Midnight stood looking at Tom Ryan's house. She wondered if this would be the last time she would see Ryan, thinking that she should have thanked him for everything. If it hadn't been for him, she would have killed herself the night Thomas had died. At least the way she was doing it she would take the leader of the Piranhas out, or die trying.

Midnight walked along the street that was the Piranhas turf. She heard them in a pool hall not far down the street. Walking into the hall, she looked around. Her eyes adjusted quickly to the dim light. She was a striking figure in all black. Her eyes were haunted, but fiery as they searched the room until they found the leader of the Piranhas.

Talma stood a towering five feet ten inches tall compared to Midnight's five feet five inches. Talma's size didn't impress Midnight, nor did it scare her. Most people made the mistake of underestimating Midnight because of her slight stature; she used that to her advantage.

"Ah, little Midnight," Talma said, strolling over to Midnight. Then she looked back over her shoulder at her followers and pulled a face. "How's the family?" The gang laughed and Talma laughed with them. She turned back just in time to catch Midnight's fist right in the face. Falling back, Talma stared wide-eyed at the smaller girl. She was shocked that her opponent could pack that much of a punch, and Midnight was advancing on her. Midnight's face was set in a grim hard line, she was determined to kill this woman. She didn't know who had killed her brother, but she knew that it was Talma's gang, so all of her hate and anger was centered on the leader.

As Midnight advanced, she saw one of the other girls start toward her. She turned, pulling out a knife, its four-inch blade glinting menacingly as she brandished it. Midnight narrowed her eyes threateningly at the other woman.

"You wanna piece of this?" she asked, her voice as cold and hard as the steel of the knife she held. The girl stopped dead in her tracks. She stood looking at Midnight for a split second then shook her head and stepped back.

Talma had recovered from Midnight's first attack and was standing ready for the Vettes' leader now. Midnight continued to advance slowly, her eyes reflecting an almost predatory look. Disturbed by the sheer determination showing on her opponents face, Talma panicked and charged the smaller woman. Midnight simply stepped aside at the last moment, catching Talma in the stomach with a booted foot. Talma fell to the ground coughing. Midnight reacted instantly, sticking her knife in her belt and launching herself at her downed adversary. Shoving Talma over onto her back, Midnight held the woman's shoulder to the floor with her left hand and proceeded to punch her repeatedly in the face with her right. Talma was attempting to block Midnight's attack, holding her hands up, but Midnight knocked them away. Finally, when she'd knocked Talma out, Midnight pulled out the knife. She straddled the other woman's chest and, holding the knife with both hands, she drew a bead at Talma's heart and drew the knife back.

"Midnight!" a voice rang out from the back of the bar. The Vettes' leader paused, her head snapping up at the sound of Tom Ryan's voice. He stood at the door to the pool hall with his weapon drawn and pointed directly at her. Their eyes met for a long second. They both knew he couldn't shoot her. Midnight's lips curled in a sardonic smile, as her eyes watched him, as if his appearance was somehow part of her plan.

Tom Ryan watched as Midnight turned her attention back to Talma who was now regaining consciousness. Talma stared up at her in terror, her eyes locked on the point of the knife that Midnight held. Midnight's eyes were pure ice as she stared down at her nemesis.

"Game point, Talma, nobody wins," Midnight growled, as she plunged the blade downward.

"No!" Tom Ryan and Talma shrieked at the same time.

Suddenly there were people blocking the way. Ryan couldn't see, he couldn't get through the crowd. If Midnight had killed Talma, he was responsible. He had known what she had wanted to do and he had let her leave the house. If she had killed Talma, he was going to have the hideous duty of not only arresting her, but being a witness against her later. But if he could get to Talma in time, maybe it would only be a flesh wound, maybe… He shoved his way through the crowd and broke through.

Midnight had moved from over Talma's body. She sat with her knees up to her chest, panting from the adrenaline running through her body. She was looking at the floor. Talma lay unconscious, but there was no blood. Ryan surveyed the scene and followed Midnight's line of sight. She was staring at the knife. It was stuck into the hard wood floor next to Talma's head, still waving back and forth from the force that had put it there. Tom thought he'd pass out with the overwhelming sense of relief he felt.

****

Ryan stayed with Midnight for a short while, not wanting to tire her too much. Once in the lobby of the hospital, Ryan turned to Joe.

"It's not your fault you know," Ryan said.

"What?" Joe said, surprised.

"It's not your fault," Ryan repeated. "Midnight is very special to me, but she's also the most headstrong, stubborn pain in the ass I have ever met. And if you think that you can control that, you're crazy. That's how she is. She was born with it. No man will ever drive that from her." Ryan clasped Joe's shoulder companionably. "And it's going to take one hell of man to live with it. But you see, that's what makes her Midnight. Otherwise, she'd just be another cop on the job. And she wouldn't be as good at that job. You know what I mean?"

"Yeah," Joe said slowly, looking at the older man with more respect, because he was able to see someone he cared about so clearly. "I think I do, and all this time I've been trying to change it. But I don't know if I can handle her going off on her own, and getting into more danger. What am I supposed to do? What if I'm not there sometime? What if—"Ryan was shaking his head at the younger man.

"Joe, if you try to stay one step ahead of that girl, and fate, you'll go crazy." He watched for Joe's reaction, unsure if he should say what he'd been thinking, but he decided that it needed to be said. "Maybe, you should consider stepping back from all this, from her. I think you're too close. You're afraid for her, and your fear is working its way around to her. That's dangerous my friend."

Joe looked at him and narrowed his eyes. "You're saying we shouldn't be together."

It was a statement, not a question, but there was no anger in his words, only quiet understanding.

"I'm saying you're too close," Ryan said, without affirming Joe's statement.

Joe nodded, his mouth set in a grim line. Ryan left and Joe returned to Midnight's room. He found her staring off into space, a very serious look on her face.

"Don't think too hard," he said, grinning as he walked over to the side of the bed. "You might hurt something."

She glanced up at him, her face still serious, but then she smiled. "I might," she said, her tone purposely light.

Joe gave her a sidelong look, knowing there was something going on in her head. He had a feeling he knew what it was. "What's up, love?"

Midnight didn't answer for a moment, obviously debating whether she wanted to tell him what she'd been thinking.

"You're thinking about us, aren't you?" Joe said. He saw the surprise in her eyes, although her face gave nothing away. Then she nodded slowly, sighing.

Joe sat down, took her hand in his, and brought his face down close to hers. "Talk to me," he said quietly.

"You're my best friend, Joe," she began, "and I love you more than anything in the world." She paused, obviously worried about what she was about to say. "I just think, that we need to step back for a while, and just see how we feel, you know?" Her voice pleaded with him to understand, and thanks to Tom, he did.

"Kind of like not seeing the forest for the trees, eh?" he said, smiling down at her.

A relieved smile crossed Midnight's face; she had been so afraid that he'd be angry or that his ego would get in the way, but she realized now that she should have known better.

"But," he said sternly, his eyes searching hers, "we stay close, and we still back each other up."

"I wouldn't allow it to be any other way," she said, her eyes misty with tears.

"I'll always be here for you, Midnight," he said quietly, as he stared deep into her eyes. "Always."

"And I for you, Joseph," she replied with equal sincerity.

He leaned down and kissed her lips. Although the kiss was tender, it was more poignant, than passionate. They had just moved to a new level in their friendship. And they had nowhere to go but up.

CHAPTER 3

San Diego, California, 1989

Joe and Midnight stayed very close, no one could interfere with their friendship. They were there for each other come Hell or high water. It's how they wanted their relationship. It worked for them, and it gave them both the comfort they needed, without the intensity of the romantic entanglements.

Midnight had relationships with other police officers from different departments and other men she met, but she never wanted them for long. The men would either become possessive of her, or they would try to change her; Midnight would put up with neither. Many simply couldn't handle how close she was to her partner. At any given time, night or day, Joe could call and Midnight would drop everything for him. The men she dated couldn't, or wouldn't, compete with that. Then there was the fact that she'd just been promoted to lieutenant; she was the youngest lieutenant in the department, as well as being one of the very few female ranking officers. The jealousy over that kept men in the department far from Midnight.

She never felt like she had to have a man around. To her, they were good for sex, but other than that they were too self-centered and self-serving to be around too long. As far as Midnight was concerned, she didn't need anyone but herself and her work. She figured if she didn't rely on anyone, they could never let her down.

The only exception to that rule was Joseph Michael Sinclair. Sometimes, if she'd allow herself to think about it, Midnight would rail at the fates that had made it so that she was not in love with the one man she cared about and trusted most.

For Joe the feelings were the same. He always knew Midnight would be there for him, if he needed her, as he was for her. Joe found that, in a lot of ways, being with Midnight was like being with his lifelong best friend, Rick. He felt the same kinship with her as he did with Rick, she knew him inside and out, as he did her. They each knew what made the other tick and they shared the same dedication to FORS.

Joe's relationships, too, were many, but usually short-lived. Often, women would only be interested in his money; it had become general knowledge in the department that Joe was worth a lot. Some women found Joe a challenge, sometimes because of his brooding silence, but usually because of his relationship with Midnight. Women seemed to think that if they could hold on to Joe longer than Midnight had, then they were somehow better than her. Joe did not understand the logic but Midnight found it amusing.

****

Midnight was working late one evening when there was a light knock on the doorjamb to her office. Looking up she saw Tammy, a shy member for FORS, standing there.

"Hi Tammy," Midnight said, smiling, "what's up?"

"Do you have a minute?" Tammy replied softly.

"Sure," Midnight replied, nodding and gesturing for her to sit down. She did, though she was hesitant.

Tammy was a member of FORS by default. She'd never been a hard-core gang member. She had, however, dated the leader of a gang FORS had taken down. Tammy turned to FORS to take him down after he'd raped and beaten her. She was a shy, quiet girl. Once her ex-boyfriend had been taken down, Joe had taken Tammy under his wing, treating her delicately and with a great deal of compassion. She'd come further out of her shell in the time she'd spent around the unit and it had a lot to do with Joe and his attention to her. He often took her to lunch or just sat and talked to her, trying to get her to open up and have more confidence. It was definitely working. Tammy didn't look or act like the same scared-to-death girl she had been when Midnight had first met her. She was finally dating again, but she was always comparing men she dated to Joe. They always paled in comparison, but the man she'd gone out with the night before had a lot promise.

"So, what's going on with you?" Midnight asked, giving her a warm smile.

"Oh," Tammy said, sighing, "I went out last night."

"And?" Midnight asked, leaning forward with interest.

"And he's very nice." She blushed and stared shyly at the floor. "And a lot like Joe."

"Really now?" Midnight said, grinning. Midnight knew that Tammy idolized Joe as if he were the perfect man.

"He's nice huh?" Midnight asked.

"Well, yes," Tammy said, her smile wider now.

"Who is it?" Midnight asked suspiciously, but her smile remained. She knew that Tammy wanted to tell her something, but she was afraid.

"It's ..." Tammy hesitated again, then she reached behind her and closed Midnight's door. As she sat back down, she took in a deep breath to calm her nerves. "It's Spider," she said. Midnight was surprised but the longer she thought about it, the more it made sense.

Spider was quiet, but he did have a certain sincere, sweet quality to him, and in a way, he was like Joe. Midnight's smile told Tammy that she approved of the match. Tammy smiled back, relieved. She was afraid that Midnight might not approve of them being together. Midnight and Joe's relationship hadn't lasted long because of the impact the job had had on it. She thought that maybe Midnight would say the same about their new relationship.

"I think that's great, Tammy," Midnight said, genuinely pleased about the union.

Tammy smiled happily. She was glad Midnight approved and she knew Spider would be relieved too.

To many of them, FORS was a family, and Midnight was the head of that family. Much like a mother's disapproval, Midnight's disapproval could spell certain death to any relationship, venture, or plan. It was their way, and they loved it.

****

The next day in the office, Joe received a call he could barely believe.

"Sinclair," he answered, his tone as always distracted as he multi-tasked trying to get everything done at once.

"Such bad phone etiquette," came the sardonic reply in an English accent much like Joe's.

"Hey!" Joe exclaimed, knowing his best friend Rick's voice better than anyone's.

"Hey yourself," Rick said, grinning at his end.

"How've you been, man?" Joe asked.

"Me? Oh, I'm fine. You?"

"Same ole, thing," Joe replied happily.

"Yeah, well, I'm 'bout to change that up," Rick replied, his smile evident in his voice. "I'm coming out there."

That had to sink in for a minute with Joe. "Coming here? Man, that's great! How long you staying?"

"Forever."

"What?" Joe asked, his voice rising as if he could not possibly have heard his friend right. "You're leaving England?"

"Yeah, they will let me out you know," Rick said, his tone wry.

"You're leaving your family? Rick," Joe said then, now sounding worried, "nothing's happened has it?"

Rick only laughed. "God, man! No nothing's happened, I'm just tired of living here and I've been thinking about a change of scenery, so I'm coming," Rick said, looking out the window of his flat, thinking of a particularly sticky situation he'd recently been dealing with. A local debutante had been trying to nail him to the matrimonial cross.

"When?" Joe asked.

"A week."

"When's your flight?" Joe asked, reaching for a pad and paper to write it all down. He couldn't believe that Rick was actually coming to California to stay.

He hadn't seen him since he'd left England. Rick had been his best friend since he was seven years old. They'd grown up together. Joe got all the details from Rick, then hung up with a big smile on his face.

He got up from his desk and walked over to Midnight's office.

"Guess who I just talked to," he said, his grin still wide.

"Who?" Midnight replied, noting his grin and canting her head to the side.

"Rick Debenshire."

"Your best friend," Midnight replied, looking suitably impressed.

"You're my best friend," Joe replied, narrowing his eyes at her, "but he was for many years."

"You're allowed to have more than one," Midnight said with a grin.

"Wouldn't be considered 'best' then, love," Joe pointed out, chuckling.

"Good point," she replied. "He'll be here, when?"

"A week," Joe answered.

"This should definitely be interesting," Midnight said, her lips twisted in a grin.

Indeed it would.

****

A week later, Joe waited for Rick at the end of the gangway. When he saw Rick walking along, he strode over to him. The two men hugged, and laughed, but Rick could see that Joe was as serious as ever. Joe had always been that way. People around them glanced at the two men. They were a complete contrast, not just in looks, but in personality as well, and it showed.

Rick was gregarious, open, and outgoing. He had a wide smile and sapphire-blue eyes that sparkled with good humor. Whereas Joe had a dark brooding air about him, he was a mystery. It had always made them an intriguing pair in their youth in London. It had also made them good partners in their gang years before.

Once they were through customs and baggage claim, and in the car, Rick looked over at his lifelong friend.

"So now what?" Rick asked, the glint in his eyes mischievous as always.

"Bar?" Joe asked, grin in place.

"And you think I'll say no to that?" Rick replied.

An hour later, they sat at a table in a bar Joe and the rest of FORS frequented. They were talking and drinking beer, Joe was telling Rick about FORS's latest case. Rick's attention was diverted at one point when he saw a beautiful blond enter the bar; he watched as she walked over the bar. She obviously knew the bartender, since all she did was hold up one finger and the bartender, nodding and smiling, handed her a drink a few moments later. As Rick watched, the woman turned, her eyes scanning the bar. They came to rest on the table where Rick and Joe were sitting. Picking up her drink, she walked in that direction. Rick found himself staring as she walked. She had a body that could stop a Mack truck, and a beautiful face to match.

Joe realized quickly that Rick was no longer listening. He recognized the look on his friend's face easily, it was pure lust. Joe turned in his chair to check out the object of Rick's attention. His eyebrow rose as he saw Midnight walking toward them.

Should have seen that one coming, Joe thought to himself.

Midnight's eyes flicked to Joe's then back at Rick, resuming the stare she'd held since turning toward the table.

Joe turned back to look at Rick, chuckling at how awestruck his friend looked.

"Uh, Rick," Joe began, his tone humorous, "this would be Midnight, my partner."

Rick's eyes widened noticeably. Joe had told him about his partner being a woman, and that Midnight was an ex-gang leader like Joe. He'd also heard tales about Midnight being able to throw down in a fight with even the toughest gang members. So this petite, copper-blond haired, green-eyed vixen was far from what he'd expected. It took him a few moments to find his voice.

Midnight noticed, and grinned at him. She knew she was never what people expected. She liked that she surprised people, it kept them guessing. She, too, was a bit awed by Joe's friend. He was extremely handsome. He had long light brown hair, worn long past his shoulders. From what she could see, his build was lean, but he looked like he was probably almost as tall as Joe. He had deep sapphire-blue eyes that sparkled mischievously.

As she reached the table, Midnight shifted her drink to her left hand and offered her right hand to Rick.

"Good to meet you," she said, her voice holding a tint of humor at the situation.

"Uh, you too," Rick said, finally finding his voice as he took her hand, holding it just a few seconds longer than necessary.

Joe hooked a booted foot around a nearby chair, pulling it over so Midnight could sit down between them. Glancing at Rick again, he could see that his oldest friend was still a bit dumbfounded. Joe couldn't help but needle Rick.

"She's something, isn't she?" he said, his eyes glinting mischievously as he looked over at his partner.

"You can say that again," Rick said, smiling too, his eyes on Midnight.

"Hullo, I'm sitting right here," Midnight said, rolling her eyes and shaking her head. Then she looked at Rick. "So, Rick, are you here for a visit or …"

"I'm here to stay," he replied, his look direct.

"I see," Midnight said, nodding, her look appraising.

The spark between them was undeniable.

"I understand you take in stray gang members," Rick said, his lip curling in a grin.

"I took in this one didn't I?" Midnight said, gesturing to Joe with her head.

"Smartest thing you ever did," Joe put in.

Midnight chuckled at that, then looked over at Rick again. "Joe said you were his second in the gang back home?"

Rick inclined his head.

"He's good," Joe said, nodding his head.

Midnight nodded too. "Well, Joe, bring him down, we'll see what we see," she said, her look once again appraising.

Rick caught the look and narrowed his eyes at it, then nodded in agreement.

Joe quirked his lips at the definite chemistry, blowing his breath out to relieve the tension he suddenly felt. He wasn't sure what to do with that, so he ordered another shot. The three of them stayed at the bar until well into the evening, only leaving when Midnight got a page and had to leave.

Rick watched her go with interest written on his face. He caught the narrowed look Joe sent him, but didn't comment on it. He wasn't worried, Joe was his oldest and best friend and Rick hadn't met a woman yet who could come between them. At least he didn't think so. Women were just a pastime, sometimes good, sometimes not.

London, England, 1988

Sheila Theland had set her sights on Richard Debenshire. She'd heard about Rick's wild side and she liked the idea of taming him; his sharp good looks and long hair excited her own wild side. It never occurred to her that he had the reputation as a player for a reason, and had she stopped to think about it, she would have shrugged and said that was with "other women" not her. Sheila pursued Rick as she had never pursued a man before. When he finally took her up on her many suggestions, she was thrilled.

Six months later, she wasn't as thrilled. Rick had kept her guessing during their time together. She finally resorted to telling him she thought she was pregnant, in a desperate attempt to hold onto him. Of course she wasn't sure that she was pregnant, in fact she had only been two days late when she told him. His reaction to her revelation wasn't what she been prepared for. She had expected either out and out anger, or sullen resignation, but she had received neither. He simply stared at her for a moment, then off into space for a long time. She could see he was considering his options, then he nodded imperceptibly, as if he had just made an agreement with himself. To her utter shock, he stood up then and left.

He showed up at her parents' door two weeks later, dressed in his customary jeans, black cotton button up shirt, and a leather jacket. He asked for her and stood leaning indolently against the doorjamb, preventing the butler from closing the door. When Sheila had reached the top of the stairs, she was breathless. She'd planned to be cool and unaffected by him, punishing him for his rebuff. Seeing him again, though, changed that. She rushed down the stairs and all her dignity went by the wayside

Once in the sitting room, Rick sat on the couch and calmly waited.

"So?" he said simply, with one eyebrow raised cynically.

"So?" Sheila replied, almost stupidly, then she realized what he was asking. "Oh!" she said, startled that he would be so crass as to bring up a subject of such a delicate nature so casually, as if he were asking after something as everyday as the weather.

When she didn't respond to his question, he narrowed his eyes at her, his mouth pursing in anger held in check. At least, she thought, he isn't rude enough to actually ask the question outright. She was always making excuses for his attitude and demeanor. She knew that she shouldn't continue to play games with him and tell him what he wanted *to know, but she just couldn't believe that was the only reason he had come. Surely he had missed her too.*

"I've missed you a great deal," she said, smiling shyly at him, pretending not to understand what he was asking. She hoped that his sense of propriety wouldn't allow him to ask her directly about the baby.

Rick didn't respond, he continued to watch her, his deep blue eyes cool, his face showing that he was unaffected by her. Finally, she had shaken her head "no," keeping her eyes on the floor. Somehow, she had expected him to breathe a sigh of relief and tell her to be more careful, and then they could get back to their relationship. But once again, he surprised her, and stood up and walked out without one word. She didn't hear from him again. She ran into him at a party his parents had forced him to attend; he and Joe had been there together. They were loud, rude, and their behavior was beyond reprehensible. When she had caught him alone, he looked at her as if he didn't even know her. She had been devastated, but had managed to convince herself since then that he had only been drunk, and that was why he pretended not to recognize her. She was wrong.

****

After learning more about FORS, Rick decided that he definitely wanted to be part of what they did. FORS hired ex-gang members and leaders, first as paid confidential informants, then if they worked out, Midnight would recommend them for the police academy. Many of her members had already become fully-fledged peace officers.

For Rick, the idea of working with Joe again, and being part of something, was interesting. He had to get a work visa first, to be able to actually get a job with the department, and even then could only be hired as a Confidential Informant. He figured if he decided to stick around, he'd work on citizenship so he could become an official employee of the department. He attended a few classes on arrest and control, and found it all fascinating. He understood quickly why Joe had become a cop. He and Joe spent some time out on the firing range, although he had carried a gun off and on for years in England for "protection." Rick knew how to shoot, but Joe, being an expert marksman now, taught him a few new things. Rick also learned how to use the shotgun the department used on raids.

A couple of months after Rick's arrival, Midnight was informed that the secretarial position she'd been requesting for months had been approved and that they could start advertising and taking applications immediately. Midnight was ecstatic; she and Joe needed help with all the paperwork that was piling up. FORS was working numerous cases and they needed some help managing it. Ex-gang members weren't exactly the best clericals money could buy. Midnight sent out the job opportunity flyer immediately.

Rick was in the office regularly now, learning the ropes and observing the goings. He found himself watching Midnight in her element quite frequently. It did nothing to dissuade the desire he had for her; it only made it stronger. She had a kind of presence that made everyone listen to her when she talked, but she was also very good at listening. He had gotten the impression right away that everyone in the office idolized her and Joe. He had talked to Tiny, who had told him that Midnight was the reason that every member of FORS was there and that they would all do anything for her. Rick could tell by the look in the big guy's eyes that he meant every word.

Rick saw how many people Midnight dealt with and how she dealt with them. She always seemed to give them exactly what they needed. She was motivational, sympathetic, understanding, or just indignant for the wrongs that had been done. Rick found out that she was an incredible person inside and out. He couldn't stop thinking about her, and he knew that he had to do something about it.

****

One night, lying in bed after a particularly long day, Rick was again thinking about his current "obsession," as he'd come to think of Midnight. He debated in his head, as he had a million times before, the pros and cons of trying to get together with her. On the one hand, she was Joe's best friend, and they had a very close relationship. So he might be treading on ground that was morally off-limits to him. She was also probably the first woman he'd ever dealt with that didn't give him an open invitation to come on to her.

That was probably the attraction, he reasoned with himself. She was a challenge, and he'd always loved a challenge. If he could get to her, he could probably get over her. Thinking along that line, however, he realized that if, in the course of getting over her, he hurt her feelings, Joe might get pissed at him. Midnight meant a lot to Joe, Rick knew this, and he didn't know if he wanted to risk what would most likely happen if he and Midnight got together and it didn't work out. Sighing deeply, he stared up at the ceiling, remembering the contact they'd had earlier in the day.

She'd been explaining a case to him, standing beside him at his desk. She'd been showing him a chart of the power base in a particular gang. When she'd leaned in to point out something on the paper, her body had brushed against him, and he had sworn she'd hit him with a live wire. He'd felt the jolt of excitement again, just thinking about it. He'd been unable to control his sharp intake of breath, and had turned his head to look at her. She'd been so close to him, her face not three inches from his. She'd looked back at him and stopped talking for a minute. It was only a few seconds, but it had seemed endless. Rick had the insane desire to lean over and kiss her. He didn't know if she'd seen that in his eyes, but her eyes had widened slightly, then narrowed as she looked away. She'd gone back to what she'd been saying, but he still felt the effects from that moment.

Thinking about it now, he was curious what she would have done if he'd kissed her. *Probably slapped the shit out of me*, he thought to himself wryly. He knew he was making himself insane. He needed to do something, anything.

Without stopping to think, he picked up his phone off the nightstand and dialed her number. She answered the phone on the second ring.

"Chevalier," she said, her tone businesslike even at home. Obviously, she was used to receiving a lot of calls out of hours.

"Midnight, it's me," Rick said, his voice smooth but soft.

"Rick, hi," she said, a smile in her voice. "What's going on?"

"I just ..." he began, hesitating as his mind asked him what the hell he thought he was doing. "What're you doing?"

"Actually, just lying here," she said, glancing at the clock; it was eleven at night.

74

"I didn't wake you, did I?" he asked, though it didn't sound like he had.

"No, I was just lying here thinking," she said.

"Yeah, me too …" he said, his voice trailing off, betting himself she wasn't thinking about the same things he was.

"What were you thinking about?" she asked, as if reading his mind.

He hesitated, closing his eyes, wondering how stupid he really wanted to be.

"Rick?" she queried when he didn't answer.

"I'm here," he said, opening his eyes and sitting up.

"So, what were you thinking about?" she asked again softly. She wasn't letting it go. *Does she have an instinct or what?* he thought.

"You," he said, throwing caution to the wind.

"Yeah?" she asked, sounding a little like a blushing teenager all of a sudden.

He wasn't sure if she had just heard something she didn't want to or not, but he'd just decided that he needed to act now, and find out what would happen.

"Midnight."

"Yes?" she asked, sounding a little breathless.

"I'm coming over," he said, his tone no nonsense

"Okay," she answered simply.

He was at her door ten minutes later. She answered wearing her usual long cotton oxford with her hair loose and tousled looking. Rick refused to take the time to think. Stepping inside, he slid his hand under her hair at the base of her neck, pulling her into him, his lips taking hungry possession of hers. Her reaction was instant and her hands entwined themselves in his hair as her lips responded to his.

She'd been waiting for this.

Her ardent response, incited him further, making him groan as his other hand slid around her waist, dragging her body to his, pressing her close. His tongue slid over her lips parting them, and it was Midnight's turn to groan. His hand left her neck, and moved to her back, both hands pressing her into him. As he kicked the door closed, he turned her around so that she had her back to the door. He lifted her, wanting to get closer to her and she wrapped her legs around his waist. His hands unbuttoned her shirt as fast as they would let him. His desire to touch her skin was overwhelming.

His lips left hers and moved down her neck, making her gasp as her hands grasped at his back. Midnight leaned her head back, closing her eyes, and giving herself up to the sensations he sent through her. She had known that the fire they'd been playing with would have to ignite eventually. Now she allowed it to burn freely, wanting to take everything he gave.

Holding her close to him, Rick moved to the couch in the living room, laid her down, and continued to kiss her. Within minutes, both of their clothes lay in a pile on the floor.

As they made love, Midnight was shocked at how her body responded to his. She had never denied she was attracted to him; the man was downright gorgeous and he exuded a sexuality that was almost tangible. She gave herself up to his attentions, refusing to examine her thoughts on it too closely. After they reached the peak he'd expertly guided their bodies to, they lay together panting from the intensity of it. Rick lay over her, his lips still kissed hers, wanting to continue the contact. Midnight responded, craving more from him.

After a few minutes, Midnight got up and led him to her room. Rick lay down on the bed, pulled her down over him, and kissed her again, re-igniting the heat. As they made love a second time, he tried to move her onto her back, but she pushed him back, positioning her body over his again, her eyes challenging him.

"I want you on your back," she said, her tone matter of fact.

Rick's lips twisted in a sardonic grin, as he leaned up to kiss her again. His hand buried itself in her hair as he held her to him. His lips devoured hers hungrily again, his tongue doing all kinds of damage to her control. His free hand slid between them, caressing her nipples, making her groan again, and pressing her body ever closer to his. Rick reveled in her reaction, his lips still not leaving hers as he levered himself up to move her underneath him again. She protested, trying to stop him, but he continued to kiss her, making her forget that she cared. He made love to her again, taking them once again to dizzying heights.

As they lay afterward, trying to catch their breath, he moved to her side, his hand still on her stomach, his fingers spread wide.

"You're pretty spoiled, aren't you?" Midnight said, still sounding out of breath.

Rick grinned, his eyes half closed as he gazed at her. "Spoiled?"

"Used to getting your own way," Midnight clarified.

He shrugged. "Most of the time."

Midnight nodded, giving him a knowing look. Rick simply grinned back at her. They fell asleep in companionable silence. A few hours later, Midnight found herself awake and watching Rick sleep. She was still surprised at how fast and powerfully she responded to his kiss, and his touch was even more exciting.

For the first time, she actually lost control over her own body and she couldn't think straight. All she wanted was to have him touch her one more time, make love to her one more time. She studied his face as he slept, taking in the strong jawline and the handsome, finely chiseled face. His long curly hair gave him a wild bad-boy look and then there was his body.

She felt her own body stir as her eyes traveled down his body. He lay on his side, his arms clutched around the pillow that his head rested on. He had a swimmers body, long and lean, with just enough muscle to keep him from being considered skinny. His arms were strong; she knew that having been held so tightly against him earlier that night. His eyes, although closed at that moment, were definitely one of his major assets. They were a deep rich sapphire blue, and when he looked at her, she could almost feel the heat in them. Then there were his lips. He had strong lips and when he kissed her she felt like her insides had liquefied.

Unable to stop herself, Midnight leaned forward and kissed his chest. Levering herself up, she moved closer, kissing his neck as he stirred. She was leaning down to kiss his lips when he opened his eyes and stared up at her. He didn't say a word, as his hand slid over her waist, pulling her close to him, his other hand instantly at the base of her neck, pulling her down to him.

Within minutes, they were making love again. Afterwards they both fell asleep again. Midnight woke the next morning, her thoughts in turmoil. She reflected on the realization that she did lose control with him, and it really bugged her. She was used to being in control all the time, being out of control set off all kinds of warning bells in her head, but her body hadn't responded to those warnings. It was like her brain had been cut off from her body, and while an exquisite high during sex, she didn't like it at all now.

Maybe it was just the fact that she hadn't been with Joe in so long and she missed just having unguarded sex. She wasn't sure what it was, but she knew that she had to be careful with it.

⋇ ⋇ ⋇ ⋇

Later that morning, Joe walked into her office, immediately seeing the look on her face and the large cup of coffee in front of her.

"Good God, what happened to you?" he asked, laughing.

She looked up at him tiredly. "Your friend happened to me!"

"He did?" Joe said. His face showed nothing, but he felt a stab of jealousy.

He knew he had no right to expect them not to get together. Midnight was single, she didn't belong to him, but something inside him just didn't know if he could handle it. He didn't think that either of them was by any means serious about the other; they were very similar in their ways of dealing with the opposite sex. Midnight had numerous little affairs, but never stayed with any man long. Rick had always moved from one girl to the next in England, usually without a backward glance.

Joe had a feeling that Rick was going to have a harder time with Midnight though. Rick was used to clingy women who dropped themselves at his feet and tried to keep him from leaving. Midnight wouldn't even bat an eyelash if he left her. It was going to be interesting to watch, but hard too, because Joe really didn't want either one of them to get hurt. He decided then that he would talk to Rick.

Midnight watched Joe's face; she recognized the jealousy in his eyes, even though he tried to hide it. She had wondered how he was going to take the idea of her being with Rick. Still she wasn't sure.

She crossed her arms on top of the desk and put her head down. "Just wake me up when the first applicant arrives."

"Well that's the thing," Joe said, his voice holding laughter as he recovered his composure, "the first one's here already."

Midnight groaned, but it was muted due the fact that her head was buried in her arms.

"Shit! I hate you Sinclair," Midnight said. Then she sighed and said, "And I hate you for getting out of this today. Tell Tammy to give me five and then show in the first one."

She picked up her coffee cup, trying to get as much caffeine into herself as she could. Spider was sitting in on the interviews with her, so was the clerical supervisor John Parks.

The interviews proceeded uneventfully. They broke for lunch and Midnight stayed in her office sleeping on the couch. Everyone was given strict orders that to disturb her was to receive a bullet between the eyes. After her nap she felt much more human.

"I guess it's my turn to get the next one, huh?" she said looking at Spider. He nodded.

The next applicant was a girl who was barely twenty; she had experience in an office setting she had an associate's degree in business. Her resume had detailed a few projects she'd worked on, showing a great deal of initiative. Midnight needed someone who could work independently, so she had set up the interview. Thinking back on it now, Midnight remembered that Randissi Curtis' voice had been very soft on the phone. She had sounded very hesitant, but happy that she had an interview.

As Midnight rounded the corner, she saw the young woman sitting in a chair, looking around her in awe. She was a very pretty girl, Midnight noted. Her hair was a golden blond and it fell in silky waves to her waist, and her eyes were almost turquoise. She looked very wholesome, Midnight thought, and totally out of place.

"Hi," Midnight said as she approached the girl.

Randissi looked up at Midnight and smiled shyly.

"Hi," she replied, not quite meeting Midnight's eyes.

Midnight decided to take a more casual approach with this girl than she had the last few candidates. This one seemed to need some special handling. Since Midnight was wearing her usual jeans and a cotton shirt, she certainly didn't look like the lieutenant of a police unit.

"You here for an interview?" she asked, making her voice sound more street style.

She sat down next to Randissi, one leg bent under her casually.

"Yes," Randissi answered.

"Why would you wanna work here?" she asked, her tone disdaining.

"Well," Randissi said hesitantly. She didn't know who this woman was, but maybe she could make herself less nervous if she talked to someone, before they came to get her for the interview. "I heard that they go after gangs here, and well, it sounds like a very noble mission, you know?" Her voice was asking acceptance.

Midnight looked reflective for a minute then shrugged. "Yeah, I guess you could say that. But you'd be working for guys like Sinclair, I don't know …" She looked Randissi up and down, like she was trying to decide if she could handle this Sinclair guy.

"Why," Randissi asked, her eyes widening, "what's wrong with him?"

Midnight rolled her eyes at Randissi. "Well he comes in hungover a lot, he has a really bad temper, and he cusses a lot too. Think you could handle stuff like that?" Midnight watched her carefully to see how she would handle the question.

Randissi nodded her head. "My older brother Darrell comes home drunk a lot and so I have to deal with him when he's hungover, and he has a pretty bad temper too." She shrugged.

"Hmmm," Midnight said. "So do you have a lot of experience and stuff? I mean, you look real young is why I ask."

"Well, I've worked in an office at the college I went to. I got so used to trying to handle a million things at once, I think I could handle just about anything now. I have three years of business in college too. But I've never worked for an office like this before. Do you think they'll hold that against me?" Her voice was concerned. Midnight smiled, the kid was definitely genuine

"Nah, I mean they called you right?"

"Yes but maybe it was a mistake," Randissi said.

"No, Randissi," Midnight said as she stood up and looked down at the girl, "I don't make mistakes." Randissi looked up at her, her eyes wide.

"But how did you know my …"

Midnight extended her hand to the younger girl. "I'm Lieutenant Midnight Chevalier," she said, smiling at the girl. She thought the kid was going to faint. "Hey!" she said, touching her shoulder. "Relax, you did just fine."

Randissi stared at her in shock. "You mean that was the interview?"

"As far as I'm concerned, yes, and since it's my unit what I think goes." She smiled again at the girl, and sat back down next to her, planting her feet firmly on the floor in front of her, staring straight ahead.

"So when can you start?" she asked casually. Randissi had to think about what she had just said.

"You mean I have the job?" Randissi asked incredulously.

"That's what I mean," Midnight said, grinning.

"Wow," Randissi said, her teal colored eyes wide.

Midnight laughed at her expression. "My second's going to have a field day with you."

"Your second?" Randissi asked, confused now.

"Oh that guy Sinclair. Sergeant Sinclair to be exact, he really is bad sometimes, but he's also a hell of a guy, even if he comes across as an asshole sometimes. Oops there's some of that cussing I said we do around here."

"It's okay," Randissi said, her smile a little wider. "I hear that around the house a lot too, with two brothers."

Midnight laughed again. "So, Randissi, can you start tomorrow?"

"Sure," she answered, still so surprised by the way Midnight had interviewed her. "Oh, and you can call me Randy … if you like. No one really uses my full name."

She was pleased by how the interview went, though she suspected that Midnight didn't interview everyone like that; probably just girls that looked so shy that they might throw up right there at the interview.

****

Fifteen miles away in south San Diego, Rick and Joe sat on a stake out; they were watching for a suspect named Robert Bondy to come home. They were going to bust him if they got the chance. A police entry team waited not too far away, but there had been no sign of Bondy or his associates. Joe looked over at Rick; he looked as tired as Midnight had that morning. Rick glanced at Joe and saw his friend watching him.

"What?" Rick said, seeing a strange look in Joe's eyes.

"I heard you and Midnight got together," Joe said evenly.

Rick looked immediately chagrined, but when he spoke his voice was calm. "You did huh? You have a problem with it?" he asked, watching Joe carefully.

Joe didn't say anything for a minute, debating about how he wanted to answer that question. "I'm not really sure yet. But I've got no say in this; you and Midnight are both adults."

"Yeah, but that doesn't mean you don't care for her, and if I'm stepping in where I don't belong, man …" Rick's voice trailed off as he looked over at Joe, concern written on his face.

Their friendship meant a lot to Rick and he didn't want anything to come between them.

"No, man, it's okay," Joe said. "I guess it's just a little weird, you know, having you here, and now having you and Midnight together."

"Well I don't know that I'd classify us as together. We spent the night together, but something tells me that doesn't make it a relationship with her." Rick smiled knowingly.

Joe chuckled, nodding his head at his friend. "Yeah, I do think I should warn you, she doesn't get serious about many people, and almost never anyone she sleeps with." Joe's look was rueful.

"Except you," Rick said, finishing Joe's sentence.

"Well, yeah, but we're friends. She's my backup, no matter what. Probably seems kind of crazy."

"Not crazy," Rick said, "probably the perfect relationship."

Joe laughed ruefully.

"Not quite," Joe said seriously. "I want you to be careful with her, okay? Both for her sake and yours."

Rick stared at his friend for a long moment, a half grin on his face. "What's that supposed to mean?"

"I mean," Joe said, looking very serious, "be careful. Midnight isn't anything like the girls you've been with before. She's probably nothing like anyone you've ever met. She'll rip your heart out, man, and you'll let her. While it's happening you'll think you're enjoying it, and she won't even know she's doing it."

"What do you mean, she won't know she's doing it?" Rick asked, taken back.

Midnight didn't seem that cruel. What was Joe talking about?

"Rick, that girl is trouble for just about every man that gets near her, especially if he gets his heart involved. She has no idea how beautiful she is; she has no idea that with just a look she can drop a man to his knees. She hates to get involved with men. She says that we're all self-centered, self-serving assholes. I'm an exception for her, but she won't even totally commit to me, and don't think I haven't wanted her to a couple of times. But she won't. That's what I'm trying to tell you, man, just be careful. I don't want you hurt, or her."

Rick was surprised by what Joe was telling him, but he knew that some of it was true. Midnight definitely had no idea of the effect she had on men, that was obvious. But he also felt that Joe was worried for nothing, because his heart wasn't involved here. At least he didn't think so.

****

Daniel stared down at the man who lay bleeding on the floor in front of him. The people around them stared in shock. Daniel raised his head, looking at each of them.

"That," he growled, jabbing a finger toward the man on the floor, "is what happens if you cross me. You got that?"

Everyone around Robbins nodded vehemently.

"Get the body out of here," Robbins said to no one in particular, "and clean up the floor." With that, Daniel walked out of the room.

Tim Bollings rushed to clean the floor after the body was removed. He didn't know what the hell he was doing there. His brother, David, had gotten them into the gang, telling him they could score some big cash. Tim wasn't so sure. What he did know was that he'd just watched Robbins knife a guy for no apparent reason. He'd practically gutted him. This was getting too dangerous.

CHAPTER 4

The day after she'd gotten the job with FORS, Randy's older brother dropped her off at the office. They didn't have enough money for two cars in the family, but Randy was hoping that this job would allow her to get one for herself. Neither spoke much on the drive to the station. Darrell was still angry with her for taking this job; he didn't like the idea of her working with cops.

Darrell had blond hair like his little sisters, but his was cropped short in a flattop style. His eyes were brown, and he was twice the size of his sister. He worked in construction, so his bulk was completely muscle. His arms and face were very tanned and weathered from the years spent in the sun. His hands were rough, and sometimes his manner was too, but he loved his sister and their little brother, Donovan, dearly. It had been just them for about six years, and Darrell had borne the burden of raising his sister and brother during those years. He had watched as his sister had blossomed into a beautiful young woman, but he had always been very protective of her. Many of his friends had been noticing her over the last couple of years and had been talking about her amongst themselves. Darrell had gotten into a fight with one of the guys for saying the wrong thing within earshot of him.

Now he sat admiring his grown-up little sister in her work attire. She looked very nice in her long straight black skirt, black flat shoes, and teal colored sweater. The sweater's color made her eyes even more noticeable. Then again, Darrell thought to himself, maybe she looked too nice. He knew what cops were like and he didn't want his sister exposed to that type, but she hadn't asked him about applying for this job, nor had she listened to him when he told her she couldn't take it. At twenty, she was developing a will of her own and he wasn't sure he liked it.

"Okay, so, you call me at lunchtime if you don't like it and want to leave," Darrell said hopefully.

Randy looked at her brother for a moment, then she smiled at him. She was glad that he wasn't going to yell at her anymore this morning.

"Okay," she told him. But she knew she was going to like working for someone like Midnight Chevalier, who had been nice enough to do what she had done to keep her from having to go into the interview.

She wasn't so sure about this man Sinclair, though. From what Midnight had indicated, he seemed pretty hard to deal with, but what Randy had told Midnight had been true, Darrell was pretty hard to deal with too. Randy kissed Darrell on the cheek and then got out of the car. She stood on the curb and watched as the beat up 1969 Camaro drove away. Taking a deep breath, she turned and went into the building. She went up in the elevator and walked out into what she would find out was the usual chaos in the office. She made her way to Midnight's office, seeing the lettering for Lieutenant Chevalier on her door. Midnight was at her desk, wearing sapphire-blue shirt, and her hair was loose and shaggy as usual. She looked up at Randy and smiled.

"You made it," Midnight said, gesturing to the chaos in the office. "Close the door."

Randy turned to Midnight, and her eyes went to the walls behind the blond leader of FORS. The walls were littered with awards and certificates.

"Go ahead," Midnight said, leaning back in her chair, glancing up at the wall, "take a look. Some of it is actually interesting reading."

Randy stepped around the chair in front of the desk and got closer to the wall. There were certificates from the Commission on Peace Officers Standards and Training, or POST as they read. There were POST basic, management, and supervisory certificates and a certificate from the Supervisory Leadership Institute from POST. Looking further Randy saw an award for Officer of the Year from San Diego PD. In fact, there were two different ones there. She'd won it a couple of times. There was a bachelor's degree in psychology from the University of California, San Diego and a degree in criminal law from Western Law University. There were awards from the California Peace Officers Association and from the California Department of Justice, Bureau of Investigation, and from the Women's Peace Officers Association for most outstanding achievement for female law enforcement officer.

There were many other plaques and certificates, but Randy decided to save those for another day. She didn't want to seem like she wasn't ready to get to work. She was however, now more impressed with her new boss. This woman had achieved a lot. Randy had never had a good female role model, not even when her mother was around. She turned back to Midnight, who was watching her. Randy's eyes were full of respect and awe. Midnight glanced at the wall, and then back at Randy and shrugged, like none of that meant anything to her. *The boss certainly doesn't seem to have a big ego,* Randy thought.

"Things are going to be a little on the hectic side today," Midnight said, glancing outside her office again. "We had a bust go south last night, and everyone's scrambling to try to catch up now. Unfortunately, you're going to have to kind of pick some stuff up as you go today, but you seem pretty quick so I'm not worried. I do, however, need you to fill some paperwork out. I want you to read everything carefully first, to make sure you understand it. If you don't understand anything, ask me, I can explain it, okay?" She looked at Randy, whose eyes had grown wider at the extent of the paperwork she had to fill out. Midnight smiled at her. "Relax it's not as bad as it looks. Go ahead and have a seat over there." She pointed to a chair in the corner next to a small table. "And yell if you need anything, okay?"

"Okay," Randy said quietly.

Midnight decided that the younger woman was just overwhelmed with all that was happening. She was still very glad that she'd hired her.

Joe Sinclair walked off the elevators and headed directly for Midnight's office; he was in a foul mood. Not only had he lost a collar the night before, but Robert Bondy had also cut him across his left cheek in the bargain. As if that weren't insult enough, that morning on his way down Interstate 5, he had been stopped by a San Diego PD patrol car for speeding. "Christ," he had muttered to himself. Obviously, this guy was new on this particular stretch of highway, because all the other guys recognized his car and his "SINCLAIR" license plate. Midnight had given it to him the year before for Christmas. "For the man who has everything," she had said.

When the officer had approached the car, he leaned down imperiously, looking in at Joe. "You rich people seem to think that because you have more money that it means you own the whole damn road," the officer said to him, his tone condescending. "Well let me tell you something, this badge doesn't see colors, black, white, or green, you get the picture? Let me see your license and registration,"

Joe had looked up at the guy for a minute, wanting to tell him to get fucked, but instead he had pulled out his police identification with the sergeant's badge displayed prominently on the other half of the ID wallet. The officer had gulped noticeably. "Sorry, sir, I didn't realize," he had said, his eyes widening a little as he recognized that he had probably just made a fatal career mistake.

"I certainly hope you don't talk to all citizens that way Officer Johnson," Joe had said, reading the officer's name tag.

"No, sir, I just … well … I," the officer stammered.

"Let your mouth run off with you, is what you did. Don't let it happen again." Joe's voice was cold and authoritative.

Joe had driven off then, leaving the officer standing in his dust, wondering if Sergeant Sinclair would report him to his Field Training Officer or not. For the final topper of the morning, Joe had driven into the PD lot and found that someone was parked in his designated parking space. Cussing and jamming the Porsche into reverse he had gone around to park in the lot across the street. His day was not off to an auspicious beginning.

So when he walked into Midnight's office he wasn't paying attention to anything, least of all a little blond female sitting quietly in the very corner of Midnight's office. Randy looked up as Joe sat down and she watched them quietly from the corner. Midnight gasped when she

92

saw his face. She stood but he waved her off. He sat down in the chair in front of her desk, extending his long legs out in front of him casually.

"Jesus, Joe," Midnight breathed, referring to nasty cut on his cheek.

Joe rolled his eyes. "Night, don't start on me this morning," he warned.

"Yeah, I heard you got stopped by La Jolla patrol this morning," Midnight said, laughing. "That Officer Johnson's about shitting his pants. He mouth off to you or what?"

"Yeah, gave me the 'you rich people' crap, I haven't decided if I'm going to talk to his FTO or not yet," Joe said.

"Okay, so what the hell happened last night?" Midnight asked curiously. There was no accusation in the question.

Joe was one of the best cops she'd ever worked with; he almost always got his man.

Joe shook his head ruefully. "To tell the truth, I don't know. He must've palmed his knife, 'cause when we hit the doors to the place, he put his hands on the bar immediately. I searched him. I looked away for two seconds and that's when he got me." Joe fingered the cut on his left cheek, his eyes narrowing as he thought of it. "Then before I could grab him he was out a back door."

"Where the hell was your backup?" Midnight said, raising her voice, but when Randy looked up in surprise, she saw that Midnight was smiling at Joe, and he was laughing. Obviously, this was some private joke between them.

Randy hadn't gotten a good look at Joe Sinclair. She hadn't looked up at him until he was seated in the chair with his back to her. She was surprised at his long hair; she expected that since he was a police officer, he'd have short hair. She was even more surprised at how casually he sat in front of Midnight, with a dirty boot resting on the end of Midnight's desk.

"Shut the hell up, Night!" Joe said

Randy wondered if Midnight would get mad, but she saw by the look on Midnight's face that she didn't pay any attention to his comment.

"Yeah, yeah, I know, you don't need backup, super-cop right?" she was saying, a smile still on her face, obviously enjoying the banter that they were engaging in.

"Yeah," Joe said sarcastically, with a wide smile, "that's me." Again, his hand touched the cut on his cheek.

"Hey!" Midnight said, her look more concerned now. "Even the best miss one every now and then, you'll catch up to him." She didn't like her partner beating himself up.

"Oh!" Midnight said then, just realizing that Randy was still sitting in the room; she was so damned quiet she was easy to forget.

Joe turned his head to look in the direction Midnight was looking and he saw the young blond woman sitting in the corner then. Had she been there the whole time? She looked shy, because when she looked up, she didn't look him in the eye, she looked like a scared doe. She was very pretty; she had part of her blond hair pulled back from her face in a braid. Her face was very delicate, with just a touch of makeup. Her eyes were a fantastic turquoise color.

Joe dropped his foot from the desk and turned his body around leaning both elbows on either knee. Randy was looking at both of them, unsure of what to say. She immediately felt intimidated by this man; he had such a strong presence, and the look he was giving her had her tongue tied instantly.

"Joe," Midnight said, "this is Randy. She's going to be our secretary."

Joe continued to look at Randy who had now plucked up the courage to look him in the eye, though she still hadn't said a word. Joe nodded his head, then glancing at Midnight he said, "When did this happen?"

Midnight shook her head in disbelief. "Joe, God, I'm going to have to get you checked out; interviews yesterday, remember, you got out of them, Spider sat in, hello?"

She picked up her baton that was always nearby and, reaching across the desk, tapped him on the head with it.

"I knew it!" she exclaimed, looking at Randy and smiling. Randy smiled back in spite of herself. "Empty!"

Reaching up lightning fast, Joe grabbed the baton from Midnight's hands and then laughed at the look on her face. She could never get used to how fast her partner was.

"If you're going to play with your equipment," Joe said wagging the baton at her, "then we're going to have to take it away."

He stood up facing Randy. Without looking back, he flipped the baton over his shoulder and Midnight caught it deftly by the side handle.

Joe walked over to Randy, stopped just in front of her chair, and stood looking down at her for a moment. She decided she better stand. Randy was five foot seven, but when she stood, her head came to about an inch below Joe's chin, so she still had to look up at him. She was also stood very close to him since he had walked right up to the chair she sat in. Randy felt very uncomfortable because the proximity of this man was very unsettling.

Suddenly, she realized, to her dismay, she was very much attracted to Joe Sinclair. Standing this close to him she could smell a mixture of cologne and leather. That, coupled with the fact that he was staring down at her with those incredible blue eyes, was a lethal combination. All Randy could do was look up at him. When a slow smile spread across his face, she thought she would die. She had never been attracted to a man in this way before and she didn't know how to handle it.

Joe could sense her discomfort, and he knew he should back off, but for some reason he didn't want to. He wanted to get this close to her and see her reaction and he had, that was what caused him to smile. They stood looking at each other for a long moment, Randy unable to look away from him, but totally uncomfortable with the idea that she was staring at her boss in this way.

Finally, Joe turned his head to look back at Midnight. "She doesn't say much, does she?"

"Well, Jesus, you've probably scared the shit out of her, Sinclair," Midnight said, walking over to where they stood.

She looked up at Joe then shoved him back a few steps. With a smile still on his face and his eyes watching Randy's, Joe stepped back and sat on the edge of Midnight's desk with his arms crossed over his chest.

"Randy, don't let this guy get to you," Midnight said, walking back over to her desk. "He's just into making people react to him." She eyed Joe, shaking her head at him as he laughed.

"Yes, but you love me," he said then, grabbing Midnight by the waist as she moved past him.

He pulled her over to him and she stood between his long legs, his hands on her hips, looking up at him defiantly. Joe smiled down at his partner and Randy saw what an attractive couple they made. Midnight was so small, especially compared to Joe. She seemed to be able to handle him pretty well though. She didn't seem phased by him at all. Randy wondered how they could work so closely together but not be attracted to each other. They clearly had a very close relationship.

Randy wished once again that she could be confident, but she was cursed with shyness. Darrell's friends had been showing up at the house lately, asking her out. She'd gone out with a couple of them, believing they liked her. In the end, however, she found that not only were they all crass, but they were also blatant about wanting to get her into bed first. They all knew that she was a virgin and they treated it like it was some kind of prize to be won. It made Randy sick. She would never go out with guys like that again, and she would definitely not sleep with someone who thought that way.

Now, Joe Sinclair probably knew how to treat a woman, without being a pig like Darrell's friends. Randy realized suddenly that within ten minutes of meeting her new boss that she already had a major crush on him. *Oh brother!* Randy thought, *Talk about a dumb thing to do.*

Randy watched as Midnight's hand went up to Joe's face and touched the cut on his left cheek tenderly. Joe looked down at Midnight, his eyes softened at her touch and he smiled. They were sharing a private moment, and Randy was embarrassed to be witnessing it, but she was totally entranced. Somehow, she couldn't look away. Midnight murmured something to him and whatever it was it made him laugh softly.

Randy thought she had to be at least three shades of red, she was afraid they had forgotten she was there. She looked down at the floor. She thought maybe she should leave but wondered at their obvious intimacy. Maybe they were a couple.

When she looked up, she saw that Midnight had turned around to look at her, still leaning against Joe. His arms were draped on either one of her shoulders. They seemed so comfortable together; Randy couldn't imagine ever being that comfortable with a man.

"Randy," Midnight said, smiling at her. "You're going to work in my office today, only because Joe here has to get his proverbial shit together, before any normal person can figure out the deranged system in his office."

Midnight laughed as Joe's arm came up around her throat, as if he were trying to choke her. Joe's eyes were on Randy, and he was smiling at her, but not a smile like he had smiled for Midnight. Randy wondered about them, but she knew she would never be brave enough to ask.

"Okay," Randy said, her voice almost cracking.

She realized then that had been the first thing she had said while Joe had been there. Obviously, he realized it too, because a mockingly surprised look appeared on his face.

"Hey, she can speak! Good, you got us a secretary that can talk, that will be useful," he said, grinning.

"Shut up, Sinclair!" Midnight said, elbowing him in the ribs. "She's shy that's all, and don't you give the kid a hard time, or I'll come after you."

Joe rolled his eyes dramatically at the threat. Then putting his hands on Midnight's slim hips, he moved her forward, so he could get up from the desk.

"Well, I guess I'll go work on my mess then," he said, leaning down to kiss Midnight on the top of the head.

With his hand on the door, he turned back with a comical look on his face. "Is this kind of like cleaning up before the maid comes?"

Midnight picked up a handful of paperclips and through them at him. He dodged them, laughing, then winking at Randy, he walked out and closed the door.

"Well," Midnight said, looking at Randy, "on the bright side, he was in a better mood than I expected this morning, but I suspect that you had something to do with that."

Randy looked at her, confusion clear on her face. "Me? Why?" she asked.

"You have no idea how pretty you are, do you?" Midnight said, sitting back against her desk.

"You think I'm pretty?" Randy asked, surprised. She thought that Midnight was beautiful, and she'd never thought of herself as pretty.

"Yeah! Jesus, kid. I'm going to have to get you into some self-esteem classes right away. You're very pretty, and the good thing is it's natural, not all that plastic and paint, you know? I hate women like that," Midnight said, walking around to sit behind her desk again.

Randy nodded, unsure of what to say at that point, so she kept quiet.

The morning progressed with Midnight working at her desk and Randy still filling out paperwork. It was noon when Randy heard the door to the office open. Looking up, she saw Joe standing in the doorway with another man behind him.

"Randy," Midnight said, as she noticed the visitors, "this is Rick Debenshire, he's also a member of FORS. Our newest member."

"Hi," Rick said.

Randy looked surprised at hearing another English accent. "Hi."

"He's English too," Midnight explained, "he was Joe's gang second back in England."

"Oh," Randy said, glancing at Joe who stood leaning against the wall. He was looking at her.

She looked away immediately, but not before she saw him smile. He really did like to see what reaction he would get from her.

"Hey," Midnight said, looking at her watch, "let's head over to The Pit for lunch, Tom will have our usual table."

"Sounds good," Rick said. Joe nodded.

"Randy, you come too," Midnight said.

As Randy watched, Midnight reached into her desk drawer, pulled out a holstered gun, and placed it in her jeans at the small of her back. Then she pulled her FORS jacket off the back of her chair and shrugged into it.

"Let's roll," she said.

Rick and Joe waited for the women to precede them, and then followed.

Once out in the street Randy noticed that both men took up rear positions on the walk over to The Pit. They were both keeping an eye on the street ahead and to the sides. Randy glanced at Midnight then, silently asking her why.

"Relax," Midnight said, "it's a cop thing."

When they reached The Pit, Joe held the door for everyone, still watching everything around them. When they all sat down Midnight and Joe sat on the same side with their backs to the wall. Another cop thing Randy assumed.

Lunch was interesting. Midnight knew the owner; he had gotten her through a pretty rough time, she explained, and he was the one responsible for her being where she was today. Tom looked like a proud father when he talked to Midnight.

"So what's happening with you these days, Sinclair?" Tom asked, eyeing Joe critically.

"Not much," Joe replied. "Just keepin' an eye on your girl's back," he said, nodding at Midnight.

"That's what I expect from ya," Tom said, grinning.

Midnight chuckled, as did Joe. Tom was very happy that she now had someone in her life she could depend on.

"Well I better get back," Tom said. Then he turned to Midnight. "You take care of yourself, young lady. I can tell you've been overdoing it again!"

Midnight threw him a mock salute and said, "Sir, yes sir!" Laughing, Tom turned and left.

Later that afternoon, Randy finally finished with the paperwork she had to read and sign, and she walked over to Midnight's desk to hand it back to her. Midnight was working on the computer and she was making a particularly nasty face at it when Randy approached. "Oh damn it!" Midnight said, hitting the desk. Then she scrubbed at her face with her hands.

"What's wrong?" Randy asked.

"Oh this goddamned file just disappeared on me. If I lost it, I'll just shoot myself now."

"Maybe I can help," Randy said, walking around to Midnight's side of the desk. She looked down at the screen for a moment.

Midnight stood and gestured for her to sit down. Randy started to work on retrieving the file as Midnight stood watching.

Randy smiled as she retrieved the lost document.

"You found it!" Midnight exclaimed. She reached and hugged Randy. "I love you, love you, love you! Now just make sure it gets saved right this time, if I lose that, I'm in deep shit."

Randy was surprised by the hug, but she was glad that she'd helped Midnight out. The more time she spent with Midnight, the more she liked her. Midnight was very down to earth, even with all the education and with her rank in the department.

It was five o'clock when Randy got a call from Darrell to tell her that he couldn't pick her up, because he had gotten stuck on a job, and they needed the extra money. Darrell hated to leave her stranded, but the house payment was coming up and they really did need the money.

"Maybe you could catch a cab or something," Darrell suggested, even though he knew they couldn't afford a cab really.

"I'll be okay," Randy said, and then she hung up the phone.

She had taken the call in Midnight's office, and Joe was there talking to Midnight. They were both watching her when she hung up.

"What's up?" Midnight asked, seeing the worried look on Randy's face.

"Well, that was my brother, and he can't come get me," Randy told them.

"Where do you live?" Joe asked.

"Pacific Beach," Randy answered, not looking directly at him.

"I can take her home," Midnight said, looking up at Joe.

"That's out of your way Night. I can take her," he said, looking at Randy. "It's on my way."

Randy was stunned. She didn't know how to answer. Finally, she nodded. "Okay, thank you."

"Come to my office when you're ready to go. Just give me a few minutes though, I need to make some calls." He looked at Midnight then. "I got some leads on our friend Bondy."

Half an hour later, Randy was waiting in Joe's office while he finished a phone call. He hung up and got up from his desk. He had his jacket off now and she saw the black leather shoulder holster he wore, and somehow she found that very attractive about him. It made him seem all the more powerful. Joe pulled his jacket off the back of his chair, looked at her, and nodded toward the door.

"Let's go, before someone else calls," he said, humor in his voice.

On the way out Joe stopped by Midnight's office. "I'm waiting for a call. Just throw it to me on my cell phone."

Once outside, Joe led her to his across the street. She was surprised when he stopped beside a newer model black Porsche. *Where does he get the money for this?* she wondered. He opened the passenger door for her, and then walked around and got in on his side, tossing his FORS jacket in the back seat. He started the engine and drove out of the parking lot. He turned on the radio and after searching through a couple of stations, he finally pushed the button for the CD player. Def Leppard's "Hysteria" flowed from the speakers and Joe sang along. Randy thought he had a nice singing voice.

He became lost in the music, so much so he forgot about Randy for a short while. After a few minutes, however, he seemed to recall he wasn't alone.

"So, is Randy your given name?" he asked, glancing over at her.

"No, it's really Randissi, but everyone calls me Randy. Is Joe your given name?" she asked.

Joe laughed at having his question turned around on him. "No," he said, glancing at her again, "it's really Joseph Michael Sinclair the Fourth." Her eyes widened at the number following his name.

"Wow," she said simply.

Joe chuckled but said nothing.

They were silent for a few minutes. Then Randy got up the nerve to say, "You said that Pacific Beach is on your way home, where do you live?"

Keeping his eyes on the road, Joe grinned and said, "La Jolla."

He looked over at her, seeing her eyes widen again.

"That surprises you, doesn't it?" he asked, having known it would.

Anyone who knew anything about peace officers knew they didn't make much money. La Jolla wasn't exactly the cheapest area in San Diego to live in.

"Well, yeah, because I thought that La Jolla was…" Randy's voice trailed off, she didn't want to be rude.

"Expensive?" Joe asked finishing her sentence.

"Well, yeah," she said.

"It is." He smiled at her, then sighed. "I guess you'll hear this eventually anyway, I'm what Midnight calls 'independently wealthy.' My parents left me a lot of money. So having a house in La Jolla is one of the benefits of that."

Randy nodded; that explained the car too. She wanted to ask what had happened to his parents. He didn't seem old enough to have parents that had died of natural causes, but she didn't want to be nosy.

"And who was it that was supposed to pick you up?" Joe asked, his eyes still on the road.

"My brother," she answered, "Darrell."

"And he's older?" Joe asked, glancing at her.

"Yes, he's twenty-four."

Joe nodded. "Any other siblings?"

"A little brother, Donovan, he's seventeen."

"I see and your parents?"

"My parents left when I was fourteen." Randy looked out the car window again.

"Left?" Joe queried in disbelief.

Randy nodded, not looking at him again. Joe grimaced, knowing he'd just hit on something very sensitive. He watched her for a few moments as she looked out the window. *Poor kid,* he thought.

His cell phone rang, and Joe reached into his pocket for it.

"Sinclair," he said, his eyes still looking over at Randy every so often. She was still looking out the window and he suspected that she was upset, and maybe even crying.

"Joe, it's me," Midnight's said.

"And," Joe said, smiling.

"And you're never going to believe who is in a bar in Mission Beach bragging about cutting you!" she said, laughing.

Joe laughed, hitting the steering wheel with the heel of his hand.

"What a dumb son of a bitch! Where?"

"Moose McGillacuddy's," Midnight replied.

"Yeah real private bar too!" Joe said, shaking his head. "Dumb shit!"

Then he looked over at Randy. "Shit, Night, I got Randy here, what am I supposed to do?"

Midnight was silent for a second. "There's a Denny's right across the way there, drop her off there. Tell her to stay there till you come get her or a black and white does."

Midnight's voice was serious, the last thing she wanted was for Randy to get involved in a bust, or get hurt in the process of one.

"Okay," Joe said, nodding.

A few minutes later, Joe pulled into the parking lot across the street from the bar where Robert Bondy was playing the big man. He parked the car, and they both got out. Randy stood watching him as he pulled his gun out of its holster, removed the ammunition magazine, checked it, replaced it, and then holstered it again. As he checked the other two spare magazines on the other side of the holster, he looked up at her.

"You stay here, Randy no matter what you hear or see. Don't come across the street unless you see a black and white or I come and get you, okay?"

Randy held up her hand. "I promise."

Joe smiled at her. Then giving her a cavalier wink, he walked across the street, pulling on his FORS jacket.

London, England, 1980

Joe had a run in with a new gang leader in town, his name was Jake and he was the leader of a gang called the Destroyers. Joe had heard about the guy; he had heard that he was a crazy Irishman and his whole gang was a bunch of lunatics that liked to hurt innocent people. He'd also heard that they dabbled in drug deals and hits on people. Joe had driven into town to meet with his father for lunch. For that reason, he wore black slacks, a white collared shirt, and black boots. The gang jacket spoiled the look of business casual, however. Joe was wearing his black leather jacket with the Black Knights logo of crossed black and silver swords and the words Black Knights written in silver in calligraphy script.

He was getting out of his car when he turned and ran right into someone coming the other way. The guy he'd run into tried to shove him back, but Joe stood firm. The man had to look up at Joe, since he was only around five foot eight. Joe recognized Jake right away from the descriptions he'd heard, and Joe could see recognition dawn in the other man's eyes as well, as his look took in Joe's jacket. Jake took a step back and looked Joe up and down. Joe just looked at the man, his face set in a mask of boredom.

"Yor Sinclair ont you?" the man said, his Irish-brogue very thick and clipped.

The man was fair-haired but it was cut short and spiked. It gave him a sharp look. His eyes looked crazed, they were such a pale blue that were almost white, and the whites around them were a mixture of a sickly yellow with harsh blood red veins. Joe wondered idly if he put tabasco sauce in his eyes to get them to look so hideous.

"Yeah, I'm Sinclair," Joe answered. He was chewing gum and smoking a cigarette looking very relaxed, but his eyes missed no detail of the man, nor the details of his surroundings.

He was aware of someone standing just off to the side, out of his direct line of sight. He assumed that person was with Jake, so he was on his guard. His hand was in his jacket pocket and wrapped around the switchblade he always carried, although he preferred to fight with his fists.

"Bin lookin' fer ya," Jake said. His smile, missing a couple of teeth, was cold and menacing.

Joe shrugged. "I'd say you found me."

His hand tightened on the switchblade as Jake looked over at the other person. Joe's eyes flicked over to take in the girl Jake was looking at. She was almost as strange looking as Jake, with red hair and fuchsia makeup.

"'e says it looks like we found 'im," Jake told the girl, and without warning went for a punch at Joe's midsection.

But Joe was no longer standing as close as he had been a second ago; he had stepped back and brought his right hand across to block Jake's punch. Jake was shocked to have been outsmarted, shocked and mad. The girl laughed wildly. Joe turned and flicked his cigarette away.

"Shut up you whore!" Jake yelled, once again making a play for Joe, this time going for his face.

Joe simply ducked and in turn punched Jake in the face, the force of which knocked Jake back a few feet. Jake stood frozen for a minute trying to figure out what he had done wrong.

Joe chuckled at him. "Give up yet?"

But Jake wasn't finished; he pulled out a knife and grinned at Joe.

Joe shook his head, as if not believing the guy could be so stupid. He kept his eyes on the blade though; he was in no mood to get stabbed. He brought his hands up in a fighting gesture, and motioned with his fingertips for Jake to bring it on. Jake hesitated, not having expected Joe to react that way. He had expected Joe to either be afraid or at least bring out a knife. He figured Joe must just be stupid or really crazy. Jake and Joe circled for a few long moments. Jake tried to fake Joe out by doing some false parries and half jabs with the knife. Joe did not react; he continued to watch the knife and its owner carefully.

There was a crowd gathering now, but Joe paid them no attention. Most of the crowd was Jake's own gang, and they were yelling encouragement to Jake, which was pumping up the smaller man's ego. Joe waited and watched, and Jake finally made his move, attempting to come at Joe from the side, lunging at him with all of his weight. With skill born of patience and experience, Joe spun, bringing his arm down in a chopping motion, and effectively blocked Jake's move. Then turning back, he grabbed the still outstretched arm and twisted Jake's wrist painfully, until he had to drop the knife. Joe stood holding Jake's wrist, while Jake writhed around, standing on tiptoes to try to relieve the pain.

"Give up yet?" Joe asked again, his eyes mocking the smaller man, his lips curling in a sarcastic grin.

"Yeah, man, yeah!" Jake yelled. Joe released him so quickly that he fell to the ground. Jake's gang laughed.

Jake's head snapped up his eyes narrowed, hating Joe more than anything at that moment.

"You basta'd," Jake spat.

Joe could see that his was readying himself for another charge. Canting his head to the side Joe simply said, "I don't think you wanna do that."

Jake realized he had been not only defeated but humiliated too. A deep burning hate started in Jake's stomach as he listened to his own gang laughing at him. He saw Sinclair standing there so cool, not even breaking a sweat, leaning against his Porsche with his legs crossed at the ankles, looking down at him.

"I'll get you fer this Sinclair," Jake said. His voice was deadly calm and so low that his gang stopped laughing. They looked at Joe, watching for his reaction.

Joe shrugged, looking confident. "I think you just tried that." And with that he walked away.

Looking back later, Joe realized that had been a turning point in his life, but he'd had no idea how crazy Jake really was, or how determined he could be.

****

Joe walked in the front door of Moose McGillicuddy's. It took a minute for his eyes to adjust to the dimly lit interior, and he looked around for Bondy. When Joe's eyes came to rest on a man wearing a jean jacket with large scorpion and the word "Scorpions" in red, he knew had found his man. He walked over to where Bondy was leaning against the bar, talking intently to a young lady. Joe leaned against the bar just behind Bondy, listening in on the conversation. Bondy was turned to the side, so he couldn't see Joe.

"So you cut him?" the girl was saying, impressed.

"Yeah, ain't no big thing, I cut cops all the time, hell they're afraid of me now." Bondy was smiling down at the girl, just knowing he was going to get some play out of this.

He was feeling really full of himself right up until the time that Joe picked him up by the scruff of the neck. Bondy was jerked off his feet and turned around to face the man he had just been bragging about cutting.

"So," Joe said looking down at Bondy, "you're a real big man, Bobby. That so?" He shook him a couple of times for emphasis.

The girl had skittered away, probably going for help, Joe thought.

"Hey, Sinclair," Bondy said, "nice slice you got there."

Bondy was still being cocky and Joe couldn't believe it. He outweighed the guy by about fifty pounds and stood about four inches taller.

"You like it, Bobby? If you want I can give you one to match ..." His voice trailed off ominously.

Joe saw Bondy's eyes flick past his shoulder, and Joe knew instinctively that someone was coming up behind him. Dropping Bondy to the floor with a resounding thud, Joe turned and ducked in the same movement, narrowly missing the assailant's first punch. He didn't, however, miss the unexpected kick to the side from a second guy he'd not seen. Wincing in pain, Joe jumped aside bringing his elbow up into the second guy's face. The man fell back, clutching his now-broken nose. The first guy came at Joe immediately though, so Joe didn't have time to recover. The guy managed to land a hard clout on Joe's left cheek breaking the cut open again; it started to bleed profusely.

"To hell with this," Joe said, bringing his foot up and kicking the first guy away from him.

He drew his gun and backed up, glancing behind him to make sure there were no more of them. Joe unclipped his badge and showed it to the bartender.

"I need a phone," he told the bartender authoritatively.

He called dispatch to request a black and white who informed him that Lieutenant Chevalier had already sent them to Joe's location and they should be in the vicinity any minute.

Joe hung up grinning, keeping a watchful eye on the three men he was holding. Bondy was still on the floor and Joe had his foot on Bondy's chest. He wasn't getting away again.

A few minutes later, the police showed up and a few minutes after that Randy walked into the bar. She looked around for Joe. She spotted him talking to a police officer holding a towel to his cheek. She made her way over to him and stood by quietly while he finished up with the officer.

"Hey," he said, once the officer had walked away.

"Are you okay?" Randy asked. She gestured to the bloodstained towel he was holding to his cheek.

He pulled the towel away and looked down at it, then looked back at her.

"I guess so. Took one good shot to the side, but that's the only new one," he said, keeping his tone light.

Randy grimaced. He smiled at her, and shrugged. He took a drink from the glass the bartender had given him, and winced at the amount of tequila the guy had put into it. He looked up at the bartender, who just shrugged.

"I figured you needed it," the bartender said.

Joe smiled and nodded his thanks.

"I better get you home," he said to Randy. "Before I stay here and order a few more." He smiled slyly at her.

He took a couple more swallows of the drink, and tossed a twenty on the bar, giving the bartender a two fingered salute. Putting his arm around Randy, he steered her to the door.

"Does it hurt?" she asked, grimacing.

Joe shrugged. "I'm used to it."

Randy shook her head. *How is anyone ever used to violence?* Without stopping to think, she reached up and touched a small drop of blood that had formed at one corner of the cut. She took in his light blue eyes that simply stared back at her. He was surprised. Suddenly she realized what she'd done and immediately pulled her hand back and looked away. She'd just touched her boss in a very intimate way. *Have I lost my mind? What was I thinking?*

113

Biting her lip, she took the chance to look back at him. She saw a soft smile playing at his lips. She wasn't sure what to think, but she felt a tug at her heart at the look in his eyes. He wasn't giving her a sarcastic, knowing look, it appeared to be appreciation. "I'm sorry, I can't believe I did that, I was just …" she began, trying to think of a reasonable explanation for her behavior. Finally, she shrugged, unable to come up with suitable words.

"Don't worry about it," Joe said softly, his eyes still not leaving hers.

Randy simply stared back at him, unable to think of something else to say.

The day was fading, the sky was a red orange color, and his eyes sparkled with the sun's dying rays. He didn't seem to mind that she had touched him. And Randy found she could barely breathe.

Joe's phone rang, breaking the spell. Joe looked almost irritated as he pulled it out.

"Yeah?" he said, his voice short. He was looking down the street now, his face lit by the sunset.

It was Midnight. "Hey, did the black and whites show up?"

"Yeah," Joe said, trying to keep the tension he was feeling out of his voice, "thanks for that."

"Figured you might like some backup," she said, then. "Is there anything left of you?" she asked, half concerned, half joking.

"Yeah, I'm fine," Joe said, glancing over at Randy.

"Good," Midnight said, sensing Joe's tension and wondering if he was making light of new injuries. She had no way of knowing about the moment she'd interrupted.

"See you tomorrow," Joe said, getting his composure back finally.

"10-4," Midnight said briskly.

She knew something was wrong, but could tell by Joe's tone he wasn't about to say anything. He hung up and started the car. He reached for his cigarettes and glanced over at Randy.

"You mind?"

"No," Randy said, shaking her head.

She wasn't sure what to make of his tension, she could feel it easily, but wasn't sure what it meant.

Joe lit a cigarette and reached over to turn up the stereo. Def Leppard was still on, but Joe hit the CD changer, changing it to Whitesnake, and the song "Love Ain't No Stranger." It was much harder driven. Once again Joe sang every word.

Joe wasn't sure what to make of his reaction to Randy Curtis. She wasn't usually the type of woman he was interested in. With women like Midnight in his life, women who took what they wanted without hesitation, this beautiful little wallflower seemed a polar opposite. Joe wasn't sure what to do with that.

After a few directions, they made it to Randy's house. She turned to Joe, to thank him for giving her a ride home. He was watching her intently again. When she smiled at him, he gave her a half grin. These odd silences seemed to be happening to them a lot. It amused Joe no end.

"Thank you, for the ride home," she said, as she noticed Darrell's car in the driveway.

Joe saw her glance at the car, and grimace.

"What's wrong?" he asked.

Randy shook her head, and tried to look nonchalant. She didn't succeed. "Nothing, I just noticed that my brother is home now, that's all."

She reached for the handle, but his hand on her arm stopped her. She turned back and he was giving her a knowing look.

"He's going to be pissed because your late, isn't he?" Joe asked.

Randy shook her head, not saying anything.

"Or is it that I gave you a ride home? A guy …"

Randy looked at him for a minute, how did he know what she was thinking? Then she nodded at him.

"My brother wasn't really happy with me for taking this job. He's real funny about cops." She shrugged.

"Why?" Joe asked. "We're the good guys, or doesn't he know that?"

"Well, he does, but, he just he thinks that cops are, um, kind of … you know."

"Always trying to score?" Joe supplied, and he knew instantly from the look on her face that he'd hit the nail on the head. "And you're so young and very innocent, he doesn't want you around guys that have such loose morals, like myself, right?"

"No!" Randy almost shouted. "Not like you, I mean well you're not like that. I mean, I don't think you are. I better go," she said reaching nervously for the door handle again.

"Randy," Joe said, and she turned back to him, "relax. Do you want me to talk to your brother?"

She shook her head vehemently. "No, it's okay, I'll just talk to him. It's okay." She then opened the door and hopped out of the car.

She leaned back down looking shyly at him again. "Thank you again for the ride, I'll see you tomorrow."

"If you need a ride tomorrow, call me," Joe said, pulling out his wallet and handing her a card from it.

She took it and smiled at him. Then she closed the door. He watched as she walked up to the house. Before she reached the front door, it opened and Joe could see a stocky blond-haired man talking to her. Then he looked over her head at Joe's car. Joe waited to see if the guy was going to come down the driveway. He could see that Randy was arguing with him, her hands held up to keep him from doing just that. Joe was about to put the car in park and go up and talk to Darrell Curtis, when Randy finally managed to turn him around and push him into the house. The front door closed and Joe shrugged to himself. *Just as well*, he thought to himself, he didn't need to get into another fight today.

CHAPTER 5

London, England, 1980

Joe Sinclair sat in a pub watching his gang, the Black Knights, celebrate. They were in their usual hangout, a place where the owner knew that most of them were under age, but served them anyway. The owner didn't care, the Knights paid for the beer they drank and they always kept their fights outside. Joe watched his second, Rick, make a move on Sherri. Rick's proposition was well received, of course; she'd had her eye on him for weeks.

Rick had a reputation for moving from one girl to the next, never staying with one too long.

Richard Debenshire was eighteen, with a magnetic personality. He was a heady combination of handsome and gregarious. Everyone liked him. He stood an even six feet, with a swimmer's-style body, long and lean. He had shaggy light brown curls that fell two inches past his shoulders and deep blue eyes. His skin tone was almost a golden color, setting off his finely boned face and eyes perfectly. He also had a perfect smile. His smile dropped them every time, and he smiled a lot. He was the perfect antonym to Joe.

Joseph Sinclair was twenty years old, with a dark brooding nature that attracted women to him constantly. His height of six foot two made him imposing to most people. His build was stockier than Rick's, with broader shoulders, but a slimmer waist. What caught many a woman's attention were his eyes, since they were almost luminescent in their color. They'd been compared to the ice that many swore flowed through his veins.

Rick was the social one, Joe was the quiet, cool one. Everyone liked Rick, whereas everyone was afraid of Joe. Joe was known for his abilities in a fight. He had a temper that, when pushed, could ignite into cold fury. Instead of making him careless in a fight, his temper tended to make him better. His anger made him hit harder, move and think faster; that's what made him dangerous.

With his arm still around Sherri, Rick walked over to where Joe sat leaning his chair against the wall. Sherri eyed Joe appreciatively, but she was equally happy to be with Rick. She'd heard a lot about both men's sexual prowess, and was eager to confirm the stories. Rick sat down, taking a chair from another table and turning it around, so he could lean his arms on the back of it as he sat.

"Hey man," Rick said, grinning at Joe.

"Hey," Joe replied, his eyes flicking to Sherri.

Sherri smiled brilliantly at him and he responded with a curt nod.

"So … what's goin' on for tonight?" Rick asked.

"Not, a lot, my parents are back in town," Joe replied

"Shit, that rules that out …" Rick said, rolling his eyes and grinning.

"Looks to me like you've got your own party goin'," Joe said, his eyes on Sherri again.

Sherri was standing next to Rick with her hand on his shoulder. Her eyes were watching the other girls in the bar. As far as she was concerned Rick was hers tonight, and she'd fight any girl that tried to say different.

Rick smiled an intense smile that had often resulted in guys calling to see what their girlfriends or wives were up to.

"You could do the same, ya know," he said, glancing around the room at all the girls. The Knights seemed to attract a crowd wherever they went.

Joe considered the idea, his eyes taking in the room.

"Come on, man!" Rick said, clapping Joe on the shoulder. "You need to loosen up."

Joe grinned at his friend. Rick was the only member of the Black Knights that wasn't afraid of him. They'd grown up together. Continuing his scan of the pub, his gaze fell on a raven-haired girl sitting at the bar. She'd been eyeing him all night. He'd never seen this one before. When he made eye contact with her, he could tell she was interested immediately. His look changed to smug confidence, as his eyes locked with hers. After a few long moments, she stood and walked over to the table. Joe's eyes never left hers.

"You're Joe Sinclair," she said, her eyes staring down into his.

"Very good," Joe responded mildly, his tone caustic.

"I saw you fight," she said then. "You're very good."

"Fightin' ain't all I'm good at," he said, taking a drink from the beer in front of him, his eyes watching her.

She was temporarily taken back by what he'd said, but then she started to smile.

"So …" she said her voice low and seductive. "You wanna show me what else you're good at?"

"Not here," Joe said, moving to stand.

She didn't step back, so she stood just inches from him. She looked up at him lustfully. Joe's lips twisted in a sardonic smile, his eyes boring into hers. She reached up, grabbing a handful of his leather jacket, and pulling him down to her. She kissed him, and Joe responded, putting his hands on her waist and pulling her flush against his body. She moaned softly as they continued to kiss. When Joe pulled away, she was staring up at him breathlessly.

"If that's a sample of what you're good at ... I don't care where we go," she said, her eyes wide, her cheeks flushed.

Joe grinned, inclining his head.

He looked over at Rick. "We all goin' to your place?"

"Fine with me," Rick said, standing and taking Sherri's hand.

They went to Rick's flat. After three hours in bed with the raven-haired beauty from the bar, Joe left. He didn't ask her name, but she remembered his for a long time afterward.

As he drove away in his Porsche, he thought about the girl he'd just slept with. She had been a hellcat in bed, and he knew he bore some new marks on his back from the encounter. Rick was right though, he had needed to let off some steam. He'd been holding on rather tight lately, and he knew that was the easy way to lose one's edge.

****

As it turned out, Randy and Darrell fought half the night about whether or not she was even allowed to continue working at the department. "I don't want you around people like that guy!" Darrell was saying to her.

"Oh, you'd rather have me around guys like your friends?" Randy replied angrily. "Those pigs that talk about me like I'm some sort of trophy."

"Hey," Darrell said looking down at his little sister, "I told you I talked to them about that."

"Yeah, well these people don't treat me like that, and I'm going back there tomorrow." Her voice was steady, but she was shaking.

"No, you're not," Darrell said, slamming his fist down on the table, making Randy jump. "Who the fuck is this Sinclair anyway? I know cops don't make enough money to drive a brand-new Porsche. What is he on the take or something?"

Randy narrowed her eyes and shook her head in disgust. "What, are you jealous?" she said, her voice full of venom.

Darrell half stood, pulling his hand back like he was going to slap her, but he turned away from her, obviously trying to reign in his temper.

He walked over to the kitchen sink, then turning to her, his eyes blazing he said. "You've worked with these people one day and already you're turning into a nasty bitch."

She stood, looking at him defiantly. "No, I'm just not going to let you tell me what to do anymore, Darrell. I'm twenty years old and I have a right to have a job if I want to and you can't say anything about it."

Darrell's mouth dropped open at her. He closed his mouth and his lips twisted in an evil, triumphant smile. "Oh yeah, miss high and mighty? And how are you going to get to work? Fly?"

Randy hesitated for a minute, she hadn't thought about that, but then she remembered the card in her pocket that Joe had given to her. Her smile at Darrell was frosty as she pulled out the card and walked over to the phone. She dialed Joe's number and hoped he was there.

Joe answered on the third ring. "'Lo?"

"Joe," Randy said, seeing Darrell's eyes almost bug out of his head, "it's Randy."

"Randy, hey, how'd everything go with your brother? He did not look happy when I left."

"Well he's not, and it seems that I have had my ride to work suspended." She was feeling braver right now, because she was mad, and because she knew Darrell was watching her. "So if that offer for a ride is still open …" Her voice trailed off, hoping that she wasn't being too forward; this was her boss after all.

"Sure, no problem," Joe said, shaking his head at the other end, knowing he was asking for trouble from her big brother.

"Great!" Randy said, smiling triumphantly at Darrell again.

She could see he was getting really mad, so she figured she better hang up quickly before he had a chance to get on the phone and cuss Joe out. She didn't think that would go over too well.

"Okay, well I'll see you in the morning then, bye."

"Okay then," Joe said, knowing she was rushing off the phone, "bye."

Joe hung up the phone. Sitting back, he reached for the beer sitting on the end table next to him. He thought about the situation with Randy's brother, amused that her brother obviously was smart enough to sense trouble. He got up and grabbed another beer out of the fridge, and walked out onto his deck overlooking the beach. He walked down onto the beach, lit a cigarette, and started to walk, mulling things over in his head.

He stayed out on the beach until well past one o'clock in the morning. When he did go back to the house, he locked up for the night and went to bed. Once in bed, he lay awake reflecting on the events of the day once again. As always, he wondered where his life was headed. There were always thoughts of what would have been if his parents had lived and he felt guilty knowing that he had ultimately failed them. His mind veered sharply away from thoughts of the accident. Only when he was drunk did his mind take advantage of his incapacitation and wallow in the pain of their death.

He pondered on Midnight and Rick then. He still wasn't sure about her and Rick being together, but he had done what he could by telling Rick how Midnight could be. Maybe she'd be different with Rick, but Joe doubted it. He didn't want either one of them hurt.

Then Joe's mind touched on Randy. He thought about how she had looked at him in the car when she had touched his cheek. It surprised him to realize that he was very attracted to her. He had been since the moment he'd laid eyes on her in Midnight's office. He had made a point of getting so close to her so that he could make her look at him. When she had looked at him, he had seen fear and timidity, but he was almost sure he had also seen interest, almost desire, but it was very diluted by the other two emotions. He had wanted to get rid of the fear and the timidity in her eyes.

He remembered the look in her eyes when they were in the car, and that had been more akin to desire. He had wanted to kiss her, but he knew it would be the wrong thing to do. It would have been too soon, and he probably would have scared her to death. Midnight's phone call had actually saved him, but he had been irritated with himself for being so impulsive. He wanted Randy, though, and there was no denying that. Joe's last thought before he drifted off to sleep was that maybe Darrell Curtis was right to worry about his sister.

The next morning Randy was waiting outside for Joe when he drove up. She almost ran to the car, looking behind her to see if Darrell would come out. He didn't, but he did watch from the house. Darrell and Randy had argued again after she had made the phone call to Joe. The argument had finally ended when she had run to her room, slammed the door, and locked it. Darrell had followed and pounded on it a couple of times, but finally gave up. Things in the house that morning were very strained. Donovan had heard them arguing the night before, and he was obviously nervous about it. Randy felt bad for putting Donovan through this, it was almost like when their parents had been there fighting all the time. But she really wanted this job, and she didn't think that it was fair of Darrell to expect her to give it up, just because he had a bad attitude about police officers.

"Hi!" Randy said getting into the car.

Joe waited until she was settled before pulling out. She'd breezed in like a breath of fresh air with her pink sweater, white skirt, and braided hair. She was clearly a morning person, something Joe wasn't used to. It reminded Joe that he was over nine years her senior. "Hi," he replied, his voice gravelly from lack of sleep.

Randy looked at him as he drove noticing he looked tired.

Once they were on the freeway, Joe reached for a cigarette and lit it. Then he looked over at Randy.

"So, I'm thinkin' I'm on your brother's shit list, huh?"

Randy looked over at him, pressing her lips together, embarrassed. "If it makes you feel any better, I think I'm higher on the list than you. I'm sorry, he's just …" She shook her head.

"Worried," Joe put in, looking ahead of him at the road again. "He probably should be."

Randy glanced sharply at him. "Why?"

Joe smiled, keeping his eyes on the road. "Because I think I'm probably about to make number one on his list."

"How?" Randy asked, her eyes widening slightly.

Joe looked over at her, his light blue eyes glinting mischievously. "By asking you out," he replied simply.

Randy stared back at him openmouthed for a few minutes. "You what?" she asked in total disbelief.

"I'm asking you out," Joe clarified, looking over at her, and blowing out a stream of smoke. "Will you go out with me, Randy?" he asked sincerely.

Randy swallowed convulsively a couple of times, so shocked that she couldn't come up with a suitable reply.

After a few very long minutes, Joe's grin turned wry. "Should I take that as a no?"

"No!" Randy exclaimed, then bit her lip at her outburst. "I mean, yes, yes, I want to go out with you."

Joe nodded, smirking at her obvious fluster.

"Friday?" he queried then.

Randy nodded, not trusting her voice again. Friday was the following day.

The rest of the drive to the office was done in silence. Joe listened to the stereo, occasionally glancing at Randy but didn't want to fluster her any further. He was, however, looking forward to the following night.

At the office, Joe went in to talk to Midnight, while Randy got started setting up her desk outside Midnight and Joe's offices.

Midnight noticed something right away.

"What did I miss?" she asked suspiciously.

Joe grinned. Midnight knew him too well.

"Well?" she prompted.

"Nothin'," Joe said, his grin still in place. "Just asked our secretary out."

"Already?" Midnight asked incredulously.

"No time like the present," Joe replied, his smile widening.

Midnight shook her head, sighing. Then she gave him a serious look. "You better be careful with that one, Joe."

Joe narrowed his eyes slightly, then nodded. "I know, babe," he said, glancing out at Randy as she worked.

"She's pretty young," Midnight said.

"How young?"

"Barely twenty," Midnight replied, "and a much younger twenty than you or I were."

Joe nodded. He and Midnight had grown up way before their time. By the time each of them had been twenty years old, they'd each lost a big piece of their lives. Then again, Joe reflected, so had Randy.

"Night, her parents walked out on her and her brothers when she was only fourteen."

"Are you serious?" Midnight queried.

Joe nodded, glancing out at Randy again, his look contemplative.

Midnight saw the look, and realized that Joe was being drawn in by Randy's plight. It was Joe's way to avoid his own. Midnight knew all about that; she'd been dodging her guilt for years. She looked considering out Randy.

"So, she may be older than her years too," Midnight said.

Joe said nothing, only nodding slowly.

After a few minutes, they talked about other things, Robert Bondy being one of them. Joe and Midnight wanted to get Bondy to roll over on the ghost leader of the Scorpions. No one knew who the guy was, outside of the gang. There was a major drug trade going on in that gang, and FORS knew that the Scorpions were the middlemen for a very big operation that was causing a lot of bloodshed on the street. But they couldn't get to the leader; no one on the outside even knew what his name was. Bondy wasn't talking, he would tell them other things, but it was obvious that the leader of the Scorpions had made sure that his minions knew the penalty for identifying him. The last guy that had been questioned by FORS had turned up dead, even though he hadn't told them anything.

"Damn it, who the fuck is this guy?" Joe said, he had really thought that Bondy would talk.

"I don't know, but we need to get him. He's causing a blood bath out there, and soon the chief's going to start calling me and I don't have anything to tell him," Midnight said, shaking her head.

The case was frustrating. Normally gang members, especially leaders wanted to be known, so they could gain notoriety, but this guy wasn't like that at all. It was a problem.

"Well, I better go and get Randy situated, poor kid has her work cut out for her," Joe said, standing and stretching.

"Good luck," Midnight said with a grin.

"Bite me," Joe said, grinning too as he walked out of her office.

As he walked into his office, he saw that Randy was sitting in front of his desk. She was looking over some of the files that he had in his "out" box.

"Diving right in, I see," Joe said, smiling down at her.

She looked up at him with a shy smile. "Is it okay for me to read this stuff, or …" Her voice trailed off as his smile got wider.

"Well I certainly hope so, one of us has to!" He laughed then at the look on her face. "Seriously, though, yeah I need you to read them over. Most of those are the case reports that we file, and I need to make sure that everything gets in there, especially all the appropriate evidence documentation."

"Okay, should I take these to my desk?" she asked, starting to stand.

Joe put his hand out to stop her. "No, why don't you just stay in here for the first couple of days or so, that way if you have questions, you can just ask me, okay?" He looked down at her, and she nodded.

When she wouldn't look at him again, he shook his head. Boy, this was going to be tough.

****

Midnight walked into Joe's office two hours later. She was putting her gun in its usual place at the small of her back and then she pulled on her FORS jacket.

"What's going on?" Joe asked, looking up from his desk.

"Well, it seems the Homegirls are getting a little feisty, so I'm going in with Kana."

"Now?" Joe asked, standing up.

"Relax, Sinclair," Midnight said, holding up a hand. "I'm going on this one with Kana, okay?" When Joe started to shake his head, she gestured to the stacks of files that Joe and Randy were still working on. "You're backed up to hell, Joe, you need some office time. I'll be fine."

Joe looked mutinous, wanting to go with her no matter what she said. He never liked it when she went on a job without him. Midnight looked back at him, a half grin on her face as she shook her head at him.

"I'm a big girl, Sinclair, I can take care of myself, you know. That's why they gave me this," she said, holding up her badge.

"Yeah, yeah, I know top of your class and everythin'," Joe said, smiling at her.

"Randy, watch him while I'm gone. He tends to be a little edgy when I go out without him. Make sure he doesn't bite the head off of someone like the Chief. See ya!" she said as she turned and left.

Randy laughed at what she had said and looked around at Joe.

"Are you really like that?" she asked.

Joe shrugged. "I can be a little uptight when my partner is out on the street without me, yes." He kept his face so straight, that Randy thought she had made him mad, but then he smiled at her. "So I guess you better do like the boss says and watch me, eh?"

Randy laughed then and they went back to work. She did notice that he seemed more on edge now though. He got up and paced the office a couple of times. He also flipped on his police radio to listen for Midnight's voice.

Midnight and Kana walked out of the building and toward the parking lot. Midnight was carrying a folder of information on the gang Kana had handed to her on their way out.

Kana and Midnight made a strikingly different pair. Midnight was petite with copper-blond flowing hair while Kana was a huge Samoan with dark skin and black hair. Anyone passing them on the street would believe that Kana was the superior between two. That was, of course, Midnight's edge on most strangers: underestimation of her abilities. Not that Kana wasn't dangerous; she'd been the leader of one of the biggest gangs in Hawaii, Sisters of Samoa. "So, what's the deal with this gang?" Midnight asked, looking up at Kana as they walked.

"Well, they fight dirty, especially the leader. That's how she got there," Kana replied.

"Okay, and what's the leader's name again?"

"They call her Oso," Kana said, eyeing Midnight for her reaction.

"Oso? You mean like Spanish for bear?" Kana nodded and Midnight made a face. "Like as big as?" Again, Kana nodded with a grim look on her face.

"Shit, just make sure you stay real close, in case I start to lose," Midnight said.

"You know I will. Hell, Sinclair will kill me if you lose!"

Midnight laughed. "Yeah he hates it when I solo without him."

"Well at least you're wearing your fighting clothes," Kana said, as they reached Midnight's Corvette.

"I always am," Midnight replied.

She opened her door, got in the car and leaned over to unlock the passenger side.

"So where are we meeting them?" Midnight asked once Kana was in the car.

"Chicano park."

"Great!" Midnight said, rolling her eyes. "Nothing like neutral territory!" She knew that Chicano Park was anything but neutral.

San Diego, California, 1978

"Give it up, puta, you'll never win!" one of the gang spat, as she looked down at her smaller opponent.

Midnight Chevalier narrowed her gold-green eyes, but didn't reply. Instead, she stood ready, her eyes never leaving Juanita's face. She ignored the taunts of the other girls, calling her juerita, puta, bitch, and whatever else they could think of. To think this had been her "family" for the last year. Bullshit Midnight thought to herself, they'd kill me to get what I'm after. What she was after was the leadership of the gang.

Midnight Chevalier was sixteen years old. She'd joined the gang a year ago, and she was not a follower. With her petite stature she didn't look like she belonged in a gang. What she had was a lot of anger to draw from and nothing to lose. Her parents didn't care what she did, as long as she didn't hassle them, or interfere with their partying. She'd grown up in San Ysidro, California, an area rife with gang activity, and she'd learned fast that either you joined a gang and learned to fight, or you'd be the victim. She was no victim.

Juanita was the leader of the Sidro Hermanas. Midnight wanted to lead the gang, and to that end had challenged Juanita to a fight. Now the two girls faced each other. Juanita was just barely eighteen, but she stood five foot ten, and weighed over two hundred pounds. She had a round face, and meaty fists that were just itching to beat this juerita into the ground.

With a banshee-like yell, Juanita launched herself at Midnight throwing a punch that should have landed on Midnight's face. However, Midnight had moved with amazing agility, tripping Juanita up. Juanita recovered herself quickly, giving Midnight just enough time to get out of her way. Juanita was angry at having been tricked so easily. She knew Midnight was a good fighter, but she'd never figured Midnight could handle her. It shook her confidence just a little bit.

"You know I'm gonna put you down, puta," Juanita taunted, as she circled Midnight. "Gonna put you down and put a cap in your ass."

Midnight nodded, her face impassive. The smaller girl's calm made Juanita nervous. Why wasn't she freaking out? She'd just told the little bitch that she intended to kill her. Juanita knew Midnight knew she could do it; she'd killed some girl in a fight just two weeks before. She looked Midnight over again, as if try to figure out what she'd missed about this girl. Midnight was quiet, but she'd proven herself in the gang, taking on and beating a lot of other gang members. She was fast, and she hit hard when she hit. She was a white girl, but she spoke Spanish with a perfect accent; she never sounded like a white girl when she talked in Spanish. She had never seen Midnight use a gun, but she knew she was good with a knife. Did she have a knife now? Is that why she was so confident?

Juanita threw another punch and missed Midnight again. Damn the bitch was fast! She threw again and again, and Midnight avoided it each time. After five minutes, Juanita was getting tired. Usually she could hit a girl a few times and the fight would be over. With her large frame, and her weight behind a punch, other girls didn't stand a chance. But this little bitch, she wasn't staying still long enough to be hit, and she didn't look at all tired.

'Bitch!' Juanita thought viciously and she charged Midnight again. This time Midnight didn't move. She waited an extra beat and, moving just a fraction of an inch back from the fist coming at her face, she threw a punch of her own. Juanita was stunned, and her lip began to bleed immediately. Midnight didn't stop with drawing first blood, her first punch was followed quickly by a yell of her own. She put her head down and charged the bigger girl, knocking Juanita to the ground, and landing on top of her. The girls in the gang watched in stunned silence. Juanita rallied, shoving Midnight off her, sending the smaller girl tumbling on the blacktop. Midnight was up on her feet again in a flash. Juanita charged at her, angry that the girl had gotten in so much. Again Midnight moved, tripping her, and when she went down, Midnight slammed a booted foot into Juanita's stomach. Going down to one knee, she proceeded to punch Juanita in the face repeatedly. Juanita was holding up her hands in defense within minutes.

One of the other girls pulled Midnight up. Another girl saw an opportunity to help her leader and grabbed Midnight's other arm, holding her. Mercy, the first girl, saw what her friend was doing and tightened her hold. Midnight knew instantly what they were doing, and she looked over at Mercy, her eyes blazing green fire.

Juanita climbed to her feet, spitting out blood and coughing. She saw that her girls were holding the blond bitch for her, and she started to grin maliciously. Now the little puta would see what happened when she crossed Juanita. Taking out her switchblade, Juanita made a show of pacing back and forth in front of Midnight. She glanced at the girl, expecting her to look scared, but Midnight didn't. Her cat-like eyes just followed her.

"You think you're tough shit, huh puta?" Juanita said. "You think you can kick my ass?"

Midnight's eyes flickered, as her lips twisted sardonically as if to say, 'I was kicking your ass.' But again, the smaller woman didn't speak.

"Got any last words, puta?" Juanita taunted, holding up the knife threateningly.

Midnight tensed, causing the two young women holding her to tighten their hold on her arms. Juanita took a step closer, drawing the knife back, ready to plunge it into Midnight's chest. With astounding agility, Midnight used the girls' hold on her arms to launch a kick right into Juanita's face, knocking her off her feet and out cold. The shock of seeing their leader go down slackened the two girls' hold, so Midnight was able to pull herself free. Turning on Mercy first, she slammed the *girl in the face with her fist, then kicked out with her right foot, catching the other girl in the stomach.*

When both girls lay on the ground, Midnight stood over them looking down. Then she turned her attention to her audience.

"Next one of you that involves yourself in my business, will get the shit kicked out of you till your own mother wouldn't recognize your ass. You got me?" she asked authoritatively.

The other girls realized that they were looking at their new leader and started nodding vehemently. Midnight looked down at Mercy and the other girl and said, "You're out. Get the fuck out of my sight, before I change my mind and kill you both."

"Midnight ..." Mercy began, getting up slowly. She and Midnight had some semblance of a friendship before this fight.

Midnight looked at Mercy, narrowing her eyes. Shook her head, and turned away from her. Midnight never trusted anyone to get too close to her. She had been friends with Mercy, but she found out how quickly that could disappear when it came to the gang. One more lesson in a long life worth of lessons. Midnight learned quickly.

****

"So what's the deal with you and Sinclair's friend? What's his name?" Kana asked after a few minutes on the road.

"You mean Debenshire?" Midnight asked. Kana nodded. "Oh, we're kind of a casual thing."

Kana looked at Midnight with a sly smile. "Is he good?"

Midnight thought for a moment and then she smiled a mischievous smile. "Oh he's fantastic, but I don't know."

"What don't you know, girl? He's good in bed, he's real easy on the eyes, and he's probably loaded like Sinclair. What's not to know?"

Midnight laughed, shaking her head at Kana. "That easy, huh?" she said with a genuine smile. She wished it were that easy for her.

"Hell yes!" Kana said, laughing too. "Shit, I still don't see why you and Sinclair don't just get back together and stay that way."

"Now that one's not that easy, believe me!" Midnight said, more serious now.

"Yeah, yeah, I wouldn't have a hard time with that man. He is Grade A, number one all the way. You're damn crazy girl!"

"I've heard that," Midnight said, nodding.

Midnight was coming up on Chicano Park. As she pulled to a stop, she looked over at Kana.

"You ready?" she asked, her eyes scanning the area around them.

Kana took a deep breath, and closed her eyes. Midnight knew that she was centering herself; it was something that Kana did often. Midnight waited patiently looking out at the street. She saw members of the Homegirls hanging around, looking at the car. It was very obvious to them who Midnight was, between the car and the size of her when she got out.

Midnight spotted Oso right away, she stood a full foot taller than Midnight and she was almost as wide as Kana. *Oh shit*, Midnight thought to herself, reaching back to touch her gun nestled snugly against the small of her back.

Midnight and Kana walked up to Oso, and three of Oso's girls closed in beside their leader. Midnight had to look up at Oso, but she managed it without looking inferior. The set of her jaw and the look in her eyes, as well as her stance, made Midnight seem bigger than she really was.

"So, juera, you wanted to meet, here we are," Oso said, calling Midnight a white girl in Spanish.

"Yeah, here we are," Midnight replied, her eyes moving to each of the three girls backing up their leader.

Midnight figured they must be a little worried if there were three of them there to backup Oso. Either that or they were ready to pound Midnight into oblivion. While she was always overly confident on the outside, Midnight never made the mistake of being so on the inside. She always treated every opponent as a very dangerous threat, that way she was never surprised.

"Look," Midnight said, trying reason first; her cop side she called it. "I need you and your girls to back off the Southside Girls."

Oso laughed at her. "Oh, and I guess we're just supposed to do you what you say, eh juera?"

Midnight rubbed the back of her neck. She knew she was going to have to fight this one. She had known it from the minute Kana had told her about the war the Homegirls had started with the Southside Girls. At an almost imperceptible nod from Midnight, Kana positioned herself at the side of both women, ready to intervene if necessary. Midnight took two steps backward. She stood with her legs shoulder width apart and her arms down at her sides, but away from her body in a fighter's stance.

"Well, we can do it that way, or we can do it the hard way," Midnight said, her voice calm and low.

Oso laughed mockingly then. "I guess I'm supposed to be shaking now, eh?"

Midnight's look didn't waver. "You don't have to be scared, you just have to know I'm serious."

Oso gave her a sharp look, she was starting to worry a little bit, this small woman, wasn't afraid of her, and everyone was always afraid of Oso. Then her eyes narrowed at Midnight.

"Yeah, you're a real bad puta with that gun in your back, aren't you?" she growled.

Midnight looked at her for a long moment, then with a look on her face that said *oh really?* she reached for the gun and pulled it out, holster and all. Without even looking at Kana, Midnight tossed her holstered gun to her. Kana caught it easily and looked at Oso as if to say *and what do you have to say now?* Midnight held up her empty hands.

"No gun," she said, but then she nodded her head at the three girls still standing with Oso, "but it's just you and me, you keep them out of this." She looked over at Kana then, nodding to her. "She'll make sure everything stays fair."

Then she moved her right foot back, planting it in ready stance, and motioned with her fingers.

"Let's go," she said, her eyes staring down the gang leader.

She could see she had already planted a seed of doubt in Oso's mind. Oso hesitated for a second. *Big mistake,* Midnight thought to herself. When Oso finally did start to move toward her, Midnight launched a kick right to her mid-section. Oso doubled over, surprise evident on her face, but then she launched herself half crouched at Midnight knocking the smaller woman off her feet. Oso's head hit Midnight's ribs, not only knocking her off her feet, but knocking the wind out of her. Coughing she rolled to the side, so that Oso couldn't get on top of her. Midnight knew if Oso could get her on the ground she was done for. Completing the roll and standing, Midnight launched another kick at Oso who was down on the ground, still stunned that Midnight had not ended up under her, as she had planned.

Midnight stood there breathing heavily. She shifted her weight back and forth, motioning again for Oso to bring it on. Oso was mad and embarrassed now. She launched a frontal attack on Midnight, which Midnight easily stepped aside from, punching Oso in the face as the bigger woman overshot her mark and fell past Midnight.

"Midnight!" Kana yelled.

Like a cat sensing danger Midnight turned, bringing her forearm up as she did. The knife her silent assailant was bringing down on her sliced through her arm. Midnight cried out, but brought her other fist up, punching the girl with the knife in the stomach. Kana immediately stepped in to help; the Homegirls weren't fighting fair, so why should they? After a few minutes, Kana and Midnight were the only two standing.

"Ah shit," Midnight said. There was blood all over her arm and a good deal on her jeans.

She turned and started walking toward her car. Kana handed Midnight her holstered gun. Midnight placed it at her back with shaking hands.

"Midnight, are you okay?" Kana asked, putting a hand out to steady the leader of FORS as she stumbled slightly.

Midnight intended to call out the black and whites, but she already heard them coming.

"Oh boy," she said, squatting down next to her car. "I feel a little lightheaded."

"Midnight!" Kana yelled as Midnight started to fall backwards, but Midnight caught herself with an outstretched arm.

"I'm okay!" Midnight said. "I'm okay."

She sat down, cross-legged on the ground, with her elbows on her knees and her head down. She was taking deep slow breaths, but they hurt too, because of the ribs that she knew were more than likely black and blue. After a few minutes, she got up slowly and moved to the driver's seat of her car.

"Are you okay to drive?" Kana asked, as Midnight started the car.

"Yeah, I'm fine," Midnight said, sounding more like herself then. "Really. Why don't you stay here and work with the uniforms, and I'll head over to the hospital, and get this stitched up."

Reaching behind her Midnight found a rag on the back seat. She wrapped it around her arm, tying it off with her teeth and her good arm.

"Midnight, if Joe finds out I let you leave without me, he'll take my head off!" Kana said, holding up her hand to Midnight. "Hold up just a minute!"

Kana ran over and talked to the officers that were just arriving, telling them that she was going with to the hospital with the Lieutenant. The officer nodded to her and waved her away knowing that it was more important for Midnight to go to the hospital than to stand around dealing with details. Kana ran back to the car. As Midnight started for the hospital, they heard the radio call that Lieutenant Chevalier was en route to the hospital. Midnight rolled her eyes and switched off her cellular phone. She knew if she didn't Joe would be on it in a minute reading her the riot act.

Two hours later, she was pulling out of the hospital parking lot when her cell phone rang. She knew it was Joe, and she knew that he had heard the radio call and had probably been trying to call since then.

"Yes," she said, flipping her phone open.

"Where the fuck have you been?" Joe yelled.

Midnight smiled at Kana, who returned the smile, it was terrible being right all the time.

"Well, thank you for your concern, Sinclair. I was just at the hospital getting checked out." She kept her voice casual, so he wouldn't go off the deep end on her.

"Checked out?" Joe repeated suspiciously. He knew his partner had a tendency to underplay things. "And what did they find?" he asked then, his voice still edgy.

He had tried for two hours to get a hold of her, and he knew that she had turned off her cell phone so he couldn't.

"They found," Midnight said, "that I have three bruised ribs, surprisingly not cracked, a nasty little gash on my arm, and some cut up knuckles. Other than that I'm just dandy."

"What's your twenty now?" Joe asked, using the code for her location.

"I'm headed back to drop Kana off in front of the office and then I'm going home, sir!" Midnight said, reeling off the information as if she were a new recruit.

"I'll be at your place in an hour," Joe said. "And you better not be lying to me, or I'll kick your cute little ass."

"Sir, yes sir!" Midnight replied, laughing.

She hung up and noticed that Kana was watching her.

"What?" Kana nodded her head approvingly at Midnight. "You did okay out there," she said, her voice reflecting her surprise.

"Yeah," Midnight said, grimacing and holding up her bandaged arm. "I did great!"

But Kana shook her head. "No, you did really good, Midnight. Hell that Oso could've taken me, but you're smarter and faster than shit!" Again, her voice reflected surprise.

Midnight looked over at Kana for a long moment; a compliment coming from someone like Kana was a compliment indeed. Kana had single-handedly taken on one of the biggest gang leaders in Honolulu and a few of her girls and won, before she had come to the mainland and joined FORS. So Kana was tough, and her applauding Midnight's fighting was impressive.

An hour later, Midnight was sitting on her couch wearing a clean cotton shirt, and her police sweatpants. Her sleeves were rolled up, so the bandage that covered her arm was exposed. She heard Joe come in and saw that Randy was still with him.

"Hey," she said, smiling up at her second and at their secretary.

"Let's see it," Joe said, his eyes looking her over.

Midnight dutifully held up her bandaged arm. Joe moved to her side, his eyes full of concern. He took her hand gently, looking at her.

"You're okay?"

"Yeah, I'm okay, I already told you that," she said, squeezing his hand.

Then she looked over at Randy, who seemed almost as concerned as Joe did.

"Oh God, not you too," Midnight said laughing.

Randy seemed to relax visibly then.

"Sit down, Randy, you make me nervous standing there," Midnight said then, motioning with her head. Randy sat on the other end of the couch.

"You need anything?" Joe asked Midnight. She shook her head. "So I take it you won?" Joe said, his voice lightening up a little.

"Of course I won. Hell, Joe if you'd seen the size of that Oso. Shit, if I'd lost, I wouldn't be here right now, I'd probably be in a box down at city morgue!"

She had meant it as a joke, but she could see from the look on Joe's face that it had reminded him she had not included him on this one. She could have paid for it.

"Yeah, I heard," Joe said shortly.

"Oh God, Sinclair, don't start okay. I've been a cop longer than you, and I did survive the mean streets before you came along! They didn't make me a fucking lieutenant because I look good in the uniform, you know!" Midnight said, her eyes flashing at him.

Joe glared at her. "Yeah I know, Midnight, but lieutenants get iced too."

"Yeah and I know one sergeant that's about to, if he doesn't back off!" Midnight snarled back at him.

Joe stood up then and strode over to look out the sliding glass doors that lead to Midnight's backyard. She lived on a hill above the beach, not quite as scenic a location as Joe's, but it was still a nice view.

Randy sat on the end of the couch; she could feel the electricity in the room. She was surprised by their anger. She had no way of knowing that they always got into an argument when Midnight got hurt. Joe always wanted to hide her away so she couldn't get hurt again, and she always fought him. It was their way of confirming that they cared about each other and also a confirmation that they were both still very much alive. Randy could see that Joe was very tense and angry, as was Midnight. It filled the air around them.

Midnight sat looking down at her bandaged arm, her teeth worrying her lower lip. After a few minutes, she took a deep breath and expelled it, looking up at the ceiling and shaking her head. As Randy watched, Midnight stood up and walked over to where Joe stood. She stood facing his side but Joe didn't look at her, and she wasn't looking up at him. Then slowly she leaned her head on his arm. Neither one of them spoke, but Joe's arm came up slowly to pull her close to him. She leaned against him, her body pressed against the length of his. They stood that way for a long time.

Tears came to Randy's eyes, because watching them made her feel the emotions that were running between them. She was glad that they had obviously made up already.

Randy realized now, that no matter what Darrell said, or did, she was now a member of FORS and nothing was going to keep her from working with these two people who in two short days had become the center of her life.

CHAPTER 6

Friday couldn't seem to come fast enough for Randy. Joe dropped her off Friday afternoon telling her he'd be back at her house by seven.

"You're going out with who?" Darrell asked incredulously two hours later.

"I'm going out with Joe," Randy told him, the second time.

"The player with the Porsche?"

"No," Randy said, her eyes narrowing as she put earrings in her ears, "the fine, upstanding peace officer who I work for, who happens to own a Porsche."

"So where'd he get the money for it?" Darrell asked. "You find that out yet?"

"It's really none of my business, Darrell," Randy replied, "but yes, I do know where he got the money for the car and the house he lives in as well."

"So where?" Darrell asked, when it was obvious she wasn't forthcoming with the information.

"It's none of your business," Randy replied, squeezing past him to go into the tiny bathroom the three of them shared. She shut the door in Darrell's face and locked it.

"You're not going out with him," Darrell yelled through the door.

"Yes I am," Randy replied, doing her best to stay calm.

The last thing she wanted was to get into some wicked fight with Darrell right before her date with Joe. As it was, she was afraid of what Darrell would do when Joe got there to pick her up.

An hour later, Randy looked outside to see Joe drive up. Darrell's friends were over and they, along with Donovan, were hanging out in the garage. Randy was completely on edge. Before she could grab her jacket and get outside, however, Joe was out of his car, even as Darrell and his friends walked down the driveway to confront him.

Joe grinned sardonically at the small group coming toward him. Darrell's friends were all construction workers, so they were brawny, like Darrell. Joe resisted the urge to sweep the sides of his jacket back to reveal the shoulder holster with the nasty looking forty-five. He knew this wasn't the time to intimidate Darrell Curtis. So instead he leaned on the hood of his car, his long legs extended in front of him, crossed at the ankles. He appeared completely at ease.

Donovan followed his brother's friends, but smiled immediately at Joe who returned the smile with a nod.

"You here for Randy?" one of the men, shorter than Darrell, asked.

Joe nodded, keeping tabs on the four of them as the spread out.

"Randy's not going out with you," Darrell said, his tone adversarial.

"That's not what she says," Joe said, his look direct.

"Yeah, well, I say," Darrell retorted.

Joe nodded, not looking the slightest bit impressed by Darrell's comment. Randy all but ran out of the house then, striding down the driveway as fast as she could on the heels she wore.

"Darrell," she warned.

"Get back in the house, Randy," Darrell told her, blocking her way.

"No," Randy said, moving to get around him.

One of Darrell's friends grabbed her arm. That's when Joe moved off the car, finally losing his calm. Darrell turned back to Joe, but Joe's eyes were on the man who had Randy's arm.

"Let go of her," Joe said, his tone no nonsense. "Now."

"Look, cop," Darrell said, his tone sneering, "just get back in your fancy car and leave."

Joe's eyes flicked to Darrell, then back to the man holding Randy.

"I said, let go of her," Joe repeated.

"What are you gonna do?" the younger man asked, his tone snide.

"I'm gonna say it one more time," Joe said. His voice still low and calm but it was an unmistakable threat. "Remove your hands from her, before I remove them for you."

Darrell debated his actions. He didn't want Randy to go out with this cop; the guy was up to no good, Darrell knew that just from looking at him. It was obvious, however, that this guy wasn't easily intimidated and the last thing Darrell wanted was for Randy to end up in the middle of a physical confrontation between Joe and his friends.

"Jack, let her go," Darrell said.

Jack did as Darrell said and Randy moved to Joe's side. Joe immediately walked her over to the passenger side, opened the door for her, and gestured for her to get inside.

"Joe," she said then, her tone cautionary. She didn't want him to get into a fight with her brother.

"It's okay," Joe said, giving her a half grin, before he closed the passenger door.

As he walked around the car, Joe said nothing to Darrell, but apparently, Jack wasn't done trying to impress.

He grabbed Joe's shoulder, but Joe was much faster than the younger man. With the lightning-fast reactions that had saved his life for years, Joe side stepped the man's hand, and reached back to clasp his would-be assailant's wrist, bringing his arm up and through. He had the younger man on his knees in a fraction of a second.

Looking down at the man, Joe narrowed his eyes dangerously. "Don't fuck with me, kid," he said, keeping his voice low. "You won't like what I'll do to you."

With that, he let Jack go and gave Darrell a pointed look. Then he strode around to get into his vehicle. The action of taking the young man to his knees had exposed Joe's weapon. It showed Darrell and his friends that Joe didn't need to use his weapon or his badge to threaten them. It was food for thought.

Even so, Darrell watched through narrowed eyes as Joe started the Porsche and turned out of the cul de sac.

In the car, Randy was mortified by what had happened. She wouldn't have been surprised if Joe had stopped the car at the end of the street and told her to get out, that she wasn't worth the trouble she was putting him through.

"Joe, I'm so sorry," she began, her hands clutched together nervously.

"Don't," he said, shaking his head, his tone harsher than he'd meant it to be, still irritated by the confrontation. To soften his words, he grinned. "It's not your fault your brother's friend isn't very bright." With that, he looked over at her and smiled.

Randy relaxed visibly.

Joe looked over at her for a long moment at the first red light they hit.

"You look beautiful," he told her. She wore a white dress that set off both her figure and her coloring nicely. Her hair was loose but pulled back at the top in a clip. She wore more makeup than she normally did at work, but just enough to emphasize her features.

Randy bit her lip, pleased that he thought so.

"You look different," she said, smiling.

"Different?" Joe asked, with a grin. "You mean you're shocked that I can clean up decently?"

Randy opened her mouth in dismay, but then Joe started to laugh. "I just meant you're dressed much differently than at work," she clarified.

"Oh," he said, nodding, his grin still evident.

He wore charcoal-gray dress pants and a crisp white button down shirt, open at the collar to reveal a simple flat linked gold chain. He even wore dove-gray leather dress boots. Handsome to the extreme.

Joe turned on the stereo and music blared from the speakers. Grimacing, he reached over turning it down.

"Who is that?" Randy asked, gesturing to the stereo.

"Skid Row," Joe replied.

Randy nodded. "You really like rock music, don't you?"

"Oh yeah," Joe said, grinning. "I wanted to be a rock star when I grew up."

"Really?" Randy asked, smiling. "I can see that," she said nodding.

"You can?"

"Oh yes," she said, nodding, "with the hair, the charisma and the presence, you'd have made a great rock star."

Joe laughed. "Except for the fact that I can neither sing nor play an instrument."

"That might be a drawback, yeah," Randy said, grinning.

"Ya think?"

"Maybe," Randy said, chuckling.

They talked for a while about inconsequential things. At one point Joe reached out taking her hand, Randy smiled shyly, but was thoroughly enjoying his attention. Her ego had no idea what to do with such a handsome man paying attention to her, but she'd already decided she was going to enjoy every minute of this date with him.

She had no idea why he'd asked her out; she couldn't believe he could find her even remotely interesting. What could he have in common with the likes of her? Randy had no idea, but she was determined to enjoy her one chance with him. Who knew if he'd ever ask her out again, after tonight?

Joe had driven south and crossed the Coronado Bridge, and Randy was shocked when he pulled up in front of the Hotel Del Coronado. The hotel, a world-famous attraction for the rich and famous, was one of San Diego's crown jewels.

Randy looked over at Joe in awed silence. He grinned, glad to have apparently surprised her.

"I thought it might be nice to have dinner here," he said, smiling.

"I've always wanted to come here for dinner," she said shaking her head in wonder.

"Really?" Joe asked, as he got out of the car. The valet opened Randy's door for her.

Joe handed the man the keys and a fifty; it was the smartest way to get his vehicle parked in a spot where it wouldn't get keyed, hit, or stolen. The valet smiled widely, nodding at Joe in appreciation.

Walking around the car, Joe offered Randy his arm and escorted her inside.

"So, you know about this place?" Joe asked as he guided her to the right and to the maître d' of the Crown Room.

Randy struggled to control herself, she couldn't believe this was happening! She'd been to the Hotel del Coronado, of course, it was a San Diego landmark and one she was always fascinated with, but she'd never had the means to eat at the hotel. The Crown Room was the most elegant restaurant they had.

"Yes," she said, doing her best to sound normal, "it was built in 1888. It's one of largest structures outside of New York to be electrically lighted."

"So, I guess you'll need to give me a tour of the place after this," he said, winking at her.

She smiled brilliantly at him as the maître d' looked up.

"Table for two," Joe said. "Sinclair."

The maître d' was a tall thin man with an equally thin mustache that gave him the perfect overly sophisticated look for his position.

"Right this way, sir," the man responded, bowing slightly to Joe.

Randy clutched Joe's hand tighter as they were escorted to table located near the large curved window in the beautifully appointed room. The ceiling was sugared pine, and glowed from the light of crown-shaped chandeliers.

After they were seated, Randy touched Joe's arm, pointing to the chandeliers. "Those were designed by the author of the *Wizard of Oz*, L. Frank Baum."

"Looks about right," Joe said, smiling warmly.

He was pleased that Randy was obviously excited about the restaurant. When they opened their menus, Randy realized she wasn't sure what most of the food was. Joe ended up helping her order, since he was familiar with the French words used.

"So, you know French?" Randy asked, intrigued.

"I'm actually part French," Joe said, smiling. "I'm not fluent in the language, but I can muddle through in a pinch," he said with a wink.

"Like when your date isn't savvy enough to order for herself in a nice restaurant?"

"Knowing how to order fancy food is over-rated," Joe said. "Besides, you know more about this place than I do," he said, gesturing around them.

He'd ordered wine for both of them, after checking that Randy liked wine, quickly stifling her comment about being underage.

After the wine and their salads arrived, Randy looked over at him. "What is England like?" she asked wistfully. "You are actually from there, right?" she asked, realizing she was assuming that since he still had an accent that he'd been born in England.

"Yes," he said, nodding, "I'm from London. What's it like?" he queried, narrowing his eyes in thought. "It's beautiful, green almost everywhere outside the city. The architecture is incredible and goes back centuries." He shrugged. "I guess it's hard for me to describe adequately, it's just home."

Randy smiled, nodding. "How long have you been in the States?"

"About eight years now," he said, "since I was twenty-one."

Randy stopped eating for a moment staring at him in shock.

"What?" he asked, a bemused grin at his lips.

"You're twenty-nine?" she asked.

Joe's grin widened into a smile. "Didn't know you were going out with an old man?"

Randy's mouth opened, then she closed it narrowing her eyes. "I'm not sure I believe you're actually that old," she said, "but in any case, twenty-nine isn't really old."

"Uh-huh, it's almost thirty." Joe said, nodding, "and you know what they say, though."

"What?" Randy asked, already suspicious of the grin on his lips.

"It's not the years, honey, it's the mileage," he said, with a laugh.

Randy laughed too. They talked on through dinner, discussing the history of the hotel, and some of the places in England that Randy had read about. Joe was a very charming dinner companion, and wasn't very impressed with himself or his money.

"It's not really mine," he said at one point. "I didn't earn it."

"But your parents left it to you," Randy said, trying to understand.

"Yeah," Joe said, nodding, "it was my father's company that made it. I had no hand in that."

Randy canted her head to the side, knowing there was more to the story than that, but not wanting to pry too much. She was still curious about how his parents died, but was afraid to ask, thinking that if Joe wanted to talk about it, he would.

They lingered over dessert and coffee, talking about books and music.

"Well, if my parents had their way, I'd never have heard rock music," Joe said, his tone bemused. "My mother never could stand it," he said, shaking his head. "Used to call it shrieking and gadding about."

Randy laughed softly. "It sounds like she was a bit more refined than you."

"She was incredible," Joe said, his eyes shining at the memory of his mother.

Randy put her hand on his, looking into his eyes. "Tell me about her," she said gently.

Joe looked at her for a long moment, then expelled his breath slowly, shaking his head in wonder. "She had this way about her," he began, smiling fondly, "even in furs, jewels, and designer dresses, she'd sit down and doctor a cut I managed to get out on my horse."

"You ride horses?" she asked, surprised at that.

"I did back home," he said, "we had a stable full of stallions and mares, Arabians, Lipizzaner's, Tennessee Walking horse, then there was mine."

"What was yours?" Randy asked, enchanted suddenly.

"I had a Friesian, Satan," he said, grinning. "Named him myself. He was eighteen hands high."

"How big is that?" Randy asked.

"Well, a hand is four inches, and you measure from their hooves to their withers, so he was six feet at the withers."

"The withers is which part?" she asked, intrigued about this side of him.

"The withers is where the neck and shoulder muscles unite, so basically the top of his shoulders was almost as tall as me."

"Wow," Randy said, widening her eyes, "what color was he?"

"All Friesians are black," he said, smiling.

"They are?" Randy asked surprised again.

"Yeah," Joe said, chuckling. It was strange to him talking about home this much.

He hadn't talked to anyone about England this much, not even with Rick. It was actually rather nice.

Later, Randy was thrilled to find out that Joe had made arrangements with a staff member at the hotel, to be allowed into the restricted areas of the hotel. Only people staying at the hotel were to be on the second, third and fourth floors. But it was Randy that was able to tell Joe about the hotel.

"The haunted room is on the third floor," she told him in a conspiratorial whisper as she got into the old-fashioned elevator.

"Haunted room?" Joe asked, leaning against the side of the rod-iron elevator door.

"Yeah," Randy said, her eyes lighting up, "this hotel is haunted. Haven't you heard of it before?"

"Not the part about being haunted, no," Joe said, wondering if she was putting him on.

"No? Well, one of the stories is that a woman killed herself in one of the rooms, back in … oh I think it was the 1800s or so. Anyway, the hotel management didn't want people to know about such a scandalous event and so they put her body in a closet …" She was watching Joe to see if he was reacting properly to what she was telling him. He was. "Well, her blood seeped out all over the floor of the closet and sunk in. Years later, they expanded the hotel and made that particular closet into a room. And even to this day, every time they replace the carpet, this strange brown stain comes up through the rug. The stain looks like old blood." She shuddered theatrically then and Joe smiled

"Blood stain, huh?" he said, giving her a disbelieving look.

"Yeah!" she said, laughing. "I swear to God!"

"But why are we going up there? We won't be able to go into the room …"

"No, but the whole floor is supposed to be haunted too."

"I see," he said, as the elevator stopped.

"Come on," she said, smiling at him. As they walked down the dim corridors, Randy took his hand in her excitement at showing him these new things. "You see how the doorways are different sizes, and how the halls change from wide to narrow?" she said pointing to another corridor as they passed.

"Yeah ..." he said. He was becoming quite interested in the hotel's history listening to how excited Randy was about being there.

"Well that's because they didn't have any blueprints when they built the hotel, they just started at one end and worked from there." Joe noticed that she was still holding his hand, but he didn't mind. It was actually nice being there with her.

At one point, they stopped to look at a print that hung on one of the corridor walls. Randy turned to continue down the hall, but Joe pulled her back. He pulled her against him, and, looking down at her smiling, he leaned down and kissed her. Her hands touched his chest tentatively. He took her hands in his and held them as he kissed her. When their lips parted, she looked up at him wide-eyed, but smiling shyly.

Randy's heart was beating a mile a minute. She'd never been kissed like that before. He had a way of making her feel special. She knew she was being far too dreamy about this entire thing, but fireworks had gone off in her head when his lips had touched hers; more had jolted through her when he'd taken her hands. The kiss hadn't been sloppy and lustful like the kisses she'd received from the few men she'd gone out with. It had been sweet, soft, and with just a hint of passion. She felt that unfamiliar fluttering in her stomach, the fluttering she'd read had everything to do with desire. And God knew she desired Joe. He'd done nothing but fan it since he'd met her. Randy had no idea if that was intentional or not.

Later they ended up sitting down in the hotel's twenty-four hour deli, talking and just enjoying the evening. Randy was fascinated by everything about him. He'd grown up in London high society, yet he was a police officer in America, in a gang task force no less. It was an odd, but interesting combination.

It was midnight before Joe took her home.

"Is Darrell going to give you a lot of grief about this?" Joe asked as he walked her to her front door.

Randy shrugged, smiling, having enjoyed herself far too much to worry about that right then.

"Probably will," she told him, "but I don't care."

Joe looked down at her for a long moment, his eyes searching hers. Sliding his hands around her waist, he leaned down to kiss her goodnight.

It took every ounce of self-control Randy had to keep from sighing. She didn't want the evening to end.

When their lips parted, Joe gave her a pointed look and touched her cheek. "If he gives you too much grief, you call me, okay?"

Randy smiled, warmed by his concern. "Okay, I will."

Joe smiled in response. "See you Monday?"

Randy nodded, biting her lip shyly.

Joe got back in his car drove away after seeing that she was safely inside. He thought about her all the way home, still smiling to himself when he walked into his house. It had been a wonderful night.

****

Things between Rick and Midnight escalated to a boiling point the next evening. Everything started out great; he went over to see her and drop off some paperwork. Midnight was reading reports in her bedroom as usual. She let him in the house through her intercom and security system and he wandered back to her room, knowing where she'd be. He watched her reading for a while, then leaned over and touched her under the chin so she'd look up at him. When she did, he smiled, and leaned in to kiss her. As usual, his kiss got both of them going, and they were in a heated embrace in moments.

Midnight pulled away first. "Rick, I have about three reports I need to finish reading tonight. I can't do this right now, okay?" Her voice was breathless from the kiss, but it was serious.

"You work entirely too hard," Rick chided, sliding his hand back around to her neck to pull her close again. His lips covered hers once more.

She pushed him back again, shaking her head, and smiling. "I need to work, go away."

"You need to learn to relax, is what you need to do babe," Rick said reproachfully.

This time as he leaned in, he slid his hands under her shirt, kissing her deeply as he caressed her skin. Midnight shuddered at the feel of his hands on her, and found herself wrapping her arms around his neck, kissing him back. *What is it about this guy?* she asked herself.

Rick reached down between them, and pushed the reports off the bed and pulled her down to lay under him. His lips never left hers. He was unbuttoning her shirt when Midnight pulled back again.

"Rick," she began, her tone sharper now. "I told you, I have work to do."

"Yeah," he replied, "and I told you that you work too hard."

With that said, he went back to kissing her again, and again Midnight lost herself in the sensation of his hands on her skin. She was fully ready to give in when the phone rang.

"Don't answer it," Rick said, his lips still covering hers. But the sound of the phone had snapped her out of her languor and she reached for it. "Damn it!" he snapped. "I said don't answer it!" He grabbed both of her wrists to keep her from disobeying him, raised them above her head, and continued to kiss her. Midnight pulled away from him, narrowing her eyes as she looked up at him.

"Let go of my wrists," she said, passion still coloring her voice, but she definitely meant it.

"No," he responded simply, kissing her again.

He kept his body was over hers, holding her captive, since he outweighed her by about forty pounds. She wrenched her face away from him again, this time anger blazing in her eyes.

"Let go, Rick. I'm serious," she said.

"What the fuck is with you?" Rick asked angrily, but he didn't move, nor did he release her wrists.

"What's with me is that I want you to let go!" she raged back at him.

Rick checked his hands holding her wrists. He knew he wasn't touching the cut. "Am I hurting you?" he asked, concerned.

"No," she retorted, "I'm just telling you to let me the fuck go!"

He shook his head. "No."

Now it was becoming a battle of wills and Midnight had no intention of losing. She wrenched her wrists from his grasp and cried out in pain, she had forgotten in her anger and desperation to be released about her injured arm. But it was too late to worry about that now. With surprising force she not only freed her hands, but shoved him off of her too. He stood up and she leapt to her feet on the other side of the bed.

Her eyes were almost wild with anger. "Get out," she bit out, her chest heaving with the adrenaline surging through her.

When he didn't move she picked up her baton. She held it in a threatening position, not breaking eye contact. Her intentions were clear as day. He stared back at her for a minute, then, shaking his head, he walked out of the room and left.

Midnight stood shaking uncontrollably. When he left she sat down on the floor and leaned against the wall trying to get her breathing under control. Her arm was throbbing painfully. She picked up her phone and dialed Joe's number. It was too late to be calling him, but she needed to hear his voice.

"'Lo," Joe answered sounding distracted. He'd been reading a report of his own at that point.

She was silent for a second, then she said, "Joe, it's me."

Her voice was weaker than normal putting Joe on alert instantly. "Night, what's wrong?"

She was silent again. She knew she couldn't explain it to him and she really didn't want to try.

"Midnight?" Joe asked, terrified that something had happened to her.

"Joe, it's okay, I'm sorry. I shouldn't have called, I'm just feeling a little weird right now. I'm okay."

"Do you need me there?" Joe asked.

"No, I'm fine, Joe, go back to what you were doing, I'm sorry." She hung up. She lay back down on the bed and stared into the darkness, her mind whirling in a thousand different directions, but it kept coming back to a certain Richard Debenshire. She finally fell asleep two hours later.

San Diego, California, 1979

Jack Chevalier was not a happy man. He'd just gotten a call from the principal telling him that his fifteen-year-old son, Thomas, was getting into fights and cutting class. Having had his current bender interrupted once too often lately, Jack Chevalier decided to play the father for a little while. He walked up to Thomas's bedroom door and without knocking walked in. Thomas was sitting on his bed, reading a magazine. He looked up when his door opened, assuming it would be his older sister, Midnight. He was surprised to see his father standing in the doorway. Jack stepped into the room, looking down at his son.

"We need to talk, young man," Jack said, his voice just slightly louder than necessary, indicating to Thomas that he was loaded, more than likely on cocaine.

"What about?" Thomas replied, his tone insolent. He already knew what Jack wanted to talk about, but he didn't think his alcoholic, coke-head father had any right to play holier than thou.

"About you cutting class and getting into fights," Jack snapped, irritated by the look of impertinence on his son's face. When Thomas didn't reply, he got angrier. "What have you got to say for yourself?" Jack asked hotly.

"I cut class and get into fights," Thomas replied sarcastically.

"You little son of a bitch!" Jack barked as he lashed out with his fist, catching Thomas totally off guard and striking him on the side of the face. Before Thomas could recover to defend himself, Jack jumped on the bed, his fist raised to hit his son again. Jack didn't see the copper blond flash that tackled him, knocking him to the floor.

With surprising agility, Midnight got to her feet, standing over her father. She was panting with the adrenaline that was surging through her veins, and her gold-green eyes blazed with anger. Jack went to grab her feet out from under her, but Midnight was faster. Using a booted foot, she shoved him away from her, and jumped over him. She moved to the other side of the bed, her eyes on Thomas.

Thomas had watched in stunned silence. His eyes followed his sister as she moved close to him, looking down. She reached out touching the already darkening bruise on his cheek.

Jack Chevalier stood up then, his eyes looking daggers at his daughter, but Midnight was not intimidated. She gave him a lethal look of her own, pointing to Thomas's cheek.

"If you ever hit him again," she said, her tone deadly low with menace, "I'll fucking kill you."

"Don't talk to me like that you little slut," Jack said, his face a mask of disgust as he took a step toward her.

Midnight didn't back away as he expected. She dropped one foot behind her in a fighter's stance, her hands dangling at her sides, her fingers working, as if itching to hurt him. She was challenging her own father. Jack stared at her as if suddenly trying to discern who she was. Indeed, he was trying to assimilate this young woman with the "little

girl" he had known years before. After a long tense minute, Jack
Chevalier shook his head, walked past his children and out of the room.

****

Monday, Joe picked Randy up for work. When she got in, he smiled at
her.

"How'd the weekend go?" he asked, putting the car into gear and
turning out of the cul de sac.

"Darrell wouldn't talk to me all weekend," she said casually. She
clearly wasn't too put out by it.

"Probably good," Joe said, grinning.

"So how was your weekend?" she asked.

"Long," he said, a smile still on his lips. Then he looked over at
her. "I missed you," he said, surprising himself.

"You did?" she asked, thrilled that he'd just said what she'd been
thinking.

Joe nodded, looking a bit chagrined. Randy noticed the look but
didn't push it any further. Still, she was happy that he'd missed her.

That day at the office, things were hectic. They were planning a
raid on a house that they suspected was the residence of many
members of the Scorpions. They had traced some information they
had gotten on Robert Bondy through the California Law Enforcement
Telecommunications System known as CLETS. It was a system used
by law enforcement to track information on felons and known
criminals including things like warrants, restraining orders; it was

linked to many law enforcement databases, including federal agencies such as the FBI.

Randy helped by typing up warrants and Joe stood behind her as she worked on the computer in Midnight's office.

"Yeah, that's good," he was saying.

He put his hands on the back of her chair and she could tell how tense he was without even looking. The raid would take place in about two hours if everything went well. "Print it," he said briskly, but he smiled at her when she looked up.

Midnight walked into the office. "Are we a go?" she asked looking at Joe. Joe nodded.

"I still think you should sit this one out, Night," Joe said, gesturing to her bandaged arm.

"Hey, I talked to the doc and he said there was no tendon damage so I can shoot fine. Besides, I tested it this morning at the range. I'm fine, Sinclair." There was no anger in her voice, although her words, like Joe's were brisk. "I'm going on this one."

What she didn't say was that her arm had hurt like crazy at the range that morning, but she was still right on target.

They looked at each other for a minute. Joe was obviously debating arguing further with her, but he could see by the look in her eyes that she was determined. He decided that at least he'd be there this time.

Rick walked in; he and Midnight exchanged an almost hostile look. It didn't miss Joe and he wondered if it had anything to do with the strange phone call he had received from Midnight the night before. He wasn't sure what had happened to make Midnight look at Rick that way, though he did notice that Rick didn't seem bothered by it. Joe shrugged to himself; there were more important things to worry about. But he would definitely talk to Midnight later.

"You going with us, man?" Joe asked, looking at Rick.

"Guess that's up to the boss," Rick said, leaning against the door-jamb, looking casually at Midnight.

Midnight looked sharply at Rick for a long moment, her eyes narrowed at him. Then she looked over at Joe. "What do you think? You've seen him in action ..." Her voice trailed off as she looked back over at Rick, challenging him to say something.

Rick only shook his head, and looked over at Joe. Randy was watching the scene from behind Midnight's desk. It was obvious things were now strained between them. Randy was beginning to realize how quickly relationships could become complicated.

Joe looked between Midnight and Rick, trying to figure out what had happened. He knew he was going to have to ask Rick, if he wanted answers. He looked at Midnight directly then and nodded.

"Night the guy was my second, remember? He can hold his own and then some," he said. It was clear from his tone he thought she was involving her personal feelings too much in the decision.

Midnight caught the inflection in his voice and nodded in agreement, pressing her lips together in self-agitation. Usually she didn't involve her personal feelings in business decisions and it bothered her that yet again Rick was the exception to that rule. She picked up the warrants, doing her best to avoid eye contact with everyone in the room.

She walked to the door. "I'll, uh, go run these by Judge Connolly. I'll meet you out there," she said, moving deftly past Rick, who still leaned against the doorjamb, as if loathe to touch him.

Rick and Joe looked at each other. Joe shrugged and shook his head.

"I'll meet you out front in a minute," Rick told Joe.

Rick went to catch up to Midnight in the elevator. He caught her as the elevator door was closing and squeezed in just in time. Midnight looked irritated. He moved to within inches of her, resting his arm on the wall just over her head.

"So what the fuck was that all about?" he asked, his voice irritated.

"That," Midnight said, her voice perfectly calm and businesslike, "was inappropriate of me. I shouldn't have questioned your ability, I'm sorry."

Rick looked at her for a second then he gave a short laugh shaking his head. "I see, you're sorry about your lack of professionalism, but you're not sorry about the other night, right?"

"Look, I don't want to go into that right now. Let's keep our private lives out of the office okay?" Her voice was still cool.

He reached over and pushed the emergency stop on the elevator, and moved even closer to her.

"And what if I don't want to do that?" His deep blue eyes challenged her. "What're you going to do?"

He watched her closely as the anger built up inside her. He knew he was pushing her, but something about her made him want to push her, to make her lose it, one way or the other. She was too damned controlled, that was her problem. He put his hand behind her neck and pulled her toward him, pressing his lips to hers in deeply passionate kiss.

He was shocked when, a couple of seconds later, she shoved him away forcefully. He was even more shocked when she slapped him. When he looked down at her again she was shaking from her anger, her eyes were blazing.

"You do that again," Midnight threatened, "and your ass is out of here."

With that, she reached over and pulled the emergency stop button back and the elevator lurched back into motion. Rick leaned against the opposite wall from her, looking totally defeated, his fingers working in agitation. He realized he had just pushed it too far. When the elevator stopped, she walked out without a backward glance. After a few seconds hesitation Rick pushed off the wall, shaking his head, and left the elevator. He waited for Joe in front of the building.

A little while later in the car on the way to the raid, Joe looked over at Rick. "So what's going on with you and Midnight?" he asked, keeping his tone casual.

Rick shrugged. "I don't know, man. You were right, she is fucking impossible to read." His voice belied his irritation.

"That she is. Did something happen this weekend?" Joe asked.

Rick didn't answer. Joe waited a few minutes, but Rick still didn't say anything. Joe realized then that something had to have happened, and Rick didn't want to tell him about it.

"Hey, man, I know it's none of my business, but she is my partner. She did not look very pleased with you this morning. So if something happened that's going to affect her, I want to know what it is." Joe's voice was serious.

Rick looked over at the man who had been his best friend for twenty-two years, and he knew that he was playing a dangerous game. He was messing with someone that Joe cared about very much and that was going to become a problem.

"Joe," Rick said hesitantly. "It's something that Midnight and I need to work out, but I think our time together is about over. I just don't want her hating me, you know?"

"She won't hate you, if you don't push her," Joe said, and Rick wondered if Midnight had already told him what had happened.

"I think I've been doing a little bit too much of that lately. I'm just going to back off," Rick said.

He knew that's what he needed to do, or else he was going to get burned, and he might lose Joe's friendship in the process. Midnight would just be the first woman that had been too much for him, and he wouldn't let himself get that close again. He could think clearly when he was away from her, he could see her as she was: a lot like him. She wanted to be in control, and if she wasn't, she wasn't happy.

"Best thing, Rick," Joe said and Rick knew that Joe's statement had a double edge to it.

Rick couldn't believe that Joe was actually threatening him. Midnight was obviously deeper in Joe's heart than he'd ever imagined. He figured it was for the best that he stay away from her. The last thing he wanted was to have a confrontation with Joe over her; he wasn't sure how he'd come out of it, but he knew he'd lose them both in the end.

****

Rick and Joe met with Spider, Tiny, Kana, and Dibbins in a parking lot not far from the house they were going to hit. Dibbins had turned out to be a very fierce ally for all his usually stoned looking appearance led one to believe. Joe and Dibbins had worked together a couple of times and Dibbins had been very quick and very smart. Joe had been pleasantly surprised. Dibbins was currently partnered with Spider, and they seemed to do all right together.

"Okay," Joe said, pulling out the operational plan that he and Midnight had worked out that morning. "Here's the plan. Midnight should be here any minute with the warrants. We're going to hit them here and here," he said, pointing to the front door and back doors. "I want everybody sharp, this group seems to be playing for keeps and I don't want anybody forgetting that." He looked sharply at the people he'd worked with for the last three years. Then he turned to Spider. "You have the shotguns?"

"Yep," Spider said. He walked back to his car, opened the trunk, and handed Joe a Benelli shotgun, leaving two more in the trunk.

"Tiny, you, Rick, and Dave are going to carry these. Dave you back Spider up, Tiny you back Kana, and Rick you're going to backup Midnight." He saw Rick's sharp look, and he shook his head at him. "Leave your personal feelings out of it, Rick. This is business now, and I've got the front door. I want you to cover Midnight, I'm counting on you." Joe's look told Rick that he was indirectly apologizing for the veiled threat of a few minutes ago.

Rick nodded, but said, "And how do I know she won't shoot me?" under his breath.

Only Joe heard him and he laughed. "You don't."

Midnight pulled up to the scene and got out of the car. She was wearing her usual jeans and boots, and a black tank top. She had a jean jacket in her hands as well as her holstered gun, and the search and arrest warrants.

"No problems on the warrants," she said looking directly at Joe and right past Rick. "Have you briefed everyone?" Joe nodded. "Good, okay ladies and gentlemen, let's lock and load."

Spider handed out the shotguns; everyone checked their magazines to make sure they were loaded, and their backup clips. Rick was watching Midnight out of the corner of his eye as he slid the shotgun's clip back into place. She was putting her clip back into her gun, and when she pulled back on the slide with her injured arm, he saw her wince. He had a feeling she'd still be feeling the effects from the damage she had obviously done the night before, and he felt responsible. She looked up as she was holstering the gun and caught him watching her. Rick just shook his head, knowing she probably shouldn't even be here, but he didn't say anything. It wasn't his place to.

Ten minutes later, everyone was in place. Tiny and Kana were at the back door, with Spider and Dibbins right behind them. Joe, Midnight, and Rick were at the front door. Joe was the entry man so he stood by the front door, but off to the side. He looked at Rick and Midnight. Midnight had her gun in one hand and a radio in the other. Keying the radio, she said two words, "Hit it."

A quick "10-4" came back from Tiny, and Midnight put the radio back on her belt nodding to Joe at the same time.

Joe pounded on the door and said, "Police! Search warrant!"

Stepping back, Joe kicked the front door open. As he did he heard back door crash open as Tiny kicked it in. Tiny was a little late was all Joe had time to think before he heard gunfire at the back of the house. Drawing his weapon, Joe waited a beat and entered the house. The gunfire was coming from the back of the house. Obviously, someone had noticed Tiny and his group at the back, and hadn't thought about the front door. Joe moved forward and Midnight followed right behind with Rick covering their backs. He swept the stairs to make sure no one was coming down them, but he didn't see anyone.

When Joe reached the back of the house, he saw mayhem. Spider was lying on the floor. Kana and Dave were trying to cover Tiny long enough for him to pull Spider out of the line of fire but they were in a bad place. They were still squatting in the doorway they had come through. The Scorpions had all the cover; they had the wall that separated the kitchen from the other rooms as well as the refrigerator and the stove.

"Midnight," Joe yelled back to her, "Spider's down! Rick, see if you can get around and lay down some cover for them!" Rick nodded moving off down the side hallway.

Midnight had come to kneel just below Joe. She looked at the scene, her heart beating a mile a minute; she saw a doorway about ten feet away and only a couple of feet from where Spider lay bleeding. They exchanged glances Joe knew what she was going to attempt. They both took a deep breath and Midnight dove forward, shooting in the direction the enemy fire was coming from. She landed very near to where Spider lay still shooting, all the while gritting her teeth because her arm felt like it was breaking apart.

She grabbed Spider by a handful of shirt and dragged him through the doorway. She propped him up against the wall and looked quickly around her. She was in some sort of laundry room, but there were no other entries, no one could sneak up behind her.

"Spider!" Midnight yelled, checking for a pulse. At first, she couldn't find one. "God no!" she yelled with tears coming to her eyes. But then she found a pulse.

She breathed a heavy sigh of relief; he was alive, at least for now. Then she checked her gun hastily. As she did she noticed that her arm was bleeding again, the blood soaking through the bandage. She shook her head; she didn't have time to deal with that now.

"Midnight!" she heard Joe yell over the gunfire that continued.

"He's alive!" she yelled back.

Then, taking a deep breath, she moved out from behind the cover, squeezing off a few shots, then pulled back quickly. She heard the shotgun behind the Scorpions and prayed to God it was Rick. Taking a cautious look, she saw his head duck out of sight into a doorway. She knew that the Scorpions would close in on a lone gunman in no time.

"Joe! Cover Rick!" she yelled and pointed toward the back hallway.

Joe was gone an instant later. Most of the gunfire had been rerouted and was now going at Rick. Midnight was worried that they'd get to him before Joe did.

"Kana! Tiny!" she yelled. "Cover me, I'm going straight through!" She pointed toward the wall that the Scorpions were using for cover.

She heard the concussions of the shotgun that Tiny held and Kana's accompanying gunfire. Midnight took a deep breath, waited two beats and moved from behind the wall. She managed to get to the other side of the refrigerator in the kitchen, the bullets narrowly missing her. She knew that one of the Scorpions was right on the other side. She waited, breathing deep. Her arm was killing her, but she couldn't stop now. She waited a beat and then, moving with the lightning speed she was known for, stood and shot the guy on the other side of the refrigerator. As she did, she saw the other guy behind the stove as he turned his gun on her, but Kana shot him dead before he could react.

Midnight moved off down the hall then, determined to get to Rick. She could tell that he was pinned down; he was in the last room down the hallway, and the Scorpions were moving in on him. She moved stealthily, and almost jumped out of her skin when Joe touched her on the shoulder. Fortunately, years of training kept her from crying out. As one, Midnight and Joe moved down the hall, behind the Scorpions. They were almost to the room Rick was in and Midnight could still hear him shooting, trying to keep his assailants back. Two of the Scorpions backed up, and found themselves backed up against two guns. Midnight and Joe both lifted their weapons bringing them down on the heads of the two Scorpions, who fell to the floor without a sound.

There were only two left and they were headed full throttle for Rick. He saw them enter the room where he was crouched beside a bed. He squeezed the trigger but the shotgun jammed. He looked up, knowing he was about to die, when suddenly the two guys stopped dead and dropped to the ground. Rick thought he'd pass out from relief, as he saw Midnight and Joe standing in the doorway, weapons still smoking.

"You okay?" Joe asked, looking at Rick, but already turning to head back down the hall.

"Yeah," Rick said, weakly, his breath coming in heavy gasps. Joe nodded, looking at Midnight. "I'll go and help secure the rest of the house and get some paramedics out here for Spider. You check him and secure this area." Midnight nodded and Joe moved off back down the hallway.

Midnight stood, holding her arm and looking at Rick. "You sure you're okay?"

Rick straightened from the crouch he had been in and she saw that he was bleeding at his side.

She stepped toward him. "You're bleeding," she said, reaching for his side.

"So are you," he said, smiling down at her. She unbuttoned his shirt so she could see the entry point in his side. He was surprised by her concern, but he was glad she even cared.

She straightened up then, looking relieved. "It looks like a graze, you should be okay," she said, smiling up at him.

"And what about you?" he said, gesturing to her arm.

She looked down and it and shrugged. "I'm alright, been in worse shape after a gunfight like this."

"I'll bet you have," he said, but his voice held no sarcasm.

"Come on," she said, starting to head back toward the kitchen. "Spider was hit. I want to make sure he's okay and that the paramedics are on their way. He looked bad."

It was clear she was more worried than her calm voice was telling. It was another facet to Midnight's personality. As he followed her back through the house, part of him sincerely hoped that they could at least be friends, if they couldn't make it as lovers.

CHAPTER 7

Spider was sent to the hospital via the Life Flight helicopter. Midnight was like ice as she brushed off the paramedics trying to look at her arm. She just held onto Spider's hand as long as she could. Rick finally had to pull her back so the paramedics could move him to the waiting helicopter. Joe came out of the house, asking her if she was going to the hospital. She didn't say anything for a minute, but finally she shook her head her eyes looking past him.

"No, I'll wrap things up here. Will you go get Tammy though?" she asked, looking at Joe. He couldn't read anything in her eyes.

Joe nodded. "Yeah, of course."

Midnight nodded and started walking back toward the house, looking like she was in a daze.

Joe walked over to Rick who was being checked out by one of the paramedics still onsite. "You okay?"

"Looks like it, yeah," Rick said, nodding.

Joe nodded, his eyes trailing back over to the front door the house. "Keep an eye on her, will ya?"

"Why?" Rick asked, not sure why Joe was worried.

"'Cause I can't see what's going on in her head, and that's usually a bad sign with her," Joe said, grimacing. "And if she breaks down, I want someone here that'll see it. Okay?"

Rick nodded, but seriously doubted that if Midnight did break down, she would do it in front of him or let her help.

****

A half an hour later Joe stood at Tammy and Spider's front door. They were renting a place together and everyone was really pleased for them. Tammy answered the door smiling at Joe, but then she saw the look on his face and her smile faded. She started to shake her head. Joe reached out and took her by the shoulders. "Tammy, he's at the hospital." She was still shaking her head, and had started crying. "Tammy!" Joe yelled, shaking her a little. He couldn't have her going hysterical on him now. "You have to come with me, Spider's at the hospital and he's going to want you around when he comes to. Now come on!" She nodded, picked up her purse and absently locking the door behind her.

He put his arm around her as he walked her to the car, and she leaned on him heavily. When they got to the car, she paused, putting off getting in.

"What if he's gone when we get there?" she said, her voice a mere whisper. "What if ..." Joe pulled her close to him and kissed the top of her head.

"He'll be okay, Tammy, you've got to believe that." His voice was reassuring, but inside he was praying that she wasn't right.

Joe managed to get Tammy in the car then and he drove to the hospital. Tammy sat like a stone, staring absently out the front window, but not seeing anything. Her hands were clasped tightly in her lap, and when Joe reached over to touch them, they felt ice cold.

He wondered if she was going into shock. Again, he prayed that Spider would be okay. He knew that the two of them were very much in love and that to lose Spider now, would kill Tammy.

When they got to the hospital, Joe again put his arm around Tammy, ushering her into the emergency room. He spoke with the head nurse at the front station and found out that Spider was in critical condition and was currently in ICU.

"You can't go in there, though," the nurse said, her tone alarmed.

"We're going in there," Joe said, holding up his badge, and giving the nurse a stony look.

The nurse looked at Joe, and at the woman who was leaning on him. She had been told that Spider was a cop, which wasn't entirely true, but that's what Midnight had told the paramedics so they'd work harder on him. She looked at Joe for a moment longer, then nodded and called over to one of the nurses nearby.

"Sandra!" She motioned for the nurse to come closer. "Take these two to ICU room 238."

"But ICU is restricted ..." Sandra started to say, but the head nurse shook her head.

"These are police officers, Sandra, just take them."

"Thank you," Joe said.

She nodded, giving Tammy a sympathetic look.

When they walked into ICU, Tammy leaned even more heavily on Joe. Spider was lying in a bed, with tubes everywhere and an oxygen mask over his face. He looked awful. Joe closed his eyes, trying to keep it together for Tammy's sake. He hated hospitals anyway but coming to see a friend who was obviously in such bad shape, made it even worse.

Joe moved Tammy to a chair next to the bed. She sat down, her eyes overflowing with tears. Joe knelt down next to her. She turned to him, putting her head on his shoulder and just cried. Joe held her stroking her hair. He knew there was nothing he could say to make her feel better. At least Spider was still alive, but that would be no consolation if he died during the night. After a few minutes, Tammy sat up, wiping at her tears. Then she turned her eyes to the man she loved and took his hand gently. Eventually, Joe sat down on the floor, leaning against the wall.

A couple of hours later, Midnight came into the room. Her eyes went to Spider immediately. She looked at Joe who was still sitting on the floor with his knees up, his arms crossed on top of them, and his head down. Then she looked at Tammy, who was looking up at her, with tears in her eyes again. Without a word, Tammy stood and walked over to Midnight and the two women hugged.

"He'll be okay, Tammy," Midnight whispered.

"I hope so," Tammy said, sobbing.

When they parted, Midnight saw that Joe was awake now. He was looking up at her, trying to determine how she was feeling. Tammy sat back on the chair, taking Spider's hand in hers again. Midnight sat down next to Joe on the floor. Her elbow nudged him. "You okay?"

"I guess," Joe answered, "you?" His head nodded to her arm.

"Yeah," she answered simply. "Everyone else is right outside. How's he doing?"

"We don't know yet, the doctor hasn't been in to talk to us."

Midnight just nodded.

About twenty minutes later, the doctor finally came in and he was very surprised to see them sitting there. "No one is supposed to be in here," he began to say, but both Joe and Midnight held up their badges as they stood.

"Well this is highly irregular," the doctor said, as if it was a personal affront to him.

"Yeah, we know all that," Joe said, his voice authoritative.

"What we want to know is how Spider is," Midnight said, her voice equally so.

"Well," the doctor said, looking happier to be talking about a subject he excelled in, "he is in critical condition, but he was very lucky the bullet didn't do a lot of damage. The entry point was in the abdomen, and it exited through his back. Fortunately, it missed his spinal cord, so given time, he should heal just fine."

Joe, Midnight, and Tammy all breathed a sigh of relief. Joe put his arm around Midnight, hugging her close to him.

"Thank you, doctor," Midnight said, tears in her eyes. Then she turned to Joe. "I'll go let everyone know. Dibbs is going nuts with guilt."

"He should be," a voice said then. Midnight turned to see Spider looking at her, grinning weakly.

"Spider!" all three shouted together. Tammy who stood closest to him leaned down, kissing him on the cheek, her own cheeks wet with fresh tears.

Midnight and Joe stood back smiling down at Spider.

"What?" Spider said, his voice quiet, but strong. "You think some little bullet's going to stop me?"

They all laughed. Midnight left the room to tell the others the good news. A cheer went up from the waiting room prompting many of the hospital staff to stop and see what all the commotion was. The head nurse smiled to herself. She was glad the police officer was going to be okay.

****

Daniel Robbins threw everything that wasn't nailed down across the room in his fury.

"They're getting too fucking close!" he yelled to no one in particular.

He began pacing, throwing furious glances at those in the room. Everyone stood by, not saying anything. They all knew that if you pissed Robbins off when he was already mad, you were likely to be dead shortly thereafter.

"We need to do something. We need to do something," Daniel repeated to himself, his voice low, dangerous. "Fuck!" he yelled, slamming his fist into the face of the nearest unlucky individual.

Tim Bollings watched from the back of the group, shaking inside. This was just getting worse.

****

In the weeks after Spider had been shot, Randy and Joe spent a lot of time together. They'd gone to a couple of movies, out to dinner, and things like antique shopping. They also spent time at Joe's house watching movies. She even cooked for them a few times.

Randy was very impressed with his home. It was a mansion to her. Although it certainly wasn't the most opulent home on the La Jolla shore, it was still huge compared to where Randy lived. The interior was beautiful, with cathedral ceilings, and beautiful tile or wood floors. The furnishings were expensive, but understated. They seemed very much like Joe, sophisticated but unpretentious. He could speak on just about any topic, but also on any level. And they talked endlessly.

Randy found that Joe had a very easy way about him, even when he disagreed with something she said. There was no arrogance in the way that he carried himself. It was something she'd tried time and time again to explain to Darrell. Darrell assumed that since Joe had money, that he was arrogant and just took whatever he wanted. It showed Randy how easy it was to make assumptions about people. She still didn't feel that she knew Joe, or much about his family and the events surrounding his parents death. He kept that to himself. It was her hope that someday he'd be willing to share that part with her.

One Saturday evening they were lying on his couch watching a movie. They'd spent the day out at the beach in La Jolla. They'd walked through the small upscale town perusing shops, then had dinner at a local pizza place. It had been a really nice day, starting at eight that morning when he'd picked her up, and ending at his house watching movies.

They'd both fallen asleep on the couch, with Joe behind her on his side, his arm under her neck, pillowing her head. The ringing of Joe's cell phone, tossed casually next to his keys and sunglasses on the coffee table, woke them. Joe reached groggily for his phone making a growling noise in the back of his throat.

"What?" he answered shortly as Randy stirred and glanced up at him.

Joe quirked his lips at her, but his grin froze as the person on the other end spoke up. Then he rolled his eyes, looking annoyed immediately.

"No, Taylor, that's not how I usually answer the phone," he said, his tone reflecting his annoyance, "but it's"—he glanced at his watch— "ten past twelve and I was asleep, so you'll have to forgive my breech of phone etiquette."

He listened to the other person for a few moments, glancing at Randy again and seeing her watching him. "You're what?" he asked in disbelief. He began shaking his head, rolling his eyes again. "Okay, but don't you think you'd be more comfortable at a hotel?" he asked. "I'm a cop Taylor, I get in at all different hours of the night," he said. Finally, he sighed loudly. "Fine," he said, his tone resigned, "let me know when you have your flight information."

After a few more moments he hung up, looking very displeased as he tossed the phone back onto the coffee table.

Randy watched him, unsure if she should ask who was on the phone. She didn't have to.

"That was Taylor," Joe said, gesturing to the phone, "my aunt."

Randy nodded. "You didn't sound really happy to talk to her."

"That's because every time I talk to her she makes sure I know how she feels about the direction of my life," he said, his tone disgusted.

"What's wrong with the direction of your life?" Randy asked, sensing this was an important point.

"Well, it's not what my aunt sees as appropriate."

"Appropriate?"

"Yeah," Joe said, his lips curling in derision, "for someone of my station."

Randy's brows furrowed. "What does she think you should be doing?"

"She thinks I should be married to some vacuous socialite, have a couple of uptight, over-indulged kids, and be running my father's company."

Randy pressed her lips together, tilting her head up at him. "So she doesn't like you being a police officer?"

Joe laughed wryly. "She despises the idea, says it's too blue collar."

Randy took a deep breath, debating whether or not to question him further. She could tell that the call from his aunt had riled him a bit. It was difficult to know if by asking questions she'd be helping, or only irritating him further. Finally, she decided to chance it.

"Do you think your parents would want you to live that life? Like your aunt wants?"

Joe curled his lips in dismay. "Well, before they died, they'd arranged for me to marry the daughter of one of their society friends."

"Really?" Randy asked, her eyes wide.

Joe nodded. "Yeah, it was all set to happen after my twenty-first birthday. My father was even going to change his will so that if I didn't marry her, I'd get nothing from his estate."

Randy was shocked, she didn't think people still arranged marriages like that, at least not in places like England.

"Did you even know this girl?"

"Yeah," Joe said, shrugging, "we grew up in the same circles."

"But, did you love her?"

Joe laughed; the sound was hollow. "It wasn't about love, Randy, it was about settling me down."

"Your parents were trying to settle you down," Randy said.

"Right," he said. "I was running with the gang, coming in when I wanted to, or not at all. Getting drunk, getting into fights, sleeping my way through town," he said, shrugging again. "My father said it was the only way they felt they could save me from myself."

****

The house Joe grew up in was a Tudor-style mansion, sitting on 120 acres of land. Inside was his father's study, a place Joe knew he would end up when he'd once again disappointed his parents. This night was much the same as many others. On this occasion, Joseph Senior cornered Joe coming in, with a fresh cut on his face from the evening's fight. Joseph beckoned to his son, gesturing toward the study. Joe followed resolutely; he knew he was in for one of those talks again.

"You keep doing that," his father said gesturing to the cut, "and the girls won't be interested for long." His smile was genuine and Joe found himself smiling back at him

"Yeah, Dad I know," Joe answered his father, sitting down in a comfortable chair and swinging his long legs up on the coffee table.

His father sat on the couch across from him. He was looking at Joe intently, searching his eyes as if to find the reason for his son's rebellion.

"What's goin' on dad?" Joe asked, not liking the look his father was giving him, feeling like he had screwed up again. But Joseph was shaking his head.

"There's nothing going on, Joe, I just wanted to talk. How are you?"

"Fine," Joe answered shortly, hoping to end this talk quickly. He was rather tired, but he could see that his dad was expecting more of an answer. "I've been just hangin' around, ya know same ole thing."

"Yes, I suppose that's part of the problem ..." Joseph said, more to himself than to Joe, but Joe heard him.

"Dad," Joe began, the words coming out harsher than he wanted. He took a deep breath to try to reign in his anger. "Don't start in on my friends again."

Joseph waved his hand. "Joe it's my responsibility to look after you, and I can't do that with you out and gone all the time ... Your mum worries herself half to death about you. And here you come dragging in here at this hour with yet another mark on your face, that she'll worry over for hours ... What am I supposed to do? Ignore it? Pretend like I don't see? Well I do see it and I don't like it." Joseph's voice was raised by the time he finished, and his eyes, much like Joe's were flashing at his son in anger.

Joe sat with his arms petulantly crossed in front of his chest listening. He waited a full minute before answering his father. He waited until he was calmer, he hated it when his dad got on this subject. The way Joe saw it, he could be out getting socialites pregnant and getting high all the time, but instead he only drank and got into fights, and only with other gang members. It wasn't like he fought with members of the royal family for God's sake.

"So, what do you want me to do?" Joe asked calmly. "You've already planned my life for me starting in four months, what else do you want from me?" Joe's voice became strident on the last part, as his anger began to ignite at the thought of what his life would become in four short months.

"Joe," Joseph began again, his voice softer now, "we love you, we just don't want to see you hurt. How are you and Roslynn getting along by the by?"

Joe smiled a fake 'I'll make it all better' smile. "Just grand, Dad, we've been shoved together for the purpose of a betrothal and we're just as happy as we can be. What do you expect?"

"Well, I would expect that the two of you would be trying to get to know each other. From what I understand, Roslynn is very lovely, and quite the lady too." Joseph Senior's eyes pleaded with his son to understand.

"Yeah, Dad, I know," Joe said, not sounding convinced in the slightest. He could tell his father a thing or two about sweet little ladylike Roslynn, but he figured now was not the time or the place.

****

"But you never married her," Randy said.

"No, my parents died, three months before my twenty-first birthday," Joe said, his tone sedate.

Randy bit her lip, unsure what to say.

"So when is your aunt coming?" she asked after a little while.

"Next week," Joe said. "On top of that, she refuses to stay at a hotel, she wants to stay here."

"And you don't want that," Randy said.

"I'd rather shoot myself in the foot with my own gun than that," Joe qualified with a grin.

Randy laughed softly.

****

It took a while for Midnight to go through all the paperwork and evidence after Spider had been shot. They had found some interesting things in the house including numerous automatic weapons and all kinds of measuring and cutting instruments used for drug sales. The members of the Scorpions who had lived through the shoot-out were still being held. The team was still hoping to find out who the leader of the Scorpions was. Midnight had run all of them through CLETS and she noticed that a pattern was emerging. A good 80 percent of the Scorpions had done time in San Quentin. Midnight was developing a theory that they had formed their alliance there and as they got out, they made their way to San Diego to join the gang. So it was a logical place to start looking for their leader. She had put the word out to all of her Confidential Informants that she wanted to find out who people like Robert Bondy, who had been incarcerated at San Quentin for robbery, had been connected with while inside. It was just a matter waiting and seeing now.

Standing and stretching Midnight looked at her watch; it was after seven o'clock at night again. She hadn't left the office before nine for the last week. She pulled her jacket off the back of her chair and walked out of her office, noticing that Rick was still there. She walked over to his desk. He glanced up at her, a pencil in his mouth; he was reading some of the CLETS runs he had just done.

"Careful," Midnight said, smiling down at him, "that'll give you lead poisoning."

Removing the pencil from his mouth, he returned her smile. "No, I think I'd have to eat the whole pencil for that."

Midnight laughed. "Well don't do that either then."

"You headed home?" Rick asked noticing her jacket over her arm.

"Yeah," she said, sighing lustily, "my cats are probably starting to think I moved and forgot to tell them."

Rick nodded and smiled. "Okay then, be careful out there in the dark alone."

"Oh I have my friend Beretta to take care of me," she said, motioning to the gun at her back. "Bye," she said then, heading for the elevators.

Once out in her car Midnight turned on the radio and started the car. Singing absently to whatever song was on the radio she pulled out of the parking lot. She didn't notice the car that pulled out behind her.

Midway home she noticed the dark gray car following her. She looked in the rearview and noticed that the same headlights had been behind her for a while. It was dark so she couldn't read the plates. She looked around her at the other cars. To her relief she saw a San Diego PD car two lanes over and about a half mile ahead.

"Who says there's never a cop around when you need one," Midnight muttered to herself.

She pulled out her phone and dialed. The San Diego PD dispatcher answered on the second ring. "Yeah, this is Lieutenant Chevalier. I need to you to patch me through to car"—she narrowed her eyes trying to see the car number on the back of the black and white—"530." She waited as the dispatcher patched the line through.

"SAM 24, go," came a familiar voice.

"Mike Harlow?" Midnight said, recognizing her old training sergeant's voice.

"Midnight?" Mike replied. "Or should I say Lieutenant?"

Mike Harlow had been one of the few men at the department who had treated her well from the beginning. They had gone out a few times, but nothing had really come of it. He was a player like Midnight, so everything had remained friendly between them.

"Yeah, yeah," she said, grinning.

"What can I do for you, Lady Midnight?" Mike asked.

"Well, I seem to have picked up a tail, Mike, and I could really use a, shall we say, routine stop?"

"I got ya," Mike said. "Just go ahead and speed up. I'll grab him as he goes by."

"You're a doll, Mike," Midnight said.

"Yeah?" he said then, his voice taking on a low tone. "Why don't you tell me that, tomorrow night over dinner?"

"You got it!" Midnight said, grinning.

"Okay, then," Mike said. Midnight could almost see him smiling. "Get on ahead, girl, and I'll see you tomorrow night. Say seven, my place."

"Yep," she said, and hung up.

She pushed her foot down harder on the gas pedal, and passed Mike. She flipped him a wave as she went by, and he nodded to her. She watched as the tail sped up with her, then she saw Mike pull in behind him and the red light came on a moment later. Midnight smiled to herself. "Hasta luego, Mr. Tail," she said gleefully. It helped to have friends.

She thought about the date she'd had with Mike. He was very easy to be with, he was also very good looking, in a cop sort of way. He had dark brown hair, and blue eyes. He was tall, like Joe, but larger in the build. Mike was in very good shape for a man of forty-five. Midnight hadn't been with anyone since Rick and that had been almost three weeks ago now, not counting the aborted lovemaking on the night they had their battle. She thought a nice diversion with someone like Mike was just what she needed right now.

Mike Harlow leaned down to look at the guy he had stopped from following Midnight. *Boy, this guy is a real winner,* Mike thought to himself. The guy had close-cropped hair, and looked pretty scummy. He was wearing shades, even though it was dark.

"Can I see your driver's license and registration please?" Mike asked, watching the guy carefully.

"What's the problem, officer?" the man asked.

As he reached over to his glove box, Mike saw the scar that ran from the man's ear down the side of his neck and down past the neck line of his shirt. When the guy's hand reached the glove box, he hesitated. Mike's hand went automatically to his holster. He un-snapped the restraining strap and rested his hand on the butt of his gun. The man obviously noticed Mike's readiness and changed his mind about something. He reached up to the passenger side visor and pulled out his registration. He handed it to Mike along with the license he pulled out of his wallet.

"Step out of the car, sir," Mike said, taking a cautious step back. "And keep your hands where I can see them."

The man stepped out. "Put your hands on the hood of the car," Mike ordered. Holding his flashlight up, Mike looked at the driver's license. It said the man's name was Daniel Robbins. Mike flashed the light into the car, keeping an eye on Robbins at the same time. He didn't see anything, but his gut told him that there was a gun in that glove box. He searched him and then told him to put his hands behind his head.

"What did I do, sir?" Robbins asked, his voice gravelly.

"Well," Mike said, putting the first cuff on him, "for starters, you were speeding while following a cop, and second of all, I have probable cause to search your vehicle. Are you going to give me consent or do I have to have it towed to the station for the search?"

He could feel the man tense, and he hurriedly locked the other cuff on his other hand.

"You ain't gonna find anything," Robbins said.

"Well, then should I take that as consent?" Mike said, as he walked Robbins back to his patrol car.

"Yeah, whatever man," Robbins said, as Mike seated him in the back seat of the patrol car. "Nice tattoos ya got there," Mike said, eyeing them. "How long you been out?"

"Hey, man, I don't gotta tell you nothin'. You haven't even read me my rights yet."

"Feeling a little guilty of something are we?" Mike said, a smirk on his face. He closed the car door then and went to do the vehicle search. He found in the glove box a Smith and Wesson .45 caliber revolver, fully loaded. He stood looking down at the weapon, and then looked down the freeway. Midnight was developing some particularly dangerous enemies.

When Midnight got home, she noticed the wind had picked up and the ocean down the hill from her house was very choppy. There was a storm rolling in. She went into the house and closed all the beachfront windows, then settled herself on her couch, with the paperwork she had brought home.

****

Randy jumped and squeezed her eyes shut as another crack of thunder rolled. Joe smiled down at her. "It's just thunder," he said, not for the first time that night.

Randy nodded her eyes still on the triangular windows of Joe's living room. The evening had started off nicely; they'd had dinner at

195

his house, Randy had cooked for them. Then they'd begun working on the laptop Joe had brought home from work. They were researching names and addresses of suspects. The storm had been developing all evening, but when the thunder and lightning display began, Randy's hands had started to shake. That was when Joe had discovered her fear of storms.

Twenty minutes later, the lights had gone out. Joe had gotten them candles and placed them all around the living room. They were sitting on the couch, Joe leaning against the arm, with her in the circle of his arms. She huddled against him, little tremors going through her every time there was another clap of thunder.

"It's okay, Randy," he said, stroking her hair. "Relax nothing's going to hurt you, you're okay here." His voice was soothing and soft.

She looked up at him, her eyes less fearful. She nodded, but she didn't move away from him. She laid her head on his shoulder, and they sat in a comfortable silence for a while. She felt very safe with Joe. She had never liked thunderstorms; they had always frightened her, even as a child. The lights going out made it even more terrifying.

It usually took Darrell and Donovan hours to calm her down during bad storms. Fortunately, San Diego didn't usually experience them.

"Does England have storms like this?" she asked, trying to take her mind off the storm raging outside.

He looked down at her, smiling. "Sometimes, mostly it's just dreary with a deluge of rain."

"You miss it, don't you?" Randy said, her eyes watching him sympathetically.

Joe nodded, his eyes coming back to hers. "Yeah, I do, but I can't go back, not quite yet." The pain in his voice surprised Randy.

"Is it because of your parents?" she asked instinctively.

Joe nodded, looking away again, the look on his face withdrawn.

"What happened, Joe?" Randy couldn't help but ask. He seemed so unhappy suddenly.

Joe was silent for a few minutes; he was looking down at the ring on his right ring finger. Randy began to wonder if she shouldn't have asked, it really wasn't her place to be asking him questions. When he did answer, his voice was a mere whisper, as if saying it softly would keep it from hurting as much.

"They were killed, in a car accident. An accident that was meant to kill me too …" His voice trailed off and he looked down at her.

She saw so much pain reflected in his eyes that tears came to hers. She reached up and hugged him.

"I'm sorry."

Joe hugged her close to him then too. The storm raging outside made him think of the night of the accident.

London, England, 1980

Joe came home to find his parents getting ready for a party.

"What's goin' on?" Joe asked, sitting down on the stairs in the foyer, watching his parents move back and forth getting ready to go somewhere.

"Oh, Joseph," Cynthia said, her voice soft and sweet, "we have the Kingston's Fiftieth anniversary party tonight."

She was dressed in a blue gown decorated with tiny jewels. Cynthia Sinclair was a lovely woman with silky blond hair and green eyes and she looked beautiful. Joe sat and admired his mother from the stairs; it wasn't often that he saw his mother dressed up.

She was looking at her son now. "Joseph, are you going to be home tonight?"

"Yeah," Joe answered absently and then regretted it when he saw the sad look on his mother's face; she always wanted to be around on the rare occasions when he was home.

Once again, he felt like a shit for never being around. The fact was he felt more comfortable in the pub with regular people, than here in this huge house, rambling around with the antiques and expensive artwork. He felt out of place.

"Cynthia," Joseph said, "I can't find the bloody keys ..."

"Dad," Joe said, "you're not planning to drive tonight, are you?"

Joseph senior looked up then, looking at his son in mock offense. "I'm not that old, young man!"

"No?" Joe said, laughing as his dad smiled. His mother laughed too. But then Joe grew serious. "Really, Dad it's nasty weather out tonight. It's been rainin' all night, maybe you should get your driver to take you ..." But Joseph was shaking his head.

"He's out, I gave him the night off. Forgot about the party, actually."

Joe grinned at his dad, as he saw his mother shaking her head and rolling her eyes at her husband.

"Well, look," Joe said standing, "I'll take you."

"Oh, Joseph," Cynthia said, smiling at her son, "that would be just lovely. We never get to spend any time with you anymore ..." Her voice trailed off, she didn't want to upset her son by starting the same old argument.

"Great!" Joe said, feeling glad he had suggested it. Finally, he was doing something to make his mother smile. "Let me clean up and grab a more formal jacket and we'll be off."

"Don't be long dear," Cynthia called up after him, as he disappeared up the stairs.

Fifteen minutes later, they were on their way with Joe driving his parents' Mercedes. They lived on the outside of London and the party was in the city. Joe took it very slow, due to the rain and wind. On a particularly steep part of the road, the car was gaining speed and Joe saw a curve coming up. He stepped on the breaks, and nothing happened. He stepped on them again, and they simply sunk to the floor. His heart leaped to his throat. 'No!' was the only thing he had time to think before the car hit the guardrail and went over the embankment. The last thing he heard as the weight of the seat shoved him painfully against the steering wheel was his mother's scream. Then he blacked out.

****

The memories seemed to hit him in waves. It took him a while to regain his composure. Randy didn't say anything, she just held him.

When he pulled back, he looked down at her, his look grim. "I guess you know my deep dark secret now, so what's yours?" He looked better now, Randy decided. His eyes were still a little haunted, but he didn't look as unhappy.

"I don't have any secrets," Randy said, smiling up at him.

"Oh yeah," Joe said, "I forgot, you're just a baby."

"I am not!" Randy said, laughing at him. He laughed too.

"Love, twenty years old qualifies you as a baby," he said, his eyes glittering mischievously.

"Maybe to someone who's almost thirty …" Randy replied.

"Oh, that was low," he said, grinning.

"Yes, well, you started it," she replied, smiling widely.

He was glad to see that she wasn't afraid anymore. They sat in silence for a while, listening to the wind howl outside. She looked down at his hand resting on the back of the couch. She took it in her own, looking intently at the ring he wore.

"What does this mean?" she asked touching the intricate design on the face of the ring.

It was a tiny detailed emblem of some sort with tiny baguette style sapphires around the edge of it. She'd noticed it many times over the last couple of weeks, but had never asked about it until now.

Joe looked down at the ring, smiling distantly. "My dad gave me this, it's our family crest."

"Crest?" Randy asked, confused.

"Yeah, it's like my family name, kind of like a symbol for our family name …" His voice trailed off, frustrated at not being able to explain it better.

"Like royalty?" Randy said, her eyes widening.

Joe laughed. "Yeah I guess. My family name goes back pretty far."

"How far?" Randy asked, obviously impressed.

"Several generations," he said offhandedly. Randy stared at him openmouthed. "Oh, I forgot Americans don't have much of a history do they," Joe said, and Randy laughed.

"Not like that. Is there any royalty in your family?" she asked, still awed.

"My uncle married a Lady, but that's about it," he answered.

"Oh," Randy said, her eyes wide. "Do you know any regular royalty?"

Joe shrugged. "Some, why?"

"Wow," Randy said, again impressed by him.

Joe laughed shaking his head.

"It's not that big of a deal, Randy. I grew up with a couple of distant members of the royal family. Hell, I'd had a duchess after me since I was fifteen. They're just regular people, you know."

"You had a duchess after you?" Randy said, latching on to that statement.

"Yeah she was a real pain too," he smiled again. "It's no big thing, Randy. Half the time it's like half of London is member of the royal family in one way or another."

"But still …" Randy said. "Can I ask you a question?" she said more cautiously now.

"I think you've already asked me a few questions," he said, but there was only humor in his voice. "Go ahead," he said then seeing her hesitate again.

He didn't want her to retreat now.

"It's kind of personal."

"Ask," he said simply.

She took a deep breath, and then looked up at him. "I heard that you and Midnight used to be a couple, is that true?"

Joe nodded. "Yeah, that's true."

Randy nodded, she wasn't really upset by the answer. "Can I ask why you two aren't together anymore?" she asked. Seeing the surprised look on his face, she quickly added, "I mean, you two just seem so close, I just wasn't sure … I'm sorry, I probably shouldn't have asked," she said then, trying to get out of the uncomfortable moment quickly.

"It's okay," Joe said, giving her shoulder a squeeze. "Midnight and I are too much alike, that's why we couldn't make it as a couple."

"Too much alike?"

"Yeah, we're both driven to avenge the tragedies in our lives. The problem is, her way was way too much for me."

"What is her way?" Randy asked.

"Balls out, no holds barred," Joe said, with a sardonic grin. "She takes chances I just couldn't handle. And that became a problem in our relationship. I tried to shield her, and she got pissed at me for it. We ended up fighting a lot, and in the end it almost got her killed."

"What?" Randy asked, disbelieving. "How?"

"A gang leader she was working got suspicious at her caution and knifed her."

"Oh my God," Randy said, shocked.

"Yeah, so we decided us being together probably wasn't the healthiest thing," Joe said.

"I guess not," Randy said, rolling her eyes.

Joe grinned at her. "You know, the funny thing is, I don't think that was the only problem with our relationship."

"What else do you think it was?"

"Midnight didn't need me," he said.

"What do you mean she didn't need you?"

"I mean, she's independent, self-sufficient, and can and will do everything for herself. She doesn't need anyone. And, I know it's pathetic but I have this knight complex. I have this need to save people," he said derisively.

"And you think that's a bad thing?" Randy asked, her tone amazed.

"It doesn't seem to suit women these days," he said, shrugging. "Women's lib and all that."

Randy laughed softly, nodding her head.

"So," he said, sliding his hand through her hair, "what about you? What are you looking for?"

Randy bit her lip, not sure if she should say what instantly came to mind. It was true, but she didn't want to sound silly and childish.

Joe watched her, seeing the doubt play across her face.

"Tell me," he prompted gently, his thumb brushing her cheek.

"I'm looking for that fairy tale," Randy said softly, "a knight in shining armor to sweep me off my feet."

Joe stared down at her for a moment, seeing the timidity in her look.

Smiling, he leaned down, staring into her eyes. His lips were within an inch of hers as he said, "Well, then I think we have ourselves a match." Then he kissed her softly and she just melted.

Randy was so relieved at his words, that she gave herself wholly to the kiss, wrapping her arms around his neck. They'd kissed a lot over the course of their time together, but suddenly this was different. Randy felt it immediately but it didn't scare her at all. In fact she welcomed the change.

Joe's hands slid through her hair, and caressed her back, his lips moving over hers so expertly she was trembling within minutes. When he pulled back and looked down at her, she could see he was very affected by the kiss too. His eyes searched hers, but he said nothing. Randy was surprised when he pulled her close to him and hugged her. She was silent for a few minutes. She could hear his heartbeat, it started out fast, but it slowed after a minute. She wasn't sure why he'd stopped. She glanced up at him and saw his eyes were closed.

"Joe?" she queried softly.

"Hmmm?" he murmured, looking down at her.

Randy hesitated, she didn't know how to ask what she'd just been thinking.

"Why did you stop?" she finally asked.

Joe was silent for a long moment, his look tender. "I guess, because I know you haven't been with many men," he said softly. "I didn't want to push you."

Randy smiled softly. "Do you have any idea how amazing you are?"

Joe looked cynical. "Amazing how?"

"Most men wouldn't care about not pushing."

"Most men weren't raised by a mother that insisted they respect women above and beyond everything else in the entire world," he said wryly.

"Oh," Randy said, smiling.

"Mmmhmm," he replied, seeing the mischief in her eyes suddenly.

It was Randy who leaned in to initiate the kiss this time. She slid her hands up his chest, then up into his hair, making him groan against her lips. They kissed on the couch for a long while, then Joe stood, pulling her gently to her feet. He led her into his bedroom; he was damned if they were going to make love for the first time on the living room couch. Standing next to the windows that overlooked the ocean, with lightning still splitting the night sky, Joe took her into his arms again, and kissed her deeply. Randy didn't notice anything but him, her fear of the storm overridden by the desire she felt. After a few minutes of kissing, Joe moved his hands to her chest, gently caressing her breasts, and Randy gasped at the fire it started in her. Joe took everything slowly, kissing her and caressing her until she could barely stand it anymore.

Eventually, he started to slowly remove her clothes, shedding his at the same time. Continuing to kiss her, he moved them to the bed. Randy was almost frantic by that time. When he finally entered her body, she tensed against the surprisingly sharp pain it caused. She'd been so caught up in him, it took her off guard. Suddenly he realized that it wasn't that she hadn't been with many men, it was that she hadn't been with any, at least not sexually.

He didn't move. He looked down at her to find her eyes were screwed shut. She was clearly in pain.

"Randy," he said softly. "Baby, look at me."

She opened her eyes, slowly. He could see the pain that he was causing her reflected in her beautiful eyes.

"Randy," he said gently, "baby, you have to relax, okay? Do you trust me?" he asked. She nodded slowly, her eyes never leaving his. "Then relax baby, it'll hurt you more if you don't. I don't want to hurt you." His voice was soft and sweet and Randy couldn't help but relax. She did trust him.

Once she relaxed, he started to kiss her again. He didn't move, he just kissed her and caressed her until her body was on fire again, and she didn't even realize he was moving in her body then. The pain was gone and all she could feel was the sensual closeness of him. She reveled in the feelings and sensations flowing within her body. When their passion reached its height, she cried out. Her voice hoarse as she said, "I love you, Joe, I love you."

A few minutes later, she lay in his arms, both of them breathing heavily.

"What was that you said?" he asked, his eyes deceptively casual.

Randy looked up at him, biting her lip. She hadn't meant to say that, and now she was worried that he'd be mad.

"I, uh said, uh …" she stammered.

"You said …" Joe said, turning on his side so he could look at her.

"I said … that I love you," she said very quietly.

She looked down, too embarrassed to look in his eyes, which she assumed would be angry. She didn't see him smile.

"So ... is it true?" he asked then evenly.

"What?" she said, her voice showing her confusion.

"Well, when a woman ... well ... When she's in the throes of passion, sometimes she says things that aren't necessarily the truth, but she gets caught up in the moment, you know."

He was giving her an out, and Randy couldn't decide if she should take it or not. She still wasn't looking at him. His finger under her chin changed that, she had to look at him then. She could read nothing in his purposely blank look.

"Is it true, Randy?" he asked, now sounding like a father.

She looked at him for a long moment, knowing that she couldn't lie to him, but the thought of him not wanting to see her again, or something worse, made it the hardest single word she had ever had to utter.

"Yes," she said with tears in her eyes.

"Oh, baby," Joe said then, pulling her to him, feeling bad that he had toyed with her.

He pulled back then, holding her by the shoulders. "Why are you crying?" he asked, smiling at her.

"I don't know," she said miserably. "I guess, because I know that you probably don't want to deal with a lovestruck secretary now, and I've ruined everything ..." She laid her forehead against his chest.

"Ruined everything, ey?" he asked, humor in his voice now. Randy looked up at him surprised.

"Didn't I?" she asked.

"Randy, I wanted to know if what you said was true, because I didn't want to be the only one," he said then, looking at her seriously.

"Only one?" Randy repeated, dumbly.

"Yeah, the only one in love," he said. He watched closely as she tried to process what he'd said.

It took her a few long moments before it sank in but when it did, her eyes widened, and new tears flooded her cheeks.

"God, what's wrong now?" he said, smiling wider.

She shook her head, her eyes not leaving his. It took her a few moments to find her voice again. "I just don't believe this. I've got to be dreaming."

"Well, if you are, we're both having it," he said. Then he looked into her eyes. "I love you, Randy."

She started to shake her head, but his lips quickly stilled her. He kissed her for a long few minutes, holding her body against his, cradling her face gently with his hands.

When their lips parted, Randy looked up at him in wonder. "But when? I mean …"

"I don't know," he said, smiling down at her and shaking his head. "I just know that when you're not here I can't stop thinking about you. And now," he said, touching her cheek and looking into her eyes, "you've given me something you can't give to anyone else."

Randy pressed her lips together looking circumspect. "I should have told you."

Joe nodded. "Yes," he agreed, "but it's too late now anyway."

"True," she said with the beginnings of a smile on her lips.

"First woman who's managed to trick me on that level," he said, narrowing his eyes at her comically.

"Really?" she said, looking pleased with herself.

"You're evil," he told her, catching her look.

"No," she said, shaking her head. "I wanted to make love with the first man I've ever been in love with."

"And?" he said, wanting to hear the rest.

"And, I was afraid if I told you I was a virgin you wouldn't want me," she said timidly.

"Why?" he asked, touching her under the chin to make her look at him.

She shrugged. "I just figured you were used to women with actual experience."

Joe nodded, his look contemplative. "Are you under the impression this was some kind of hardship for me?"

"I …" she began. Then she shrugged, not knowing what to say.

"Randy, I've wanted you since the first moment I met you," he said, touching her cheek to emphasize his words. "I've just been waiting until you were ready."

Her eyes widened at his first statement, then narrowed slightly at the second. "So I was ready," she said, with a slight grin.

"I guess," he said, grinning too.

Randy was still shocked that he'd said he loved her, but then things were all new to her that night. She fell asleep in his arms wondering if she would wake up in the morning and find that it was indeed a dream.

CHAPTER 8

The next morning Joe took her home, fortunately after Darrell had left for the morning, to change and get ready for work. As they drove to work, Joe's cell phone rang.

"Joe, it's me," came Midnight's voice.

"Hey Night, what's up?" he asked cheerfully.

"Tried your house last night, but the storm must have knocked the line out," she said, wondering what had Joe so cheerful first thing in the morning. "Last night when I left the office I picked up a tail."

"What?" Joe said, all humor gone from his voice now.

"It's okay. I ran across Mike Harlow, you know my old training sergeant. Anyway, he stopped the guy for me. So he didn't follow me all the way home or anything. I just thought you should know, so you can watch your back too."

"Well, what did Mike find out?" Joe asked, concerned. "Who was the guy?"

"I don't know yet, I have date with Mike tonight, as a result of his favor, so he'll tell me then."

"You can't call him now?" Joe asked, impatient to know who this guy was.

"Joe, calm down, it's not that big a deal. I just thought you should know."

"Night it is a big deal. If you hadn't noticed the guy, and he'd followed you home … I don't even want to think about it."

Midnight smiled at the protective tone in his voice. Sometimes it was nice to have someone always worried about her.

"Well, he didn't so you don't have to think about it. I'm fine. Okay?" Her voice was softer, she didn't want to argue with him, and she knew this would be a likely subject for them to argue about.

"I'll be there in a while. We'll talk then, okay?"

"Okay," Midnight said.

They hung up. Joe looked over at Randy; she hadn't said much this morning. He hoped that she wasn't going to be shyer around him because of the night before.

"You okay?" he asked, his eyes glancing over at her.

She nodded, smiling at him.

"Just not sure what to do with all this?" he asked gently.

"Pretty much," she said, smiling again.

"It'll come to ya," he said, winking at her. She smiled.

When they got into the office, Randy went to her desk and Joe went to Midnight's office. He stayed in there a few minutes and then went to his own office. Things were still jumping from the Scorpion house raid, and reports were coming in constantly. Randy was surprised when she looked up and it was almost two o'clock. Midnight came out of her office and walking by her desk. "Let your boss know that I have a meeting with the head honcho, and I'll be back around five. Okay?"

"Okay," Randy said, smiling.

Midnight was so unpretentious. She was meeting with the chief of police, and she treated it like it was nothing. Randy was still constantly impressed with the leader of FORS.

About an hour later, Randy was in Joe's office. She was at his desk trying to find a report, and he was over by the door looking in a stack on the table there. "It's here somewhere," Joe said, his voice matter of fact. "It has to be."

Randy laughed. "I hope so, I don't want to have to retype that little sucker."

Joe's phone rang, and Randy automatically picked it up.

"Sergeant Sinclair's office."

"Joseph Michael Sinclair the Fourth, please," asked an extremely cultured English-accented voice.

"Yes, ma'am," Randy answered automatically, handing the phone to Joe.

Joe gave her a perplexed look, taking the phone.

"Sinclair," he answered. He listened for a few moments, then rolled his eyes. "Alright, I'll be there in a few."

When he hung up, he reached over to pick up his jacket. "Look Taylor is here. I need to head to the airport to pick her up. She's only about," he said, glancing at his watch, "six hours early. Can you catch a ride with Rick or something?"

"Sure, no problem," Randy said. "Is everything okay?"

Joe nodded, not saying anything, but Randy noticed as he picked up his jacket that he immediately reached in for a cigarette and she had already learned that he only smoked when he was stressed about something. "You're still coming tonight, right?" he asked, his tone entreating.

"Of course," she said, smiling. "I'll see you at seven."

Leaning over he kissed her quickly on the lips, then he was gone.

An hour later Midnight came back. She looked around for Joe. "Where'd he go?" she asked Randy.

"His aunt arrived early," Randy answered.

"And the siege begins," Midnight replied.

"Siege?"

"Taylor hates everything about Joe's life now. It's her goal in life to change him back."

Randy bit the inside of her cheek nervously, not sure what that evening would hold.

Midnight headed over to her office, having no idea the angst she'd just caused.

A little while later a young man walked up to Randy's desk.

"I need to see Midnight Chevalier," he told her, his voice quiet.

Randy looked up at the younger man. He looked about eighteen. He had blond hair and brown eyes. He looked a little on the rough side; his hair was longish and wild, and he didn't look like he'd shaven in a few days. He was wearing faded jeans and a ripped t-shirt with a flannel shirt over it. He was the epitome of the "grunge" look. But when he looked at Randy, he smiled a little and she smiled back.

"Okay," Randy said nodding, "can I tell her your name?"

"She won't know me," he said, his lips tugging in disappointment.

"Then, can I maybe tell her what it's about?"

"It's about the leader of the Scorpions," Tim said.

Randy stared back at him, re-evaluating him. He knew something about the elusive leader of the Scorpions? Then he was definitely more than he appeared to be.

Three minutes later, Tim was sitting in Midnight's office, and already in awe of her.

He watched her as she sat behind her desk. She was surprised how shy he was, being from a rough group like the Scorpions, but he had already told her that he really was only a member because his brother was, and that he didn't like the kind of stuff they did. That's why he had shown up on FORS's door. He thought it was time they were stopped.

"Hey," Midnight said softly. "It's okay you know, you're doing the right thing. This gang has already killed a few people and they almost succeeded in taking out one of my people. So don't feel like you're betraying good people, you're not. And you said your brother is already thinking about getting out right?" Her voice was concerned.

She didn't want to have to take the kid's brother down, but she'd have to if he'd committed a felony; if he'd been involved in the killing of the last member they'd interrogated. That made Midnight think this time she needed to be more careful. This time she'd make him a member and that way he'd be safe. Besides the Scorpions wouldn't know that he'd given them the info on this next house, they'd guess that they'd gotten the information from all the reports run from the last bust. Which was partially true, the address he'd given her was one of the ones turned up in the CLETS DMV runs. But Tim's information was going to pinpoint that house and give them the extra they needed for the warrant.

"Yeah, I know," Tim said, his eyes on Midnight. "Are you really a cop?"

Midnight smiled at him. He seemed so sweet. She had a feeling he already had a bad case of puppy love. "Yes, I really am," she said, unclipping her badge from her belt and tossing it to him.

He caught it and sat looking down at it, as if it were a valuable heirloom. Midnight watched him, and smiled to herself. He reminded her a little bit of Thomas. Of course, every young man in a gang reminded her of Thomas.

"Hey, Tim," she said, "we need to get to work on this, so I can get it over to the judge. Come over here and stand behind me as I type it. I want you to tell me if it's accurate. Okay?" She motioned him over to behind her desk. He did as she asked, trying to act casual. He handed her back her badge and she clipped it back to her belt. After about half an hour, she had the warrant done.

"Can I go with you?" Tim asked, his eyes wide at the prospect of playing a police officer and helping this blond woman.

"No, Tim, I think you better sit this one out. Your ex-friends will be there and I really don't want you to be seen by them. Okay?" Her smile was warm as she looked at him, trying to soften the rejection a little.

"Okay," he said, shrugging. "I guess I'll see you later then?"

"Well, I probably won't be back in the office tonight, but, how about you come by tomorrow. We'll see what we can do about putting you to work on some other stuff okay?" Her smile was on her face again and Tim nodded excitedly. Again, Midnight found it hard to believe that this kid had been a member of the Scorpions, but one never knew.

"Debenshire," she called.

Rick's head snapped up from his desk. "Yeah?"

"I need your help."

"If you need me, I'm there," Rick said, his voice holding a double meaning, to which Midnight smiled.

"Yes, well, this will be work related unfortunately," she said, winking at him as he entered her office.

They had finally gotten to a point where they could joke about the great sex they had together. Though neither side made any moves to rekindle the relationship.

He stood, picking up his jacket and followed her to the elevators.

Tim watched them leave. He wondered if they were a couple, they seemed awfully friendly with each other. He thought that Lieutenant Chevalier was the most incredible woman he'd ever laid eyes on.

As they walked out of the building, Midnight looked down at her watch. "Oh shit," she said.

"What?" Rick asked.

"It's getting on toward five o'clock. Shit, shit, shit," she said shaking her head.

"Is that a problem?" Rick asked, confusion on his face.

"Oh it's no big deal, I have a date at seven, and I'll probably be late as usual," she said, looking at him.

She saw the slightest flash of jealousy, but it didn't bother her. She saw it in Joe's eyes a lot too; it was just some kind of man thing, she figured.

"Who're you going out with?" he asked, trying to keep his voice sounding normal.

"Oh, he's my old training sergeant."

"Old?" Rick asked, raising an eyebrow at her.

Midnight laughed. "I mean old as in a long time ago not in terms of age."

"Oh okay I was going to say with the way you are," he was smiling now.

"And what's that supposed to mean?" Midnight said, eyeing him in mock offense.

"Well, just that you tend to be insatiable," Rick said, looking up at the sky nonchalantly. They had stopped at Midnight's car and she was looking at him over the roof.

"Maybe for you," Midnight said then, her eyes watching him for a reaction.

He looked directly at her, trying to determine if she had meant it or not. He saw no malicious intent in her eyes, so smiled at her. She was the first woman he had ever slept with that had not turned nasty and vindictive when the relationship ended. And that was something considering the way their relationship had ended. She returned his smile and then got into the car.

"So where did Joe go?" Rick asked.

Midnight shrugged. "Randy says his aunt got here early."

"Oh shit," Rick said, rolling his eyes. "She wanted to get a head start on him, then?"

Midnight laughed. "Yeah, probably."

Rick just shook his head. "I understand Joe's gonna have Randy with him."

Midnight nodded. "I think he's pretty serious about her."

"Taylor will not like that at all," Rick said seriously.

"Because Randy's poor?" Midnight asked, her hackles up instantly.

"Because Randy isn't Roslynn Ellington," Rick corrected.

Midnight pressed her lips together in annoyance, but said nothing else.

A half hour later, they had the warrant and were headed over to serve it. Midnight radioed ahead and had two or three black and whites meeting them there.

The service went surprisingly easy considering the way that the last raid had gone. Midnight ended up having to run down and tackle one of the guys that tried to make a break for it, and Rick was right behind her. Midnight sat straddling the guy's back and she reached behind her for her cuffs. She looked up at Rick and she could see he looked surprised.

Midnight was right, he was surprised that, one: she had managed to catch the guy, and two: she had managed to tackle him alone. She was constantly surprising him with her strength and determination.

This one he had definitely not figured out yet.

Joe had been right; Midnight was totally unlike any woman Rick had ever met. There was nothing coy, or wilting about her, she was not shy, nor was she overly tough as to be too masculine. She managed to keep an even balance between being a woman, and doing a job that was geared more for men. And Rick found it very interesting. He constantly found himself watching her to see what she'd do next that would shock the hell out of him.

Now she was watching him, as she sat on the two hundred pound man on the ground. She had cuffed him and was now standing to pull him up. Rick stepped in, and she let him. He took the guy by the arm and walked him toward the waiting patrol car.

As he patted the guy down he couldn't resist saying, "Fast little thing, isn't she?"

The guy didn't say anything. Rick could tell he was mortified at having been run down by a woman, and one of Midnight's slight size, no less. Rick laughed, shaking his head. He put the guy in the patrol car and turned to look for Midnight. She was talking to one of the uniformed officers. He watched her as she placed her hand on the officer's arm talked animatedly. The officer was looking down at her with obvious interest. Midnight didn't seem to notice at all.

She looked up at one point and saw Rick watching at her. Her eyes locked with his and from the look she gave him, he realized she did know what effect she was having on the officer, and she was obviously using it to her advantage.

Ten minutes later, she was motioning him to her car. He walked over, his smile wide. "And just what kind of spell did you put on that poor patrol officer?"

"The 'oh please god I don't want to do all this paperwork or I'll never get to my date on time!' spell," Midnight said, laughing.

"You are the worst, Midnight Chevalier!" Rick said.

"Yeah, I know but hey I didn't pull rank or anything, I just asked and ... okay I batted my eyelashes a few times but I didn't promise him anything so what's the big deal? Right?"

He could tell that she didn't like to use her feminine wiles too often, and she was basically asking for him to agree with her so she wouldn't feel like she'd done so unfairly.

"We men are pigs, Midnight, and if he gets stuck doing extra paperwork 'cause he thought it might get somewhere with you, that's his mistake," he said, his voice sure and supportive.

Midnight relaxed a little. Yet another huge difference between Midnight and every other woman he'd ever dealt with; she did not like to use her body or her face to get her anywhere.

"I'm just going to drop you by, I hope that's okay," Midnight said, as she drove back toward the office.

"No problem, but do you have time?" he asked, looking at the clock on her stereo; it was already six thirty.

"Mike's used to me being late. I always am, I guess I'm kind of a lousy date," she said, her voice holding a bit of chagrin.

"You are a perfect date, Midnight, and this Mike is very lucky to have one with you," Rick said, his eyes on her.

He wasn't sure what had made him say that, but he didn't like her getting down on herself. In his opinion, she was pretty fantastic, and she shouldn't believe anything different.

Midnight looked over at him, her eyes disbelieving, but she smiled at him. "Thanks," she said simply. She certainly wasn't a gusher either.

She dropped him off a few minutes later, waving as she drove off. He watched her go, standing in the parking lot. He felt a little pull at his heart, but he shook his head, and turned and walked into the building.

****

Randy arrived in a taxi at Joe's house at seven. She looked beautiful in a soft blue dress. Joe handed the driver cash as he opened the door for her, smiling.

"You look incredible," he told her, leaning down to kiss her softly.

"Thank you," she replied looking a little apprehensive.

"So she arrived okay?" Randy asked.

"Yeah … You ready for this?" Joe said, eyeing her.

"No!" she said. Then she sighed. "But will I ever be?"

"Probably not," he said. He touched her under the chin then, and looked her straight in the eye. "Just remember that I love you."

She smiled at him and he took her hand to lead her into the house.

Taylor hadn't joined them yet. Joe poured Randy a glass of wine. He noticed that her hands were shaking as she took the glass. He took her other hand in his, giving it a quick squeeze. Just then Taylor swept into the living room, always one for grand entrances, even in limited company.

Randy was very surprised at how young Taylor looked. Joe had told her that she was his mother's youngest sister, and that she was forty-five or so. Apparently, she always lied about her age. Looking at the beautiful, petite blond woman, as she reached up to hug Joe, Randy thought she didn't look a day over thirty.

"Joseph Michael," Taylor said in the most upper-class English accent. "You look so handsome," she said, standing back to look at him, "but that hair … Don't they have hairdressers here in America?" She eyed him critically, shaking her head.

"Yes we have hairdressers. I just got it cut about a week ago."

"Good Lord, Joseph, the girl must have been blind, she missed your hair altogether!"

Joe laughed, knowing his aunt was serious. She had never liked his long hair, and it was about an inch longer than it had been when she'd seen him last.

"Taylor …" Joe said then, turning to Randy, who was standing just behind Joe, wishing she was somewhere else. He reached out, taking her hand and pulling her forward. "This is Randy. Randy this is my Aunt Taylor."

Taylor stood stock still, looking at Randy. After a few long moments, she slowly extended her hand to the younger girl. "Lovely to meet you, dear," she said, her smile not quite reaching her eyes.

Randy shook her hand, and tried to smile, but she was dying to get away from this woman with the cold blue eyes.

Joe could see Randy was reverting back to her shy habits. He reached out, touching her waist, and squeezed it just slightly to let her know he was there with her.

"Taylor, would you like a drink?" Joe asked.

"Wine, please, Joseph," Taylor said, even as her eyes stayed on Randy critically.

Joe poured the wine and handed it to Taylor.

"Why don't we sit down?" Joe suggested.

They sat down; Joe and Randy sat on the couch and Taylor sat across from the in the Eastlake chair. *Like the judge*, Randy thought to herself.

Joe's cell phone chimed. Joe merely looked down at the display, then put the phone down on the table.

"That job of yours?" Taylor asked, her tone disparaging.

"Yes," Joe answered, trying to keep the conversation light. He didn't need his aunt starting in on his profession now too, but it was too late.

"Well, I don't think much of your work, Joseph. I don't see why you don't just come back and manage your father's company like he wanted ..."

"Because I don't know anything about running a publishing company, Taylor," he answered, gripping Randy's hand a little tighter. "Besides, I like what I do."

"Getting calls at all hours of the night? Getting stabbed, shot, and Lord only knows what else?" Taylor remarked, raising an eyebrow at him.

"I do a little bit more than that Taylor. Getting shot and knifed are just some of the fringe benefits." His voice was sarcastic now, and Randy could feel that he was losing his cool.

She put her other hand on his leg, trying to calm him down. It didn't go unnoticed; Taylor looked at Randy's hand on Joe's leg for a moment, then she looked at Randy.

"So what does your family do, Randy?" she asked, her look innocent enough, but her eyes belied that innocence.

"Well ..." Randy said, not sure how to answer.

"Don't bother, Randy," Joe said, his voice calm again. His eyes narrowed at Taylor. "Drop it, Taylor."

"Joseph," Taylor said, her eyes widening at his words. "I think that it is perfectly reasonable to want to know what kind of people you're attaching yourself to." Her voice was the epitome of upper class.

"Not now, Taylor," Joe responded, his voice still calm.

"I see," Taylor said, her gaze sliding to Randy again, then back to Joe. "Have you spoken with Roslynn lately?" she asked, her eyes boring into her nephew's.

"Not since I left England nine years ago, Taylor," Joe said, some of his irritation showing through again.

"Well, you should call her, Joseph. She's been asking about you."

"I thought she was married now," Joe replied.

Taylor shrugged delicately. "She is, but … things aren't quite working out …" On the surface she seemed so casual, just making conversation, but the way she looked at Joe said otherwise.

Joe narrowed his eyes at her. He knew exactly what she was getting at and he was pissed at her for bringing Roslynn up with Randy in the room. "Well things *are* working out for me."

"Joseph," Taylor said, obviously surprised at his response.

"Taylor," Joe said, in a good imitation of her tone of voice. "Randy is the woman I'm with."

"But your parents …" Taylor began to say, but her voice trailed off as she saw the anger flash in Joe's eyes.

"My parents what, Taylor?" Joe asked coldly.

"Well frankly Joseph, they just wouldn't approve. It was their wish that you and Roslynn—"

"Well they're not here are they?" Joe said, cutting her off.

"Joseph Michael Sinclair!" Taylor said. Her eyes flashed at him indignantly and her voice rose angrily. "I will not have you mocking the dead!"

"And I," Joe said, his voice equally strident, "will not have you presume to tell me what they would have wanted! I'm not who I was before, I've changed and that has changed everything around me."

"It certainly doesn't change your status, Joseph," Taylor countered, her voice sneering. "Nor does it change the class to which you should associate yourself!"

Joe grinned a sardonic grin then, shaking his head. "That's where you're wrong, Taylor. It does change it. Before, I only wanted to make my parents happy, now I want to make *me* happy!"

"And never mind your duty," Taylor again countered.

"What duty, Taylor?" Joe asked, sighing. He knew they were getting nowhere, and he could feel Randy trembling beside him. He could only imagine what this conversation was doing to her self-esteem.

"To your family name, Joseph," Taylor said, as if speaking to a dull-witted child. "If you'll pardon my saying so, the Sinclair name has seen generations of only the finest caliber bloodlines."

"Good God, Taylor! You make us out like we're Goddamned race horses!"

"Joseph!" Taylor exclaimed.

"Taylor!" Joe sighed again, leaning back against the couch. "I never did fit into this family very well, did I? I was always the wayward son." His voice was quieter then, and Randy knew that he was feeling very hurt by what Taylor was saying.

"Yes, that's true enough, Joseph, but you were young, and no one remembers the sins of youth …"

"They don't, do they?" Joe said, his voice growing sarcastic again. "Do they remember a young man killing his own parents so he could inherit their money?" Randy looked at him sharply and could see the fire burning in his eyes.

"What?" Taylor responded, her eyes widening.

"That's what they all think isn't it, Taylor? That I killed them?"

"Joseph, all charges were dropped …"

"I know that, but that doesn't mean that I was innocent, right?"

Taylor didn't answer for a long two minutes. Her eyes stared at Joe's, but then lowered to the ground. Randy looked at Joe, and she could see a flash of pain cross his eyes.

"You don't even believe me, do you?" His voice was so quiet, like he was trying to lessen the impact of what he was saying, on himself.

Taylor looked at him then. "Joseph …" she started to say, but her voice trailed off, as her eyes once again dropped from his.

Randy felt his sharp intake of breath and saw how devastated he looked.

"I don't fucking believe it!" he said after a few moments. His eyes shone with tears, but his face contorted in a cynical mask.

"Joseph Michael! I will not stand for that kind of language!" Taylor said, and Randy knew she was trying to avoid the subject, and divert Joe.

"You won't, eh?" Joe said, standing and taking a menacing step toward his aunt.

Randy stood too, putting her hand on his arm. Joe stood staring down at Taylor, his eyes pools of light blue fire. "Tell me, Taylor," Joe said, his voice pure ice, "did you ever believe me?"

Taylor sat looking fearfully up at her nephew, but Randy could see her warring with the emotion. Taylor stood suddenly, her eyes flashing indignantly at Joe.

Randy felt Joe's arm tense under her hand. "Joe," she said, her voice cautionary.

Joe's eyes were still on Taylor, but at the sound of Randy's voice he looked down at her. His eyes softened as she looked up at him shaking her head slightly. Taylor was astounded that such a slight girl could have such an impact on her bull-headed nephew. She had never seen him react to any woman as she had just witnessed. After a few tense moments, Joe stepped back allowing Taylor to pass. Without a word, Taylor left the room.

Joe walked over to the bar and poured a succession of shots.

"I'm sorry," he said, "I need to take you home." His words were short and he still looked so angry. Randy just nodded. There was nothing she could say in that moment to make it any better.

The ride to her house was quick. Randy got out of the car, and Joe left without a word. She had no idea what was going on in his head, but she was afraid for him.

****

Midnight got to Mike's at seven fifteen. She was pretty proud of herself for only being fifteen minutes late, and Mike, as usual, didn't say anything. He had dinner ready. Mike Harlow was a very good cook; over the years he had cultivated a fair repertoire of recipes that were fantastic. He was still single at forty-five, and he said he refused to eat take out all the time, so he'd learned to cook.

Midnight took up her usual place on his couch; she never liked to eat formally at his dining room table. Mike had a nice comfortable house. It was cozy in a warm cluttered kind of way, much like Tom Ryan's house. Mike hadn't even bothered to set the dining room table this time; he remembered her habits.

As she took her first bite she exclaimed, "Oh, Mike this is great!"

"Midnight Chevalier, all you eat is take out, it's no wonder you think a homemade meal is good," Mike said, laughing at her.

"Now, Mike, that doesn't mean I don't have taste!" Midnight replied between bites. "I'll have you know that I have had some of the best take out in San Diego." Her voice was haughty, but her eyes reflected humor.

"Yeah, I'll just bet you have," Mike said. He looked at her seriously. "How come you haven't found yourself someone to settle down with yet? Somebody who'll cook for you and take care of you."

"Oh God, Mike who says that's what I want?" she said, still smiling. She knew that he was just as bad. "And what about you? How come you haven't found yourself some little woman to take care of you, Sergeant Harlow?"

"Touché," Mike said, knowing they were a lot alike in this way. They were silent for a little while. Then Mike looked at her again, as always trying to figure her out. "So, Lieutenant," he began, emphasizing her rank, "what have you been up to lately?"

"Same shit, different day, Mike. What about you?"

"Oh, same old, same old, making the streets safe for women and children, robbing from the rich to give to the poor, rescuing damsel lieutenants in distress … Which reminds me," he said, his voice growing very serious, "you need to start watching your back, little girl."

"What do you mean, my friend last night?"

"Yeah, Midnight, that guy was carrying, and we aren't talking some little pea shooter either he was carrying a forty-five."

"Really?" Midnight said, looking appropriately shocked.

"Really, Midnight, and he seriously considered pulling it on me so he isn't messing around here. I want you to be careful." His voice was very stern, his 'training sergeant voice,' Midnight called it.

"Yeah, Mike, yeah." He could see her mind clicking away as she mulled it over. "You run him?" she asked after a few minutes.

"Yeah I ran him, he didn't have any warrants, but he's been in."

"Yeah? How do you know?"

"He had the tattoos," Mike answered.

"Notice any scorpions?" she asked, holding her breath.

"No, but I doubt I saw them all either. He was a real scumbag, Midnight."

"Yeah, I wonder if he was from Quentin … Did you book him?"

"'Course I booked him," Mike said, looking at her like she was nuts for asking. "But the DA's office kicked him loose this morning. Possession of a firearm is only a misdemeanor."

"Not if he's on parole," Midnight countered, she knew her laws inside and out.

"He isn't on parole, he's just out I guess. He didn't show up as a parolee."

"Hmm," Midnight said, her eyes going unfocused. Mike could tell she was mentally going over all the information he had just given her.

She had a damn quick mind, he had to give her that. She shrugged then, realizing that she was being rude, and that she was here because she owed him for the stop he'd made, she didn't want to turn it into an office visit.

She turned the conversation to more social topics and they spent the next two hours talking about minor things. It was almost ten o'clock when there was a muted ring, and Midnight looked chagrinned as Mike looked around trying to identify the source of the ring.

"It's me," she said, reaching for her jacket lying on the back of his couch.

"So important," Mike said, raising an eyebrow at her, but his smile held no reproach. She smiled at him apologetically.

"Yes?" she answered.

Mike watched as she listened, her lips tightening in worry.

"Okay, thanks, I'll be there as fast as I can," she said, hanging up a moment later.

"Look, Mike, I have to go, Joe needs me." She stood up and picked up her jacket. Mike's hand stopped her.

"What happened?" he asked.

"Don't know for sure, but that was La Jolla patrol. Joe's been drinking all night and just got himself into a fight. I gotta go see what I can do," she said, touching Mike on the arm. "I'm sorry," she began.

Mike nodded. "He's your partner, go."

Midnight expelled the breath she hadn't realized she'd been holding. "Thanks Mike, you're a doll!" She leaned down, gave him a quick kiss him on the lips, and was gone.

Midnight drove as fast as she could up the freeway. She headed to the last bar Joe had been reported in. She found him at the bar, blood streaming from a cut on his eye. He was drinking straight from the bottle. She noticed that his shield was on the bar, so it was obvious he was warning the bartender off of trying to cut him off. That was not a good sign.

She sat down next to Joe, grabbed a shot glass from in front of him, took the bottle out of his hand, and poured them both a shot.

"What are we drinking to?" she asked, her eyes on him.

Joe looked at her, his eyes narrowed, but he picked up the shot glass. "To murder and all its benefits," he said, his tone low.

Midnight was shocked by what he said, but she drank the shot anyway.

"What happened, Joe?" she asked, as Joe picked up the bottle and poured two more shots.

He shook his head miserably. "Just fucking shit," he slurred. His accent was always thicker when he was drunk

"To fucking shit then," Midnight said, lifting her glass again.

It was two hours before they stumbled out of the bar. Midnight had wisely had the bartender call them a cab. On the drive to Joe's house, he looked over at Midnight.

"Whyn't you need me?" he asked her, still slurring his words..

"Need you?" she asked, feeling the effects of the alcohol in her veins.

"You should, ya know, I'm your bloody partner," he said then and leaned over to kiss her.

At first Midnight kissed him back, but she sensed something else was going on and pushed him away. She was stunned when he took her wrists, holding them away from their bodies so he could kiss her again.

"Joe, stop it!" she yelled, trying to rest her wrists from his grasp. He tightened his hold.

She cried out, wondering remotely if he was capable of breaking her wrists with his bare hands.

"Joe stop!" she yelled and she shoved her foot against his chest, breaking his hold on her.

Joe's head hit the side of the cab, and he shook it, as if trying to clear it. The cab driver had pulled over by that time, and Midnight jumped out, eager to get away from Joe.

"Night?" Joe said, looking like he'd just come out of some kind of trance.

She shook her head, slammed the cab door, and then turned to walk away.

The cab driver took off again, heading toward the address he'd been given, glancing back at Joe a few times. Joe's head was in his hands. He couldn't believe what he'd just done.

In the end, Midnight caught a black and white and had them take her home. At home, she climbed into her shower and sat on the floor, letting the water stream down on her head. She cried hard. She had no idea what was going on, but she couldn't believe her partner had just attacked her the way he had.

Chapter 9

The next morning, Midnight got out of bed feeling the effects of the night before. She showered and got dressed, then headed into the office. When she got there, Tim was waiting at her door for her. She sighed, not sure what to do with him. She saw that Randy had made it into the office and was relieved.

"Randy, why don't you go work on Joe's in mail, see if there's anything we need to deal with right away. I doubt he'll be in today." Randy nodded. *What did that mean?* She noticed that Midnight didn't look very lively that morning either.

"Okay," Randy said, heading for Joe's office.

Midnight turned her attention to Tim. "Hi there," she said, stooping to get under his downcast eyes.

"Hi," he said, his voice soft.

"Come on in my office and I'll get the things you need to fill out to get the background started." They went into Midnight's office and she put him in the same place she had put Randy when Randy had filled out her background information.

Rick came in about twenty minutes later to talk to her about a case.

"What happened to you?" he asked, grinning, thinking that her date had gone a bit long from the looks of her.

He tried desperately not to be jealous. As Joe had done a little over a month ago, he didn't notice the person sitting quietly in the corner.

"Joe lost it last night," Midnight said, her look pointed.

"Oh shit," Rick said, "what happened?"

"I have no idea," she said, shaking her head, "but I got a call from La Jolla patrol. He was drinking his way through the town and getting into fights."

Rick took a deep breath and blew it out slowly. "Taylor must have set him off."

"That's probably it," Midnight said, her tone flat.

Rick detected her tone and looked more closely at her. "So what did you do?"

"I went and drank with him, hoping I could get him to talk," she said, her look closed now.

"And?" Rick asked, his tone becoming much more serious.

Midnight just shook her head.

Rick stepped closer and reached down to take her hand. That's when he saw the dark bruises on her wrist. He grabbed the other one and saw that both wrists were black and blue.

"What the fuck did he do?" Rick asked, his eyes searching Midnight's.

Again, Midnight shook her head, not looking at him.

"Son of a bitch!" Rick said as he turned and headed out of the office.

"Rick!" Midnight yelled, realizing too late what Rick was going to do, but she couldn't catch him, his stride was too quick.

Outside in the parking lot, tires squealed as Rick accelerated out of the lot. He put his foot down hard on the pedal of his Mustang.

He pulled into Joe's driveway, skidding to a stop. Joe's Porsche was there, so Rick knew Joe was too. Rick found Joe on his deck. He was drinking again. Joe turned at the sound of Rick's boots on the wood deck. He suddenly became guarded and his body tensed. Rick's eyes blazed and he knew what that meant.

"Rick, what's going on?" Joe said, trying to sound casual.

"What the fuck's wrong with you man?" Rick said, his voice loud and barely controlled.

"Wrong with me? Nothing," Joe said, leaning casually against the railing of the deck.

"Well, then tell me this, who the fuck do you think you are? And before you answer that, I saw Midnight's wrists …" His voice trailed off with the threat he had so far left unspoken.

Joe shrugged indolently. "So you saw them, what about it?" he asked, watching Rick's reaction carefully.

Rick just looked at him dumbly; he couldn't believe that this was the man that had been his best friend for twenty-two years.

"What about them? Are you fucking nuts? Do you even know what you did to her?" Rick's voice was incredulous.

"I kissed her, it got a little rough. So what that's got to do with you?" Joe said, his voice purposely cool.

Rick was so mad he could almost feel his heart pumping adrenaline to his body.

"You fucking son of a bitch, you attack her and think it's nothing?" Rick's hands were tightened into fists, as he fought to control his anger.

He knew Joe's tactics, he'd been his second long enough. He knew that Joe was baiting him into getting mad and losing control, and then Joe, who was always cool in a fight, would kill him.

"I guess that all depends on who bitches first, doesn't it?" Joe said.

Rick lost it, launching himself at Joe, catching him in the midsection. They fell to the ground, Rick coming out on top. Rick punched Joe in the mouth twice, and then Joe moved stealthily to get out from under him. Joe twisted around, grabbing Rick's arm and bringing him up with him, but Rick was faster, and sober, and he brought his left arm around and punched Joe again. The force of Rick's blows stunned Joe. Rick had never actually hit him before, and they'd fought side by side a number of times, but never each other. Rick's foot lashed out then, knocking Joe to the ground. Rick straddled his body and Joe looked up at him with bleary eyes. Rick grabbed a handful of Joe's shirt, and pointed a finger at him.

"If you ever touch her like that again, I'll personally break your neck, you got that?" Rick's voice was like steel and his breathing was ragged from the exertion of the fight.

He stood, and walked away. Joe lay on his deck, unable to move. He could not believe what had just happened. Rick had just beaten him in a fight. He hadn't even thought it possible, and his usual tactic of making his opponent blind with anger hadn't worked either. Well, it had, but obviously he had gone too far, and it had made Rick stronger.

The next day at the office, Midnight immediately noticed the bruises on Joe's face as he walked in. She also noticed, to her utter shock, that Rick did not have an apparent mark on him. She hadn't thought that Rick could beat Joe. She realized she might have been wrong. The whole office was tense; it was like a film covering everything and everyone.

The bruises on Joe's face had shocked Randy, but she knew this wasn't the time to ask. She hadn't talked to him since the night at his house. She wasn't sure what to say. She noticed too that Rick had a very deep scowl on his face. Now she was really confused, but she knew she couldn't ask anyone. Joe was stone cold; he didn't speak to her when he came in. He just walked into his office and closed the door. Randy didn't like this side of Joe and hoped she wouldn't see it too often.

Midnight stayed in her office, and Joe stayed in his. Tim was in the office again, and watched Midnight doggedly until she motioned for him to come in.

Tim looked at Midnight timidly. "Are you okay, Lieutenant?" he asked, lowering his gaze dutifully to the floor. Midnight couldn't help but smile, despite her horrible mood.

"I'm fine, Tim, and it's Midnight, okay?"

Tim nodded. "Do you have anything you need me to do today?" he asked, his eyes darting shy looks at her. Midnight sighed, leaning back in her chair.

"Not really, Tim. Your background's not through yet, and procedurally—" Tim was nodding.

"I understand," Tim said.

"Tell you what," Midnight said as she steepled her fingers in front of her. "How about you stay in here with me, and sit right there"—she pointed to the chair right across from her desk—"and write down all the names and information that you can possibly think of about the Scorpions. Will you do that for me, Tim?" Midnight looked at him, smiling sweetly. How could he say no?

"Sure, Lieu—I mean Midnight." He said her first name shyly, as if afraid she would change her mind.

"Wonderful," Midnight said, giving him a winning smile. "There's a pad of paper over there and here's a pen."

They worked together in the office the rest of the day. Midnight would often catch him staring at her. A couple of times she would catch his gaze and smile at him, he would smile then, as if she had professed undying love. Midnight found it very sweet, and it helped to balance all the bad things going on in her life. By the time she stood to leave the office, she felt better. Tim was still working away; he had been for four hours. He had at least ten pages of information. Midnight figured maybe one page worth would have any real value, but she didn't mind letting him think that he was giving her the moon.

She picked up the pad, and looked at it appreciatively. "Hey, you got a lot here," she said, her voice purposely awed.

"Well, a quiet person seems to blend into the woodwork better so they don't notice me as much," Tim said, cautious with taking too much pride in all that he knew.

"Well, thanks a lot, Tim. It will help us out a great deal."

Tim stood from the desk and ended up right in front of her, looking very nervous. Midnight realized that he was almost as tall as Joe, and the comparison jabbed at her. She looked up at Tim and smiled.

On impulse, she reached out and hugged him. She thought she heard him suck in his breath as he put his arms around her, but he barely touched her, as if he was afraid she would break if he did. When she moved back, she saw that his face was flushed.

She smiled at him again. "Thanks again, Tim."

She went back behind her desk, and locked everything up. Then she reached over and pulled her jacket off the back of her chair, and while shrugging into it she told him that he could go home if he wanted to.

"I think I'll stay a little while longer if you don't mind? I want to finish some stuff up on these notes. Okay?"

"Sure, Tim, go ahead. I'll see you tomorrow."

"Okay, bye," Tim said, watching her walk out of her office.

After Midnight left, Tim worked dutifully on his notes. After he was finished and was standing to leave, he noticed the wall behind her desk. He stood and admired all the certificates and awards. *She's one hell of a woman ...*

San Diego, California, 1980

Thomas came home to find his sister sitting on the couch in their darkened living room. The stereo was on and Midnight was drinking, which was something she wasn't given to doing alone.

"What's going on?" he asked as he turned the lamp on.

Midnight narrowed her eyes, but didn't turn her head to look at him. She was indeed drinking, and she looked like she'd been doing it for a while. When Thomas walked around the couch and saw her face, he knew why. It was obvious that she'd been in a fight; she had a nasty cut on her cheek, a dark bruise on her jaw, and a split lip.

"Damn, sis!" Thomas breathed, sitting down on the couch next to his sister. "What happened to you?"

"What d'ya think, Thomas?" Midnight said. Her tone was ice cold.

"Yeah, but...." Thomas said, his voice trailing off because he didn't want to make her mad.

Midnight glanced up at him, her eyes narrowed. "Yeah, but what?" she asked. "Yeah but it looks like I lost. Well I did okay?"

"Okay..." Thomas said, taken back by her admission.

It was very rare that Midnight lost a fight; she was a damned good fighter.

"The bitch jumped me," Midnight said, turning back to her drink, and taking a long swig.

"Who?" he asked her.

"Talma." Midnight spat the name out like it left a bad taste in her mouth.

"The leader of the Piranhas?" Thomas asked, not totally surprised.

Talma and her gang had been making noises about trying to take over Vette territory for months.

"We gonna smoke 'em?" Thomas asked then, looking excited suddenly.

Midnight glanced sharply at her little brother. She didn't like the aggression he was starting to show. The last thing she wanted was for him to turn out like the animals she ran with. She wanted him to go farther than San Ysidro, California.

"Don't give me that look, Mid," Thomas replied, his tone irritated. "The bitch jumped my sister, what do you expect me to want?"

"Okay, fine. And yeah, I'm gonna reciprocate," Midnight said, looking more like herself again.

She got up from the couch, and walked into the kitchen to refill her glass. Thomas noticed a piece of paper that Midnight had been sitting on.

"What's this?" Thomas asked, as he reached over to it up.

Midnight walked back into the room, eying the paper in his hand, with a look on her face that Thomas didn't understand. Then she regained her composure and shrugged.

"Nothing," she said. She went to take the paper away from him, but he was already opening it and scanning the writing on it.

"This is from a college …" Thomas said, sounding shocked as he looked up at his sister. "It says you've been accepted to UCSD."

Midnight looked back at him for a long moment, giving nothing away.

"I know what it says," she said finally, her tone blasé, "I can read you know."

"Yeah, but … I didn't know you applied to college," Thomas said, looking dumbfounded.

"I didn't," Midnight said, her tone cool, "some do-gooder teacher did. Okay inspector?"

"Okay," Thomas said, still trying to understand, "but you got accepted …"

"Yeah, and I'm not goin', so what," Midnight said, sitting back on the couch, her face closed off, her eyes averted from his.

"Why not?"

Midnight looked over at him, the look on her face disbelieving. "College costs money, Thomas. They don't just hand it out for free. Besides what would you do? Stay here in la-la land with Jack and Carrie?" Her tone was sarcastic, and Thomas didn't know how to reply.

Midnight took another long swig from the glass in her hand, her eyes fixed on a spot on the carpet in front of her, her foot moving in agitation.

"Well, I'm goin' to college," Thomas said finally. "Or maybe I'll join the Navy and fly jets. I don't know yet," he said, sounding very young in his ambition.

Midnight looked over at him, grinning despite her mood. "You are, huh?"

"Yep, I'm gettin' the fuck outta here that's for sure," Thomas said, sitting up a little bit straighter.

"Good," was Midnight's only comment.

Thomas left a while later; he said he had a date with Sandy. Midnight sat alone for another hour, drinking and thinking about her life. She was feeling very depressed, feeling trapped by circumstances and she was angry about it. College was impossible; she wasn't even sure how she'd gotten accepted to a college like the University of California at San Diego. It was a prestigious private college that took the best of the best. Midnight figured someone must have screwed up in admissions office. She also knew that taking care of Thomas was her future. Trying to figure out how the two of them were going to make it was the concern that kept her awake at night. She knew that she could make it on her own, but Thomas was her responsibility and she wouldn't let him down. She was deep in thought when her parents arrived home after a night out at the bars. She didn't hear them come in.

"What are you doing?" Jack snapped.

His voice made Midnight jump, but she recovered quickly. She stood up and turned around giving them a cynical look.

"Why Jack, you wanna join me?" Midnight asked, using her father's first name.

She hadn't called him "Dad" in many years. She also knew it irritated him.

"You're under age, young lady," Carrie chimed in, doing her best to sound parental.

"And you're crocked, Carrie," Midnight replied, her tone derogatory.

"Don't talk to your mother like that!" Jack yelled, tensing as he did, as if he wanted to hit his daughter.

Midnight looked at him for a long moment, noting the movement. Then she started to grin, the look in her eyes telling them what she thought of them.

"Try it, Jack, and you're drinking days just might be over," she said, her voice light, but the look on her face indicating that she meant it.

"Get out of my house you little bitch!" Jack screamed, feeling very impotent, but not willing to take on his daughter.

Something in the way Midnight looked at him made him sure she would kill him if she got the chance. He wasn't going to give it to her.

Midnight stood in the living room looking at them for a full minute longer, a challenge in her eyes.

It was a moment Carrie Chevalier would recall for years to come. It was the moment when she saw her daughter as clearly as she'd ever seen her. Midnight was one hundred percent a gang leader, in look and stance, her body spoke the most serious of challenges. Carrie doubted anyone could hurt her at that moment. Neither she nor Jack dared to call their daughter's bluff, if it was a bluff, and Carrie doubted that it was.

Without another word, Midnight walked past her parents, her eyes on them the entire time, then she walked down the hallway, picking up her Vettes jacket on her way out. Outside she stood leaning back against the doorway, blowing her breath out. She made her way to the café, and went to the jukebox first, selecting a song that had been going around in her head since she'd left the house. The song was Pat Benatar's "Invincible." It made her think of her and Thomas against the world. As the song started, she sat down in her usual booth, and closed her eyes, listening to the words.

She sat there most of the night. No one bothered her, no one dared. The owner of the café knew her and liked her, so he told the waitress to take her coffee and not bug her otherwise.

****

Joe, who was still in his office, noticed the tall blond kid, looking at Midnight's awards and he watched him for a while. It was obvious the kid had a crush on the leader of FORS. Joe shook his head ruefully, not wanting to think about Midnight one second longer than necessary.

He was now genuinely pissed off that she had told Rick about their business. He was even more pissed that Rick had the nerve to stick his nose in where it didn't belong. The fight had been between Midnight and himself, and where Rick got off pulling that possessive act, Joe hadn't the faintest notion. Without realizing it, Joe snapped the pencil he had been holding in half as his angry thoughts ran the course they had run all day. When Randy came in, she saw the anger on his face. She picked up the work in his out basket and turned to leave without a word. Joe watched her walk out and his thoughts turned to the night of the storm. It seemed like a hundred years ago, a different time, a different life even. The events of the last two days had numbed him to the point of not feeling anything. Somewhere in the smallest place in his heart, he sincerely believed that this wouldn't be a permanent condition.

Taylor had been gone when the cab had dropped him off. He couldn't have cared less. All he could do was wonder how many people had never believed him. It was eating him alive. His ghosts were coming back to haunt him, taking shots at him over and over again.

****

That night, Midnight was working in her little-used kitchen. She was cooking herself chicken soup, a recipe she had learned when she was taking care of Thomas and herself. She often made it when she was feeling down, or upset. It seemed to cure everything and she hoped it would heal her ailing heart. Her whole world was turned upside down; her best friend in the world had not only abandoned her, but also kicked her on the way out.

She stood in the kitchen, the stereo was on, and she was listening to the soundtrack from Flashdance. She liked dance movies, and therefore thoroughly enjoyed their soundtracks. She was leaning against the island in her kitchen with her arms gripping the counter top behind her. Her face was turned up toward the ceiling and her eyes were closed as she listened to the music.

She didn't notice Rick standing in the kitchen doorway watching her. After a few minutes, she sensed his presence and her head snapped around to look at him.

He saw that she had tensed, but when she saw him, she relaxed.

"My front door unlocked?" she asked, smiling weakly at him.

"It's a bad habit," Rick said, smiling back at her. "What're you doing in here?" he said, indicating the kitchen.

Midnight laughed. "I can cook, you know," she chided him. "Just because I don't choose to most of the time doesn't mean I can't."

"Okay," Rick said, holding up his hands in defense. "I believe you."

"Okay," Midnight said, looking at him. Her face grew serious then. "You and Joe got into it yesterday." It was a statement, not a question.

"Yeah," Rick said. He held her gaze. Looking away would make him look guilty and he certainly wasn't. Not in his mind, anyway.

Midnight shook her head. "I don't know how I'm supposed to feel about that."

Rick shrugged. "You don't have to feel anything. He was mouthing off and I got mad, so I hit him."

247

Midnight didn't respond, she just nodded sadly. She didn't like the idea that Joe and Rick, who had been friends almost as long as she'd been alive, were now fighting because of her.

With a sigh, she walked over to the stove and stirred the soup. "Will you at least stay for dinner?"

Rick smiled at her, nodding.

Later they sat on the couch. Flashdance was still playing on the stereo. They didn't really talk, they just ate and mulled over their own thoughts. Then the song "I'll Be Here Where the Heart Is" began to play. Rick watched as Midnight sang the words, feeling his own heart torn out from the emotion and pain he saw on her face.

As the song faded away, Rick saw a tear roll down Midnight's cheek and he felt the knife twist in his heart. He knew she had been singing about Joe, and he knew that she would always hold Joe in her heart. If he thought about it long enough it would drive him crazy. How she could still care about him after what he did to her? But it obviously wasn't enough to make her hate him, even if she seemed like she wanted to. Rick was, however, grateful to be here with her now, to be there for her.

He realized that he was starting to fall hard for this woman, and the idea tore at him even more. He knew that falling for her would probably mean a life of misery, because she didn't seem to have any deep feelings for him or any man, other than Joe. Again, Rick cursed Joe and his damned luck. He had someone like Midnight devoted to him, and instead of treating her with the tenderness and love she deserved, he attacked her and bruised her. Yet she still loved him, obviously.

They sat and talked for a while, but it became increasingly obvious to Rick that she was exhausted. The strain of the last few days was starting to tell on her face.

"Midnight, you look beat," Rick said.

Midnight looked at him and nodded. "I am, but … I really don't want to be alone." Her eyes pleaded with him to understand. Rick thought he did.

He nodded at her and without a word, Midnight moved closer to him. He put his arm around her, and she leaned against him. After a few minutes he noticed that her breathing had become even, and he looked down to see she was asleep. He knew the position she was sleeping in couldn't be comfortable so he gently picked her up in his arms. He carried her to her room, and laid her gently on her bed. She stirred, and opened her eyes. Her hand reached out and took his.

"Stay, please," she said, and Rick knew that wild horses couldn't keep him from doing just that.

Again, he nodded. "I will, but I want you to get some sleep, I'll be right here," he said softly.

She nodded, closing her eyes. Her hand still clasped his. He knelt next to the bed watching her. Eventually he moved to lie next to her. Again she stirred. She looked up at him, and smiled, and then she moved to rest her head on his chest. His arm encircled her shoulders and his other hand came up to stroke her cheek. She sighed and fell asleep again. Rick spent the night holding her, and tried to convince himself that the events of the past few days were going to come to some positive end. As it stood, he was at serious odds with his best friend, and he was falling hard for a woman who he was sure wasn't capable of loving him back. Things were not going well at all.

Things got worse at FORS the next day. Joe came into the office looking particularly hungover and very hostile. When Rick and Midnight came in together, Joe's eyes narrowed at them, the look of disgust on his face indicating his distaste for them being together at all. Rick stood across the room and glared at Joe. Joe did the same, and they were trying to stare each other down.

"Fuck it," Rick said, flicking his hand in a dismissing gesture at Joe.

That triggered Joe's temper. He strode threateningly toward Rick. Midnight witnessed the whole thing and immediately insinuated herself between the two of them. She held up her hands to Joe, and gave him a stern look.

"Get out of the way, Midnight, this is between me and Rick," Joe said, his eyes flicking coolly over her, in a possessive way. Midnight felt Rick tense behind her.

"No, Sergeant, this isn't between you and Rick. It's between you and me. And I'm telling you that if you continue, you're going to be in a shit load of trouble. So it's my advice to you that you go and cool off." Her voice was the epitome of authority.

Joe hesitated, but she could see that his anger was still burning, and his eyes narrowed at her use of his rank. His eyes flicked to Rick, who stood ready behind Midnight.

"You going to let her fight her battles for you?" Joe said, his voice derogatory. "Or are you afraid to fight me when we're both sober?"

"Fuck you, Joe. I'll fight you anytime, anywhere," Rick said, keeping his voice cool. "I'm not worried, you seem real tough against a woman, but you aren't shit to me."

Joe's temper flared and his fist came up. Midnight managed to dive out of the way and she heard the impact of Joe's fist. Rick fell to the floor, and Midnight turned to see Joe going after him again. She moved with lightning speed getting to Rick first, and kneeling next to him. She threw a deadly look at Joe that stopped his forward movement. Even in his anger, he knew better than to confront her.

Rick was lying on the floor; he was conscious, but it was obvious that he was dazed. Midnight looked down at him.

"Are you okay?" she asked, her voice concerned.

Rick nodded, his narrowed eyes on Joe as he started to stand.

But Midnight stopped him. "No!" she said harshly, holding her hands on him to keep him down.

Her head snapped to look at Joe. She saw that the temporary hesitation on Joe's part had worn off and he was heading forward to drag Rick up. She jumped to her feet, and shoved him back. Tiny, who had come up behind Joe, grabbed him roughly by the arms and held him firm.

"You," Midnight said, sputtering in her anger. "I warned you. You're out of here pal, you've just crossed the line."

Joe's look was indifferent. "That so?" he said, his voice antagonistic.

Midnight nodded at him, her eyes blazing. "Yeah that's so. Get the fuck out, and don't come back." She looked at Tiny and gestured to the door with her head.

Then she turned her back on Joe. He was still looking like he didn't care.

"Get him the hell out of here, Tiny," she said, her voice cracking on the last word.

There were tears in her eyes as she knelt down next to Rick again. But Joe didn't see them. Tiny ushered him out the door, and Joe didn't bother to fight him. He knew that Tiny would do anything for Midnight and that included doing him some serious damage if Joe said or did the wrong thing to Midnight.

Randy had watched the entire scene from her desk. She felt frozen in place. She couldn't believe what was happening. Tears came to her eyes when Midnight told Joe to get out and not come back. She wanted to run after Joe, but she also wanted to go to Midnight who was crying as she knelt near Rick. Randy watched as Rick got to his feet, bringing Midnight to her feet with him. He hugged her, and then turned and guided her to her office, holding her close. Rick kicked the door closed behind them. The whole office was silent for a full five minutes. Everyone was shocked by what they had just seen. Nobody was sure if Midnight was serious about Joe not coming back, but she had sounded serious. When people started to move about the office again, everything was very subdued and the whole office seemed to feel depressed.

Once outside in his car, Joe sat staring at Midnight's Corvette that was parked right across from him. He closed his eyes against the deep pain that was starting in his heart. He knew he'd gone too far, he knew that she was serious. He thought it might kill him. It took a long time for him to calm down enough to drive out of the parking lot. No sooner did he get home than he went to the bar. Joe proceeded to drink until he passed out. When he woke up, he started drinking again.

The rest of the day at the office was very tense and very quiet. No one dared to say anything about the scene between Joe, Midnight, and Rick. After about half an hour, Rick had left Midnight's office while she stayed behind working on reports. No one entered her office and no one approached Rick. He sat at his desk working. There was a bruise starting at his jaw, and the sight of that kept everyone away from him.

Later that night, Rick called Midnight wanting to check on her. She asked him to come over and he did. They spent the evening much as they had the night before; Rick held her and they talked a little bit. They avoided the topic of Joe altogether, both sensing that the other didn't want to talk about it. They talked about the cases they were working on, and they even talked about Tim.

"He's a nice kid," Midnight said, her head resting on Rick's chest. They were on her couch listening to the stereo.

"Yeah, he is, and he's got a major crush on you," Rick said, smiling down at her.

Midnight laughed. "I kind of thought so," she said, with no conceit.

"Kind of?" Rick said, incredulously. "That kid is so far gone I think if you touched him he'd fall over dead from happiness."

"I wouldn't go that far," Midnight said, smiling.

"Well, I would," Rick replied. "Smart kid, though, knows a beautiful woman when he sees one." He tightened his arms around her for a moment.

"I see," Midnight said, looking up at him. "Well I've always known men were blind."

Rick looked at her for a long moment, and he shook his head disbelieving. "You have no idea how beautiful you are." His voice was soft and low. Midnight looked away from him, embarrassed. He touched her face, bringing it back to face him. "I didn't think anything could embarrass you."

She wouldn't look at him, her eyes staring over his shoulder instead.

"Midnight, look at me," Rick said, smiling.

When she looked at him, he smiled even wider; it was obvious that his complement had really embarrassed her. She laughed and he did too. The rest of the evening was comfortable and in a way healing for both of them. They didn't make love; Rick didn't even try and Midnight liked him even more for that. Joe was the only man that she had ever spent the night with without sex.

She was glad that they had become good enough friends now that he could sense that she wouldn't want that kind of closeness right then. She was still emotionally wounded from the incident with Joe and the last thing she wanted was to have sex with anyone. Rick seemed to sense that, and while he held her close to him as they slept that night, his hands never wandered. The kisses he placed softly on her lips weren't tainted with passion, they were tender. Midnight felt very comfortable in his arms, and this time it didn't bother her that he was like Joe in that respect.

The next day, the office was a little less sedate, although Joe's absence was very noticeable.

Tim was in the office and again he tended to want to work with Midnight, and as usual, she indulged him. Rick watched her talk to him, and smiled to himself remembering their conversation of the night before. Midnight looked up and saw him smiling and she smiled too. She was having Tim clarify some of the information he had written down a couple of days before. She had been very surprised to find that he did indeed seem to know a lot about the Scorpions' operations. He didn't know the leader's name, but he had seen him a few times and he described him to Midnight.

"He's tall, kind of like Joe," Tim said, then grimaced at having brought up what he knew was a sore spot. Midnight shook her head smiling at him, motioning for him to go on. "And he's got like a crew cut, brown hair, and I think his eyes are brown too, but it's real hard to know 'cause he wears shades a lot. Probably 'cause he's got scars and stuff on his face. Oh and speaking of scars, he's got this one scar that runs like from his ear, down his chest, all the way to his waist." Tim ran his index finger from his left ear down his chest to the right side of his waist.

Midnight widened her eyes; she could imagine what kind of fighter would get a cut like that. "Anything else? Tattoos? Anything?"

Tim nodded. "Yeah, a bunch of them."

"Like what?" Midnight said, trying to keep the excitement out of her voice. She knew she was getting close to something, but she didn't want to push too hard.

"Well he has a cross on his back, and a lion on one of his arms—"

"Upper or lower?" Midnight asked.

"Upper. He has a bunch of them though. I try not to look at him much when he's around, 'cause he might call me out or something. He fights dirty. I saw him knife a guy in the back when the guy wouldn't fight him. He killed him. He's real mean."

Midnight nodded, knowing she had yet another reason to arrest the guy.

"Oh, yeah!" Tim said. "He does have one tattoo I can remember, he has a red scorpion on the front of his left shoulder. It's really a cool tattoo, lot of detail and stuff ..." Tim's voice trailed off, as Midnight looked at him sharply. She didn't want Tim to think anything about this guy was "cool." It reminded her of Thomas, with his "cool" long hair. Tim looked down then, knowing he had said something wrong, to make her mad.

Midnight shook her head. "Hey, Tim." She looked at him, waiting until he raised his eyes to her again, then she smiled at him. "You've been a great help, we'll get this guy, don't you worry." Tim smiled at her, glad that she wasn't mad at him.

Tim left the office a few hours later, telling her he had to go see his brother, and do "some stuff." Midnight had nodded absently, her attention on a report she had just gotten from the Bureau of Investigation's Criminal Intelligence Section. Tim stood in her doorway watching her for a few minutes. Midnight realized that he hadn't left, and looked up and saw him watching her. She smiled at him warmly, and his heart soared. He left the office with a spring in his step.

Midnight went back to the report, shaking her head and smiling to herself. She remembered a time when Thomas had been trying for her approval.

****

Midnight sat in one of the booths of the restaurant. One jean clad leg rested on the seat of the booth, her back to the wall, as usual, keeping tabs on everything and everyone. Many of the members looked in her direction, but didn't bother to try and talk to her. They knew she wasn't the social type. She grimaced as she noted Thomas walking toward her with Sandy in tow.

"Shit," Midnight said under her breath, as her gold-green eyes tracked their progress toward her. She didn't notice the young man come up beside her, until his voice made her jump ever so slightly.

"Hola, chica ..." he said, his voice full of innuendo.

Midnight controlled her immediate reaction, which was to grab him by the throat for sneaking up on her. Instead, she narrowed her eyes as she turned her head. "You do that again, and you're gonna be breathin' outta new hole," she said, her voice pure ice.

"Hey, juerita, lighten up!" the young man, Manuel, said, giving her a suave grin, but moving pointedly out of her range. He attempted to sit next to her, but she stared back at him, refusing to move her foot.

"So when are you and me gonna get together?" he asked, wisely choosing to sit across from her.

"We're not," Midnight said, her tone matter of fact.

"Not what?" Thomas asked, smiling at his sister, as he walked up. The girl he was with all but hid behind him.

"Never mind," Midnight said, giving Manuel a cool look. "What is it you've got there, little brother?" she said then, her tone not warming in the slightest.

"Midnight, this is Sandy," Thomas said, pulling the girl forward to face Midnight. The girl looked terrified. "Sandy, this is my sister, Midnight."

Midnight's eyes flicked from Thomas to the girl, and then back to her brother, when "Sandy" said nothing. Finally, Midnight shrugged and said, "Okay." After that, she turned back to Manuel, dismissing Thomas and Sandy. Thomas walked away eventually, feeling very put out by his sister's attitude.

As they walked home that night, Thomas complained about Midnight's behavior.

"You were a total bitch, Midnight," he said, not for the first time in the argument.

"I told you, I don't converse with members. That makes 'em think I'm their friend and I'm not," Midnight said, not looking at her brother.

"But Sandy's different, she might end up being my girlfriend or something. Doesn't that count for anything?" Thomas asked, his tone imploring.

"Thomas," Midnight said, stopping in her tracks, and staring up at him. "I'm not their friend okay, I'm their leader. If I start being miss congeniality then no one's gonna respect me. This is my gang, I run it. You wanted to join, now you're in, but don't expect me to change my ways for you. I got a reputation to uphold here, this ain't fun and games ya know. If one person thinks I'm soft, if one chick decides she wants to make a play for my spot, and I lose, I'm dead, and where will that leave you?"

Thomas lowered his head, his lower lip stuck out in an over exaggerated pout, his green eyes looking at his sister through a veil of brown hair. "Jesus, Midnight, I didn't realize that my finding a girlfriend was going to get you killed ..."

Midnight stood in the middle of the darkened street and stared up at him dumbfounded for a long moment. Then she started to laugh.

"Just shut the hell up, will ya!" she said, reaching out to shove him. He fell back, laughing too. He started to chase her, and she ran, her boot heels striking the pavement and her copper-blond hair flying wildly around her. It was one of the rare times when they were brother and sister, not leader and member.

Midnight was so distracted by their game that she didn't see the police car drive up until he was right next to them.

"Good evening, Miss Chevalier," Tom Ryan said from his squad car.

Midnight turned to look at him, a guarded look dropping over her face like a mask. "What do you want, Ryan?" she asked, her tone mildly defiant. She actually liked the guy, he was pretty cool in her book, but she had no intention of letting him know that.

"Hey there Thomas," he said, smiling at the young man, ignoring Midnight's question. It was rhetorical anyway.

"Ryan," Thomas said, his face serious as he took his cue from his sister.

"So, what's on the agenda for this evening, Midnight?" Ryan asked keeping his tone of voice conversational.

"As a matter of fact," Midnight said, smiling a false sweet smile at him, "we're on our way home, Officer Ryan." Her tone was that of an obedient schoolgirl.

"Uh-huh ... and where've you been tonight?" Ryan asked.

"At Barney's over on Bay View," Midnight answered her look openly defiant now.

She knew she was guiltless this time.

"Okay ... I heard you had a run in with Talma Hooks, that true?" Ryan asked, his tone taking on a more intent tone. Midnight knew he was fishing.

"Couple days ago. Why?" Midnight asked, her gold-green eyes narrowing at Ryan.

"Word on the street is she wants to take you down," Tom said, sounding concerned.

"Yeah," Midnight said confidently, "she'd like to try, so what."

"Midnight," Ryan began his tone almost fatherly, "Talma Hooks is playing for keeps... I think you should take her threat seriously." He watched her face, seeing that she was listening, even if she was acting like she wasn't. "Maybe," he said cautiously, "now would be a good time to get out. There's a program with the department—"

"Don't bother, Ryan," Midnight said, shaking her head, "I'm no charity case. I don't need to be rescued, thank you very much." Her tone indicated anything but gratitude. "I can handle Talma."

She started to walk away then, and Ryan felt the need to get out of his car and intercept her. He was surprised once again by how small she really was, dwarfed by his six-foot frame.

"Midnight," he said, standing in her way, "be reasonable," he told her, holding up his hands to block her from moving away from him. "What kind of life is this for Thomas?" he asked, knowing that was a chief concern for Midnight.

"I can take care of myself and Thomas," Midnight said, staring defiantly up at him.

Thomas stood by, watching the exchange. He was fiercely loyal to his sister and would believe anything she said. Ryan knew he was fighting a losing battle.

"Okay, okay, so you won't quit the gang, but at least promise me you'll be careful around Talma Hooks."

"Yeah, yeah, okay?" Midnight said, giving him an irritated look now.

Ryan knew it was time to back off. He stepped back, allowing her to pass, and watched as she and Thomas continued down the street.

Ryan had been keeping an eye on her for over two years now. He had seen in the young woman a great deal of potential. He knew that she was very smart, and that, given the right opportunities, she could do a lot with her life. It bothered Ryan to see her running the streets. He'd ascertained that her parents were drug addicts and that they basically paid no attention to their children. The first time Tom Ryan had met Midnight Chevalier, he had been responding to a call about a gang fight. He had driven up to find that the fight had broken up, but there were still people milling about. He had approached a young woman leaning against a wall.

"Did you see what happened here, miss?" Ryan had asked her politely.

Midnight had looked up at him, her look wry as she grinned.

"Yep," she had responded, her tone indolent.

Her eyes had stared right back into his, surprising him.

"Would you like to tell me what happened then?" he had asked her, smiling in spite of himself.

"Nope," she had replied, her eyes never leaving his.

"Would you like me to haul you down to the station for question-ing?" Ryan had asked authoritatively.

Midnight's grin had grown wider at that point. "For what? Hang-ing out on the side of building?"

Ryan had known then that she was far from the average gang member. She hadn't resorted to cussing and being difficult, she'd used her quick mind to diffuse his attempt to squeeze her for information. That was the day that he decided to watch this particular young woman. He had found out her name and that of her gang, and knew that their territory fell within his patrol area. He'd been stopping and talking to her since that time. She always acted like she didn't want to be bothered by him, but she had also always talked to him. Ryan thought she probably liked him more than she'd ever let on.

He was worried about her, however. She seemed so fragile, and he had seen Talma Hooks, the woman was twice Midnight's size. She was also eager to make a name for herself. It was a bad combination.

****

Midnight got a phone call around five thirty. It was Tim, he told her he'd found out more about the leader of the Scorpions, and asked her if she would meet him at his apartment. She agreed, writing down the address. She picked up her gun and her jacket then left the office. She really hoped that all the information Tim had provided so far would help but she sincerely hoped that he knew the guy's name now. As she drove over to his apartment, she dialed Mike Harlow's office number.

It had occurred to her while Tim was giving her the leader's description that she hadn't gotten a description of the guy that had followed her a week or so ago. Mike wasn't in his office so she left a message for him.

As she got closer to the address, she noticed that the neighborhood wasn't the greatest. When she found the address, she parked in front and as she got out, slipped her gun into its usual place and clipping her radio to her belt. Then she walked up to the front door of the apartment building. She went up two flights of stairs, noticing the graffiti and garbage in the stairwell. When she got to the correct apartment number, she knocked. She heard a sound from inside. She wasn't sure what it was, but it made her nerves jump. She pulled the radio off her belt.

"This is Lincoln-10," she said into the radio.

"Lincoln-10, go," replied the dispatcher.

"I need a black and white at 3124 Home Avenue, apartment 24."

"10-4 Lincoln-10," the dispatcher answered.

Midnight put the radio back on her belt and reached back to pull out her gun. She reached out and tried the doorknob; it was unlocked. She opened it cautiously and stood back out of the doorway for a moment, then swung into the apartment, her gun at the ready.

"Tim," she called. No answer.

She moved into the room, her arms extended in front of her holding her gun. Her steps were cautious and her eyes darted around, trying to secure the area. She wondered if Tim had just had to leave, and would be back. But her instinct told her that something was wrong. She made her way through the room and stepped into the living room. That's when she saw Tim. He was lying on the floor. Then she saw the blood. She screamed as she ran to his side, skidding to a stop and dropping to her knees.

"Tim!" she yelled, tears already in her eyes.

There was blood coming from his chest; he'd been shot a few times. He was breathing and she checked for a pulse. He had one, it was weak, but he had one. Still holding her gun, she pulled the radio off her belt.

"This is Lincoln-10, I need an ambulance at 3124 Home Avenue, apartment 24, now!" Her heart was beating so fast, she could barely breathe.

Still on her knees she lifted Tim's head to rest on her lap, her tears dropping on his face.

"Come on, Tim, don't do this to me. Come on!"

He opened his eyes, and his hand came up to touch her hand. She took his hand and held it tightly. "You're going to be okay," she said softly.

She could see he was having a hard time breathing, and she could see fear in his eyes. "Oh God, Tim, you're going to be okay, you've got to be."

He looked at her, and she could see pain and sorry in his eyes. She leaned down and kissed him; his lips were cold, and he squeezed her hand. When she pulled back, he smiled just slightly at her. His hand went limp then and she knew that she had just lost him too. Her screams pierced the silence.

"No Tim! Goddamn it! No!"

The police found her a few minutes later, with Tim's head still in her lap. Her head was down, and she was crying and rocking back and forth. Her gun was still in her left hand. The police approached her cautiously with their weapons drawn, not knowing who she was.

"Drop the gun lady!"

Midnight's head came up and she looked at them blankly, tears still streaming from her eyes. One of the officers recognized her and held up his hand to the other officer. "It's okay, she's a cop." He walked over to her then. "Are you okay, Lieutenant?" he asked. She nodded.

The paramedics arrived and moved to Tim's limp body. The police officer helped Midnight stand, but she shrugged off his hands. Her jeans were bloody, as was her right hand, but she didn't notice. She stood by while the paramedics tried to revive Tim. Her eyes grew more and more distant. The officers didn't notice that when she walked out she was still holding her gun in her hand. They also didn't see just how devastated she was.

She drove back to her house with her gun resting in her lap. In a haze she locked her front door and activated the alarm. She still held her gun. She opened her bedroom window, letting the cold wind blow in. After a few minutes, she moved back into her room and removed her boots and jeans, putting her gun down on her bed in the process. She looked down at the jeans lying on the floor. She looked at the blood, as if not understanding where it had come from. She picked up her gun again, as if it were a security blanket and lay down in the center of the bed. She curled into a ball, her arms crossed in front of her, the gun cradled against her breasts. She lay there staring off into space.

CHAPTER 10

Rick got a phone call from the duty sergeant telling him the FORS's Lieutenant had called in a black and white, and then subsequently an ambulance. Rick got the address from the sergeant and all but ran to his car. It had been two hours since she had left the office; she hadn't said where she was going. Rick got to the apartment and was informed that Tim Bollings was dead, and that Lieutenant Chevalier had been the one to find him. A cold fear gripped Rick that only deepened when the officer said that she had wandered out of the apartment and driven away without saying a word to anyone.

Rick ran down to his car and sped off toward Midnight's house. When he got there, he pounded on the door, but no one answered. Her car was in the driveway so he knew she was there. He tried the door, but it was locked. He jumped the fence and tried her back door, but it was locked tight too. He went back to his car and radioed for any black and whites in the area. Two police cars arrived a few minutes later. They all tried the door, and even attempted kicking it open, but to no avail. Midnight's security system included a solid steel door making "breaking in" impossible. All of her windows were barred too. Rick went to her bedroom window and looking in, he could see her on the bed. She was curled into a tight ball shivering.

"Midnight!" he yelled, but she didn't move. He tried a few more times, but she still didn't answer. He was really worried now. He needed to get in there, before she did something stupid. He had no way of knowing that she cradled her gun against her. It occurred to him then that Joe had a key to her house and knew the access code to her alarm. Rick knew then what he had to do.

Telling the officers to stand by, he ran to his car. He threw the Mustang into reverse and backed out of the driveway. He drove as fast as he possibly could to Joe's house. To his relief Joe's car was in the driveway. He jumped out of his car, ran to the front door, and pounded on it. There was no answer. He went around the house and found Joe on the deck. As Rick skidded to a stop on the deck, Joe's head snapped up.

"What the fuck are you doing here?" Joe began to ask angrily.

"Joe, it's Midnight. We need you," Rick said, with enough intensity to make Joe jump to his feet.

"What happened?" Joe asked, his concern for Midnight, far outweighing any antipathy he had fostered for Rick.

"Tim Bollings was killed, Midnight found him …" Rick's voice trailed off as Joe started to move toward him.

"Oh, Jesus," Joe said worriedly. "Where is she now?"

"At her house. She won't answer the door, Joe."

"Well she doesn't have to," Joe said, pulling his keys out of his pocket. "Come on." They both walked in long hurried strides to Rick's car. They drove down to Midnight's house in silence, both men tense and worried.

When they got to Midnight's house, the police were still waiting, but had made no progress at opening the front door. Joe motioned them aside, as he pulled out his keys. As he turned the key in the lock, the dead bolt slid back easily. Then he unlocked the other lock, and turned the knob. The chain was on the door too so he stood back and kicked the door open. He walked in, stopping at the alarm to deactivate it. Rick brushed straight past him and headed down the hallway to Midnight's room. Her back was to the door, so he moved to the other side of the bed, and knelt down beside it. That's when he saw the gun and her finger firmly on the trigger.

"Oh, God," Rick said, closing his eyes.

"What?" Joe asked, entering the room.

He walked around to where Rick stood. His eyes went to the gun gripped in Midnight's small hands. Her eyes were closed and her whole body was shaking.

"Let me handle this," Joe said, looking at Rick.

Rick nodded numbly, too afraid for Midnight to take offense to Joe taking over. Joe lay down on the bed next to Midnight.

He looked down at her, reaching out to gently touch her cheek. "Midnight." His voice was soft.

She opened her eyes to look up at him. Her eyes registered no emotion.

"Babe, give me the gun," Joe said, his voice still soft, but she shook her head, her eyes growing wary of him. "Come on, Night just give me the gun," he said again, his eyes searching hers.

He knew he was putting himself in a dangerous position, especially with what had happened between them. He knew in the emotional state she was in and she could easily turn the gun on him. But he was willing to take that risk, to keep her from hurting herself. He saw her hand tighten on the gun, and he held his breath. Her eyes were still looking at him, they were narrowed, as if suspicious of his motives. It tore at his heart to see that look in her eyes. He wondered if she was considering shooting him.

"Midnight," Rick said, looking down at her, "give Joe the gun."

Midnight's gaze shifted to Rick and her eyes misted with tears. She looked back at Joe then, and he could see her trying work through all of the emotions she was feeling.

"Come on, Night, just give me the gun, we'll get through this, I promise," Joe said, reaching for the gun. She pulled back, tightening her grip on it again, her eyes narrowing again. "Okay," Joe said, shaking his head. Then he pinned her with a serious look. "Then shoot me." Her eyes widened at his words. "You heard me right," Joe said, pointing to his chest, "shoot me, I deserve it, for what I did to you." His eyes misted with tears then. "Just don't hurt yourself, baby, please."

Midnight closed her eyes, tears starting to run down her cheeks. In what seemed like slow motion, she turned the gun toward him. Both Rick and Joe held their breath, then, opening her eyes, she extended it to Joe and took her finger off the trigger. Joe took it, his eyes not leaving hers, and slowly moved his hand to his back so Rick could take it from him. Joe reached out and pulled Midnight into his arms. She was crying now, hysterically. Her hand gripped the front of his shirt tightly. Her whole body was shaking from the sobs. Joe held her, stroking her hair, tears of his own running down his face.

"He's dead, Joe," Midnight said, her voice broken, and hysterical.

"I know, I know," Joe said, squeezing her tighter. The tone of her voice scared him.

He knew she was on the edge and if he didn't handle this just right, they could lose her.

"I hate this job," she sobbed, her hand tightening on his shirt. "I hate these people. I don't want to do this anymore." She sounded defeated and hoarse.

"It's okay, baby," Joe said, still stroking her hair. "We'll get through this, it's okay."

"They killed him, Joe, the bastards killed him."

"I know, baby, and we'll get them, we will," Joe said, sounding determined.

"I can't do this. I can't do this," she said, shaking her head. "Not again." Her voice was a harsh whisper.

"You aren't alone this time, baby. I'm here, Rick's here, we'll get you through this."

She nodded, still crying. Joe looked up at Rick and they both realized that all of the fighting and anger of the past week was over. The harsh words, the anger, the wounds, were all forgiven and forgotten as they both prayed for Midnight to be okay. Rick left the room and called for a doctor. When the doctor arrived, Rick explained the situation to him. The doctor indicated that a sedative would help to keep Midnight from trying to hurt herself. Rick gestured to Midnight's bedroom. Joe still lay on the bed, with Midnight in his arms; she was still shaking and a crying. Joe looked at the doctor and nodded to him. When the doctor touched Midnight's hand, she pulled it away, looking suspiciously up at him.

"It's okay," Joe said, tightening his arms around her again. "He's just going to give you something to calm you down, he won't hurt you."

She looked up at him and shook her head, becoming in moments a little girl trying to avoid a sharp needle stick.

"It's okay," he repeated. His hand touched her under the chin, keeping her focused on him to distract her. "Just look at me, I'm right here. It won't hurt you." He nodded imperceptibly and the doctor got the shot ready. Joe continued to talk to her, her eyes shifted to the doctor again as approached her and Joe felt her tense. "Baby," he said, making her look at him again. "It's okay, this will make you sleep, I'll be right here when you wake up, okay? I promise." His voice was sincere.

The doctor stuck the needle in her arm as she nodded, her eyes flickering at the sharp stick. The doctor left and Rick followed him out. He gave Rick a bottle of pills. "They're sleeping pills; she looks like she's going to need them."

Rick went back into the bedroom, watching Joe, as he stroked Midnight's hair and talked softly to her. He was glad that he had gone to get Joe, he wasn't sure if she would have responded to him. Joe and Midnight had been friends for so long; he knew her and he'd known exactly what to say. Rick had been very concerned when he had told her to shoot him. He was half-afraid she would. He had been prepared to grab the pistol away if she really looked like she was going to do it. At this close range, she would more than likely have killed Joe, and he couldn't let that happen no matter what had happened between them. He watched as Midnight drifted off to sleep. Joe looked up at him, and the look they exchanged was one of mutual concern. Rick walked over and stood by the bed.

"I'm going to have to go into the office in the morning, and take care of some arrangements for Tim's funeral but I don't want her alone," Joe said.

"I'll stay with her," Rick said, his eyes on her sleeping form.

271

"Yeah, that's what I was hoping," Joe said, his eyes shifting from Rick's face to Midnight's.

He could see the depth of Rick's feelings for Midnight in his friend's eyes. And in a way, he was glad; he knew that Midnight was going to need as much support as she could get, and maybe Rick would be able to give her what he himself, obviously, could not.

Rick nodded again, his eyes still on Midnight. Rick and Joe spent the night watching her, and they didn't talk much. Rick sat in a chair he had pulled over to the bed. Joe continued to lay with Midnight in his arms.

After a few hours, Joe carefully got up. He looked at Rick, and without a word, Rick moved to take his place. Rick sat on the bed and leaned against the headboard. Midnight stirred, her hand reaching out, touching his chest. He put his arm around her and drew her up to him. She didn't open her eyes, but she settled against him, her head on his chest, her arm resting across his stomach.

Joe watched, as Midnight settled with Rick, and then left the room. He walked out to the living room, pulled open the sliding glass doors, and walked outside. He went to sit on the edge of the hill. The wind blew his hair from his face, as he looked out at the ocean. The impact of the evening's events started hitting him. He knew that Midnight could have easily killed herself, and he would have been arranging her funeral. *No*, he corrected himself, *I would have killed myself next.* He'd spent a lot of time mulling over the incident of a few nights before. He realized now that he had done a lot of damage to their relationship and he cursed himself for it. He'd stepped over that line of trust they'd established, but he knew that there was nothing that he could do now. All he could do was be there for her, now that she needed him, and hope that she'd forgive him later.

Joe stayed outside for almost an hour, thinking about what could have happened, and thinking what an asshole he had been, and how lucky he was that Rick had come to him. Eventually he went back into the house, and back into Midnight's room. Rick's eyes shifted to him as he walked in. Joe looked at his lifelong friend, with his partner; they looked good together, Joe decided. He wondered if it would last this time, and he found himself hoping it would. He sat down in the chair beside the bed, making no move to trade places with Rick. It was as if in changing places the first time, Rick had taken his place in Midnight's life. Joe felt the pull at his heart as the thought came to him.

Early the next morning, Joe showered and made coffee for himself and Rick. They stood in the kitchen drinking it, neither one of them speaking, both lost in their own thoughts.

"I guess I'll get going," Joe said finally. Rick nodded. "You call me if you need me here, okay?" Joe said, his voice stern because of his concern for Midnight.

"I will," Rick said, then he looked pointedly at Joe. "Is she going to be okay?" he asked, seeking reassurance from the man that knew her best.

Joe sighed, shaking his head. "I don't know, man, I really don't know. It's a lot like when her brother was killed." Rick looked at Joe for a long time, wishing he had been more positive, but he knew that Joe was just as concerned about Midnight as he was, and that Joe was just telling the truth.

"I'll keep a close eye on her," Rick said. He saw a pained look cross Joe's face.

"You've cleaned up after me a lot lately, haven't you?" Joe said, his voice self-depreciating.

"Some," Rick answered honestly, "but we've all been through a lot of shit lately."

Joe didn't answer for a minute and then he slowly extended his hand to Rick. Rick regarded his outstretched hand for a few moments, but Joe did not pull it back. Joe watched Rick, and after a few tense moments Rick's hand came out to clasp Joe's. They both smiled as they shook hands and in that moment their friendship was healed, a little different, but healed.

After checking on Midnight, and kissing her tenderly on the cheek, Joe left the house. He stopped at Randy's house. Darrell answered the door, his look instantly wary.

"We've never formally met," Joe said as he extended his hand to Darrell. "Joe Sinclair." His voice was matter of fact and in no way apologetic.

Darrell reluctantly extended his hand and the two men shook hands. Darrell glared at Joe the whole time, evidently challenging him. Joe was almost amused, silently daring him to say something. Randy approached them and broke the ice.

"Joe?" she said, very surprised to see him. He looked very haggard and tired.

"Randy, we have to talk. Can we go somewhere?" he asked, looking at Darrell and then back to her.

"Sure," Randy said, taking his arm, "we can go in the living room."

She led Joe to the small living room. Joe looked around, taking in the old, but well-kept furniture, and the faded curtains. Randy sat on the couch, and looked up at him. She seemed even more fragile here, in this place, like a waif that needed a shining knight to take her out of all this. Something pulled at Joe's heart at the sight of her. They needed to talk about what had happened a few nights before, but now was not the time.

He sat down on the couch next to her and took her hands in his. He was clearly hesitant to say what he needed to and Randy knew that something bad had happened.

"Joe?" Randy said, her voice a mere whisper. Her eyes were wide with fear for what he was going to say.

Joe swallowed, his eyes not leaving hers. "Randy, look, a lot has happened and I'm going to need your help so you're going to have to try to hold it together for me. Will you try?" His eyes pleaded with her. He didn't know how she was going to take Tim's death, or Midnight's subsequent state. He knew it was going to be shock for her. She nodded, her eyes still wide.

"Randy, Tim's been killed." His voice was soft, but Randy still felt the impact of what he had said.

She sucked in her breath in a ragged gasp, tears coming to her eyes immediately. Joe pulled her to him, hugging her. After a few moments, she sat back and looked up at him, waiting. She had the feeling that there was more.

"Midnight found him, Randy, and she's in a bad way right now, so I'm going to need you, now more than ever." He watched her closely, checking her reaction. He needed to know that she could handle what was going on. She nodded numbly.

"Is she okay?" Randy asked sounding scared.

"I wish I knew ..." He hesitated. He wasn't sure how much he should tell her. She was going to be important in helping him in the next few days. She deserved to know everything. "When Rick and I found her, she was curled up with her gun, and her finger was on the trigger."

"Oh God," Randy said, realizing the severity of what he had said. Randy couldn't believe that someone who seemed so strong, as Midnight always did, could in the blink of an eye become unstable.

It made the impact of Tim's death seem even harder. When Randy looked up at Joe, her eyes told him that she trusted him to get them all through this. After all the turmoil of the last week, her unwavering trust in him buoyed his failing spirit. He hugged her to him again, drawing some strength from her faith in him.

"This is going to be a really hard few days for everyone, Randy, and we're going to have to be the strong ones. Do you think you can do it?"

Randy tried to process everything. He was relying on her and she knew that she would be strong through this, for him, because he needed her. She nodded to him and he smiled at her, squeezing her shoulders that he still held.

Two hours later in the office, Joe met with the chief of police. He requested a funeral with honors for Tim. After some consideration, the chief agreed. Joe then had the unfortunate responsibility of calling Tim's parents in Oceanside. He had their phone number from the paperwork that Tim had filled out only a few short days before. With Randy sitting across from him, her eyes glued to his, Joe dialed their number. A woman answered on the fourth ring, sounding out of breath.

"May I speak to Mrs. Bollings?" Joe asked, his voice calm and clear, but his eyes told Randy a different story. She could tell he was dreading having to tell Tim's parents. She reached out and took his hand. He looked at her, a smile twitched at his lips. He held her hand in his, and Randy found herself looking at his ring.

"This is Mrs. Bollings," the woman answered, her voice a little hesitant.

"Mrs. Bollings this is Sergeant Joseph Sinclair, of the San Diego Police Department. Ma'am, I'm sorry to have to inform you that your son has been murdered."

"Oh my God!" Mrs. Bollings said, crying. Randy saw a look of pain cross Joe's face. He closed his eyes, and Randy squeezed his hand to remind him she was here for him. "Was it Timothy or David?"

"It was Tim, ma'am," Joe said.

"When? How? Why?" Mrs. Bollings was asking, her voice bordering on hysteria.

"Ma'am, he was murdered by a gang that he and his brother have been involved with. He was trying to help us take down their leader. They killed him, ma'am, I'm very sorry."

"That gang! I knew that David was involved, but he promised me that Timothy wouldn't be part of it. He promised me he was getting out …" Her voice trailed off, as she cried.

"Ma'am, both David and Tim were trying to get out," Joe said gently. "It's just not that easy."

"Did you know my son?" Mrs. Bollings asked then, her voice hopeful.

"Not very well, ma'am. He was mainly working with my partner, Lieutenant Chevalier. She's the one who found him …" Joe's voice trailed off, he wasn't sure if she would want to hear the details.

"Would I be able to speak to her?" Mrs. Bollings asked.

"I'm sorry, ma'am, Midnight—Lieutenant Chevalier, isn't here today. She's very upset about your son's death and I'm afraid she's not going to be up to talking to anyone for a while." The sorrow in Joe's voice conveyed his worry about his partner, and Mrs. Bollings heard it and took solace in the fact that this Lieutenant Chevalier was upset by the loss of her son too.

"I understand," Mrs. Bollings said.

"Ma'am, we've arranged for Tim to be buried with honors. I hope that will be okay."

"Yes, that would be very nice. Is that really allowed?" Mrs. Bollings asked.

"Yes, ma'am, in special cases. Tim was well thought of here, and we feel that his death is a great loss to us all. If there is anything I or any member of the department can do to help you through this time, I sincerely hope that you will call me." Joe's voice held all the sincerity that it possibly could, because he knew what it was to lose a loved one, and he knew how hard it could be.

They talked about the funeral arrangements and after a few minutes they hung up. Joe looked at Randy and she smiled at him. Tears were running down her face and Joe softly brushed them away.

"You okay?" he asked gently.

"Yes," Randy said, nodding, her eyes on him. "That was very nice. You handled it so well I think you made her feel better."

"Well, I thought this would get easier to do with experience but it doesn't. It's always hard, and it always hurts."

His eyes took on a faraway look and Randy knew he was thinking of his parents. She sat holding his hand, not saying anything, but just being there with him.

****

After Joe left, Rick went back into the bedroom, and stood looking down at Midnight. She was still asleep, her face buried in the crook of her arm. Rick lay down next to her, beginning to feel the sleeplessness of the night. Midnight stirred, as if unconsciously sensing his presence again and she moved closer to him. Rick fell asleep holding her and thinking of how nice it felt. He woke four hours later, lying on his stomach, his arms wrapped around the pillow under his head. He realized, with a start that Midnight was not in bed anymore. He jumped up, strode into the living room, and found her curled up on the couch. The stereo was on, but it was very low. Rick shivered at how cold the room was but she didn't seem to notice it.

"Babe," Rick said, reaching for the afghan that lay on her loveseat. "It's freezing in here," he said as he draped it over her.

She looked up at him, her eyes were sad, but she didn't seem as out of it as she had the night before. He touched her cheek as she closed her eyes. He knelt down next to her, looking into her eyes.

"You scared the hell out of us last night." She just looked at him, her eyes showing no emotion. "Are you okay?" he asked, his voice soft.

She nodded and leaned back against the couch. *She looks pale,* Rick thought to himself. "I'll be right back." He went into her kitchen.

A little while later, he came back carrying a mug. Sitting down, he handed it to her. "Drink this, it'll make you feel better," he said.

Midnight looked at the cup. "What is it?" she asked, her voice weak and hoarse.

"Just try it, love," Rick said. She took a drink and looked at him.

"Is it tea?" she asked, her voice surprised.

Rick laughed. "Yes, it's tea. It'll make you feel better, trust me."

"How'd you find tea here?" she said then, gesturing toward her kitchen.

"Joe must've had it here at one point or another. This particular blend has sentimental value." Rick smiled then, in a melancholy way.

"Why?" Midnight asked, sipping at the tea again, her eyes on him.

"It's the tea that my mum makes for us whenever we're not feeling well, mentally or physically. She thinks it cures everything. It does seem to have a calming effect," he said then, looking at her.

"Is that why the English drink tea?" Midnight asked, almost smiling.

"Probably," Rick said, smiling down at her.

They sat in companionable silence for a while. Eventually, she leaned against him, and his arm went around her comfortingly.

"Where's Joe?" she asked. She was still leaning against him but facing away.

"He went to the office. He's taking care of things there." Rick's voice was gentle, not wanting to upset her again.

Midnight nodded, understanding what "things" Joe would be taking care of.

"Are you two ... did you ..." She didn't finish as Rick's arm tightened around her.

He was surprised that with everything she was going through, she was still worried about his and Joe's friendship.

"Yes everything is okay. You're more important to us than any argument." His voice was strong, and she felt stronger because of it.

They spent the day sitting together in her living room. Rick would get up every so often to get Midnight something to eat, or answer the phone. Joe called three times; Rick assured him that Midnight was fine, over and over. Midnight slept off and on during the day. When she slept, she lay against Rick. Rick would lean against the arm and the back of the couch, and Midnight would snuggle against his chest, her hand on his shoulder. It was very comfortable, for both of them, and Rick found that he couldn't hide his protective feelings for her anymore. He was beginning to realize that he didn't care if she loved him or not. Just being with her made him feel complete, and he wasn't willing to give that up, even if she never loved him. He'd stay with her as long as she'd let him.

****

When Joe and Randy left the office late that afternoon they were both exhausted. They had worked steadily almost frantically to tie up the loose ends that surrounded Tim's death. Joe wanted everything wrapped up so that Midnight wouldn't have to deal with anything painful when she returned to the office.

He sincerely hoped that she would be of a state of mind to return. He wasn't totally sure of her anymore. Her words of the night before rang in his mind. "I don't want to do this anymore," she had said, and even though Joe knew that she had been hysterical, part of him was terrified that she had meant it. He wasn't sure what he would do if Midnight quit FORS. She would be quitting him because that's what it really was. The thought ran through his mind a number of times that day. Looking over at her empty office, he had felt a sick feeling deep in his stomach. He was anxious to get back to her house and see how she was. Rick had told him that she seemed fine, but Joe knew that Rick would not worry him on purpose.

When Joe pulled up in front of Randy's house, he shut the car off, looking over at her. "We did good work today," he said, smiling over at her.

She nodded, and then she reached out and touched the fading bruise on his cheek, her teeth worrying her lower lip. "Is everything okay now, between you and Rick?" she asked, her voice quiet.

Joe considered the question for a moment and then nodded. "Pretty much. There was just a lot of underlying shit going on."

Randy nodded, taking on a shy look. Joe had come to know that look meant she wanted to ask something, but was afraid to. "What is it Randy?" he asked gently.

She hesitated for a moment, her eyes looking into his. "Are you and Midnight okay?" she asked, and Joe knew what she was asking.

He sighed then. "Randy, I did something that I don't know if she can ever forgive me for. Right now, though, she needs me, so I guess we'll deal with the other stuff later."

Randy looked at him, feeling sad, for whatever rift had been caused between him and Midnight and sincerely hoping that they could work it out.

"It'll be okay," Randy said then, trying to make him feel better.

He looked at her, a grin on his face as he shook his head. "Ever the optimist, aren't you?" he said, but there was no derision in his voice.

"Someone has to be," Randy said, smiling at him.

"I guess so," Joe replied, and then he looked up and saw Darrell standing in the driveway, his fists planted firmly on his hips, his feet apart. "Oh, boy," Joe said, and Randy followed his gaze.

When she saw Darrell she got out of the car, and Joe did the same. Keeping the car between them, Joe leaned against the driver's door, facing Darrell. Darrell eyed him as Randy came up the driveway.

"Darrell, you're home early," Randy said, trying to sound casual.

"Yeah," Darrell said sarcastically, "so you and your boyfriend boss will have to say goodbye here."

"Darrell!" Randy said, surprised at his words.

Joe strode around the car, and right up to Darrell. They stood eye to eye.

"Just what is your problem, man?" Joe said angrily.

"Well, Mr. Rich Cop, you're my problem," Darrell said, his voice just as angry.

"And just what is it I've done to you?"

"You're screwing with my sister's head, and don't think I can't see it either!"

Joe's eyes went to Randy. She was standing beside him, looking up at Darrell in surprise. "She looks fine to me," Joe said, his voice calmer.

"Yeah, well she isn't fine. She walks around the house depressed half the time, other half she's moody. It's all been since she's been dating you. So I figure that you're to blame," Darrell said, his meaning pretty clear.

Joe looked at Randy again, surprised at what Darrell had said. He knew that the timing with them had been bad. He worried now that it had been worse than he realized. Suddenly, he felt like a world-class bastard.

"Randy?" he said, his voice concerned.

Randy looked up at him, clearly upset by what Darrell was saying, but unable to lie to Joe. She nodded slowly. The look in Joe's eyes was pained, and he shook his head.

"Randy, I'm sorry, I didn't realize. I just ... I didn't think." He was looking at Randy apologetically.

"Yeah, you don't think," Darrell interjected, not liking the way his sister was looking up at this cop. "You're just some slick bad ass in a Porsche who drops her as soon as he gets bored!"

Neither Joe nor Randy was looking at him; they were looking at each other. But they heard what he was saying.

Randy turned her attention to him and scowled. "That's not true, Darrell. Joe has been going through a lot lately and he certainly doesn't have the time to worry about how everyone around him is dealing with something that is really his business!"

Randy's voice was angrier than Darrell had ever heard before. He looked down at her seeing the fire in her eyes, and he was taken back by it. Why was she defending this man? He was obviously totally self-involved if he couldn't see how Randy had been feeling lately, so why would she want to defend him? Darrell wasn't sure, but he knew he didn't like it. He looked at Joe then, his eyes blazing with his own anger.

"Are you happy now?" Darrell asked. "Now my own baby sister is defending you. Does that make you feel like a man, Sinclair?" His voice took on a derogatory tone.

Joe had to stifle the desire to punch Darrell in the face; he didn't want to upset Randy further.

After a few tense moments, Joe shook his head, his eyes on Randy again. She was looking at him, tears in her eyes. He could see fear there too, and he assumed that she was afraid that he and Darrell would get into a fight. In actuality, Randy was terrified that Joe would think that she was too unstable to handle the pressures of dating and working for him and would break it off with her to make Darrell happy.

Darrell stood tense and ready for a fight; he was shocked when Sinclair put his hands up, in a surrendering gesture. "I'm not going to fight you Darrell," Joe said, sounding defeated. Randy swallowed hard, afraid of what he was going to say next. "But by the same token, I'm not letting your sister go either. She means a lot to me and, regardless of how things have been lately, she continues to mean a lot to me. I'm sorry if it's causing you problems but I'm not giving her up." Joe's voice was sure and calm. Randy watched him with a smile on her face.

Darrell looked back at Joe for a long time, not saying anything, realizing that he had no answer to what Joe had said.

"Fine, then," Darrell said, his face a mask of anger. He gave Joe one more measured look, and then turned on his heel and walked back up the driveway. Randy watched him go, a sad look on her face.

"Randy, why didn't you talk to me?" Joe said, putting his hand on her arm. She looked at him and shrugged. "Well, I guess I've been a little out of touch lately," Joe said, his voice self-depreciating. Then he looked at her, his eyes holding hers. "But from now on, I want you to talk to me, do you understand?"

Randy nodded, her eyes very serious. Joe hugged her and kissed the top of her head.

"When this all blows over, we'll talk, okay? I'll see you tomorrow," he said.

"Okay," Randy said, smiling up at him.

Joe walked back over to his car, and before getting in he flipped her a casual salute, to which she laughed. He got into his car and drove off. Randy hugged herself, glad that he had cared about how she was feeling. She knew that Darrell would probably be harder to deal with now, but she didn't care, because she knew that Joseph Michael Sinclair cared about her.

When he got to Midnight's house, he used his key to unlock the door. He found Midnight and Rick on the couch in the living room. Midnight was asleep, and Rick was holding her. Rick looked up as Joe entered the room.

"Hey man," he said.

"Hey," Joe replied, sitting down across from where Rick and Midnight were. "She okay?" he asked.

"She's a lot better today. How did things go at the office?" Rick asked, taking in Joe's haggard look.

He knew that this wasn't going easy on Joe either, but Joe was hanging on, and Rick was amazed once again at Joe's tenacity.

Joe scrubbed at his face with his hands. "Okay, I guess. His mother took it pretty well. She wanted to talk to Night though."

"Did you tell her that Midnight is a little indisposed at this time?" Rick asked, worried about Midnight having to deal with a hysterical mother.

"Yeah, and I think it made her feel a little better. You know, that we're upset about his death too …" Joe's voice trailed off, as Midnight stirred. She opened her eyes, and looked at him.

"I thought I heard your voice," she said, her own voice quiet.

Joe smiled at her. "Sorry, love, I didn't mean to wake you."

"It's okay," Midnight said, sitting up.

Her hair was tousled and she looked very young, but the sorrow in her eyes told a different story.

"Midnight," Joe said, looking at her seriously, "are you okay?"

She nodded, tears coming to her eyes.

Joe shook his head, grinning at her. "Yeah, I can tell." He stood, moving to kneel in front of her, his eyes pained. "Night I'm sorry about everything." The sorrow in his voice made the tears in her eyes spill over. She reached out to him and he hugged her to him.

Rick watched the exchange with a lump in his throat. He was glad that they were friends again. He hated the idea that their relationship had been destroyed because of something as uncontrollable as unchecked anger and emotion.

Midnight reveled in Joe's embrace. Between Rick and Joe, she felt cocooned in security, like nothing could intrude and hurt her anymore. She knew that she was going to have to deal with her feelings about Tim's death, and would have to attend yet another funeral for a boy who died way before his time. She took comfort in knowing that Joe and Rick would be there to support her through all of it. She also knew that soon she would have to deal with her feelings for Rick, but she didn't want to do that just now. She was too sensitized to everything right now. The last thing she wanted to tackle were feelings that were absolutely foreign to her. For now, she was happy to have the security of these two Englishmen and their gallant ways.

Chapter 11

Two days later, Midnight stood in front of her mirror with haunted eyes. She wore a black dress of Victorian lace. Her hair was pulled back from her face, held by pearl combs and she wore the lightest amount of makeup consisting of mascara, blush, and a touch of lipstick. Rick was stunned by her appearance; he couldn't help but think about how beautiful she looked, despite the sobriety of the day. Midnight turned and looked at Rick, her eyes sad and full of dread. Rick went to her and she stepped into his embrace.

"Are you going to be okay, Night?" he asked, his lips near her ear.

She looked up at him, her face set in determination. "I have to do this, Rick, I have to. He was …" Her voice trailed off as tears came to her eyes again.

"Okay babe, okay," Rick said soothingly, as he hugged her again.

Joe walked in. Both he and Rick were dressed in dark suits. At any other time Midnight would have been amazed that they could dress up so nicely, but today, she wasn't seeing anything.

Rick looked over at Joe, his concern for Midnight's well-being reflected in Joe's eyes. Midnight stepped away from him and looked at Joe.

"We need to go," Joe said, his voice very sober.

Midnight nodded as she walked to the door. Joe and Rick looked at each other for a long moment. Both men had been very worried about how she was going to handle the strain of this day. They made a silent agreement to watch her carefully and protect her from everything they could. But Midnight was remembering another funeral, another time.

Joe drove the Jaguar that he had bought years before. It was still in mint condition, and was appropriately black, befitting the occasion. He drove to Randy's house first, and went to the door to get her. Randy answered the door; she too was wearing black. Her dress was black cotton with a black jacket over it. Her hair was pulled back into a French twist, and much like Midnight wore the smallest amount of makeup. She looked very subdued. Joe put his arm around her as they walked out to the car. He looked back over his shoulder, catching sight of Darrell in the front doorway, but he didn't say anything.

They arrived at the church where the service was to be held and walked inside. Midnight and Randy walked in front with Joe and Rick behind them. They made a very striking foursome, and many heads turned despite the sad occasion. They were very surprised to see that there were at least three hundred police officers in dress uniform standing among the pews of the church. All twenty-five members of FORS were in attendance. Midnight hesitated, her eyes taking in the officers, and then going to the coffin in the front of the church. Randy reached over and touched her hand. Midnight looked at the younger woman, her eyes showing a little bit of surprise at Randy's apparent strength. Midnight smiled slightly at Randy and squeezed her hand. Joe and Rick exchanged a surprised look behind the two women. Midnight, still clasping Randy's hand, started to walk again. Many of the officers inclined their heads to Midnight in a gesture of respect. She inclined hers in response. She saw Tom Ryan then and went over to hug him.

"I'm sorry you're having to go through this again, little one," Tom said in her ear.

Tom had realized the minute he'd heard about Tim, what would be going through her mind. When they parted, Midnight had tears in her eyes again. Rick stood behind her, his hands on her shoulders comfortingly.

"Thanks for coming, Tom," Midnight said, smiling at him through her tears. Tom nodded, eyeing Rick, Joe, and Randy who were standing around Midnight like a shield.

"It looks like you've got a good support group this time, but if you need anything, you call me," Tom said, his eyes on Midnight. She nodded to him.

There was movement in the back of the church then and Joe saw that it was what must be Tim's family arriving. Joe and Rick ushered Midnight and Randy to a seat in one of the front pews. Joe and Rick flanked Midnight and Randy.

During the course of the service, silent tears fell from Randy's eyes, and at seeing them, Joe reached over and took her hand in his. She didn't look at him, she just held onto his hand with both of hers.

Rick glanced at Midnight frequently. She wasn't crying, but he could see by the faraway look in her eyes that she was reliving her brother's funeral. After a few minutes, he put his arm around her, and felt her lean heavily against him. He knew this was hitting her hard, but he also knew how strong she was. She was determined to make it through this, and Rick was determined to help her.

After the service, they made their way to the gravesite. When Midnight got out of the car, she hesitated again, leaning back against the car with her eyes closed. Rick noticed it first, he turned to her his eyes filled with concern.

"Midnight," he said.

She was shaking her head with tears flowing from her eyes. "I can't do this I can't do this, not again," she was saying softly as if she were talking to herself. Rick looked at Joe who had come up beside him.

At an unspoken agreement, Joe moved to Midnight. Without a word, he took her in his arms. She held him tightly, holding on to him as if she were drowning.

"Shhh," Joe said.

She was crying now. He was stroking her back, his head bowed down to hers.

"I can't, Joe, I can't," she said, her voice desperate. "It's my fault, I can't."

"It isn't your fault," said a voice from behind them.

They all turned to see a young man of about twenty-three standing with an older couple. None of them had noticed the three standing just off to the side, watching the scene. The young man who had spoken was obviously David Bollings. He was looking at Midnight with regret and sorrow in his eyes.

"It's my fault he's dead, don't blame yourself. You were trying to help him." His voice was shaky, but calm.

Midnight regarded this young man for a few moments, tears still in her eyes. She shook her head at him. "It's not your fault, either then," she said, her voice stronger now. "Your brother joined the gang on his own and actually, you probably kept him alive longer by being in it with him. Tell me …" Midnight's voice took on a mentoring tone. Rick and Joe exchanged a knowing look over her head. "How many times did you step in for him, and save his butt? How many times before he joined the gang, did he tell you that if he didn't join your gang, he'd join another one?"

David Bollings was looking at her with surprise on his face. "How did you know that?" he asked quietly.

"Trust me, I've been there. You can't blame yourself, David. It's very sad that Tim died, but if there's anything I've learned, it's that everything has its meaning, so we have to find out what that is." Midnight looked at the older couple then. "Are you Tim's parents?"

They nodded.

"You should be very proud of both of your sons. Tim was working with me to try to stop this gang, at his own personal risk …" Her voice trailed off, as she stated the obvious. "I understand that David was doing his best to extricate himself from the gang's hold but it's never as easy as it sounds. What David is going to need right now is his family around him. Please don't blame him for what has happened. He had no way to control it I know these kind of people, and if David had done anything, you'd be burying him today too." Midnight's voice was soothing, but firm. She didn't want David's parents to hate him, like her own parents hated her.

Mrs. Bollings looked at Midnight for a long moment with tears in her eyes; she had realized when she had seen her at the church that this was Lieutenant Chevalier. She had been surprised at her slight appearance.

She had been very impressed with Sergeant Sinclair's demeanor on the phone the day he had told her that her son had been killed. He had been sincere in his sympathies. And now Midnight Chevalier had just put aside her grief to try to help the Bollings work through theirs. She was very impressed by what the young woman had said. She was also touched at how much the death of Tim had affected her. But even so, she was able to be strong for David. Emma Bollings made a mental note to write to the chief of police about this astounding young woman and her staff.

"Thank you," Emma Bollings said, tears in her eyes. Then she looked at Joe. "You are Sergeant Sinclair?" she asked. Joe nodded. "Thank you so much for the lovely service you arranged, and everything you've done to make this day go easier on us all."

Her eyes showed sincere gratitude. Her husband, who had yet to speak, nodded. It was obvious that he was very upset by the death of his son. Emma Bollings moved to Midnight and to Midnight's surprise hugged her.

"Thank you," Emma said again, in Midnight's ear.

When they parted, there were tears in Midnight's eyes again. She nodded to Tim's mother.

The gravesite ceremony was punctuated by a brief statement from the chief of police. Midnight had declined to speak simply because she didn't feel that she could pull it off with the dignity that she felt Tim deserved without becoming a tearful mess. An American flag was retired and given to Tim's mother, who cried and nodded to the chief when he handed it to her and saluted. Taps was played and a twenty-one-gun salute signaled the end of the funeral. Midnight stood with her eyes staring straight ahead and her chin up in quiet dignity. Every so often a tear would stream down her cheek, but she was no longer outwardly hysterical.

Rick stood behind and slightly to the side of Midnight, his hand behind her elbow, his eyes watchful for any sign that she might not be able to handle all of it. But she did.

Randy stood by watching the funeral with a quiet dignity of her own. She could feel Joe standing right behind her and she drew strength from his presence. At one point, she glanced back at him and saw the stricken look in his eyes. Knowing that he was thinking of his parents, Randy reached her hand behind her and took his hand, squeezing it gently. When she glanced at him again, he gave her a small smile, but continued to hold her hand.

The members of FORS looked like a gang that somebody had tried to dress up. They looked very uncomfortable, but as professional as the motley group could look. They were very respectful of the sadness of the occasion. Spider and Tammy were even in attendance. Although Spider had not returned to work yet, and had not known Tim, he still felt the loss.

After the funeral, the members of FORS congregated around Midnight and Joe, lending their support to their fearless leaders. They reluctantly made way for the chief, who had come over to speak with Midnight, but they all stood by warily. They were ever protective of their boss, even with the chief.

"Lieutenant Chevalier," the chief said, taking her hand. "I'm very sorry about your loss."

Midnight nodded, looking down, trying to keep her tears from starting again.

"I just spoke with Mrs. Bollings and she wanted me to be sure to convey to you and Sergeant Sinclair"—the chief glanced up at Joe— "that she appreciates your efforts and your gestures through this whole incident. She also wanted me to let you know, Midnight, that she in no way holds you or any member of FORS responsible for Tim's death."

"Thank you, Chief," Midnight said, her voice quiet. The chief nodded.

"Now, Midnight, I want you to let me know if you need anything from the rest of the department to catch this gang. I want them taken down, and I know that your unit," his eyes touched on each and every member of FORS, "is capable of doing it." His voice was strong and sure, and every member of FORS stood a little bit taller at the sound of them.

"Damn straight!" someone said, and the everyone's surprise, the chief laughed.

"Keep me apprised of your progress, Lieutenant," the chief said then, squeezing her hands.

She nodded again. "I will, sir." She looked up at him, her eyes burning with the usual fire that he saw in them, and he truly believed she would not fail him.

As the chief walked away, he thought about Midnight Chevalier. She had certainly proved to be a valuable asset to the Department. When she had first brought the idea of FORS to him, he had been a little skeptical that the unit would work. How did one recruit and control gang members? But FORS had worked, very well indeed. There had been a couple of incidents when someone from the team gotten too rough with a gang member, but Midnight kept a pretty tight rein on her people and they were obviously devoted to her.

The chief found it astounding that these young people, many of whom had run with a gang for a long time, could be so loyal and determined working for a law enforcement agency. In fact, Midnight had recommended a couple of them for the police academy and the chief was seriously considering approving those requests. Midnight had been nominated for a statewide Officer of the Year award by the attorney general. The chief found himself ever happy that he had approved Midnight's idea from the get go. It made him look good to have officers of their caliber working for him, and he knew it.

Joe, Rick, Midnight, and Randy were getting into Joe's car when Mrs. Bollings approached them. They had been invited back to the Bollings house, but Midnight wasn't sure she could handle anymore, and so Joe had let them know that they wouldn't be coming. Mrs. Bollings approached Midnight who was standing with her back to the car, her hands holding tightly to the door handle behind her.

"Ms. Chevalier," Emma Bollings said with a warm smile, "I just wanted to thank you again, for everything, and to tell you that I think that you are a very incredible woman. In my quest for knowledge about my son's activities, I had occasion to learn of your own beginnings, and subsequent achievements, and they are astounding. You should be very proud of yourself."

There was no derision in the older woman's voice, only warmth and understanding. Midnight smiled at her, still feeling guilt over Tim's death. "But you're not proud of yourself are you? You're thinking that you could have done something to protect my son, but you're wrong. Your words to David proved that, and perhaps it would have been your funeral your friends here were attending today. Ms. Chevalier, my son was very special to me, I loved him very much, but blaming the person that is trying to keep things like this from happening again, isn't going to bring Tim back and I know that. It wasn't your fault, Ms. Chevalier, and I sincerely hope that you will come to believe that soon." Mrs. Bollings looked at Midnight for a few minutes, her eyes concerned and sad.

"Thank you, Mrs. Bollings. That does mean a lot to me. I only hope that you will stay in touch with us, so we can let you know when we catch your son's murderer. And be assured, ma'am that we will catch him." Midnight's voice was strong and determined and Emma Bollings didn't doubt her for a minute.

Joe, Midnight, Randy, and Rick went back to Midnight's house, none of them wanting to be alone. It was Midnight that went to the wet bar first. She picked up a bottle of Southern Comfort and a shot glass, and sat back down on the couch. The other three watched her as she poured and downed three shots in a row. Joe got up and went over to retrieve a bottle of tequila and two shot glasses, one for him and one for Rick. He looked at Randy, holding up a third glass.

"I'm only twenty," she said softly.

"There are two cops in this room that didn't hear that, and we won't tell them," Joe said, smiling at her.

"Okay," Randy said, nodding.

Joe and Rick knocked back a couple of shots. Midnight was now nursing the half glass of the Southern Comfort she'd poured. Randy ended up with Baileys. Everyone sat around in a comfortable silence for a while. Every now and then, someone would say something and a small discussion would start. For the most part, they mulled over their own thoughts. After a couple of hours, they all decided that they were hungry.

Midnight suggested they order Chinese food. "I know the best take out Chinese in the world!" she said, and that reminded her of

Mike. "Hey," she said, looking at Joe, "you know I don't remember seeing Mike Harlow at the funeral today."

"Maybe he was on duty. He usually works days, doesn't he?" Joe replied.

"Yeah, but he's not one to miss something like this. Besides even if it was his regular shift, he's a training sergeant. I don't know, it's just a little weird." Midnight shrugged, it was hard to know why he hadn't shown up.

They ordered dinner and ate when it arrived. An hour later Joe stood looking at Randy. She was half-asleep.

"I better take Randy home, before her brother calls missing persons or something." He grinned down at Randy and she stood up.

Midnight stood too and reached up to hug Joe. "Thanks, for everything," she said, her voice soft. Joe squeezed her a little tighter in response.

"Anything for you, love," he replied, his lips right next to her ears. The sound of his voice brought tears to Midnight's eyes, as well as to Randy's who had overheard him.

Midnight turned to Randy and hugged her. When they parted, Midnight took both of Randy's hands. "You've been a kind of silent party in all of this, but I want you to know, that I appreciate everything you have done these last few weeks. I know you've helped Joe through some of this too, and I also appreciate that. I know that this job is causing some friction for you at home, and, I just want you to know that if you ever need anything, a place to stay, a shoulder to cry on, whatever, I'm here, okay?"

Randy nodded, with tears in her eyes. Randy respected Midnight more than anyone she had ever met, for all she had accomplished and all she had gone through, especially recently. It meant a lot to her that Midnight was willing to be there for her. She hoped that someday she'd be able to return the favor.

Joe and Randy left, and Midnight turned to Rick.

"And, as for you," Midnight said, smiling at him.

"What? You're kicking me out too?"

"Would you be real hurt if I told you I wanted to be alone to-night?" she asked, her eyes showing her concern for hurting his feelings.

"No, I wouldn't be mortally wounded, but if you need me I expect you to call me," he said sternly.

"God," she said, making a face. "Do you realize that you're start-ing to sound exactly like Joe?"

"What do you expect? I've been friends with the man for twenty-two years!"

"Yeah, I guess that would tend to warp someone," Midnight said, smiling.

"Warp, that's a good word for it." They laughed then.

Rick stood up and she walked him to the door. Before he opened it, he turned to her and held out his arms. She stepped into his embrace and he hugged her to him.

"Hey," Midnight said, stepping back and looking up at him, as if she had read his thoughts. "I will see you tomorrow, you know. You hug me like you're never going to see me again."

Rick laughed. "Yeah, I guess you're right."

"I'll see you tomorrow then," Midnight said.

"Yes, ma'am," Rick said, flipping her a little wave as he walked to his car.

She watched him drive away, and then she closed the door. She leaned against the door for a few minutes with her eyes closed. Then she went to take a shower. When she went to bed an hour later, she found, to her dismay, that she missed having Rick there to hold her. That bothered her; she hated the fact that she had become so dependent on him. It wasn't fair to him. She was surprised at how nice he had been over the last few days. She didn't know about him though, he could be so intense sometimes. Midnight was one of the people who believed that there was one person in the world for every other person, and that when you met that one person you were meant for, you just knew it right away. Since she had not felt an instant kindred spirit in Rick, she chalked him up to yet another man in her life that would come and go.

Her thoughts turned to Joe, she was glad everything seemed back to normal with him. She knew that what had happened between them had permanently changed their relationship. But in a way, she knew that it was good for both of them.

As if he knew she'd been thinking about him, he called her.

"Hey," he said smoothly, "Rick tells me you're soloing it tonight."

"News travels fast around here, doesn't it?" Her voice held no anger, only surprise.

"Well, he worries about you, just like me."

"So what is the story with Rick, anyway?"

"What do you mean?"

"Well, when I first met him, I thought he was a player like you. Then when we slept together, I was convinced he was a player. But now, with all that's happened … he's been here for me. I mean, do all Englishmen have that damned gallant streak in them?"

"Yeah, they breed it into us," Joe said, laughing. "Actually, you were right the first time, Rick is definitely a player. Hell back home he'd have three or four girls on the hook at a time, all dying for his attention. But, I think the thing is, you are different from any girl he's ever dated, and maybe you're the kind of change he needs."

"Whoa, hold on there now partner, I'm not looking to be anybody's change, okay? I mean you know my philosophy and Rick just isn't him so don't go off buying a wedding dress or anything."

"Alright, alright," Joe said, knowing that he shouldn't bug her too much. "You win."

"So what about you and Randy?" Midnight asked then.

"What about us?" Joe asked, grinning at Randy who sat next to him.

"Oh come on, Sinclair, I can see things have changed there," Midnight said curiously.

"Okay, you're right," he said, realizing that Midnight had missed a few things where he and Randy were concerned. But he didn't want to talk at that point, since Randy was there. "We'll catch up soon on that, okay?"

"Okay, that makes sense," Midnight said, catching his tone, and guessing Randy was still with him.

She was happy about that. Joe needed someone and it wasn't a place Midnight felt was right for her to be anymore. It was time for both of them to move on with their love lives.

"So, are you okay?" Joe asked, concerned.

"Yes, I guess I am. Today was a killer, but we made it through."

"Yeah what you said to Tim's mother, that was good."

"Well, I think her attitude helped a lot, but I was determined to try and keep David from getting the blame. I've been there, and it's not a good place to be."

"I know, love, but it was nice of you to be so strong for them. I was extremely proud to be associated with you today."

"Gee, like you're not any other day," Midnight said, in mock anger.

"You know what a meant."

"Yeah, I know." She stifled a yawn then.

"Look I'm keeping you awake, I'm going to go. I just wanted to check on you myself."

"Okay, boss, I'm fine," she replied.

"Goodnight."

"Byc."

Joe hung up the phone, looking over at Randy. They were parked at the beach. Joe had decided they needed to clear things up between them before another day passed.

"Now," he said, turning to her as he slipped his cell phone into his pocket, "we need to talk."

Randy nodded, somewhat worried about what that meant.

Joe moved forward on the seat, reaching out to touch her cheek with his hand.

"I'm sorry," he said, surprising her, "I shouldn't have allowed Taylor to get to me like she did."

"Joe, she basically accused you of killing your parents for their money," Randy said, reaching up to touch his face. "I can't blame you for letting her get to you."

He smiled, blowing his breath out. "Okay," he said, nodding, "but I could have handled things better. I shouldn't have shut you out."

"You did what you needed to do."

Joe looked back at her for a long moment, narrowing his eyes slightly. "You're far too used to people treating you badly, Randissi Curtis," he said, his tone chiding. Randy started to shake her head but his finger on her lips stopped her. "You are, and you need to stop," he told her firmly.

"Joe, I can't ask too much of you," she told him.

"Why not?"

She didn't reply. She just shrugged, her eyes dropping from him.

"What are you afraid of, Randy?"

She shook her head, still not looking at it.

"You're afraid I'll leave you," he said, his tone matter of fact.

"Everyone does," she said softly, tears in her eyes.

"Well," he said, turning her eyes up to him with his finger under her chin. "I'm not goin' anywhere," he told her, leaning down to kiss her lips softly.

Her hands reached up to wrap around his neck. It was exactly what she'd needed to hear from him. They kissed for a little while, then talked a little more. When he dropped her off at home, Randy watched him drive away, hugging herself. She couldn't believe she was lucky enough to meet a man like him.

****

The next morning, Midnight was feeling very refreshed and ready to face the day that lay ahead. After a quick shower, she blow-dried her hair, partially, because she was already in a hurry to get to her day's tasks. She was in her car on her way to the office within forty-five minutes of waking up.

Once in the office, she posted a notice that she was calling a unit meeting in the conference room at ten that morning. Many people were surprised to see her in the office, more still at the fact that she seemed okay. People that knew her better chalked it up to her usual strength of spirit. Midnight worked industriously until Joe wandered into her office at nine.

"Hey," he said, sitting down in his usual spot, "what's this meeting about?"

Midnight looked up at him, smiling at his boots that were, as usual, up on her desk. "Well, it's kind of a pep talk slash strategy session actually."

"I see," Joe replied. "You need me to do anything?"

"Nope," Midnight replied, "got it all under control."

Joe looked at her for a long moment, not sure if this was even the same woman he had talked to the night before. She was all business and the epitome of focus. "Okay then," he said slowly, as he stood. "I guess I'll see you in there."

Midnight nodded, already going back to work at her computer.

Rick met Joe coming out of Midnight's office.

"What's this meeting about?" Rick asked, his head nodding toward Midnight's office.

"She says it's a pep talk," Joe shrugged. "I don't know."

"She seem okay?" Rick asked then.

"Yeah, she's back to her usual intense, distracted self," Joe replied, grinning at Rick.

"Well then, I guess we'll just see what our Lady Midnight has up her sleeve then."

An hour later, Joe and Rick lounged by the head table in the conference room as everyone filed in. There was a lot of murmuring going on; somebody had started a rumor that Midnight might be resigning from FORS. Rick and Joe had tried to kill the rumor before it really got going, but it was obvious from all the tense faces in the room that they hadn't managed to nip it soon enough.

A few minutes after ten, Midnight walked in. She was wearing black jeans, black boots, and a sapphire-blue shirt. Rick couldn't help but admire her as she walked in. For all that was going on, she just looked so beautiful. She also looked very determined and both Rick and Joe were relieved. They had kind of wondered if the rumor might have some truth to it. She had said some things the night Tim had been killed that made the rumor possible. But the way the carried herself as she entered the conference room and made her way to the head table put instant death to that rumor. Everyone in the room seemed to relax simultaneously.

Midnight stood in front of the room. She put the folder she was carrying on the table in front of her, and she looked at the members of her unit. Her face was very serious.

"Thanks for coming everyone," she said evenly. "I'm sure you all know that Tim's death hit me pretty hard and I'm sure that you also know who killed him, our elusive leader of the Scorpions." She looked down and took out a page, and held it up.

"I was just informed this morning that Sergeant Mike Harlow was in a serious car accident yesterday on his way to the funeral. It was of a suspicious nature ..."

Joe and Rick moved toward her, but she held up her hand, looking at them, and shaking her head as if to tell them that she was okay.

She turned to the group again. "Fortunately, Sergeant Harlow is going to be okay. I'm sure all of you know that Mike Harlow is a personal friend of mine. But what many of you don't know is that he helped me out a week back, by stopping a guy that was tailing me and subsequently arresting him." She looked around at everyone then.

"It is my belief that the Scorpions tried to kill Mike for assisting me, to keep him from talking to me about the person he stopped."

Everyone in the room started to talk; they were uncomfortable with the direction of the meeting. The Scorpions were putting hits out on cops? How crazy was this leader anyway? Midnight held up her hand for silence.

"The thing here is, folks, these guys aren't playing games, and they've been hitting real close to home lately and you know what?"

Her eyes turned to ice then, as did her voice. "They're really starting to piss me off."

Everyone cheered. They knew that Midnight wasn't the type to run from a fight, but her reaction to Tim's death had shaken some of their confidence in her invulnerability. That confidence had now been restored. Joe and Rick exchanged a look of surprise at her vehemence, but Joe shrugged, shaking his head. He knew how strong she could be, but his unwavering belief in her strength had been damaged by her emotional state the night of Tim's death too. It was obvious now that she was definitely back to her old self, and Joe was glad. The last thing he ever wanted was to lose her over something as impossible to predict as Tim's death had been. It had terrified him and shaken him to his very core. She could have killed herself before any of them knew what was happening, and her subsequent overwhelming grief had made it difficult to believe she would ever be the same. But here she was, the same old Midnight, ready to take on the world again.

She talked about the Scorpions; what they knew so far, what she had ascertained from Mike's comments the night she had been to his house. She gave them the description of the guy that Tim had given her and explained how the police mug shot at the county jail had matched that description.

"Unfortunately for our little Scorpion friends, they can't kill off the whole police force," Midnight said, with a nasty glint in her eyes.

It was obvious that she was out for revenge. They had killed Tim and tried to kill Mike, and they were going to pay. Midnight announced then that they were going to run twenty-four-hour surveillance on three different houses.

"I think this Daniel Robbins, might be at one of them, or will show up there," she said.

She read off the list of shifts she had worked out and partnered people up. Rick and Joe were partnered. Midnight's name was not on the list. "I'm going to keep an eye on things from here," she said, by way of explanation. She had always made a point of doing the same dirty work she assigned her people to, and she always felt it necessary to explain when she wasn't included in one of those duties. No one ever faulted her though. "And as for the rest of your cases, boys and girls, this one is top priority. I've got tons of overtime already allocated for this case, but I don't want anyone overdoing it, okay."

Many in the group laughed ruefully, and Midnight smiled in response. It was well known that if anyone overdid it on a regular basis it was either Midnight or Joe, or both. "Okay, point taken," Midnight said, smiling at her group, "but let's be real careful out there guys. I don't want any more incidents, okay?" Everyone nodded seriously. She adjourned the meeting and everyone filed out, talking amongst themselves.

Midnight went back to her office. Her phone was ringing when she walked in. "Lieutenant Chevalier," she answered. There was a moment of silence. "Hello?" she said into the receiver.

"Midnight," came a vaguely familiar voice on the other end.

"Yes, who is this?" Midnight asked, glancing up as Rick and Joe entered her office, with Randy not far behind.

"Midnight, it's me, your father."

Midnight closed her eyes for a moment, sitting down heavily in her chair. Joe and Rick were at her side immediately, but she shook her head at them. They both stood by, watching her anxiously.

"What do you want?" Midnight asked, her voice shaky.

"We saw your picture in the paper this morning from that boy's funeral," her father said hesitantly.

"So you called to tell me again how I killed your son?" Midnight's voice had turned to ice and she narrowed her eyes.

Joe looked at her sharply, his face showing surprise. He knew who she was talking to.

"No, Midnight, can't we start again? Thomas's death was so long ago."

"And you think you can just call me and I'm supposed to come running home now?" Midnight asked, disbelieving.

"We are your parents, Midnight it's only right that—"

"Hold on here!" Midnight interrupted him, making a cutting gesture with her hand, her eyes flashing angrily. "Who the fuck do you think you're talking to? I'm the daughter you cut out of your life, remember? I'm the one that killed your baby boy, remember?" Her voice was thick with anger, even as her eyes filled with tears at the memory of that painful day over eleven years before. Joe moved around the desk, and kneeled next to her chair, taking her free hand. She shook her head but didn't pull her hand away.

"Midnight, you have to understand we were upset we had just lost our son," Jack Chevalier said sternly.

"Your son? My God, I was your daughter, he was my brother, I watched him die." Her voice broke then, and her tears started to flow.

"Yes, but why was that, Midnight? Why was he there, because of your gang. Your gang, Midnight. You let him join it and you let him fight. Can't you see our side of this?" her father said desperately.

Midnight didn't reply for a few moments, she was having trouble breathing, with the shock of the emotions she was feeling. She felt betrayal, anger, hatred, sadness, and an overwhelming need to hit someone. Her hand tightened in Joe's grip, but he was ready for that, and held her hand tightly. She looked at him and his eyes bore into hers, as if willing her to calm down, and handle this. She took a couple of deep breaths, glancing at Rick, who was also watching her, concern written all over his face. She swallowed hard, as if swallowing her anger.

"No, I guess I can't see your side of it, Mr. Chevalier. I do see that this conversation is over, however." She hung the phone up. She turned and looked at Joe, her eyes still affected by the emotions running through her. He held his arms out to her and she moved into them.

"Who was that?" Rick asked.

"Her father, I believe," Joe said, and Midnight nodded affirmation, as she sat back in her chair. Her eyes were guarded, but it was obvious she had been shaken badly by the call.

"You haven't talked to him since your brother's funeral?" Rick asked, making a good guess.

Midnight shook her head, looking up at him.

"And he just called you out of the blue?" Rick asked then.

"No," Midnight said, expelling her pent up breath, shaking her head, "they saw my picture in the paper, at Tim's funeral. I guess it made them homesick for someone to kick around."

"What did he say, Night?" Joe asked.

"He said they wanted to start again with me." She laughed ruefully then. "Yeah, start accusing me of killing Thomas again, is what I guess he meant. He said that I should try to see it from their side, bastard." The last word was said with much venom, her eyes were flashing angrily again. "Jack and Carrie don't realize that they lost the right to dictate anything to me when I was eight and they decide to go back to the party life they'd led before they had us," Midnight said, disgusted. "We were nothing to them, nothing, just people in the house with them. They didn't care who we were, what we did, or how we survived, as long as we didn't interfere with their binges."

Joe nodded, having heard from Midnight what garbage her parents were. Nothing like his parents had been. Midnight's had been alcoholic drug addicts who apparently overnight forgot they actually had kids. It had been a wonder social services had never stepped in. Joe supposed it was because Midnight had taken care of herself and Thomas. She'd made sure Thomas had something to eat, clothes to wear, and a place to live, such that it was. Midnight had also made sure that Thomas had gone to school, wanting better for him than she'd had. It had all been for naught when he'd been killed.

Now Jack Chevalier thought he could contact his daughter after all these years and she'd welcome the contact with an open heart. Not likely.

"What a jerk," Randy said from behind them.

Midnight, Joe, and Rick looked over at her and Randy looked chagrined, thinking she'd spoken out of turn. But then she drew up her courage, and walked over to Midnight's desk.

"I mean, what kind of parents can abandon their child, especially when she needs them the most. Don't they care about what you went through? What kind of people are they?" Her voice indicated her distaste for them.

"Not very nice people," Joe enjoined.

"Really," Rick added.

Midnight looked at the three of them, gathered around her like a human shield. It felt good to have these people care about her so much that they would stand with her no matter what happened. She smiled and the other three laughed nervously, not sure what to make of her change in moods.

"Oh, God you guys lighten up!" Midnight said, laughing. "Jesus, I guess old Jack was feeling a little brave. Hopefully he won't get his courage up again anytime in the near future, I hate bad PR." She made a face then, and the other three couldn't help but laugh.

CHAPTER 12

The surveillance started that night. Joe and Rick had the first shift at a house in East San Diego. Nothing turned up, and after five hours, both men were really bored.

"So, is everything between you and Midnight resolved?" Rick asked, looking over at Joe.

"Yeah, I think so, although I don't think our relationship will never be the same as it was. It's okay though, I think we need to move on, you know?"

"Yeah, maybe," Rick said.

"So where's your head at when it comes to her?" Joe asked.

"Well," Rick said, his eyes trailing out the window, "you know, when I met her, she blew me away. She's so incredible looking, and she's got some serious fire. But then we got together, and I decided she had too much fire, even for me, so I tried to stand back. But man, she's damn hard to stay away from, isn't she?"

Joe nodded in response, grinning, knowing what Rick was saying; he'd had a hard time with that himself a few times.

"Anyway," Rick continued, "then when all that shit happened with you and her, and she needed someone, I knew I had to be there for her. I told myself it was out of loyalty to you, but I found myself feeling very possessive of her. You know me, Joe, I don't ever care about a girl that much, not to the point of fighting my best friend over her!"

"And that you did," Joe said, with no anger in his voice, only irony.

"Yeah, but I guess what surprised me, was how I felt that night she locked herself in her house. Joe, I didn't care what I had to do to get to her, and when we got in, and I saw her with that gun, that scared the hell out of me. I guess I knew then that I was falling for her ..." Rick's voice trailed off then, as he looked at Joe for something akin to sympathy.

Joe shook his head slowly, as if not believing that Rick could be so dumb. "Oh man," Joe said sighing deeply, "yeah, that's what I thought. Damn, Rick, I warned you not to start up with her, now you're stuck." He shook his head again, looking out the window.

"And she doesn't feel the same, does she?" Rick said, his voice very matter of fact, but Joe could see in his eyes that he was begging him to differ.

Joe looked at his best friend for a long time, then he slowly shook his head. "I tried to warn you, man," Joe said lamely.

Rick gave a short laugh. "Yeah, it's kind of like saying that breathing will kill you. It's little hard not to, but it will kill you." Rick shook his head then leaned against the passenger side window. "Shit man, what am I going to do? I can't stay away from her, and I can't make her feel something she doesn't. I'm fucked, aren't I?"

"Basically," Joe said.

Rick was silent for a while, then he shrugged. "Well, to hell with it, I'm just going to be with her, if she'll even let me, and to hell with love."

"Now, there's a healthy attitude," Joe said, sarcastically, shaking his head, but smiling at Rick's determination.

"What choice do I have?"

Joe shook his head and laughed. "Really, none."

They were silent then, each lost in thoughts of the woman they cared about. The rest of the night passed uneventfully.

****

The following night started out much the same. Joe and Rick once again sat in front of the house they were staking out. They had been out there for four hours so far. Many members of the Scorpions had entered the house, but none of them matched the description they had of Robbins. They were talking about other possible directions they could go to get information on Robbins when they heard a scream. It sounded like a young girl, and both Rick and Joe were out of the car in seconds.

Neither one of the them saw the man that stood twenty yards away, pointing a gun at Joe's head. Joe didn't hear the shot, nor did he feel the bullet as it hit him in the back. Rick heard it and skidded to a stop, turning in time to see Joe fall. "Joe!" he yelled, as he ran back to his friend. He fell to his knees, feeling for a pulse on Joe's neck. He felt a slight one.

"Son of a bitch!" he yelled, but Joe was unconscious.

With tears of frustration and rage starting in his eyes, Rick looked up and saw the man standing there, with an evil smile on his face. He was now pointing the gun at Rick, and Rick waited, sure he was going to die in the next instant. But as the man pulled the trigger, nothing happened. The man looked down at the weapon, and saw that the slide was locked halfway, the gun had jammed. He threw the gun aside in frustration.

Rick was watching him to see if he had some sort of backup weapon, so he didn't notice the man stealing up behind him with a switchblade in his hand. Rick felt a searing pain as the blade sliced through his shoulder. Moving with lightning speed, he jumped to his feet, putting himself between his assailant and Joe. He glanced over his shoulder and saw that the man with the gun had disappeared. Rick was mad now. These bastards had set him and Joe up and they had tried to kill him and may have already killed his best friend. With strength born of blinding rage, Rick lunged at the knife wielder. The guy never had a chance, but he put up a valiant fight, cutting Rick a number of times in his efforts. Rick didn't feel anything, the adrenaline running through his body keeping him moving.

He beat the knife wielder into unconsciousness then turned to Joe. He knelt next to him, again checking for a pulse. As his own pulse slowed, Rick started to feel the searing pain in his shoulder, and from the other assorted cuts he'd sustained. He was feeling a little light-headed from his blood loss, but his main concern was Joe, who was still unconscious. Keeping a close eye on his surroundings to make sure that none of the Scorpions came out to finish him or Joe off, Rick moved to Joe's car.

He reached inside and grabbed the portable radio.

He moved back to kneel by Joe, then spoke into the radio. "I need help," he said, knowing he wasn't using the right terms. "I need an ambulance at 2244 Home Avenue!"

"Identify yourself," the dispatcher replied.

"I'm Rick Debenshire, Sergeant Sinclair has been shot, hurry the fuck up and get an ambulance here!"

He put the radio down so he could keep his hand on Joe, hoping the contact would keep Joe with him. There was a cold hard knot in his stomach; he knew that Joe could be dying as he waited for the ambulance. He didn't have the strength to move Joe, and doing so would possibly do more damage. Rick reached over and pulled Joe's gun out of his shoulder holster. Leaning back against the front bumper of Joe's Porsche, he rested his uninjured arm on his knees, watching watched for anyone approaching, the gun in his hand with his finger on the trigger. The light-headed feeling and now nausea was getting worse, but he was determined to stay conscious until the police arrived. He was almost unconscious when the police car and ambulance came skidding around the corner. Seeing them, he closed his eyes, leaning his head on his arm and blacked out. He didn't see the paramedics examine Joe; he didn't hear the exclamations about how much blood Joe had lost or about how much damage it had done. He didn't hear that Joe's pulse was thready or when they lost Joe's pulse altogether and had to initiate emergency resuscitation procedures.

****

Midnight was in her office when she heard Rick's radio call. Her heart stopped. She grabbed her gun, and hit the stairs at a dead run. Once in the parking lot, she jumped into her car, and started it simultaneously. She didn't notice the dark gray car that fell in behind her as she drove at a frantic pace toward the hospital they'd be taken to. She had no

318

idea that Rick had been hurt too. As she drove, she called dispatch to ask for an update. The dispatcher informed her that both men were down, and that at their last update, they had lost Joe's pulse.

"Oh, my God," Midnight said to herself as she hung up the phone.

She was speeding down the freeway, her mind going a mile a minute. This couldn't be happening, she couldn't lose Joe and Rick, not after everything they had all been through. Remotely she thought she had better call Randy. If the girl really did care about Joe, she may not even get a chance to say goodbye if … Midnight couldn't finish the thought. She reached over and picked up her phone again to dial Randy's number. Darrell answered.

"Darrell, it's Lieutenant Chevalier, I need to talk to Randy."

"Well Lieutenant, my sister is asleep, so you'll just have to—"

"Don't give me shit, Darrell!" Midnight yelled into the phone. "Just put her on the line!"

Randy came on the line a minute later. "Midnight what is it?"

"Randy, Joe's been hurt, and he might be …" Midnight steeled herself to say the word, "dead. I'm headed to Scripps Mercy Hospital. Meet me there as soon as you can."

Randy hung up the phone in shock. Darrell was staring at her, having seen her go white when Midnight had told her about Joe. "Randy, what is it?"

"I've got to go, I need the keys to your car," she said, holding out her hand.

"Go? Where?" Darrell said looking perplexed, even as he pulled the keys out of his pocket.

"It's Joe, he's been hurt. I've got to go, Darrell. Give me the damned keys!" She snatched the keys out of his hand and ran out the car.

She couldn't believe that Joe could be dead. It just wouldn't be fair, Joe was the first man she had ever loved and trusted, and now if he was gone … She didn't even want to think about it. She jumped into the Camaro and started it with a roar, noting as she did that Darrell had come to the front door. Without looking back at him, she backed out of the driveway and sped off toward the hospital. She frequently had to wipe at the tears that continued to fall. All she knew was that she needed to get to the hospital. Nothing would stop her.

Midnight's phone rang a few minutes later. It was Spider calling from the scene. He told her that Joe had been shot with a nine-millimeter caliber pistol and that from what witnesses had said, Joe had never had a chance; the guy shot him in the back. Midnight steeled herself against the mental image of Joe lying dying in the street, like her brother.

"Midnight!" Spider said, concerned about her mental state, knowing how close she was to Joe.

"What about Rick?" Midnight asked, her voice a dead whisper. She didn't want to know if Joe was dead or not, not now, not yet, she had to get to the hospital first.

"Midnight, Rick's okay, he received a few nasty cuts, and one real bad one on his shoulder, but he'll be okay."

"Okay, okay," Midnight said, nodding, her tears starting again. "I'm on my way to Scripps, that's where they went right?"

"Yeah," Spider replied, knowing that she shouldn't be driving. "Midnight, be careful, okay we don't need to lose you, too."

Midnight let out a sob, at the word "too." She hung up the phone, putting her foot down hard on the gas pedal, determined to get to the hospital.

Midnight arrived first, with Randy not too far behind. Midnight jumped out of the car and hit the doors at a dead run, with Randy right behind her. She flashed her badge at the security officers outside the emergency room, barely slowing. They ran down the corridor and, turning a corner, Midnight caught sight of Rick. She skidded to a stop fifteen yards from him, as if not approaching would change the outcome of what he'd tell her. He was leaning against a wall with his arm in a sling. His head was bowed.

"No!" The single word ripped from Midnight's throat as she started to run again, toward Rick.

His head snapped up at the sound of her voice, and she could see the cuts on his face as she approached. She ran straight to him, and into his arms. Rick held her against him as best he could.

"He can't be, he can't be," Midnight said, over and over.

Then she looked up at him, her eyes begging him to tell her different.

"Night, he's not dead, but they said it doesn't look good," Rick told her.

"Oh God, no!" Midnight said.

She turned to Randy who had gone white, and was shaking her head in denial.

"No, he can't die, Midnight. No!" Randy leaned against the opposite wall, with her arms crossed in front of her as if she was trying to literally hold herself together.

Rick slid to a squatting position, his head on his arm, his sorrow increased seeing Randy's reaction to the news. Midnight knelt next to him, trying desperately to hold on to her control. Her hand stroked his hair.

"I tried, Midnight, but there was nothing I could do. The bastards shot him in the back, sons a bitches." Sobs racked his body then, and Midnight took him in her arms.

He leaned against her, holding her with his good arm. Midnight was crying now too, and looking at Randy. Pulling Rick with her, Midnight moved to a couch nearby. She nodded to Randy to come sit with them. Midnight held Rick against her with one arm and with the other hand reached out to touch Randy's hand. Randy took Midnight's hand and held it tightly. They stayed that way for two hours, waiting for the doctor to come out and tell them if Joe would live. When he finally came out, it was Midnight who stood. Rick and Randy looked up with haunted, terrified eyes. The doctor looked at all of them, his eyes cool and businesslike.

"How is he?" Midnight asked, her thumb rubbing the palm her hand in agitation.

"He's alive, for now. There was a great deal of damage. He was shot with a large caliber weapon and it did a number on his insides. He's lost a lot of blood, but we've tried to stabilize that. His condition is still critical. I wish I had better news."

Midnight just stared up at the doctor, watching his mouth move, and wishing she wasn't hearing what he was saying, knowing that Joe's chances were almost nil. Suddenly, the doctor's face became unfocused. She tried hard to focus, but then everything went black. Rick saw Midnight starting to waver and jumped up, catching her before she fell. He laid her on the couch. She had passed out cold. The doctor called for a nurse, checked her pulse, and told the nurse to get some smelling salts. Midnight woke to find Rick holding her hand, and Randy standing by with a worried look on her face. She jerked her head away from the smelling salts the nurse was putting under her nose.

"Midnight, are you okay?" Rick asked.

She nodded, absently, then she remembered why she was here and what the doctor had said about Joe. She started to shake, her breathing came in short gasps. Rick held her, trying to calm her down. The doctor suggested a sedative for her, and Rick nodded without letting Midnight go.

Randy watched the scene feeling like she was far above it all, like she was watching a movie. This couldn't be happening, no, she was just a normal person, and this type of thing didn't happen to normal people. They didn't fall in love with their boss, who then got shot and died. This just couldn't be happening. She was terrified when Midnight blacked out, she couldn't believe what the doctor had said. Joe made it through surgery, but he could still die, that wasn't right. If people made it through surgery, they were supposed to be okay. Randy wished that things would just stop, so she could change them around to the way she wanted them to be. She wanted to keep that doctor from saying "I wish I had better news." He had said he wished it was better news, but Randy found that hard to believe. How could this doctor be sorry, he didn't know Joseph Michael Sinclair, he didn't know all of the terrible things that his patient had been through over the course of his life. To have Joe die now, would be like a cruel joke, and Randy just couldn't believe that it could happen so easily. She watched as the doctor gave Midnight a shot to calm her down. Midnight didn't seem to notice. After a few minutes though, she became noticeably calmer.

"Mr. Sinclair will be in recovery for a number of hours, so there's really no point in keeping her here," the doctor said, gesturing to a shell-shocked Midnight. "Why don't you take her home and we'll notify you of any change in his condition."

Rick nodded then and looked over at Randy.

"I'll stay here," she said quietly.

Again, Rick nodded. "Call me if he wakes up or if anything happens …" There was a sadness to his eyes that no person should ever experience.

He walked Midnight back out to her car. He put her in the passenger side, and got behind the wheel of her Corvette. He started the car and drove off toward her house. After a few minutes, she looked at him.

"You don't have to stay with me," she said quietly.

Rick looked over at her, surprised that she was still awake.

"I'm okay. I won't do anything, you know," she said.

"All the same," Rick said glancing over at her.

"All the same, nothing Rick, he's your friend too, and you should be there, in case he comes out of it." Her voice was hopeful then, and Rick smiled over at her.

"Are you sure?" he asked, really wanting the chance to be with Joe. He figured that she'd be asleep a good eight hours or so with all the stuff the doctor had given her.

"Yes, I'm sure, but if he wakes up tell him I love him." There were tears in her eyes as she whispered the last part.

"I will, babe," Rick said, reaching over to touch her cheek, tears in his own eyes.

He knew what she was thinking, but he didn't want to think about it himself. She was afraid that if Joe did wake up it might be for the last time, and she wouldn't be there to tell him that she loved him, so she was entrusting Rick with the duty of doing so. He understood, and felt the weight of the responsibility heavy on his heart.

When Rick pulled up in front of her house, Midnight got out of the car. "Midnight," Rick said, getting out of the car.

"It's okay, I can get myself inside. My house keys are separate from my car keys. You get back to the hospital, I want you there when he wakes up." She said the last part with determination that it was going to happen. Rick looked at her for a long moment.

"Go, already!" she said, smiling at him, even though her eyes were incredibly sad.

"Midnight," Rick began, wanting to tell her how he felt about her, but she was shaking her head at him.

"Will you get out of here, come back and get me if he wakes up, okay?" Her voice indicated that she didn't really expect it to happen, but she wanted him back at the hospital fast, and she was trying to prove to him that she was okay to be alone.

Finally, Rick nodded and got back into the car. He drove off a few minutes later. Midnight walked up her driveway, feeling the effects of the sedative, but feeling the weight of the night's events more. She couldn't believe that she might actually lose Joe, the man that had been there for her, almost since the beginning of FORS. She could wake up in the morning and he could be gone. From what the doctor had said, the chances of him pulling through were low. Suddenly Midnight couldn't believe she was there, opening up her front door. She should be at the hospital with her partner; he needed her, now more than ever, but she had gotten carried along with the river people wanting to shelter her from the shock of the possibility that Joe could die. She wouldn't get to see his face again, to look into those light blue eyes that had stared down at her so many times. She'd never feel his arms around her again, as he held her for comfort, or in passion.

Suddenly, everything was too much. She opened the front door and headed for the phone to call Rick and tell him to come back and get her. She never saw the man waiting in the darkness, nor did she see the butt of the gun he brought down on the side of her head. She was unconscious before she hit the floor. Daniel Robbins stepped out of the darkness, smiling evilly as he looked down at the motionless form of Lieutenant Midnight Chevalier.

****

Midnight woke with the most awful headache and she instantly knew she wasn't anywhere familiar. She looked around cautiously. But she couldn't determine where she was. She felt her head, she saw the blood as she drew her fingers back. Her hand reached automatically for the small of her back, but her weapon was gone.

"Shit," she said, to herself.

She took in her surroundings. She was lying on a bed, in a semi-dark room. She could make out a window beside her, but there were bars on it. There was a nightstand, and she could make out a door at the other end of the room with a slit of light showing at the bottom. There were no other furnishings. She wasn't bound, and she was grateful for that. Especially a few minutes later when the door opened and a man walked through, turning on the light. Midnight recognized Daniel Robbins from the police photographs she had seen at the jail. She sat up, leaning against the wall, her watching Robbins warily.

"Ah, Midnight, you're awake, I'm glad." Robbins' voice was gravelly.

Midnight said nothing, her eyes narrowing at his use of her first name.

"Oh," Robbins said, grimacing. "You're not talking to me and why's that?"

"It was you, wasn't it?" Midnight said, her voice coming out hoarse.

"Me, Midnight? What are you talking about?"

"Listen you son of a bitch, don't try to play games with me. It was you that tried to kill my partner, wasn't it?"

Robbins' eyes narrowed at her, his eyes growing cold, but then he grinned maliciously. "Yeah, and I tried to kill your boyfriend too, but"—he shrugged—"it just didn't happen."

"You bastard," Midnight said, her voice filled with venom, her eyes narrow points of green fire.

Robbins nodded as if she were praising him. "Yeah, I know, but you people are gettin' in my way, so I took care of things."

"In your way?" Midnight asked, her a malicious grin tugging at her lips.

"Yeah, you see, I'm making this high-powered deal to distribute for the cartel, and all this shit FORS has been doin' is gettin' in the way of that. The Riveras don't like loose ends, or cops." Robbins' voice lost its calm tone, and became angry during the course of his tirade.

"Well, that is our job, you know," Midnight said calmly.

"Yeah, well it ain't Sinclair's anymore," Robbins said, watching her for reaction.

Midnight just stared at him. Robbins smiled gleefully.

"What are you talking about?" Midnight asked, all tone gone from her voice.

"Sinclair's dead," Robbins said, his smile purely evil.

Midnight closed her eyes, swallowing hard. She opened them again and looked at Robbins. "You're lying," she said, praying that he was.

"Nope, I just called the hospital myself, he died a half hour ago ... Complications, you know nine-millimeter slugs can cause a lot of damage to a man's insides. Terrible thing ..." Robbins' voice trailed off as Midnight lunged for him. He hit her in the face, picked her up, and threw her back on the bed.

She landed with a yelp, and Robbins jumped on the bed and straddled her. She struggled against him, but he weighed too much.

His hands held her arms, and his weight centered over her pelvis, pinned her legs down. She stopped struggling then, tears were flowing down her face. She couldn't believe that Joe had died, and now this bastard had her locked away here. She couldn't even be there to say goodbye. Then she looked up at Robbins, and she suddenly realized he was looking at her in lust. Her throat constricted as she realized he intended to rape her. She tried to get away then, her arms flailing. She managed to get one had free and clawed at his face just missing his eye. He slapped her then, so hard her head snapped back.

"Bitch!" Robbins said. He turned to look over his shoulder and said, "Hold her down."

Midnight suddenly realized that two other men had come into the room while they were struggling. She knew then that she had no chance, but she was damned if she was going to give up. Robbins pulled her jeans off and ripped open her shirt open. Midnight squeezed her eyes shut; she didn't want to see his face.

She heard him whistle appreciatively. "Have you guys ever seen a body like this? Damn, lady, you're wastin' your time as a cop, you should be in Playboy or somethin'. Hot little number. Tell me, Midnight, which one were you getting it on with, Sinclair or the other guy? Or was it both of them? It doesn't matter, we'll kill the other one when we're done with you."

"No," Midnight said weakly, "please." She was thinking of Rick, she didn't want him to be killed too.

"Oh, you hear that guys, she's beggin'." Robbins put his lips close to her ear. "I like it when they beg." His gravelly voice made her sick.

His hands touched her and she couldn't help but try to shrink away from them. Her eyes were still closed, and tears were sliding

329

silently down her face. After a few moments, Robbins entered her body with force. Midnight screamed feeling like her whole body had just been raked over hot coals. She started to struggle again as he moved inside her. The bile was rising in her throat as her body struggled to get away from the searing pain he was causing. She managed to wrench her arm from one man's grasp, and her nails raked Robbins down the throat. He yelled, the bloody welts already starting on his throat. He hit her with his fist and she sank into unconsciousness gratefully.

When Midnight woke again, she was curled into a tight ball. As she straightened, she cried out involuntarily at the searing pain between her legs. Looking down she saw dried blood. She closed her eyes trying to regain her control. Her head was pounding, her whole body hurt, and she was still there. And Joe was still dead. The tears started again, for the man who had been her best friend, her only love. She was still crying when Robbins came in, looking very pleased with himself. Midnight moved away from him, watching him closely in case he tried anything else.

"Now, Midnight, are you telling me you didn't enjoy it when I fucked you? I have to be better than those Englishmen. Maybe you just weren't paying attention. I guess I'll have to try it again, I do want you to enjoy yourself." His smile was cruel.

Midnight's eyes widened, but she said nothing.

"But first I have a request of you," he said, and from his back he pulled out her gun. She eyed it, as if willing it to go off and kill him. "You see, Midnight, I want the names and addresses of all the members of FORS."

She looked at him as if he were crazy.

"And," Robbins continued, turning her gun to the side and looking at it as if he were addressing it rather than her. Then he pointed it at her, his eyes boring into hers. "You're going to give them to me."

"Over my dead body," Midnight said, staring at her own gun.

"Oh, Midnight, that's inevitable, but I can hurt you a lot more, before I kill you." His head nodded toward the blood on her legs. Midnight shuddered, but she didn't respond.

"Now are you going to give them to me, or do I have to beat them out of you."

"What do you think you're going to do with them?" Midnight asked, trying to bide her time.

Robbins looked at the gun again. "Kill them of course."

"If you've killed Joe," Midnight said, her voice faltering on his name, "and you kill me, why would you need to go after them?"

"Come on, Midnight, what do you take me for?" Robbins said, laughing. "I know how stupidly loyal those people are to you. Even if you're dead they'll keep coming at me, and I don't need the bother."

"You're afraid," Midnight said, her voice stronger now.

"No, I'm careful."

"You knew we were closing in on you, and you got scared, so you cheated."

"All's fair, bitch," Robbins said, wagging her gun at her. "Now, are you going to give me that information?"

Midnight looked at him steadily, she didn't care what he did to her, she wasn't going to jeopardize the lives of her team. She had protected them this long; she would go to her death doing so.

"No," she said simply. His face grew red then with suppressed anger. She was pleased she was getting to him.

"Well, it's obviously time for another lesson then," Robbins said, putting the gun down on the nightstand and grabbing her by a handful of her hair.

He twisted her head around, and started to kiss her, she bit down on his lip; to her satisfaction, she tasted his blood. He grabbed her arm, and she struggled, bringing her hand up to claw at him, but he whipped his arm back and slapped her. He stood and dragged her off the bed, and pulled her up against him. Her mouth was bleeding and she could taste her own blood. He tried to kiss her again, and she tried to bite him again. He was enraged now, and threw her against the wall. She cried out as a nail in the wall bit painfully into her shoulder. She slid to the ground. He picked her up, and dropped her on the bed so he could cover her body again. Then Midnight heard the most wonderful thing she could have ever imagined.

"Get the fuck away from her!" said Rick.

He was standing in the doorway pointing Joe's gun at Robbins. Robbins jumped up, pulling Midnight up with him, his forearm around her throat.

"Forget it Robbins, you aren't going to hurt her again. So why don't you get smart and step away from her."

"No, I don't think so. Why don't you just get the fuck out of here before I kill her."

"You even twitch like you're going to and I'll nail you from here." Rick's tone was icy. He watched Robbins but didn't look at Midnight. He knew the sight of her so battered would distract him, and he didn't trust Robbins.

Even now, Robbins was moving back. Midnight knew he was going for her gun lying on the nightstand, out of Rick's sight. She knew she had to do something; the last thing she wanted was for Rick to get shot with her gun. She carried her duty weapon loaded with Black Talon ammunition, which would do some nasty damage to a body. She couldn't let that happen.

"Rick, he's going for my gun!" She gasped as Robbins tightened his hold on her throat, all but cutting off her air. "Kill him!" she whispered harshly, tears in her eyes. But Rick was shaking his head; he wouldn't take the chance of hitting her. Robbins took another step backward, but Rick's voice stopped him.

"You pick up that gun and I figure you're going to kill me and her. Then I will shoot you because I figure if you think you're going to kill my girlfriend, you'll probably do it. I think she trusts my aim better."

Midnight nodded affirmation then. Robbins halted, realizing he'd die either way.

"Yeah, well I ain't goin' out like that, so I'm just gonna move past you and you're gonna let me or I'll kill her. I don't think you want that, do ya? See if I get away, then no harm no foul, but if I kill her she's dead for a real long time." Robbins' voice was low and evil.

Midnight could see that Rick wouldn't risk her getting killed. She wanted to scream at him; they couldn't let Robbins get away. Robbins was moving past Rick now, and Rick was keeping a bead on him, but he didn't stop him. Robbins pulled Midnight with him through the house. Rick followed, the gun still pointed at Robbins. Midnight's eyes were locked on Rick, she was more afraid for him than she was for herself. She felt that she had gotten herself into this, and he was here trying to rescue her. If he was killed trying, she'd never forgive herself. When they got to the front door, Robbins tightened the pressure on Midnight's throat to the point where Rick was sure he was planning to kill her.

"Robbins!" Rick bellowed, tightening his finger on the trigger of the gun. "You do it, you die. I swear it!" He could see Midnight starting to fade with the pressure around her throat.

Robbins hesitated. Rick's eyes narrowed but the gun he held never wavered an inch. Suddenly, Robbins shoved a now unconscious Midnight at Rick, blocking his shot. Rick pulled the gun up, and lunging forward, caught Midnight with his injured arm. He cried out at the searing pain it caused. Robbins darted out the door, but Rick was too concerned about Midnight to follow him. He heard a police car pull up, and he hoped that maybe they had caught Robbins. He had purposely kept the police out of it up until this point, because he was afraid that if Robbins heard a siren, he would kill Midnight immediately. Holstering the gun he held, Rick picked Midnight up and carried her out to the police car. He laid her down in the back seat, and sat down with her head rested in his lap. He checked for a pulse and found a strong one. Rick breathed a sigh of relief. He touched her face, his look pained at the bruises that Robbins had inflicted. Midnight stirred and looked up at him.

"Night, are you okay?" he asked her.

She nodded, but then he could see the memories flood back to her and she began to cry.

"Midnight?" he said worried that she was more injured than she appeared. "What is it? Talk to me." His eyes were searching her face.

"Rick," Midnight said incredulously, "he's gone. Joe's gone ..."

334

ACKNOWLEDGEMENTS

Thank you to Marianne Warren, who was the first person brave enough to tell me I needed to change the titles of the books to better represent them!

Thank you to Christine Hooker and Fatima Martinelli for being awesome beta readers for me, I was really nervous about this one and you both made me feel better.

As always, thank you to my wife, my life, my love... I love you Tirzah!

You can find more information about the author and series here:

www.sherrylhancock.com

www.facebook.com/SherrylDHancock